EREC REX

THE SEARCH FOR TRUTH

EREC REX

THE SEARCH FOR TRUTH

KAZA KINGSLEY

Illustrations by Tim Jacobus

Simon & Schuster Books for Young Readers
New York   London   Toronto   Sydney

Check out the other books
in the Erec Rex series

The Dragon's Eye
The Monsters of Otherness

EREC REX

THE SEARCH FOR TRUTH

SIMON & SCHUSTER BOOKS FOR YOUNG READERS
An imprint of Simon & Schuster Children's Publishing Division
1230 Avenue of the Americas, New York, New York 10020

Book design by Lucy Ruth Cummins
The text for this book is set in Adobe Caslon.
The illustrations for this book are rendered digitally.
Manufactured in the United States of America
2 4 6 8 10 9 7 5 3 1
Library of Congress Cataloging-in-Publication Data
Kingsley, Kaza.
Erec Rex : the search for truth / Kaza Kingsley ; illustrations by Tim
Jacobus.—1st ed.
p. cm.—(Erec Rex ; [3])
Summary: When twelve-year-old Erec Rex learns that his friend Bethany is in
trouble in Alypium, the magical kingdom he is destined to rule, he rushes to try to
save her and to find the five Awen in order to protect the Substance.
ISBN: 978-1-4169-7988-3
[1. Dragons—Fiction. 2. Fantasy.] I. Jacobus, Tim, ill. II. Title.
III. Title: Search for truth.
PZ7.K6153Ers 2009
[Fic]—dc22
2008036934
erecrex.com

For my uncle Alan, keyboard player extraordinaire, who gave me a true appreciation of music in general and the Beatles in particular. I hope you are jamming with John Lennon somewhere right now.

'Beauty is truth, truth beauty,—that is all
Ye know on earth, and all ye need to know.'

—Keats, "Ode on a Grecian Urn"

I am a stag of seven tines.
I am a wide flood on a plain.
I am a wind on the deep waters.
I am a shining tear of the sun.
I am a hawk on a cliff.
I am fair amongst flowers.
I am a god who sets the head afire with smoke.
I am a battle-waging spear.
I am a salmon in a pool.
I am a hill of poetry.
I am a ruthless boar.
I am a threatening noise from the sea.
Who but I knows the secret of the unhewn tomb?

—"The Song of Amergin," A.D. 400

CONTENTS

CHAPTER ONE

The Substance Channel

I T MUST HAVE been a dream. That was the only explanation Erec Rex could think of for what had just happened. Yes, a nightmare. That's what it was.

Thirteen-year-old Erec blinked a few times, waiting for his bedroom to appear. It did not. In fact, his skin still looked disturbingly green. And his fingernails—were they shrinking before his eyes? They hadn't really been long claws a moment ago, had they?

After waiting another minute, Erec squeezed his eyes shut, wishing he was anywhere else. The sad fact had sunk in—he was not in bed after all. He was lying on his back in Fork-Out Grocery. Heaps of sparkling pink notebooks and toppled stacks of diaper boxes were scattered all around him in a big mess on the floor.

At first he thought he was covered in snow. Then he saw the slashed boxes. Torn white fluff from shredded Lil' Dumpling diapers covered everything around him like a Christmas display. But who would have shredded the diapers all over like that? He ran his hand through his dark hair, which was straight in front and wildly curly in the back, shaking diaper fuzz from his head.

Then Erec noticed gray dust sprinkling down from a black, charred hole in the side of a nearby case of spaghetti boxes. It looked like someone had blasted it with a flamethrower. Who could have come in here and done this? Someone really ransacked this place.

Erec gulped as a realization dawned on him. If he truly was here, in the grocery store, and he had not been dreaming, then maybe . . .

Could *he* have done all this?

This was not good.

A little girl stood staring at him, her lip trembling. She tugged on her mother's skirt and pointed at Erec. The mother glanced at him with disgust, as if he was a delinquent who made a mess of store displays for fun.

Erec wished that were true. Because what really happened was far worse than a bout of bad behavior. What had just happened, in fact, should never have occurred here, in New Jersey, in plain sight of normal people.

Erec hid his eyes with a diaper fluff–covered hand. He had to face the facts. He had begun to turn into a dragon.

His adopted siblings had seen it too. All five of them had been swarming around the grocery store, dumping unhealthy sugared products into their adoptive mother June's cart faster than she could take them out. Danny and Sammy, thirteen-year-old twins with sandy brown hair, and Nell, eleven, had watched Erec grab hold of a shelf when his head began to spin. Nine-year-old, redheaded Trevor had popped around the corner just as Erec's vision faded out. And Zoey, just five, with wild blond curls and hazel eyes, was staring at him when he woke up on the ruined store display.

But it was what happened in between his vision fading and waking up among diapers that made Erec's heart race. He'd had a cloudy thought.

Cloudy thoughts were what Erec called the strange commands that took him over at times, forcing him to do whatever they said. His whole life he'd had to deal with being overcome, when he least expected it, with orders appearing in his head. Cloudy thoughts made him do things like run to the bottom of a staircase and hold his arms out. He would feel like an idiot crouching there, but then a little girl would tumble down the stairs into his arms. He would have saved her without even knowing she was coming. Cloudy thoughts had also saved his own life many times, giving him extra strength and telling him what he needed to know to survive.

But things changed. Erec inherited first one and then the other eye of his dragon friend, Aoquesth, who died saving Erec's life in a battle. The dragon eyes were now attached to the back of his own eyes, and carried special powers that he looked forward to discovering. The first one made his cloudy thoughts more intense, with visions like premonitions. But this was his first cloudy thought since he had gotten two dragon eyes, and it was different, more powerful than any he'd had before.

Erec took a breath. What *had* just happened to him in the grocery store? Right when he picked up a carton of his favorite cookies, Chocolate Springballs with cherry centers, everything had turned green. His eyes had swiveled around so that his dragon eyes were facing forward. His mind seemed to race through time so fast he couldn't make out what was happening. He remembered grabbing the metal shelf for support.

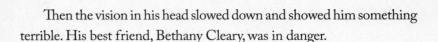

Then the vision in his head slowed down and showed him something terrible. His best friend, Bethany Cleary, was in danger.

Thick white ropes and webs hung in the air. Bethany was panting, long dark curls plastered against her sweaty face. She was backed against a wall, trapped. She had been running away from three boys, one with white, fuzzy hair covering his head and neck, another with an odd gray cap that stuck high over his head, and the third with black hair and an evil glint in his steely blue eyes. Now she was cornered.

Erec gasped. It was Dollick, Damon, and Balor Stain. They were the triplets working with evil Prince Baskania to overthrow the Kingdoms of the Keepers, the unseen magical realms connected to ours. Erec had been amazed when he found the strange place, and more shocked to learn he had been born there, in Alypium.

Balor Stain pointed what looked like a normal television remote control at Bethany. Her body stiffened as she was magically lifted from the ground.

A shadow appeared, morphing into a tall man with silver gray hair that grew into a sharp widow's peak. A cold blue eye peered from his face with a dark gap marking where his other eye should have been. Today his forehead was wider than the rest of his face. Across it gleamed seven more eyes, each from a different former owner.

It was Thanatos Argus Baskania. The Shadow Prince, as his followers called him. A smirk snaked across Baskania's face. "Ah, Bethany Cleary. Daughter of the great seer, Ruth Cleary. Too bad she had to go so young, too, eh?" His voice sounded like nails on a chalkboard, making Erec's bones shiver.

Bethany glared at him, unable to speak or move.

THE SEARCH FOR TRUTH

"But Ruth was in my way. Just like your friend Erec." Baskania cackled. "Soon he will join your mother and you, along with everyone else who is an obstacle to me."

Erec filled with rage as he watched the horrifying vision unfold. He clawed the air around him, vaguely aware that his skin was turning scaly and green, and claws were sprouting from his fingers.

Bethany looked furious. She struggled with her invisible bonds.

Baskania sucked in his breath. "Well. The Fates have smiled upon me at last. I was fascinated to hear the secret you just told your friend. So you hold the key I have been searching for." His voice lowered to a whisper. "Somehow, you will teach me how to use the Final Magic. Control over everything I desire, life and death. Amazing." He smiled, the corners of his mouth twitching. "If I can't find the answers I need from torturing you alive, I'm sure I will discover them when I remove your brain."

Erec roared in fury at the image in his head. He lost control, thrashing and clawing. Something hot came out of his mouth. It made him feel better for a moment, but not for long.

A rope spun out of Baskania's palm and wrapped tightly around Bethany. "Say good-bye to the world, Bethany Cleary. You'll be safe in my fortress for the remainder of your short life." He snapped his fingers. Baskania, Bethany, and the Stain triplets disappeared.

That's when Erec opened his eyes into the white diaper fluff, the would-be snow of Fork-Out Grocery.

* * *

Nell appeared at Erec's side with the help of her walker. "Erec, you . . . you . . ." She pointed at the charred hole. Black strands of spaghetti poked from the boxes around it. "Fire came out of your mouth."

Erec stared at the boxes. He had breathed fire?

But how? Erec shook his head. So this was what his dragon eyes were doing to him? Turning him into a dragon? He shouldn't be here, in Upper Earth. If people saw him shooting fire here, they'd lock him up.

He gulped, thinking about what he had just seen happen to Bethany. Had she already been captured? Did Baskania really find out her secret—that somehow she carried the key that he could use to learn the Final Magic?

Baskania not only wanted to rule the Kingdoms of the Keepers, but he also owned huge megacorporations all over the nonmagical world, and led a political movement trying to take over the United Nations. If Erec had not stopped him, Baskania would have taken over the Kingdoms already and destroyed them. That was reason enough for Baskania to want to kill Erec—but he also craved Erec's dragon eyes for himself.

What Baskania wanted most of all was to learn the Final Magic, magic so powerful that nobody could ever stop him. King Piter, ruler of Alypium, had told Erec that the Final Magic would make Baskania lose control and destroy the world.

Erec froze. His cloudy thought wasn't over yet. A message filtered into his mind that told him the rest of what he needed to know.

Bethany was not captured yet. Baskania had not found out her secret. But he would. Erec's vision would come true, and Bethany would die—if he didn't get to Alypium immediately and stop his friend Oscar Felix from ruining everything.

Panic seized him. How would he ever get there in time? He knew that in just three hours Bethany would tell Oscar the secret, one that nobody should ever know about her. And somehow because of this, only three minutes later, she would be captured by Baskania and would die.

"Mom," Erec snarled between gritted teeth, "we have to go *now*. Buy the food later." He took a breath. Maybe she didn't understand. "I'm telling you, Bethany is in danger. I have to get there fast. I don't think I'm going to make it in time."

June nodded, but kept putting groceries onto the conveyor. She glanced around to see if anyone was listening, then said, "Relax, Erec. I'll get you there as soon as we get home."

"But, Mom . . ." He wanted to yank her out the door. "It takes time to catch a train to New York. And to get to FES Station. Then I still have to take the artery there, and then find Bethany, wherever she is. We have to go now."

June tossed a box of Flying Count cereal onto the counter, her brown hair pulled into a ponytail. The cashier lazily scanned cracker boxes and put them in a bag. She seemed to be moving in slow motion. June said, "I understand, Erec. That's why I'm going to get you there immediately. As soon as we get home. Let me just pay for this. You'll have plenty of time."

"How can I get there immediately? It will take hours." Frustration filled him. She just didn't get it.

June looked around and then whispered, "I have a way to get you to Alypium straight from our house."

"But—" Erec's breath caught. He knew his mother was not supposed to perform magic in Upper Earth. If she did, the wrong people might find her again. Normally he would never want her to do that. But Bethany would die if he didn't get there right away.

She noticed the look on his face. "What's wrong? I thought you'd be happy that you don't have to go through FES Station."

Erec shrugged. "There's no choice. You're right. You'll have to send me there by magic. I just worry about you getting caught."

June smiled. "But I won't be doing magic. I got a new Vulcan product that will take you. They're not trackable."

Erec's mother had bought things before from a store called Vulcan, in the Kingdoms of the Keepers. Strange things, like an alarm clock and toothbrush that acted like they were alive. Well, Erec thought, whatever this new thing was that June had bought, it had better work, and fast.

After paying the cashier, they walked through the parking lot, zipping up jackets against the chilly January air. A heavyset woman with dark hair, a very white face, and too much makeup bumped into Danny right as they were leaving. She turned her head away quickly before Erec could get a good look at her. Danny looked up and said, "Oh, excuse me," but she was gone.

In the car, Danny and Trevor played keep-away with an apple. Danny made Trevor list statistics of his favorite sport, springball, each time he caught it. That was easy for Trevor, until Zoey intercepted the apple and ate it.

Erec barely noticed what was going on around him. All he could see was a scene from the future where Baskania captured the best friend he ever had.

June pulled a small silver ring out of a box. "Amazing," she said. "Hard to believe this could actually work."

Erec raised an eyebrow. "It better." The little shining band did not inspire confidence.

"Don't worry," June said. "Vulcan products always do what they're supposed to. It'll be interesting to see what happens. This"—she held out the ring—"makes a Substance Channel. The ring carves a wormhole into the Substance around us, and it can take you anywhere. You direct it as you go." She turned the ring over and frowned. "Well, you should be able to understand this better than anyone else. You can see the Substance when your dragon eyes are out."

Erec nodded. His dragon eyes let him see the nets and webs that carried channels of magic all over and through the earth.

June rubbed the ring in her hands until it began to glow. Then she pulled, stretching it until it was bright and thin, like a glittering hoop for a circus animal to jump through.

"Ouch!" June jerked her hands away from the ring. It hung in the air, glimmering. She rubbed her hands together. "That felt like an electric shock."

Erec pointed into it. "Am I supposed to climb through there?"

Suddenly, the ring began to spin. Soon it was whirling so fast that there was no way Erec could go near it. He was afraid it would slice into him if he touched it.

The faster the loop swirled in the air, the wavier it looked. Instead of a circle, it became ripply, glowing as it grew until it was Erec's size. Then it stopped suddenly and hung still. It was round again, but now it pulsed with greenish light. Erec carefully put a hand through the ring. An invisible force pulled his fingers, as if to guide him in.

"You're supposed to think of the place you want to go while you're in the Substance Channel," June said. "Focus on it. And let me know you got there okay."

"Sure," Erec said. "After I find Bethany, I'll e-mail you on the MagicNet."

"Okay. I can always check on you with my Seeing Eyeglasses." June had a pair of glasses that let her see whoever she missed the most, anywhere they were. For a while the glasses had been stuck on their alarm clock. June had to send the clock to a Vulcan store to get them removed.

Erec put his arms through the ring, then he slid his head through.

Instead of coming out the other side into the room, he was surrounded by darkness. Before he knew it, he was sucked into space.

It was a strange feeling, floating on nothing in the blackness. He was hanging in stillness. And he didn't seem to be going anywhere. How much longer before he would arrive?

Then Erec realized he had not given the Substance Channel any directions. *Alypium.* He focused his mind on it. He had to get to Alypium, fast.

Suddenly he felt himself whizzing through space. It was as if a tunnel were being carved around him as he went. Relief surged through him. Good. He would get there soon and find Bethany. But where in Alypium was she? And how would he find her?

Then a thought occurred to him. Maybe the Substance channel would take him straight to Bethany if he concentrated on her instead of a specific place.

He thought about Bethany, saying her name in his head. *Take me to Bethany Cleary.* He thought about her tanned face, her dark, wavy hair. Then his head filled with the image he had seen of her in the future. Frozen against a wall. Ropes around her. Scared, helpless. About to die.

Please, he begged the Substance, *get me there fast.*

The memory of his cloudy thought haunted him. The man he hated more than anyone in the world was going to hurt Bethany. The one who had killed his dragon friend, Aoquesth. Erec pictured Baskania, seven eyes across his forehead, standing before Bethany, ready to torture and kill her because he thought she had the secret of the Final Magic.

Erec felt a jerk, as if he suddenly had shifted direction. He was yanked sideways, then thrown into the light on a hard floor. When he looked up, the ring hanging in the air above him vanished.

He dusted himself off, relieved. He was indoors. But this place did not look like the Castle Alypium. It wasn't a shop, either. The room he was in was large. The air was thick and hard to breathe, but then again he always felt this way when he first arrived in the Kingdoms of the Keepers. He had to get used to it.

A group of people stood nearby. They were all looking at him.

But only one of them stepped forward and smiled—the one with seven eyes across his forehead.

CHAPTER TWO

The Ghost Surgeon

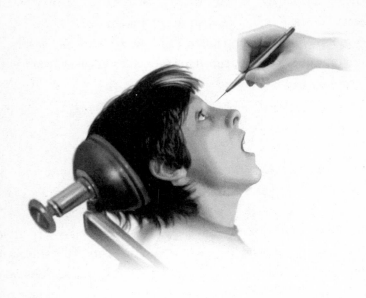

THICK CURTAINS HUNG around the stately atrium that
was scattered with plush furniture. An ornate reception
desk sat at the back of the room. People walking by
stopped and stared at Erec, then noticed Baskania and
rushed away.

"Well," Baskania said to Erec, "what a nice little present." He
laughed. "Two little presents, actually." He tapped the empty space
on his face where his own eye once had been. "Looks like I'll get to

fill this gap with your dragon eye sooner than I expected. And now I'll have your other one to match it too."

Baskania pointed a finger at Erec. "Say good-bye to the world, boy. There's no dragon to save you now."

Erec squeezed his eyes shut, waiting for a shock of pain, blackness, or something that told him his life was over.

He cursed himself. Why did he mess up in the Substance Channel like that? His mother had told him to concentrate. All he had to do was think about Bethany or a place in Alypium. And instead he had let his mind wander to Baskania, of all people, which brought him here.

He could not believe how badly he had messed up. Soon Bethany would tell Oscar her secret. And somehow, just three minutes later, Baskania would know, and Bethany would die.

There was another problem too. Even bigger, if that was possible. Erec had been the only one competing with the nasty Stain triplets to become a new ruler of the Kingdoms of the Keepers. Three kids were to be crowned soon. For some reason Erec had been the only one chosen by King Piter's scepter during the ceremony. That didn't seem to matter to Baskania, though, nor to the Stain triplets who were competing with Erec for the throne. If Erec died now, they would take over, Baskania would become the emperor, and his madness and power would drive him to destroy the world.

And it was all Erec's fault.

Surprised that he was still alive, Erec cracked his eyes open. Baskania frowned at his finger. "No," Baskania murmured. "The dragon eyes. How careless of me." He saw Erec staring with shock and confusion, and smiled. "I must be careful with your eyes so there will be no mistakes. I had two dragon babies before, but by the time I took their eyes out they were worthless. They had been dead too long. No, I'm not going to kill you yet. We'll have the surgeon take your eyes out first, correctly, and then I will have the pleasure."

Baskania closed his eyes in thought, then a glowing silver man appeared at his side wearing a silver laboratory jacket. A stethoscope hung from his neck. It was hard to see him in detail. When Erec looked straight at him, he became blurry. An intense radiance glimmered around him.

Erec recognized him as a silver ghost, like the first bus driver that had taken him to Alypium. *So this would be who would cut his eyes out right before he died,* he thought.

He tried to remember anything he could about silver ghosts. They were vain, didn't like people, and would do almost anything for payment. But there was one other thing Erec remembered about silver ghosts that flooded him with hope.

They could not touch him.

June had told him that he was charmed, and he knew from experience that ghosts could not hurt him. But that didn't stop his heart from racing when Baskania zapped him and the ghost into a room with a dentist's chair. Erec shuddered thinking about what might happen next. If the ghost took a swing at him, he would probably be safe. But if the ghost touched him with something else, like a surgical tool, would he still be protected?

The ghost slid around the room gathering small drills and saws, and filled a jar with a clear liquid. Suddenly, Erec found himself floating through the air toward the dentist chair, which rose up and lay flat. Thick chains pinned his body to the chair.

Erec jerked back and forth to break free. He had to get out of here. He looked around the room. There was one door and one window. He could see a treetop through the window, so they were probably up high.

"Where are we?" he asked the ghost.

"In one of the surgical suites in the Green House." The silver ghost sounded bored. "Won't be here for more than a few minutes, though. Of course, you won't actually see where you are going after that, so it won't matter, will it?"

Erec's heart pounded, thumping in his chest. Was this really happening? His eyes were going to be taken out and handed to Baskania? He struggled against his chains, but they were too tight.

The ghost picked up a sharp silver instrument and long, skinny scissors, then sat near Erec's face. He sighed, seemingly annoyed to be wasting his time, and jabbed the knife at Erec's right eye.

Erec squeezed his eyes shut. His body clenched in anticipation of the pain. He was afraid to open his eyes in case the ghost was waiting for him to do so. But finally he peeked, out of curiosity.

The silver surgeon was frowning in frustration. He kept poking again and again with the knife, the scissors, and the other tools around him. He could not get any of them within inches of Erec's face. They stopped in midair, as if they were hitting a force field.

Erec just about melted with relief. Not that he was even close to being safe. But at least he had a few more moments to figure out what to do.

But what could he do, chained flat on a dentist's chair, with Thanatos Baskania down below?

The ghost sneered. "You're making this difficult, aren't you? Well, no worries. We'll figure out a way to take those eyes out. I'm not going to tell the Shadow Prince he can't have what he wants." He disappeared out the door into a hallway.

The oppressive air of Alypium was suffocating him. Why hadn't he remembered to take a bottle of Upper Earth air with him for little breaths, until he got used to it? The Substance, the network that carried all the magic of the world, had been messed up somehow in the Kingdoms of the Keepers. It made the air feel thick and nasty, tinged with sadness. He couldn't wait until he grew accustomed to it so it wouldn't bother him anymore.

If he lived long enough for that to happen.

Erec felt sick. Everything he had done had been for nothing. He had finished two of the twelve quests that would let him become king. Around his neck hung the Amulet of Virtues which had appeared after his first quest, marking the number of quests he had done. Two of its twelve segments glowed with color. He had finished these quests even though he'd had serious doubts about being a king at all. But he knew what would happen otherwise. The Stain triplets, Baskania's helpers, would become kings and would destroy Alypium. And Baskania would be in charge. He couldn't let that happen.

Unfortunately, Erec had more than doubts about becoming king. He was terrified of it. Because he knew that if that happened, he would be given a scepter. As much as he wanted one, as much as he craved a scepter after using King Piter's, he knew it would corrupt him completely, turn him as evil as the Stains, and Baskania himself. What would be worse, letting his enemies crush the world or doing it himself? He still was not sure.

Erec pushed with all of his might against his chains, but he could not budge them. He dug his heels into the chair. Maybe he could slide his way out. Sure enough, after shimmying against the vinyl seat, he managed to inch just high enough to free one of his hands.

At that moment the ghost surgeon appeared with three others just like him. Erec froze. They did not seem to notice that he had slid upward in the chair.

Each of the ghost surgeons tried various ways to remove Erec's eyes. None was able to touch him, though, with anything they picked up. A short, paunchy one ran a hand up and down over Erec's arm. "Look at this," he said to the others. "I can't even come close to this pathetic boy at all."

They launched into a discussion, referring to Erec as a "rotten human" and "waste of space."

"We must figure out how to fix this ourselves," one said. "If Baskania finds out there is a problem, we'll all pay the price."

"Wait," another said, pointing at Erec. "We cannot touch him. But is he really protected from everything? Or just from us silver ghosts? Let's try calling in a human doctor to take his eye out."

Erec's heart sank. They had figured it out. How would he get out of here now? Even if he worked his way through the chains, he would never escape all of the people in the Green House—especially Baskania—once they knew he was free.

The ghosts went out into the hallway to find a human doctor. Why had he been so stupid? If he had just controlled his thoughts in the Substance Channel he'd be safely with Bethany now, warning her not to make her deadly mistake.

There were still things he wanted to learn about himself, but now it was too late. He would never meet his father, whoever he was. And his birth mother. Where was she? And why did she leave him? Now he'd never know why he had been chosen to be king and do the quests. He would die knowing nothing about himself.

Erec tried to push farther through the chains, but he could barely move. He wished he had a cloudy thought now to save him. Why wasn't he getting one? Maybe there was no way to save himself. If only he could escape, fly out the window or something.

Erec bit his lip. Fly out the window . . . Maybe there *was* something he could do. Something that had saved him once before. At least he could try.

But first he needed to bring his dragon eyes forward. He took a deep breath and focused as hard as he could on one thing. Love. The love that was deep inside him. He thought of Aoquesth and all that the dragon had done for him. His family, his friends. But mostly just love for the world. Because that was what he had to protect now.

Soon he felt his eyes turn in his head. Everything became a vivid green. Thick white ropes hung throughout the room. It was the Substance. Now that his dragon eyes were out, he could see it again.

Not much time was left before the human surgeon would come to take his eyes. This was his last chance.

He concentrated deeply on the love he felt inside. Then Erec looked out the window and focused all of his feelings into the sky, into the great networks of Substance that filled the air.

Aoquesth had taught him how to call dragons with his eyes. Using all of his strength and love, he called to them for help. *Dragons!* he pleaded. *Save me! If Baskania takes my eyes, and I can't find Bethany soon, our world will end.*

The door opened. Erec's dragon eyes swiveled back into his head. The room was no longer green. A tall, thin man walked in, followed by the silver ghosts. A few dark hairs were slicked over his bald head, and others stuck straight in the air. He wore a monocle over his pinched nose.

"Hmm." The man stared at him and frowned. "I've seen you before. Don't know where, but I'm pretty sure you were up to no good."

Erec shoved his heels against the chair and inched farther up through his chains. The ghosts tried to grab him, but could not touch him. They did not have to worry, though. He was far from being able to run away.

He wondered if any dragons had heard his call. If only they would come. Where were they? He tried to stall a minute longer. "I have met you," he said, trying to think of what to say. "Wasn't it . . . at the coronation ceremony?"

The man frowned. "I wasn't there. Now hold still." He grabbed a scalpel and put a hand on Erec's eyebrow.

Erec jerked his head away. He wiggled up more in the chair, but his free hand became caught again in the next chain. *Come on, dragons,* he thought. If they did not hear him he was lost.

The man grabbed Erec's head. "Here we go now. Won't be a minute."

Erec twisted and fought, but he was pinned down. The man brought the sharp point of the knife to Erec's eye.

An ear-splitting crash made everyone jump. Glass and bricks flew through the room. A stream of fire tore through the air over Erec, blasting a wave of heat around him. A roar echoed through the noise of smashed plaster and wood clattering to the floor.

A dragon had broken through the wall around the window. The front half of its body twisted around the room, shooting blasts of fire. The surgeon backed away, yelping in fear. The ghosts watched, unafraid, yet unable to stop it.

The dragon reached a claw toward Erec. He jolted, suddenly realizing that even though he had called it, it might not recognize him. He held his breath.

The dragon slid a talon under his chains and yanked. In a moment he was free. It grabbed him with its claws and backed through the hole in the wall.

The dark-haired man watched, aghast. He looked back and forth as if he were trying to think how he could possibly stop a dragon. Then he grabbed a camera from his pocket and took a picture of Erec. "You're not supposed to do this!" he shouted. "This picture is evidence—you're a criminal. We'll find you, boy."

The dragon whisked Erec into the sunlight and blue sky. Erec trembled, seeing the ground so far below him as the dragon whizzed higher toward the clouds. The rhythmic beating of its wings soon calmed him, and he realized he would not fall. Feeling the wind on his face while the earth sailed below him was incredible.

This was not the same feeling he'd had when he was riding on Aoquesth's back, holding one of his spines. Erec felt more like a mouse caught by a hawk. But the trees under him blended into a blur of yellow-green and lakes swirled into patterns with the shadows of mountains and valleys. Above him, the dragon's jointed black wings shot back and forth across the blue sky. He felt himself relax completely, absorbed by the beauty all around him.

Soon they landed on a rocky outcrop. Erec sat up and looked around. He was sure they were in Otherness. The dragon's purple-red scales and gleaming ruby red spines shone in the sunlight. But not until she spoke did he recognize her.

"Erec Rex," she said. "We meet again."

"Patchouli?" He looked at her reddish face, then he was sure it was her. He ran over and hugged her around the neck. "Thanks for rescuing me. You don't know how close I came to—"

"It's the least I could do. I still owe you for saving my babies and all the other missing hatchlings." She snorted and a stream of smoke billowed from her nostrils.

Erec sat down and caught his breath. He was alive. Safe.

But he still had no idea where Bethany was. Now he was far away in Otherness. He knew he had to find her fast, before it was too late.

CHAPTER THREE

Mrs. Stain's Rumors

EREC SAT ON a rock and rested his head in his hands. He had to clear his mind and figure out what to do. His heart pounded, and his breath was still ragged, plus the tension racing through him made it hard to think. He wondered if he was more driven and stressed about finding Bethany from the command of his cloudy thought, or if it was because he knew she would die if he failed.

"Patchouli," Erec said. "Could you fly me back to Alypium? I need to find Bethany right away. It's urgent. Maybe you could scout around with me from the air and look for her?"

Patchouli sighed. The heat from her breath was so intense Erec had to step back. "I wish I could," she said. "But it's very dangerous for dragons to be there now. The Alypium army is under orders. They have detonation bombs poised at the sky, ready to kill us on sight." The corners of her mouth curled down.

"But . . . why?" Erec didn't understand. "I thought things would be better there now, after the battle in Otherness. Didn't the Archives of Alithea show everyone the truth, that dragons were good?"

"I wish that were true," Patchouli said. "But the only ones who saw the scroll were the soldiers. And what they learned was that the Hydras and Valkyries, who they were fighting, were really good people. I'm afraid it didn't tell them a thing about dragons."

"Baskania is behind this, isn't he?" Erec said. "He's scaring everyone about the dragons." The thought of Baskania made him shiver. He had to hurry. "Look, Patchouli, Bethany's life is on the line. The whole world is on the line."

Patchouli lifted her head and gazed into the clouds. "If it's that important, Erec, you should look into the future with your dragon eyes and decide what to do."

Erec remembered how Aoquesth read into the future. Now Erec had both of his eyes, but he had no idea how to use them in that way. He shook his head. "I can't."

Patchouli tilted her face, curious. "Why not?"

"I don't know how." Erec wished Aoquesth was alive. He would tell Erec everything he needed to know.

"For us dragons it comes naturally," Patchouli said. "We're just guided a little by our parents when we're young. Maybe I could work on it with you someday."

Erec kicked a rock across the dirt. Then he looked at Patchouli. "Could you look into the future for me?"

"I'm not sure if Aoquesth told you," she said. "But we dragons don't use that power, except for emergencies. It is not easy, and it takes a lot out of us. Plus, sometimes seeing the future makes you want to change it. If you live your life seeing and changing the future it soon becomes no kind of life at all."

That was what Aoquesth had said. Erec knew it was also just what Baskania would do if he had dragon eyes. He walked in front of Patchouli and put his hands on her snout. "Please, Patchouli. This is an emergency. For you as well as me. I mean it when I say our world will end if I don't find Bethany, and soon."

Patchouli closed her eyes, then opened them. "All right. I will trust you, Erec Rex. The great Aoquesth placed more than his trust in you. He placed his hope for the future in you when he gave you his eyes."

She rested on the ground, her head on a tuft of grass. "I'll need quiet."

Patchouli closed her eyes. When she opened them at last, beams of green light shot from them, joining to form a spotlight. It shone on a bush in front of her, making it glow. She held so still that it looked like she was not breathing. Then, all of a sudden, she exhaled and shut her eyes. She sprang to her feet.

"Erec, I was right to believe you. You will always have my trust from now on," she said. "What I have seen—" She stopped suddenly, and Erec knew why. He had seen it himself with his cloudy thought.

"Climb on my back," Patchouli said. "I'll take you to the fields behind the Castle Alypium. I know now where I can drop you off safely."

Erec scaled up her tail to her back, hand over hand, then wedged himself between two bloodred spines. She arched her back and the earth soon sank below them. Massive black, jointed wings stretched far on each side of him, and below them he saw trees and ponds getting smaller until they were tiny. He grabbed the red spine, squeezing, as they dove into a blinding white cloud.

"Patchouli?" he whispered. "I hope you know the right way." With the loud wind rushing into his face he was sure she could not hear him.

So he was surprised when she answered, "Of course I do, silly boy."

"You can hear me?" The rush of wind was so loud in his ears he could barely hear himself.

But the dragon's voice boomed loud. "Our hearing is a little better than yours."

They burst from the cloud. Mountains shot by below them, covered with green pine forests. It was breathtakingly beautiful.

"Patchouli," Erec asked, "when you looked into the future, did you see anything you would change?" Aoquesth had said that dragons could change the future that they saw, if they felt it was necessary. But Aoquesth had accepted his future willingly, even knowing he would give up his life for Erec.

"Yes, I did," Patchouli answered. "I am changing it. I would have dropped you off too far away, and you would not have found Bethany in time." He could feel her shudder through her scales. "I found a way to work it out."

Erec was enjoying the ride when the spires of the castle finally rose below them. They started soaring downward, and the ground lifted fast to meet them. He felt dizzy and had to squeeze extra hard to be sure he didn't fall off.

They made a soft landing on the ground. Patchouli's voice was quiet. "Bethany is with your friend Oscar in the castle gardens, right near the flagpole garden, close to the castle maze. Now go. She will tell Oscar her secret in just two minutes."

Erec slid from her back and stumbled, trying to regain his balance. He jogged away, then turned to Patchouli. "Thank—"

"Run!" she boomed. Then the dragon soared into the clouds.

Erec ran as fast as he could past the maze and into the gardens. Oscar was a good friend. He was one of the first people Erec had met in Alypium, and he had been at Erec's side all along. It didn't make sense that he would put Bethany in danger. But Erec knew that's what would happen if he didn't get there fast.

Right past the singing flagpoles, he saw two figures on a bench. Oscar and Bethany. Oscar's head was on her shoulder, his red hair gleaming in the sun.

"Nooooooo!" Erec ran toward them, screaming.

Bethany and Oscar froze, staring at him in shock. Then a grin spread across Bethany's face. "Erec! You're back? That's great! I was wondering when you'd get here."

The smile left her face as she glanced at Oscar sitting on the bench. His eyes were red and his lip was trembling.

Erec's insides froze. Why was Oscar so upset? Had he done something terrible? Like let Baskania know Bethany's secret? Was he too late? "Wh-what's wrong?" he stammered.

Oscar looked up at Erec, and hot tears began streaming down his face. "My . . . my . . . dad." It was all he could say.

Bethany put an arm around him. "Oscar's father died, Erec. It happened four weeks ago, but I just found out. Oscar came here today from Aorth."

"Did you . . ." Erec pointed at Bethany. "Did . . . you tell him . . ." He grabbed her arm. "Come here. Quick. I need to talk to you."

"Erec!" Bethany looked shocked. "Could you be a little more

sensitive? Did you hear what I said? We should help Oscar feel better now."

"I know . . . I will . . . Ugh!" Erec smacked his fist into his hand. "Listen! Both of you! This is urgent. I came here because I had a cloudy thought. Something terrible was about to happen. I *have* to make sure it won't happen. So I have to talk to you privately, Bethany. Now! Then I want to catch up with you, Oscar."

Bethany stood, sending Erec a disapproving glance. "I'm so sorry, Oscar. We'll be right back."

Oscar put his head in his hands. His voice sounded strangled. "Just go. Nobody cares, anyway."

"But why would telling Oscar my secret have mattered?" Bethany asked. "It doesn't make sense. Three minutes later Baskania would have appeared? Why?"

"I don't know why," Erec said. "I just know it would have happened. For sure." He searched her eyes. "You promise you won't tell him now? It's important."

"Yeah, sure," she said. "It is funny. The thought had just occurred to me to mention it to him, right before you showed up. I thought I could trust him. He was confiding in me about how he felt. It seemed like telling him something that worried me might make him feel less alone." She shook her head. "I just don't get it."

They walked back to the bench, but Oscar was gone.

"Oh, no!" Bethany cried. "We have to find him. What must he think? You show up and rush off with me, even after hearing that his dad died." She looked around. "Oscar!" she called.

Erec sat on the bench. "I don't know, Bethany. I thought we could trust him. But he must be helping Baskania. Can we be sure his father even died?"

Erec heard a bush rustling. He turned and saw a shadow move.

"Oscar?" Erec cleared some leaves out of the way, and Oscar's tear-stained face appeared.

"Go away! I heard what you said. My father *did* die. Not that you care. You were never my friend, obviously."

Erec crouched in front of the bush. "I'm sorry." Looking at Oscar through the leaves, fierce and defiant, it seemed impossible that he was lying about his father. "Oscar, what happened to your dad? I feel awful."

"He died." Oscar sniffed. "Nobody knows why. But you don't feel awful. You don't even believe me. And you think I'm helping Baskania?" He sounded stunned by that idea. "How could you?"

"Oscar," Erec said, "come on out, okay? I'll tell you everything that I can, and maybe we can figure this out together."

Oscar crawled out from under the bush, face puffy and eyes red, and took a seat on the bench, arms crossed. Bethany and Erec sat on either side of him.

Erec had to think fast. How much could he safely tell Oscar? Obviously not what Bethany's secret was. But he couldn't see why Oscar could not know the rest. "I had a cloudy thought," he explained. "I had to find you and Bethany before she told you . . . something, and stop her." He described what had happened in the Green House, and with Patchouli. "I don't know why, but if Bethany told you that . . . that certain secret, then Baskania would know right away and capture her three minutes later." He looked into Oscar's eyes. "Have you talked to Baskania at all?"

"Never!" Oscar said, outraged. "I've never even seen him in person! He doesn't know I exist. Your cloudy thought was wrong."

"Maybe it's because someone else you know is connected to Baskania. What about Rosco? He worked for Baskania." Erec breathed a sigh of relief. "That's it! You would have told Rosco, and he'd have let Baskania know right away."

Oscar's face wrinkled into a ball, lips sticking out. "No!" he growled. "I would *not* have told Rosco anything. I haven't seen him in a month, ever since we found out he kidnapped your brother and sister. I'll never speak to that jerk again. I hate him." He glared at Erec. "I am *not* talking to Rosco, or Baskania, okay? I don't even *want* to know that dumb secret anyway. So don't even tell me. Just leave me alone."

Oscar got up and stormed down the path. Bethany rushed after him and threw an arm around his shoulder, but Oscar brushed it off and ran away.

Erec and Bethany walked through the castle gardens past brightly colored daisies in blues, yellows, greens, and pinks. Their huge tops spun into the air like small helicopters, then landed on the stems of neighboring plants, like a giant game of musical chairs. Some of the daisy tops couldn't find anywhere to land and had to spin back up again and again.

They brushed leaping lizards from their faces as they walked. Then Bethany held up a finger and her dark brown eyes shone. "I got a cell phone, Erec! Usually they put them in your finger, like a tiny cell, when you're born. King Piter let me get one last week. It didn't hurt at all, just a pinch. So now I can make calls here." She tucked a curly strand of long, dark hair behind her ear. "I'm worried about Oscar. I think we should find him. Maybe I'll call him on my cell. He's a mess."

Erec nodded. "I'm sure. He must feel awful. I know how I'd feel if—" But then he stopped. How would he feel? He had no idea what it was like to have a father. Of course he would be upset beyond thinking if June, his adoptive mother, died. But a father? Oscar was lucky at least to have had a dad as long as he had. Bethany took it for granted too. Not that she had a real one. Her parents had died when she was young. But King Piter had become just like a father to her. It was almost the same thing.

Erec shook those thoughts from his head. He was just jealous of Oscar and Bethany, which was ridiculous now, after what had happened to Oscar. He should figure out ways to help.

Bethany bit her nail. "You know what he was saying, Erec?" She hesitated a moment. "I guess it's okay if I tell you. I mean, it wasn't a secret, I think. You knew Oscar never got along too well with his dad, right?"

"Yeah." Erec remembered Jack saying that Oscar's father was pretty rough on him. He had sent Oscar away to boarding school when he was young. And whenever he did see him, he'd always seemed disappointed in him. "Oscar was afraid to tell his dad when he lost the third contest in Alypium last summer. His dad made him think he had to win all six of them."

"That was a bit high of an expectation," Bethany said. "Considering there were over six hundred kids competing and only three could win." She shook her head. "Oscar tried so hard to impress him. He told me his father was finally coming around. After Rosco taught Oscar how to do magic without a remote control, his dad was actually impressed.

"But then when we all found out Rosco wasn't such a great guy, I guess Oscar's dad caught wind of that too. Oscar had to go home. His father told him his magic lessons were over. No more tutors. No living in Alypium. His dad had had enough of his bad luck. He said Oscar would have to stay at home and learn to do something he could handle, like bagging groceries."

"Oh, that's nice." Erec couldn't believe it.

"Well, it gets worse," said Bethany. "They got into a huge fight about it one night. Oscar threatened to run away if his dad didn't let him learn magic. And just then, after Oscar went to bed all angry and miserable, his father died. Nobody saw it happen. It was like a big mystery. On the table the next morning, they found an envelope with a ton of money in it. A note said that it was to pay for a new magic tutor for Oscar in Alypium. It was just signed 'a relative.'"

"Weird." Erec frowned. A huge blue daisy head whirled by his face. On it sat a small leaping lizard, riding it like a spinning spacecraft.

"Can you imagine how Oscar feels now?" Bethany asked. "I was glad he opened up to me about it. It's a lot for him to deal with. He's still angry at his dad, but so sad, too.

And worse, he feels guilty, like it was his fault. I told him that he had to forget that completely. But he can't shake it."

"Poor Oscar." Erec felt terrible. The oppressive gloom in the air of Alypium, from its messed up Substance, made everything seem even worse. It would take him a few days to get used to it again. And then the feeling would still come back unbidden every now and then, stray cries of sadness from the air.

They reached the house of Erec's pet wenwolf dog, Wolfboy. The house had been padded for the dog's safety during full moons. The big, mangy, dark gray mutt jumped all over him until he finally knocked Erec over. A big pink tongue covered Erec's face in slippery kisses until he pushed him away. "Good dog." Erec scratched behind Wolfboy's pointy ears while he nuzzled up by Erec's side.

"You know," Erec said. "I know just what might cheer Oscar up."

Even though it was January in Upper Earth, and the Asian mountains upon which Alypium was perched were covered in snow, the temperature was perfect. The golden dome covering the kingdom kept the sun's rays filtered in the summer and held heat in during the winter.

But Erec still wore a sweatshirt jacket, with the hood as far over his head as he could pull it, when he walked into town with Bethany, Wolfboy, and Bethany's fluffy pink kitten, Cutie Pie. He hoped that with his hood up, nobody would recognize him. The last time he had been spotted in Alypium, a huge mob had chased him back to the castle. That was thanks to Baskania spreading word around Alypium that the Stain brothers were the true rulers, and Erec was an imposter. Everyone seemed to believe that Erec was some power mad intruder trying to become king, and messing up everything for the poor Stain boys.

They strolled into the agora, where most of the shops were. In a pet shop, they found a furry yellow kitten for Oscar. Erec thought a puppy might be more fun, but once Bethany saw the kittens there was no changing her mind.

They got in line to pay, behind a tall, thin woman. Everything about her was pointed. Her chin, nose, and even her teeth looked sharp and nasty. Gray hair was shorn very short around her face, dangling longer from the middle. When she bent to look in her purse, the lock of hair hung down into a point, making her look like a curved fishhook.

She didn't bother turning around when the kids walked behind her. Her thin lips pressed into a stern line as she talked to the cashier. "Thank you for ordering these, Mabel," she said, inspecting the gleaming, deep silver horseshoes on the counter. "Have someone carry the feed bags through my Port-O-Door, please."

Mabel, the cashier, looked just the opposite of the other woman, short and round in a bright red sweater. When the tall woman bent over her purse again, the two of them reminded Erec of a hook poised next to an apple. "Yes, Mrs. Stain," Mabel said, nodding.

Bethany nudged him, eyebrows raised. Erec had not thought much of their conversation, but now he listened closer.

Mrs. Stain sighed. "Those boys and their dragon horses." She shook her head. "We had to make their little friend, Rock, give his horse to Dollick. It really wasn't fair that Dollick didn't get one, you know. And we don't like to upset Dollick much. He makes terrible noises and starts to butt his head into people."

Erec's eyes shot wide open as he looked at Bethany. Mrs. Stain! How had he not recognized that name? So this was the mother of the Stain triplets: Damon, with the strange bone that protruded from his head under his gray hat; Dollick, who *baa*ed and looked quite a bit like a white, fluffy sheep; and Balor, their ringleader, who was just pure evil.

Mrs. Stain clicked her tongue. Erec noticed that no bone shot from her pointy head, nor did she have fuzzy, white sheep's wool all over her face and neck. It made Erec wonder what her husband must look like.

"You know," she said as she bent over the counter, hook coming closer to apple. "We're trying to fix the disarray that Rex boy seems to have caused."

Erec shrank farther into his hooded jacket. He was glad Mrs. Stain was oblivious to his presence right behind her.

She continued, "Spread the word, Mabel. The Rex boy is still up to no good. We think he's going to keep butting into the quests that the Fates are sending up from Al's Well. Which means he's still trying to be king. Even though he knows the whole kingdom is against him. We want to let everyone know that they shouldn't worry."

"But . . ." Mabel leaned forward timidly, obviously itching to ask a question, yet nervous. "I heard you already tried to fix things. That your boys went to the Labor Society when Erec Rex was out of town, and they tried to get the next quest without him. Is that true? But the Fates weren't ready to send the quest, so they had to leave without getting it." She shrunk back, as if Mrs. Stain might bop her on the head.

Mrs. Stain's thin lips disappeared into a tight line. "*That* was just a test run," she said. "Nothing to be concerned about. It doesn't mean we aren't ready with other ideas."

She looked at her watch, seeming to have lost interest in the conversation. "Get me help with the feed bags. Now, please. I've had enough here." Erec turned his back quickly when she looked around, but she was too caught up in herself and the feed bags to notice who was around her.

A scrawny boy with snowy white hair and black eyes lugged the feed bags in and out of the wooden Port-O-Door that led into Mrs. Stain's house. She watched with her arms crossed, tapping her foot. Erec recognized the boy from this summer's contests in Alypium, where kids had competed to see who would be the next rulers.

"Just think," Bethany whispered. "Balor, Damon, and Dollick are probably right through that door."

Erec's mind flashed to an image of Damon and Dollick fighting over who got to be the first to kill some dragon babies. He almost threw up.

They took turns carrying the new kitten to the apprentice boarding house where Oscar was staying. Cutie Pie rode on Wolfboy's back, an arrangement that looked like it was to Cutie Pie's liking much more than the dog's. On a few occasions Wolfboy tried to shake her off, but her claws just gripped him tighter.

"I can't believe they tried to get the next quest from Al's Well without me." Erec still felt stunned.

"How can you be surprised?" Bethany asked. "Think who we're dealing with. The thing is, how are you going to know when the next quest is going to start? Do you think Erida will actually come tell you again?"

Erida was the Harpy who had invited Erec to draw his first two quests from Al's Well. Erec had not thought about what she would do. "I don't know. Maybe she has to."

"I wouldn't count on it," Bethany said. "We're going to have to figure out another way to find out when Al's Well is ready for you."

A strange feeling rose in Erec. It was one he was getting used to, but not one that he liked. This feeling was exactly why he had not been thinking of Erida or his next quest at all. In fact, he'd spent a whole month at home not thinking about it, just enjoying his time with his previously lost siblings—the twins, Danny and Sammy—and putting off coming back to Alypium. Every now and then he wondered if Erida might try to find him, if the next quest might start before he got back. But then this feeling would hit him, and he'd push the whole thing right out of his head.

The feeling. It was a strange mix of opposites. Insane craving and terrific fear. Wanting and dreading. Clinging and pushing away.

It was all about the scepters. Erec had such an intense experience in the past using King Pluto's and then King Piter's scepter. But those experiences were nothing compared to the lingering feelings they left behind in him. Still, months later, there was not a day that Erec did not imagine the scepter's power coursing through him again. There was not a night that he did not dream of wielding one, controlling all he saw.

But with those cravings came a deep terror. He knew that if a scepter was offered to him he would not be able to refuse it. And he saw, from his own dreams of conquering the world, that it would bring out the worst in him. Like King Pluto, who had once been a good kid, he would turn self-serving and evil.

And doing more quests meant just one thing. Moving closer and closer to the day when a scepter was handed to him.

"You know," Erec said, turning to Bethany. "I was thinking. It seems pretty safe for me to bow out now. I mean, I've got the Amulet of Virtues. That shows I've finished the first two quests." He held the shiny gold disc on the chain around his neck in front of him, two of its twelve segments glowing red and purple-blue. "The Stain brothers, and Rock Rayson, if he's still with them, don't have these. I bet that means they can't really win the scepters. So let them just do what they want without me."

"What?" Bethany stopped walking and squeezed the cat carrier to her chest. "You have to be kidding! If you don't compete, they'll take that as a forfeit. The only reason the Stains haven't officially become kings is that old law saying that twelve quests have to be done before the scepters are claimed. And if you aren't doing them, they'll be able to do the quests without you."

"I don't think they could," Erec said. "Al's Well has only let me draw the quests, not anyone else."

"That's because you haven't quit," she said. "If you quit, the Stains would probably be able to take over." She started walking again, and Erec joined her. "Listen, is it worth taking the risk? Knowing what would happen if Balor, Damon, and Dollick get the scepters? They'd hand them over to Baskania. And you can imagine what life would be like then."

Erec didn't have to imagine. He'd had a glimpse with his dragon eyes in his last cloudy thought. It would be the same thing that would happen if Oscar found out Bethany's secret. Baskania would get the scepters, throw the world into slavery, and soon end life as they knew it.

"There's another problem," Erec said. "Even if I do become king, there are two more thrones that need to be filled. The kingdoms need three new rulers. Who do you think will end up being the other two kings? Looks like Balor and one of his brothers have it pretty well wrapped up. I don't see anyone else in the running."

Bethany kicked a pebble and sent it flying into a small patch of shrinking violets. The purple flowers jolted away from the stone, quivering. "I'll rule with you."

"But you can't. King Piter said the new rulers have to be chosen by the scepter and the Lia Fail stone. The scepter only went to me, nobody else."

"Well, I wasn't in the castle then," Bethany pointed out. "Maybe one of the scepters would have come to me if I had been there. Anyway, the Stain brothers weren't picked, and they were there then."

"Yeah, but they have Baskania behind them, and he can make anything happen," Erec said.

"Maybe." Bethany bit her lip, concentrating. "But I wonder who the other two rulers are *supposed* to be. I guess they must be two people who weren't in the room during the coronation." She looked at Erec. "So it's possible that I could be one, I guess."

Erec shook his head. "King Piter made it sound like I'm the only one." He wished Bethany was right, though. No doubt she would do a better job of ruling than he would, given the way the scepters affected him.

Bethany looked as disappointed as Erec felt. "Maybe the other two kids will turn up somewhere. All we can do is hope."

So, what were Erec's options? Letting Balor and friends ruin the world? Or getting the scepters, and ruining the world himself? Great choices. "I still think I should just give up," he said.

Bethany studied his face. "I know what it is. You're afraid of getting the scepter again, aren't you?"

Erec nodded.

She sighed impatiently. "I thought we talked about that. You can just not accept it. When it's all done we'll bury it somewhere. Or I'll hide it from you if you want."

Yeah, sure, Erec thought. *Right.*

CHAPTER FOUR

A Smug Harpy and a Helpful Ghost

OSCAR HELD THE small yellow kitten to his cheek. His eyes were red and puffy. "Thanks, guys."

Erec tried to cheer him up. "We saw Balor and Damon's mom in the pet store. Looks like she made Rock Rayson give his dragon horse to their brother Dollick. She said it 'wasn't fair that Dollick didn't have one.' I guess it's only fair for her sons to have things, not other kids."

"What about their friend Ward Gamin?" Oscar asked. "He won a dragon horse too. You think they'll take his away?"

"Who knows." Bethany looked disgusted. "Those Stain triplets don't care about anyone but themselves." She glared at Erec, an unspoken reminder that he couldn't drop the ball and let the Stain boys become kings.

The three of them were sitting by a brook in Paisley Park. All around them kids were paired with tutors, brandishing remote controls and making useless things happen in an attempt to harness their magic. Bethany had called her session off today, and Erec had no tutor arranged yet. His previous one, Pimster Peebles, had taught him nothing—had not even allowed him to try using his remote control. He said it was too dangerous.

Erec smiled at Oscar. "Well, one good thing about Rosco Kroc— at least he showed me how to use my remote control to move things. He's the only one who taught me anything about doing magic. I bet he would have shown me more, too, if—"

"If what?" The smile dropped from Oscar's face. "If he didn't turn out to be an evil kidnapper? How could you even think anything nice about that guy? I hate him. *Hate* him." He glared at Erec with defiance. "It was your brother and sister he kidnapped. Remember?"

Erec rolled his eyes. "Of course I remember. I don't like him either, believe me. But we used to. Remember how you talked about how great he was? How much magic he taught you?"

Oscar's face was bright red. Erec immediately felt bad for making a point of it.

Oscar growled, his eyes slits, "Don't ever speak another word about Rosco Kroc to me. Ever. He ruined my life."

Erec nodded, but Bethany tilted her head, puzzled. "We all can't stand him, Oscar. We know what he did. But how did that ruin your life? Just forget about him."

Erec knew why Oscar felt his life was ruined. He had looked up to Rosco, loved him like a father, probably. And Rosco had disappointed him. It must have humiliated Oscar to find out that the person he respected most was a kidnapper and a spy for Baskania, and had lied to him about it. And when he was sent home, he'd gotten in fights with his father about getting another tutor, right before his father died. Maybe Oscar thought that if it hadn't been for Rosco, his father would have lived. He probably blamed Rosco for the whole thing.

Oscar wiped his eyes on the kitten's yellow fur and squinted at Bethany. "Because of Rosco, I'll never get to do any quests with Erec. That's the only thing I really want to do. I could have learned all that magic from anyone."

Erec had forgotten about that. One more reason for Oscar to hate Rosco.

Bethany held a finger up. "Why can't you do a quest, Oscar? Just because Rosco said so? He's wrong."

"No," Erec said. "He's right. Ugry said that he'd make sure Oscar would never go on a quest with me, just because Oscar had been associated with Rosco."

Oscar's face was pinched. "If I ever see him again, anywhere, he better watch out."

Erec figured it was time to change the conversation. "Well, I'm probably not going to go on another quest again, anyway. Looks like Balor and crew are working on ways to get the next one without me even knowing about it. We'll just figure out our own fun things to do here instead."

The edges of Oscar's mouth twitched into a smile. Bethany glared at Erec, but didn't bring the quests up again.

"How long have you been here?" Erec asked.

"Just got here yesterday," Oscar said. "I have a bunch of money that I found at home. Some unknown relative left it for me to get a tutor. I still need to find one though. Are you getting a new tutor?"

"I better," Erec said. "Peebles stunk."

Oscar grinned and Bethany broke into a smile. She took Oscar's kitten from him and rubbed noses with it. A second later Cutie Pie, pink fur on end, dove from a bush right at her hands. If Bethany hadn't jerked away in time, the kitten would have flown to the ground. "Cutie Pie!" she exclaimed, jaw dropped. "I'm allowed to hold other kittens. Shame on you!"

She handed the yellow kitten back to Oscar. "I want you and Jack to have dinner with us at the castle tonight. King Piter will be there. He'll be so glad to see Erec again. We should make it a party. Sound like fun?"

Oscar nodded. "I still have that autograph the king gave me, from the first time I met him."

A loud, strangled screech made all three of them jump. In front of them appeared a creature with the body of a vulture and the head of a woman. Shiny black hair plastered on her head wound into a tight bun, and her nose shot out like a beak. Erec wasn't sure if she wore black lipstick or if her lips were naturally that dark. But either way, he recognized her, and her ferocious expression, immediately.

It was Erida, the Harpy.

Erida, from the Committee for Committee Oversight, in the Bureau of Bureaucrats, was supposed to be in charge of the quests. She had invited Erec to draw his first two from Al's Well. Erida thrust a claw toward him, holding a crisp parchment roll. He reached out toward her to take it.

As if he was not right in front of her, Erida shrieked, "Erec Rex! Erec Rex! Erec Rex!"

Erec jerked his arm back in shock. "Is that for me?"

"Erec Rex! Erec Rex! Erec Rex!" she squawked, a glint in her eye, as if she enjoyed making them recoil. Bethany covered her ears. With a flick of her claw, the parchment flew into Erec's face. "Watch out, Erec Rex," she said. "President Inkle made us the police here now. We've got our eyes on you. See you soon . . . sucker!" she cackled. Then she swooped through the air and flew away.

Erec shuddered. How could President Inkle have made those awful Harpies the police of Alypium? Then again, the president seemed to do whatever Baskania wanted. Maybe this was another way of scaring the people of Alypium into doing whatever they wanted.

He unrolled the thick crinkled paper. It read, "It is with the utmost pleasure that the Committee for Committee Oversight invites Erec Rex to the Labor Society this Friday at 7:00 p.m. to accept his third quest." At the bottom, a smug-looking smiley face was engraved next to the words, "Our Mission—PIPS: Pleased, Inspired, Pleasantly-surprised Service."

"Friday? That's tomorrow. Well, this is a surprise," Erec said, staring at the invitation in his hand. He fingered the gold amulet around his neck, not thrilled about drawing another quest. "I can't believe that Alypium is going to be run by screaming Harpy police with their dumb committees and red tape."

Bethany's lips fluttered back and forth between a smile and a frown. "I don't know, Erec. I don't like it. You heard Mrs. Stain. What if they have some kind of plan to trick you? But, then again, you can't quite turn it down, can you? Doing another quest is your only chance to be king and get rid of Baskania for good."

"I *can* turn it down, Bethany. You saw Erida's face. And the words, 'Pleased,' 'Inspired,' and 'Pleasantly-surprised'? They want me to go. That's not a good sign. I better stay away."

"So you'll quit and let Baskania get the scepters? Destroy the whole world?" Her eyelids narrowed and she put her hands on her hips.

Erec felt guilty. He was just thinking about himself. She was right. He had to put aside his fears of being given a scepter and actually do something to keep them away from Baskania. He shrugged sheepishly. "You're right. We just have to think about a safe way to do this."

"Don't forget," she said, "your Amulet of Virtues will protect you more with each quest you do. It kept King Piter, Queen Posey, and King Pluto safe from Baskania when they were young, after they did enough quests."

Erec nodded. It also gave Baskania more reason to get rid of him now, before he got any stronger.

Oscar had been quietly watching them. His voice sounded distant as he said, "Just go without me. Nice to know you."

Erec stared at him. "You know what, Oscar? Who cares what Ugry says? Who cares about these dumb rules? All the rules are being made against me now, anyway. I want you and Bethany to go with me on this quest. Let's see someone just try to stop you."

Oscar sat up straight. His kitten almost dropped from his lap, and had to cling on to his pants with her claws. "You . . . you mean it, Erec? I can do a quest with you?" He stood. The kitten tumbled to the ground but landed on her paws. "I can't believe it!" A grin filled his entire face. "Maybe I'll solve the quest myself! Maybe I'll even end up being king with you!"

"I don't think—" Erec stopped in midsentence when he saw Bethany shake her head at him. She was right. Oscar deserved to feel happy.

It had been a month since Erec had been in the Castle Alypium, and it felt strange being back. It was so big and imposing compared to the New Jersey apartment he shared with his five adopted siblings and their adoptive mother, June. On his way to the west wing, Erec

caught a whiff of something foul. Around the corner stood a man with a vertical crease running up the center of his bulging forehead.

Balthazar Ulrich Theodore Ugry, King Piter's AdviSeer, leaned on his dark carved walking stick. The scarab amulet on his black cape was glowing. "Ahh," he said, eyelids narrowing. "I can see I'll be busy again."

Erec frowned at him. "Not on my account. Just do your own thing. I'm fine."

As many times as Erec had been suspicious that Ugry was up to something nasty, though, he had been proved wrong. As unpleasant as he acted, and smelled, it seemed that Ugry meant no harm. In fact, he had saved Erec from a shadow demon. He could not let himself forget that.

"So are you saying you don't need a babysitter anymore?" Ugry looked perpetually annoyed. "Because that's not how it seems to me. Each time you're here you get in trouble."

"I'll be fine. Just . . ." Erec waved as if to shoo him off.

Ugry smirked and drifted down the hall. Erec found Bethany in the west wing dining hall. Its soaring ceilings, stained glass windows, chandeliers, and fancy china on the long table made Bethany look tiny.

Jam Crinklecut, the butler in charge of the west wing house staff, walked in. He carried a silver tray stacked high with cheeseburgers, pizza, and stuffed potato skins. His gray vest, long black dinner jacket with tails, fancy white shirt, and even his white gloves looked perfectly pressed. Fortunately, his hair was no longer slicked to the side with thick grease as it had been when Erec first met him.

Jam was more than a butler to Erec, he was a friend. He had followed Erec into Otherness and fought by Erec's side against the entire Alypian army. Not that Jam would ever brag, or even admit that he had been brave. He was too humble, and noble, for that.

Jam broke into a grin when he saw Erec. He put the platter down, rushed over, and put his hands on Erec's shoulders as if he were about to give him a hug. Then he thought better of it and instead bowed again and again.

"Aw, cut it out." Erec boxed Jam's shoulder playfully, then gave him a quick hug. "How've you been, Jam?"

"Most pleasant, young sir," Jam said in his crisp British accent. "And how may I best serve young sir today? Are there any special requests you might have?"

Erec thought a moment. "Yes, Jam, I do."

Jam straightened, ready as usual to serve.

Erec smiled. "I request that you join us at the table for dinner."

Jam's eyes flew wide open. "But . . . young sir." He looked around uncomfortably. "This is highly irregular."

Before Erec could answer, King Piter came through the doorway. His long white hair was pulled back under his crown, and his eyes twinkled. The king's magnetic presence made everyone turn to him like needles in a compass.

Or was it what he was carrying? In his hand glimmered a golden scepter. Erec's breath caught when he saw it. For a moment he forgot that everyone else in the room existed. It was just him and the scepter.

"Well, Jam," King Piter said, "I think it's a wonderful idea. I'm sure Erec would enjoy a meal with you."

Jam bowed to the king. "Yes, sire. If you say so, sire." He looked around uneasily as if wondering what to do next, then stood a moment, staring at the plates. Finally, he sat next to Erec.

Bethany flew across the room and gave King Piter a hug. "Hey, Daddy!"

A smile played on the edge of Erec's lips. Bethany used to catch herself when she called King Piter her father, but she must have given into it finally. Erec was happy for her. She had wanted parents so badly, and King Piter was pretty close, basically adopting her. Bethany had seemed over the moon when the king told her he thought of her like a daughter.

The king patted her head, the corners of his lips tipping into a wistful smile. Then he looked at Erec. "Come here, boy."

Erec approached him, as he had when he'd first dined with the king, unsure what to do. The closer he came to the scepter, the more he began to squirm. He wanted to touch it badly but was also terrified of it.

Then something inside him relaxed. It was better this time. The urge was less. He was sure of it. No doubt his cravings for the scepter were still there, but its grip on him was loosening. Finally! He stayed on the other side of the king as he came close, feeling slightly more in control.

King Piter planted a thick palm on his head and mussed his hair, then walked to his seat at the head of the table. As Erec sat down, a woman's voice sounded in the room. "Erec?" The voice sounded familiar. He looked all over, but no woman was there.

Then it was louder, making him jump. "Erec? Can you hear me?"

Erec stood up and looked around. "What was that?"

Bethany and King Piter watched him with quizzical looks. "What was what?" Bethany asked.

"That voice!" he said.

And then it sounded again. "Erec? It's me. Your mom. Remember? The Seeing Eyeglasses?"

The Seeing Eyeglasses let their wearer see the person who they missed most, and talk to them. His mother had them on now and could see Erec clearly, even though he couldn't see her. His jaw fell open. "So, this is what it's like? You can spy on whatever I'm doing with those things?"

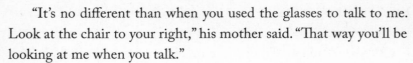

"It's no different than when you used the glasses to talk to me. Look at the chair to your right," his mother said. "That way you'll be looking at me when you talk."

Erec laughed. "All right."

Bethany looked stunned. King Piter, on the other hand, munched some cloud rolls without taking any more notice.

"Is everything okay?" his mother asked. "Looks like you found Bethany all right."

"Yeah. And I got an invite to do another quest. So I guess I'll be here awhile."

"I figured that would happen soon," she said.

Bethany asked, "Erec, who are you talking to?"

"My mom. She has the Seeing Eyeglasses."

"Ohhh." Recognition showed in Bethany's eyes.

"I'll check in on you later, then, Erec," June said.

"Okay, bye, Mom."

The king cleared his throat. "Good to see you back, Erec. I'm glad to hear the Fates are ready to give you your next quest tomorrow."

"I have a question," Bethany said. "Why was there so much time between Erec's last quest and this one? They're so important, it seems like there shouldn't have been any wait."

King Piter laughed. "I've actually been surprised at how fast Erec's quests have been coming. Ours were spread out much more. The quests aren't just contests that can be planned in advance. They are a part of Erec's real life. His quests will affect all of our lives, really. Things happening around us will shape into the right lessons for Erec to become a good king.

"There are no time limits on quests. Some of the great quests in history took many years. Some of them might require a while to prepare for as well. The Fates would not rush the making of a king." He winked at Erec. "And they know when it's time to give breaks, too, when they're needed. I think Erec was ready for some time at home this last month."

The king sighed. "I've been busy with some problems. I'm sorry I haven't had time to check up on your situation much. Things are getting worse on Upper Earth, and it's all I can do to figure out what's wrong."

"What problems on Upper Earth?" This caught Erec by surprise. It didn't seem possible that any problems large enough to interest King Piter could be happening on Upper Earth.

The door flew open. Jack Hare and Oscar Felix walked into the dining hall. A servant appeared seconds later and held the door open, too late. He looked around as if to announce them but was unsure what their names were.

Jack marched straight to Erec's side. Erec jumped up and grinned. "Hey, Jack! How's it going?"

"Better now." He clapped Erec on the shoulder. "Glad you're back. You gonna get another slice of that amulet filled?"

Erec looked down at the Amulet of Virtues on the chain around his neck. Another of the twelve slices would fill in if he completed the next quest. The thought also reminded him that the quest itself might not be pleasant.

Both Oscar and Jack approached the king, bowing and thanking him before sitting down.

Erec looked at the king, averting his eyes from the scepter. "What problems are happening in Upper Earth, King Piter?"

The king looked down as a servant whisked a plate of what looked like green slop before him on a golden plate. "Bees, Erec. The latest problem is the bees. I've had some very upsetting news about them from my plants in Upper Earth."

Erec, Bethany, Jack, and Oscar all looked at one another as if they must have heard wrong. "Killer bees?" Bethany asked.

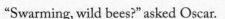

"Swarming, wild bees?" asked Oscar.

"No." King Piter shook his head. "Worse. Vanishing bees."

Erec frowned. "You mean invisible attack bees?"

"No, Erec," the king said. "Disappearing bees. They're not even leaving a trace. No dead bodies, nothing. The bees in Upper Earth are just going away somewhere and not coming back."

Oscar raised an eyebrow as if the king had gone crazy, then quickly stopped before the king noticed. "So what's wrong if they disappear? They just sting people anyway, right?"

"No, Oscar." King Piter sighed. "They do much more than sting people. Bees are vital to life in Upper Earth, at least as we know it. You like apples, strawberries, melons, cherries, pears? Bees pollinate most of the crops out there, and many wild plants as well. If the bees disappear and the crops don't make it, it would affect the food chain and many other species would die out. It would be hard to say how people would survive if those plants and animals start to go.

"But the problem is even worse than that," he said. "If the bees are vanishing, it can just mean one thing. The Substance is starting to drain out of Upper Earth. The bees are the most sensitive to it. They fly along the network of the Aitherplanes that hold the Substance. It helps them find their way around. But if bees are starting to disappear, they will not be the only ones. Another creature will be next. And then another. It won't happen right away. But if things keep going this way with the Substance, one of these days Upper Earth won't be able to sustain life at all."

Erec, Bethany, Jack, and Oscar walked down into the catacombs below the castle after dinner. The maze of twisty passages had been covered by the wall of the castle when it was on its side for ten years, keeping everyone out.

"I just can't believe it," Bethany said. "Upper Earth is dying? The bees are disappearing, and soon other animals will too? We have to help King Piter stop whatever is going wrong there."

Erec nodded. "It has to do with the Substance. I'll talk to the dragons about it. They can see the Substance all the time. Maybe they have some ideas."

"Don't you think King Piter already tried talking to the dragons?" Oscar asked.

"I guess." Erec shrugged. "I know the Substance is different on Upper Earth than here. When I have cloudy thoughts I can see it hanging in the air like ropes here. There is a lot more of it. On Upper Earth it looks more like cobwebs."

"King Piter said it's draining away from there," Bethany said. "What if it's gone soon?"

Erec sighed. "What is it about the Substance that makes it so important?"

"It carries the magic we all need to live," Jack said. "We learned that in grade school. You can't survive without the Substance around you."

That made Erec remember the Nevervarld. In the Nevervarld there was absolutely no Substance. No magic could enter it at all. And no living things could stay alive in it except dragons—and even they could not live there for long. So would Upper Earth turn into a Nevervarld?

"That's why it feels so awful to come to the Kingdoms of the Keepers from Upper Earth," Bethany said. "There is so much more Substance here it makes us feel all heavy and depressed."

Jack nodded. "But it's not just that there is more of it here. It's that it's messed up here. Sad or something."

They all nodded, each knowing the feeling the upset Substance gave them. Erec was glad that he was finally starting to adjust to it.

"You know, there is one other person who knows a lot about

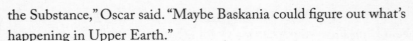

the Substance," Oscar said. "Maybe Baskania could figure out what's happening in Upper Earth."

Erec stared at him in shock as they walked, and almost hit his head as he rounded a rocky corner. "Baskania? My mortal enemy? The guy who almost tore my eyes out and killed me just before I came here? I don't think I'll be going to him for help." Erec shook his head. "It wouldn't surprise me if he was the cause of the problems."

"Here we are! The coolest room in the castle," Bethany announced with a grand swish of her arm. Before them was a door with a gold handle. She opened it, and they walked into a cavernous room. A golden glowing figure materialized before them. He looked like a cross between a man and a cloud. It was the golden ghost guarding King Piter's most treasured possession, his Novikov Time Bender.

The ghost's voice wavered. "Hello, Erec."

"Hi, Homer." Homer was the only golden ghost that Erec had ever met. As far as Erec knew, he never left this room.

"A golden ghost!" Oscar looked whiter than usual, which was impressive given his pale skin typical of the people from underground Aorth. "I never thought I'd see one. This is such good luck!" He stepped forward, arm outstretched. "Can you help me, ghost?"

Homer, the ghost, seemed to radiate warmth, drawing them all closer. A chuckle arose from the glowing apparition. "I'm afraid we're not good luck charms, Oscar Felix. It's true we may help humans at times, if we so choose. And that would be only if we feel those humans are right in their motives. But really, the only one who can help you, and bring you the luck you need, is yourself."

Oscar did not look disappointed, only amazed, as he stepped closer to the smiling image.

"And look." Bethany pointed at a tall, thin box that looked like an upright coffin. It was made of solid gold, except for the front, which was a sheet of glass. "There is King Piter's time machine."

THE SEARCH FOR TRUTH

They all turned to look at the Novikov Time Bender. It seemed too simple to send people traveling through time. Fascinated, Erec walked closer to take a look. The last time he had been down here, he had just lost his dear dragon friend, Aoquesth. He had been too exhausted to fully take in the concept of a time machine.

A small television screen jutted from the side of the golden box, connected by a tube. The glass front was hinged like a door, with a gold handle. Peering inside, Erec could see some sort of dials hanging against the wall.

Bethany looked around. "Why isn't King Piter here? Last time you called him right when we showed up. Aren't you guarding this for him?"

Homer slid toward the Time Bender. "I do guard this room for the king and keep his Time Bender from the wrong people. I was with King Piter even before he had this built. But I'm not a paid servant with orders to report whoever walks in here. The king trusts that I know how to handle things.

"I called him here the last time you came because Erec and Jam were exhausted and you had a bad case of helmet hair. I knew the king would want to be with you, to help you, and to say good-bye. I did not call him because I thought you were a danger to his Time Bender." The ghost chuckled.

"How does it work?" Jack asked, gazing at the box.

"Simple really," Homer answered. "Neat little device. You just climb in and turn the dials to the date you want to go to. Then you fit into your old body that was there at that time, stay for as long as you like, and come back when you're done.

"Someone in this room could see you in two different ways. We could see your current self, laying in the Time Bender, through the glass. Of course, you change to look like you were at the age you went to. And we could also look through the viewer to see exactly what

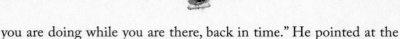

you are doing while you are there, back in time." He pointed at the television screen.

"I don't get it," Erec said. "You go back into your body at that time? What does that mean?"

"Well," the ghost explained, "say you went back three years. You would appear three years younger through the glass. But also you would be there, back then, walking around in your old ten-year-old body. You'd fit right in with people who knew you at that time, except that in your case, Erec, you were not here three years ago. So people might be suspicious."

This sounded amazing. "You mean I could go to any time that I was alive?"

"Exactly," the ghost said. "But I would not recommend going back to when you were too young. Like an infant. Your mind would stay the same as it is now, of course. But you would not have enough physical strength to get around, or get back into the machine when you were ready. You'd be stuck there for years."

"Could someone go into the future?" Bethany asked.

"Very dangerous," the ghost said flatly. "I don't recommend that at all."

"Why?" Erec asked.

"You might make a mistake and choose a time when you are no longer alive. There are no guarantees on anyone's future, you know."

Oscar looked intrigued. "And what would happen if someone went into the past, before they were born? Or went into the future, after they had died? Could they do it?"

"They could," the ghost answered. "But their body would disappear from the machine. They would be transported to that date, at the age they are now, but they would never be able to get back. You might see them for a little while with the viewer, but their image would soon fade away."

THE SEARCH FOR TRUTH

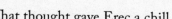

That thought gave Erec a chill.

"I guess King Piter has it locked up so nobody can use it?" Oscar asked.

"No." The ghost sounded casual about it. "He trusts me to do what is right, of course."

"So," Erec said, "you would never let anyone use it, I guess?"

The ghost fluttered in front of them in at least ten different shades of gold. "That would be up to me."

CHAPTER FIVE
The Torn Quest

EREC'S MIND KEPT flitting from one thing to another. At one moment he would feel stunned, wondering what new trouble awaited him when he drew the next quest from Al's Well. The last one had thrown him into a battle where he'd almost died and had lost Aoquesth. Then, just as that seemed overwhelming enough, he would start to think about the bees disappearing, Substance leaking out of Upper Earth, and the normal world turning into a Nevervarld death zone where nothing could live. How long before that would happen? Centuries? Decades? Years?

Then, right when he was sure his head would explode, images of the Novikov Time Bender would pop again into his mind. Now that was one cool device. Imagine, to be able to go back in time like that. Where would he go?

Then an idea hit him. Maybe he could go back and save Aoquesth. It seemed like Homer, the golden ghost, might actually let him use it. Didn't he say that he helped people who were "right in their motives"?

Well, nothing was more right than Erec going back to save Aoquesth's life. That dragon had given up everything for him. The only problem was that Erec had no idea how to do it, even if he could go back to that battle where Aoquesth had lost his life. Baskania's death blade had been coming right for Erec. If Aoquesth hadn't stepped in and intercepted it, Erec would have died. It seemed it was either Aoquesth or him.

Erec, Bethany, Jack, and Oscar met in Paisley Park at ten o'clock in the morning. Bethany and Jack took the day off from their tutors.

"All right, guys," Jack said. "Erec is drawing his quest tonight at seven. We need to figure out a plan in case there are problems. I agree with Erec. Erida's invitation sounded a little too cheerful. What was that? 'Pleased, excited'...?"

Erec smirked. "'Pleased, Inspired, Pleasantly-surprised Service.' And when she flew away she said, 'So long, sucker.' Kinda makes you wonder."

"I know," Oscar said. "I'll pose as you. I'll find someone who can change my looks. Then if anything happens, they'll have the wrong guy."

Erec felt touched that Oscar was willing to protect him. He really was a good friend. "No way, Oscar," he said. "I can't let you risk your

life like that. You know what would happen if they captured you?"
He shook his head. "Plus, you wouldn't be able to draw the quest,
even if you did look like me. It won't work for anybody else."

Bethany stared at the ground, not saying anything. Erec looked
at her questioningly. She shrugged. "I'm kind of all mixed-up about
all this."

Erec was too. It was hard to charge into something that felt like
a setup.

"I mean, I know you have to get the quest," she said. "I just wish
there were another way. It's obvious that Baskania expects you to
go there. Maybe he's planning on . . ." Her words hung in the air.
It seemed obvious what Baskania planned to do to Erec when he
caught him. Take his eyes out and then kill him.

Jack's jaw dropped. "I have an idea. No clue if it will work, but
it's worth a try. Oscar, come with me. We'll meet you back here in
two hours."

Erec and Bethany brought a lunch basket, packed by Jam, back
to Paisley Park to wait for Oscar and Jack. Of course, given Jam's
expertise, it had everything they could want. Egg salad, tuna, and
turkey sandwiches sat atop cut fruits, snack bars, cheese and cracker
stacks perfectly lined up, and bags of fresh, homemade brownies,
cookies, and cake slices. And, even though it was healthy, there was
not a crumb of cloud loaf in sight.

As they munched sandwiches and popped bites of honeycomb,
spun sugar birds nests, and divinity, Bethany kept starting to talk,
then stopping. "I mean—" She looked frustrated, sighing.   •

"Is something wrong?" Erec finally asked.

Bethany nodded, blushing. "I don't want you to go."

Erec twisted to look at her. "But you were the one arguing me
into going in the first place."

"I know. I mean, you have to do it. I think. I just don't want to . . . lose you." Her face flushed bright red.

Erec looked away, not wanting to embarrass her. "Look, I don't want to lose me either," he joked. "I don't know what the right thing is to do. But hey," he said, offering her a chocolate-chip cookie, "you're my best friend no matter what happens. Always remember that."

Maybe that hadn't been the right thing to say. Bethany's eyes turned red. "I'm sorry," she said. "I'm just worried something bad will happen."

"Hey, I've got this thing." He held the Amulet of Virtues out toward her. "It's got to help a little."

Jack and Oscar appeared with big grins on their faces. "Problem solved," Jack announced, dusting himself off like he was a trophy. "We got you safe passage, man. Now you owe us."

Oscar beamed. "This'll work extra well, since I'm going on the quest with you too!"

"Huh?" Erec looked at them. "What's going on?"

Jack strutted forward and peered into their basket. "Hmm, I don't know, Oscar. I think they should give us a few brownies and some of those chocolate honey drops if they want to hear our good news. What do you think?"

Oscar reached into the basket. "You're right, Jack. A little food might make me more talkative." He giggled and stuffed a cinnamon cookie into his mouth, but he couldn't wait to tell the story of what had happened. With a full mouth, he said, "We talked to Janus! We can go early today and draw the quest before anyone else knows we're there!"

"What?" Erec could not believe his ears. "How did you get through to Janus? I thought he was locked up in the Labor Society building." He felt better right away. Janus was the odd man who looked like he had been stranded for years on a desert island, who guarded the side door of the Labor Society, the passageway to get to Al's Well. He was the perfect person to help Erec.

Oscar puffed his chest as if it had all been his idea. "You know how Jack's gift is that he can talk to animals? Well, he got a mouse to take a note into the building. Mice can always find a hole or some way in. And it brought our note right to Janus. He opened the door and talked to us."

"He wouldn't let us in," Jack said. "The guy seemed scared by the whole thing. He thought this might make him lose his job. But he knew what was going on, and he wants to help. He said that Baskania took Balor Stain into the Labor Society through the front door. The side door you go through wouldn't let him in. And he marched him right up to Al's Well. Al told him it wouldn't work for Balor, but Baskania pushed Al out of his way and made Balor stick his hand into the well."

Oscar added, "He couldn't find anything in it though. So Baskania performed magic on the well to make something come out of it. And you know how powerful Baskania is."

"Yeah," Bethany said. "But is he more powerful than the Fates?"

"I guess not," said Jack. "Because the thing that Balor found and grabbed out—" Jack and Oscar burst into laughter.

"Yeah?" Erec leaned forward.

"Well," Jack said, still laughing, "you know how Al's Well looks just like a toilet?"

Erec's eyes widened. "You don't mean he pulled out a . . ."

"Yup!" Oscar said gleefully.

Imagining Balor's face looking at what he had pulled from the toilet made Erec grin.

"Eww!" Bethany almost rolled off of the bench she sat on, laughing.

"So anyway." Jack chuckled. "We're going at five o'clock. Two hours early. Nobody will know we're there. Janus said the only one that really has to be there is Erec, at least according to the Fates. So he's not breaking any rules. Except the million new rules that the Labor Society made up."

"You guys are awesome." Erec beamed. "Thanks."

The four of them strode through Alypium to the gleaming turrets of the Labor Society. Erec, wearing the hood of his jacket over his head, walked in the middle of the group. He looked down, hoping not to be spotted. People rushed by them on the street, in and out of shops, but luckily nobody seemed to notice them. Erec was relieved. He was sure if they went at seven o'clock, when people expected him, he'd be booed and shouted at again, like he'd been the last time he'd come to draw a quest. Baskania had turned the people against him.

They crossed the lawn to the side of the Labor Society. The wooden door seemed out of place on the glistening silver building. A sign hung on it read OPEN AT SEVEN O'CLOCK.

Erec checked his watch. It was a few minutes before five. He tapped on the door, holding his breath.

In a moment, it swung open. Janus popped his head out and looked both ways, dust flying from his long scraggly gray hair and beard. He was filthy and bony, wearing a shaggy gray prison smock. Erec wondered if that was because he had been locked away in the little shop, or if he would look like that anyway.

Janus whispered, voice trembling, "Oooh, I don't like this. No, sir. I'll get fired for this or worse, I tell you."

"Sorry, Janus," Bethany said. "But Erec is being set up by Baskania. This will really help him."

"I know it." Still, he looked around nervously.

"I thought you'd want to be fired," Oscar said, blunt as usual. "I thought you didn't like being locked up in here."

"I don't, but I do!" Janus shook his head harder, dust flying. "This is my job. I've always done it," he said proudly. "I just don't like the new changes that the Committee for Suppressing Change made to it." He stepped back and Erec entered the shop, followed by Bethany, Jack, and Oscar.

They waited for their eyes to adjust. Thick dust covered the shelves of the shop. The odd items set on them were too hard to make out through the caked-on grime. A gray cloud poofed from the shaggy carpet with each step they took, and all of them began coughing.

Janus walked behind his desk and slid out a pad of paper, creating a small dust storm.

Erec knew he had to sign the pad. That would let him through the force field into the building to get to Al's Well. "Will they be expecting me in there this early?"

A wild cackle jolted through the room and everybody jumped. Then an unnaturally loud, deep voice boomed, "Yes, Erec. They will."

Erec spun around. Behind him stood Thanatos Argus Baskania.

Baskania had one eye open in the center of his forehead and another on his chin. Both of them were blinking and looking wildly around, seeing things that Erec could not. One of his natural eyes was still missing; a terrible, dark hollow sat in its place. He had removed it to make room for Erec's dragon eye. But his other natural steely blue eye bored straight into Erec's. His silver-gray hair formed a perfect widow's peak in the center of his forehead, right above the eye there. A narrow, crooked nose jutted above his thin, pinched lips. His long, black cape hung over his tall, strong frame. He caressed a small silver ball, which he then dropped into his pocket.

Next to him stood Balor Stain, lips tight in a grin, and a terrible gleam in his icy blue eyes. His jet-black hair made his pale skin look even whiter. Erec thought he saw a hint of fear in Balor's face, behind his bravado. Balor whipped a remote control from under his blue apprentice cloak. "Howdy, Erec Rex."

Erec's eyes narrowed at him.

In a moment, rope shot from Baskania's palm and coiled tightly around Erec, from his shoulders to his ankles. Erec cringed. Now what would he do? He struggled against the ropes with no success. How did Baskania find out they were here?

He was stuck. Or was he? Erec had a thought. There was one way he might be able to get out of these ropes—summoning dragons again with a dragon call, as Aoquesth had taught him to do.

But Baskania gazed at him. "Interesting thought. I'll have to put a shield around the building to block any transmissions to dragons." He drew a few markings in the air with his finger. "That should do it." His thin lips twisted into a smile.

Erec stared in shock. Baskania had read his mind. He almost kicked himself. Of course Baskania could do that. Now what would Erec do? His heart was pounding. He would never get away.

Bethany ran to Erec, fumbling with the tight rope as if she could possibly free him. Two large men strode through the door. Erec recognized them as players on Baskania's Super A springball team. One was the burly John Arrete. He had the magical gift of stopping time, which made him perfect as the team trapper, a position similar to a goalie. The other was Gog Magnon, the team's batter, who looked more like a caveman than ever. Gog locked the door behind him.

Baskania laughed. "Nobody leaves here, understood?"

Gog Magnon and John Arrete bowed their heads. "Yes, Shadow Prince."

Jack and Oscar seemed frozen, dazed.

Baskania turned to Oscar with a smug smile. "Thank you, Oscar, for letting me know where to find Erec. I couldn't have done this without you."

Oscar's jaw dropped open, and some squeaky noises came out. Jack and Erec looked at him in horror. Bethany stopped trying to untie Erec, a useless endeavor, and sat on the floor in shock.

"But . . . but . . ." Oscar's face flushed red.

"Now." Baskania turned to Janus, who shrank under his gaze. "As for you—"

"I'm sorry!" Janus blurted out. "Don't kill me, please! I was just trying to help."

"I know you were, Janus." Baskania's voice was calm. "I'm not upset at all. Quite the contrary. You've helped me quite a bit here. Now you will just continue to follow my orders and you will be rewarded." He smiled.

A strangled shout burst from Oscar's mouth. "I didn't tell you anything! You liar! I've never even seen you before." He was panting, and his fists were opening and closing.

Baskania turned to him, eyebrows up. "But of course you did, Oscar, or how would I know to be here? You're my good friend now. Don't be ashamed to admit it." He laughed, a wild cackle.

Oscar ran at Baskania and tried to kick him in the leg. Before his foot hit, Oscar sailed backward and slammed against a wall.

"Now, now, Oscar," Baskania said. "That is no way to treat a friend." His eyebrows lowered. "I would not advise trying that again." He turned to Janus. "Now that we know Al's Well is ready, Balor Stain will be drawing the quest today. Erec will stay here in case I need him to help Balor. And when I no longer need Erec here, I will bring him back to my fortress. Come, Balor."

Balor walked to the paper pad and picked up the feathered quill. He signed his own name, and Erec's name, several times. The signatures did not fill with light as Erec's had.

Balor looked at Baskania, and this time the fear in Balor's face was unmistakable. He opened the door that led into the Labor

Society. A shimmering bubble filled the door frame, the same one that only Erec had been able to pass through. Balor stepped back, then rammed himself at the membrane. He fell back, unable to get in.

After a few attempts Baskania sneered. "I'll get you there my own way." He snapped his fingers, and he and Balor disappeared.

All eyes in the room focused on Oscar. "How could you?" Bethany asked.

"I didn't do anything!" Oscar yelled, enraged. "He lied. I never saw him before today."

"How did he know your name, then?" Jack asked, his voice cold and hard.

"How do I know?" Oscar put his hands over his face. "Aargh!" he shouted. Then he looked at Jack. "I can't believe this. It's not my fault! Why won't you trust me?"

Jack stared at him. He said slowly, "So help me, Oscar. If you're lying—"

"I'm not!" Oscar grabbed his shoulders, frantic. "Believe me."

Jack sighed. "I do believe you. I just don't get it though." He looked at Erec. "Hey, I know Oscar really well. I think he's telling the truth."

Erec and Bethany nodded. Erec had his doubts, but it didn't seem like arguing would help.

Oscar started to calm down. "Now," he said, determined, "let's think of a way out of here." In a flash, he grabbed a large dust-covered item off a shelf and swung it hard at Gog Magnon.

Erec could not believe his eyes. Either Oscar had been telling the truth, or he was truly sorry for what he'd done. Attacking a massive oaf like that was pretty bold, or stupid.

Before the object, which may have been a lamp, hit Magnon in the head, Arrete performed his famous trick of stopping time. One second later the lamp was back on the shelf, and Oscar was crumpled on the floor across the room.

"Huh?" Magnon grunted, confused. He looked like he was thinking about clobbering Oscar but decided not to, as he hadn't been touched.

Erec thought about trying a dragon call, even though Baskania had blocked the building against it. But before he began to focus on it, Baskania and Balor appeared again. Balor looked angry, wiping a hand on his blue cloak. He must have reached into Al's Well and not had any luck. Erec remembered what Balor had pulled from the well last time and gave him a smirk.

"All right, Erec." Baskania's eyebrows lowered at him. "It seems you will be necessary. Sign the paper."

The ropes fell instantly from Erec's sides and he picked up the feather quill. He hesitated a moment, wondering if he should do it. But he realized that he was unable to fight. If he drew the quest from the well, he would at least know what to do. Maybe if he survived, he could attempt the quest—although surviving did not look likely.

As he signed the pad, the letters of his name cracked deep into the paper. Bright light shone from the words into the shop.

"Take Balor with you through the side entrance," Baskania said.

Erec walked with Balor to the bubblelike material that glistened in the door frame. He passed his hand through easily. Balor stepped in front of him, blocking him, but bounced off the force field like it was rubber.

Then Erec slid right around Balor and into the Labor Society building. He filled with new hope. Was this possible? He had escaped! If he could just get—

But something yanked him right back into the shop. Balor had grabbed Erec's jacket and kept part of it from crossing the barrier, using it to pull him back. "Oh, no you don't, you loser. Let's try this." He shoved Erec behind him and threw Erec's arms over his shoulders. Then, holding his wrists, like Erec was some kind of cape, Balor tried to butt his way through the membrane. Erec's hands slid in, but Balor bounced off.

"Forget it, Balor," Baskania said, disgusted. With a nod, he and Balor disappeared from sight.

Seizing his chance, Erec charged through the doorway into the huge glass and steel Labor Society lobby. Was he free? He looked around. Nobody seemed to notice him.

But a hand fell heavily onto his shoulder. Of course Baskania would not let him go that easily.

Balor was waiting by the elevators. They rode down to the bottom floor. Baskania followed Erec and Balor up the hill to the well. He tapped on the gravestone marked JACK that they passed at the bottom. "Looks like it's time for Jack to have some company."

When they got to the top of the hill, the door in the stone was open. Al lumbered over, waving them in. He looked just like a plumber in his overalls and tool belt, and was carrying a big plunger. "You two back again?" Al said, eyeing Baskania and Balor.

The stench hit Erec right away. He had forgotten how awful it smelled here. Al had called it the "smell of life" because "people's fates weren't always that sweet." He had said Erec would get used to it, but Erec doubted that was possible. Balor and Baskania were disgusted, not liking the smell any more than he did.

"I gotta finish polishing it, after that last mess." Al shot a look of disapproval at Baskania, then walked through an opening in the round shower curtain around the well and bent over it. The back of his overalls were loose, so his shirt came up and the top of his rear end showed over his pants. Balor snickered.

Al backed out and closed the curtain. "Let's do it right this time," he said. Erec was amazed that Al did not seem afraid of Baskania.

He yanked a cord and the curtain flew open, revealing the gleaming white toilet that was Al's Well. Servants behind Erec stood in a row and bowed deeply before it. Erec thought he heard a distant chorus singing a single note: "Aaaahhhh."

Al gestured toward the toilet. Balor followed Erec and stood next to him.

"You want to go first?" Erec asked Balor, smirking.

Balor scowled at him.

"You will both reach in at the same time," Baskania's voice boomed. "Balor will take the paper, either in the well or as soon as it's out. Balor—before he sees it."

Erec got onto his knees before the porcelain commode. The inside was a straight drop into blackness, like a never-ending latrine. He reached a hand inside. The air within it was misty, and the water seemed boiling hot and ice cold at the same time. He almost jerked his hand out, until he realized that it did not hurt him.

Balor crouched next to him, plunging his hand in. Both of them fished around in the strange liquid. Chills raced through Erec. What would the quest say? Would Baskania let him find out? Would it be something dangerous? He knew the quest was meant for him. It didn't seem right that it was being taken away.

A thick, warm paper entered his grasp. This was it! He tugged, but it was caught on something. Was it Balor? Did he have it?

Balor looked like he had something, but from the look on his face he wasn't sure what it was.

Erec tugged, and he felt the paper rip. He fished around a moment, but the other piece was gone. Both Erec and Balor pulled their hands out at the same time.

In Erec's hand dripped a piece of paper, torn at the end. In Balor's hand was a smelly, slimy piece of poop.

Balor shrieked and flung it into the grass. Almost in the same movement he grabbed the paper from Erec's hand. He wiped his hand on the grass and read the quest. Confusion filled his face. "'Get behind?'" he said. Then he gasped in shock, and looked from Erec to Baskania, aware that he had read it aloud. "I'm sorry," he sputtered to Baskania. "It just didn't make any sense, or I wouldn't have said it. Look, the end is ripped off."

Baskania turned over the paper as Balor again wiped his hand on the grass and then the shower curtain, to Al's annoyance. *"Get behind"?* Erec thought. What kind of a quest was that? Only part of one, it seemed. Get behind what? He snickered at Balor. "Looks like the Fates sent you a message, too."

"Reach back in," Baskania commanded. "Find the other part."

Balor sat poised to grab the paper, this time not bothering to reach into the liquid himself. Erec stuck an arm all the way into the toilet. He could feel nothing except for the strange liquid.

Al, standing in his line of sight, mouthed something at him. Erec could not tell what he was saying. He seemed to be repeating a word, but what was it?

Then Al made a little motion with his hand. And Erec suddenly understood.

Flush.

Erec put his left hand up by the toilet handle, pretending to grasp so he could reach deeper in. Then he grabbed the handle and pulled.

CHAPTER SIX

The Pool Table

A HUGE ROAR FILLED Erec's ears, and he was sucked headfirst into the toilet. As he flew in, he caught a glimpse of shock on the faces of Balor and Baskania.

Erec choked and sputtered in the liquid as he shot through a long tunnel. He felt pops in both of his wrists and then something opening there. His breathing became regular again. With a jolt, he realized that his Instagills had opened, and he was breathing through them. Erec and Bethany had won the Instagills—automatic gills that opened when they were in water—in Queen Posey's Sea Search contest when he had first come to Alypium.

Colors that Erec had never seen before whirled around as he spun through the liquid in Al's Well. He had the sensation of being surrounded by fire and ice, a feeling that almost burned yet did not hurt at all. As he plummeted through the giant tube, the liquid around him was replaced by regular water. It sped him around bends and curves gently, rushing past other openings and forks, carrying him through an underground network, as if he were a tadpole. He looked for the other half of the paper with his third quest written on it as he swirled on, but even if it were somewhere in the water, it would have been nearly impossible to find.

A smile burst across Erec's face. He was free and soaring safely away, somewhere. If only he had seen the whole quest he would know what to do. But, then again, Balor would have seen it too.

The tunnel felt like a giant water slide, whipping and turning him this way and that. Erec began cheering. He found that he could hear himself, even though he was underwater. Maybe the Instagills had that effect too. In the end, he slipped up through a thick, dark pipe and into a shallow pool. His head popped out of the water and he took a breath. The feathery gills in his wrists shut back into slits.

Erec tried to absorb what he saw around him. He was indoors, in a small rectangular pool of water that sat on a pedestal—the pedestal being the tube he had just come through. The water was only up to his chest as he sat on the bottom. Around the room were shelves stacked with games and books. The room felt oddly familiar. Erec was sure he had been here before.

Then he realized. This was the game room. He was in the castle! Bethany and he had fallen onto the wall in this room when the castle had been on its side. The games and furniture had been piled on the wall then. Only the pool table had remained fixed to the floor.

Erec remembered what had happened when Bethany accidentally flipped a shelf up with her foot. The top of the pool table had opened and loads of water had dumped right on top of her.

He was in that pool table! Erec looked around, amazed, and then climbed out, dripping water all over the rug. He found the same shelf that Bethany had kicked on the side of the room. It was pushed up against the wall. When he pulled the shelf flat, a green felt top covered the water in the pool table. The shelf was marked with a few wavy lines—a water symbol. He flipped the shelf up and down a few times and watched the water appear and disappear under the felt top. It must have opened automatically when he shot out of the tunnel.

Now he understood why the table had dumped tons of water on Bethany when the room was on its side. It was a passage out of the castle, leading into endless water tunnels.

Dripping all the way, he walked to his room in the west wing, dried off, and changed. He was safe now, and nobody knew where he was. If only he could find a way to figure out the rest of his third quest.

Erec called Jam on the house phone in his room, then met with him in the west wing dining hall. He figured it was a good place to wait for Bethany, since they hadn't eaten dinner yet. After Erec told Jam about what had happened, the butler looked faint. "Young sir, I believe you have had enough near-death experiences for all of us. Maybe it's time to relax a while. Rest in your room if you like. I'm more than happy to bring you anything you want there."

"I'm fine, Jam," Erec said. "I just want to find out what my quest was supposed to be. How will I ever know?"

Jam studied him. "Well, young sir, you do have those dragon eyes. Maybe you could learn to use them."

That was it! His dragon eyes could show him the future—and let him change it. That was exactly what he needed to do. Patchouli said she could teach him how to do it. Now he would just have to find her.

Bethany walked in, then stopped, staring at him in shock. "Erec? You're okay?" She threw her arms around him and then Jam, as if hugging one person wasn't enough to show her relief.

Erec grinned, thankful that she was safe as well. "Bethany, do you remember that pool table in the south wing near the castle armory that dumped water on you?" He told her how he had been catapulted there, flushed through Al's Well.

She laughed. "That explains one more thing I saw. Janus helped Jack, Oscar, and me escape from his shop after you and Baskania were gone. We hid behind some trees and bushes nearby, just in case you showed up and needed us. After a while we heard this noise. It was Balor, bursting out of a ditch filled with water. He was soaking wet, coughing and choking. I couldn't understand how he got there, or why. But I bet he flushed himself after you and ended up there."

Erec grinned. Of course Balor would try to follow him. "I wonder why we ended up in different places?"

Bethany thought a moment. "I bet the Fates had a hand in it. It is their well, right?"

"Yeah," Erec agreed. "And guess what they sent him when he reached into Al's Well?" They both laughed until their sides hurt.

"How did Janus help you guys escape?" he asked.

Bethany sighed with relief. "He was babbling, and kept pointing to different things around his shop. I thought he was just nervous. But then he made a big fuss about one of the dusty things sitting on a shelf. He acted all worried that someone was going to steal it, said it was really valuable and nobody should touch it, and we weren't really supposed to be in there anyway.

"I thought he had gone overboard from all the stress. But he was pretty crafty after all. John Arrete picked the thing up, whatever it was, and he froze like a statue. Gog Magnon looked confused. He's not too bright, because when Janus begged him not to take the thing out of Arrete's hands, he grabbed it too, and froze. We just ran out of there."

"I hope Janus doesn't get in trouble for that," Erec said. Then he thought of something that made him frown. "I don't understand why Oscar is telling Baskania where I am. I can't believe it. I never thought he would do this to me."

Bethany shook her head. "I don't think he did anything, Erec. That's the strange thing. I believe him. Just looking at him, how upset he got at Baskania—"

"It was all an act," Erec scoffed. "Why would Baskania make up something like that? And how else would he know we would be there early?"

"I don't know," she said, puzzled by that too. "It's not like I have a good explanation. I just know Oscar."

"I don't think you do." Erec felt impatient. "What about my cloudy thought? If you had told your secret to Oscar you'd be dead right now. He has to be talking to Baskania."

Bethany could see Erec was still tense, and she changed the subject. "So the only part of the third quest you heard was 'Get behind'?"

Jam served Erec some macaroni and cheese, and Bethany loaded her plate with some of the goodies that were now in front of them. "Yeah. 'Get behind.' That really tells me a lot."

"I'm going to find King Piter." Bethany stood. "Wait here. Maybe he has an idea what we can do."

Jam disappeared for a while, and he was just returning with three cloud cream sundaes when King Piter walked into the room with

Bethany. "I'm glad you caught me, Erec," he said. "I'm leaving tonight for Upper Earth and won't be back for a few days."

"Jam." Erec motioned toward a chair. "Get a sundae for yourself, too, and join us, okay?"

Jam sheepishly nodded. Erec thought he looked grateful even though he was embarrassed.

The king listened to Erec tell about the ripped quest. "That's a shame," he said. "That never happened to Pluto, Posey, and me when we did our quests." He frowned. "Which reminds me, you are still doing them all alone." He shook his head. "I wish there was a better way."

"I've taken friends with me," Erec said.

"I know, Erec. That's not the same." The king shook his head. "I think you understand."

Erec did understand. His friends' help was important, necessary even. And it felt good to have company. But it was different than truly sharing the burdens with someone. All of the big decisions had been his alone. King Piter had done his quests to become king with his triplet siblings. Erec thought it must be nice to be part of a real team.

"How can we find out who the other two future rulers are, who are supposed to be doing this with me?" he asked.

King Piter didn't answer. Instead, he studied the wooden table. Erec watched him carefully. Something in the king's face struck him as odd.

"You know who they are, don't you?" Erec asked.

The king looked up at him guiltily, and anger rushed through Erec. How could he? The king did know who they were, and he was holding back that information too.

"Why is everything a secret? If there are two others out there who can help me, tell me who they are now."

"There is nobody who can help now, I'm afraid," the king said. "There are problems with both of them, you see."

"Problems?" Erec said, enraged. "What problems? Who are they? Where are they?"

King Piter sighed. "Yes, problems. One of them is missing, you see. And the other—"

"The other is not missing?" Erec felt faint. "Who is it?"

"No." King Piter shook his head. "The one who is not missing cannot help you. I want her to stay hidden, for her own safety."

Erec sat down, stunned. Two kids somewhere could be doing the quests with him right now. Two other suckers who, for whatever reason, were also chosen to be the rightful rulers. Well, they were smarter than he was, staying away from the scepters and the dangers of the quests.

King Piter cleared his throat. "You need to find out what your third quest is, first and foremost. I think you'll need to consult the Oracle."

Erec thought he had heard of the Oracle before. He tried to clear his mind, swallowing his anger.

"What is the Oracle?" Bethany asked.

"It's the one place where you can speak directly to the three Fates," King Piter said. "I think you were meant to go there. They are the ones who design your quests, knowing how the thread of your life entwines with all of ours around you. If they gave you only a part of your quest, I think that means you need to go to them to find out the rest."

"So they know my future, then?" Erec asked. That sounded interesting.

"They know everybody's future. The Fates are the only ones who can give real prophecies." He looked pensive. "Except one seer from long ago. Bea Cleary, the one who foretold the future rulers of Alypium. But she was very rare."

"And not part of my Cleary family tree, I found out," Bethany said with a scowl.

"Where is the Oracle?" Erec asked.

"It's in Delphi, Mount Parnassus," the king said. "Central Greece."

"Greece? In Upper Earth?" Bethany was surprised. "But I thought magic things don't exist in Upper Earth."

"On the contrary," King Piter said. "Life itself is magic, Bethany. But if the Substance gets messed up any further, I'm afraid you may be right."

Erec did not want to think about the missing bees and life on Upper Earth coming to an end. All he could deal with was thinking about surviving this next quest—if he ever found out what it was. And, of course, wondering who and where the other two chosen rulers of the kingdoms were. On top of his usual questions about who his real father and birth mother were, and why they had left him. Just a few small things to worry about.

"What about my dragon eyes?" Erec asked. "Maybe if I learn how to use them to tell the future, I can figure out what to do."

"That may take some time," King Piter said. "It's not a bad idea, though. Why don't you take the Hermit with you to the Oracle? He could probably teach you how to use your dragon eyes along the way."

"The Hermit?" Erec tried not to sound as shocked as he felt. "He's a little . . . strange, don't you think? I mean, I never could tell what he was talking about. I'm not sure if he's the right one to teach me."

"Well, you better get used to him," the king said. "Because I appointed him to be your new magic tutor."

The next morning at breakfast, Erec noticed that Jam had slipped some classic Alypium dishes in—ambrosia, a fluffy white pudding sprinkled with nuts and berries, and nectar, a drink that tasted like sparkling honey. They actually tasted great, and after he ate he could feel energy surge through him.

"I can't believe King Piter knows who the other two future rulers are, and he won't tell me," Erec said. "Can you believe that guy? We'll have to come up with a way to find them."

Bethany nodded, uncomfortable. Erec felt guilty complaining about her father figure and decided to drop it. "Do you want to come with me to the Oracle?" he asked instead. Jam was nearby, adjusting a chafing dish of scrambled eggs. He seemed to be listening. "Jam?" Erec asked. "Could you come too?"

Jam's face flushed with excitement. "Sir! Young sir! Well. I don't know if I'm worthy of your newest trek, but I assure you there would be nothing more . . ." He stopped, at a loss for words.

"Great!" Erec said. "So you'll come, then!"

Jam muttered something about making arrangements and rushed from the room. Bethany grinned. "I'm in. This will be fun! Hey, can we invite Jack and Oscar? I know that's more than three people, but since you're not exactly doing the quest yet, it shouldn't matter."

Erec couldn't believe his ears. "Oscar? Invite Oscar? Bethany, do you want me to get killed? How could you begin to trust him with this?"

Bethany crossed her arms. "But you told him you'd let him come. You saw how excited he was. I'm telling you, there is no way he's been in touch with Baskania. I think Baskania's trying to split us up. That poor kid just lost his dad. How do you think he'd feel if we all went off without him?"

Erec felt awful, but how could he take the risk of letting Oscar know his plans? But he agreed to discuss it with Jack. Bethany lifted the finger where her new cell phone was implanted and stuck it in her ear.

"You look really cool like that." Erec laughed.

"Shh." Bethany stuck her tongue out at him. "I have to listen for the tone." Then she put her finger to her mouth and said, "Jack Hare," and put it back in her ear. Erec grinned as she stuck her finger back and forth from her ear to her mouth. "It looks like you're eating earwax."

"Really funny," she said.

"Yeah, it is." Erec chuckled.

"Shut up." Bethany took out her finger and looked at it. "Something strange happened. I told Jack to come to the castle, but the phone was all garbled. Then there was a fizzy sound and a pop. And it stopped working." She tried to call her friends, Melody, and Darla Will, but her cell phone would not work at all. "Darn. I just got the thing too."

"Hey." Erec had an idea. "Before Jack gets here, let's go to the library tower and look up the Oracle. We should get as much info as we can about it, then pack up and leave soon."

Jam returned to the room. "I have taken care of the arrangements, young sir. I found my Serving Tray, made by Vulcan. It serves up some wonderful dishes. So this time I won't have to find nuts and berries for your meals."

"Awesome, Jam! Does it make desserts, too?"

"As many as you wish, young sir." He bowed.

Carol Esperpento, the librarian, had just arrived. Her narrow eyes looked lost behind the thin granny glasses that jutted from both sides of her face. She pointed to the fifth floor, where the books on the Oracle were kept. "The books must stay here," she warned sternly.

"Good thing she was here," Erec said.

"Nah," Bethany said, shrugging. "Piter gave me a key. These books are kind of all mine."

All hers? Erec wondered if this idea she had about King Piter becoming her father was going to her head.

They found the section on the Oracle under "Books about the Fates," and browsed through section headings such as "Great Oracle Vacations for under 400 Gold Rings" and "Famous Oracle Prophecies Through History." Bethany found a section called "Real Adventures to the Oracle—What to Expect."

"Check this out." She laughed, pointing at a book called *Oops, I Fell in Again: One Boy's Story of Continual Spills into the Oracle of Delphi*. She pulled *The Total Loser's Guide to Getting Life-Altering Prophecies at the Oracle of Delphi* and *Everything You Always Wanted to Know About the Oracle but Were Afraid to Ask* off the shelf and sat down.

Erec found a section heading called "Oracle, Shmoracle: Is It Really a Miracle?" and pulled out a book called *Fate or False? Is the Oracle a Real Channel to the Famous Three?*

"It says here that the Oracle is a person," Bethany said. "It's someone who gives a message from the three Fates."

"No, it's a place." Erec pointed at his book. "It's in Delphi, like King Piter said."

"Oh, wait, I see that too. But look—here it says the Oracle is a message. A prophecy sent from the Fates." She looked at Erec. "It's a person, place, and thing? That's really clear. I wonder if the people who wrote these books have actually been there."

"So, we're going to the Oracle to meet an Oracle and get an Oracle?"

"Something like that." Bethany flipped a page. "This book says that there is only one real Oracle, the one in Delphi. You can still visit the ruins of the ancient Temple of Apollo there. But the Oracle isn't in the ruins. It's nearby in a short stone well right next to Mount Parnassus. Man, the pictures of that place look beautiful!"

"Uh-oh." Erec pushed his book toward Bethany. "Looks like there's a catch. This book says the whole thing might be phony. You want to know why people aren't lined up for miles waiting to get their futures read?"

"Hmm." Bethany crossed her arms. "I hadn't thought of that. I guess it would be a pretty popular place to go. What, is it guarded by a monster?"

The word "monster" made Erec flinch. After befriending Tina, a Hydra, he had changed his opinion about that word. "No, it's not guarded. It just won't work at all unless you bring a 'medium' with you. And, according to this book, nobody's ever seen the thing work."

"A medium—like a psychic?" Bethany dropped her book, then looked up something in the other one, furiously. "I see it here. 'A true medium is necessary for communication with the Fates through the Oracle.' Oh, that's great. Now what do we do?"

Dejected, they returned to the west wing dining hall and found Jack waiting with Jam. "Hey! You're okay! That's great," Jack said when he saw Erec. "I was worried about you. Did you get the quest?"

After Erec filled him in, Jack shook his finger. "My cell phone is dead. It's been messed up since we were near Baskania. I wonder if he did something to it."

"Mine won't work either," Bethany said. "Now how are we going to get ahold of Oscar?" She looked at Jam.

"Unfortunately, modom, I am a bit old-school. I never got a cell phone."

"Are you still thinking about inviting Oscar along to the Oracle?" Erec asked. "Do you maybe have a death wish?"

Bethany smiled at Jack. "Before King Piter went to Upper Earth he said we should visit the Oracle to try and find out the rest of Erec's quest."

"The Oracle? Can I come?" Jack said. "I called Oscar and told him to meet us here right before my cell phone died."

Erec stood up. "What? Oscar is on his way? Does he know that I'm here?"

"Not yet." Jack shook his head. "I didn't know you were here until now. But what's the deal? You still don't trust Oscar? Look, I've known him since he was little. He's a good kid, really. You truly think Oscar is hanging out with Baskania?"

Erec regarded his two friends in puzzlement. "Look, whatever you think of Oscar, there are some facts we have to face. I like Oscar too. But I can't overlook those facts." He paced. "Everything tells me this is stupid. But to prove you wrong, and to give him one more chance, I'll let Oscar see me here again. I just need to be ready to get out of here fast. So let's get set to leave now. As soon as Oscar knows I'm here, I'm in danger." He shrugged when Bethany crossed her arms. "If I'm wrong, I'm wrong. But we have to be ready, in case."

Jam bowed from across the room. "I'm already prepared to go, young sir."

"I've got backpacks at my place," Bethany said. Erec was sure she had everything in the mansion that King Piter had given her, attached to the castle. "I'll bring one for you, too. Meet you back here in ten minutes."

Erec looked at Jack. "I'm going to get a few things too. Jack, promise me you won't tell Oscar I'm here until I get back."

Jack shrugged. "Whatever."

First off, Erec put on his magic Sneakers that let him run soundlessly, throwing distracting noises elsewhere. He took a sack of some of the money he had stashed under his bed, plus his Magiclight, a prize he had once won that could leave beams of light hanging in the air.

Then he had an idea. Before going back to meet Bethany, he fetched Wolfboy from his doghouse. "C'mon, boy. Wanna go on an adventure with me?"

Wolfboy wagged the whole bottom half of his body, then jumped on Erec, knocking him down. "Whoa, boy. I take that for a yes." Erec grabbed two bags of dog food and led Wolfboy into the castle.

Oscar was waiting, looking forlorn. But he smiled when he saw Erec. "You're okay! What happened to you?"

Everybody in the room seemed afraid to answer. Erec did not want Oscar to know anything. This was Oscar's final test as far as Erec was concerned. "I need to know, is there *anything* that you are telling anybody that could be getting back to Baskania somehow?"

Oscar threw up his hands. "No! I have no clue why Baskania said that. Maybe he's trying to split us up."

Erec really wanted to believe him. He looked sincere.

He took a backpack from Bethany and put his things in it. A strange feeling came over him, making the back of his neck prickle. He felt his eyes swivel until his dragon eyes faced forward. Everything looked green. In the distance he could hear his friends gasp, but that felt too distant to absorb.

Then it happened. Images whizzed before his eyes in reverse order, too fast to make out. He had the feeling that he might swirl away, as if the ground had dropped from under his feet. He tottered, with nothing around him to grab, and then latched on to something— might have been Jam's arm.

Suddenly the vision slowed down and he could make it out. But he did not like what he saw.

The west wing dining hall hung thick with white ropes and coils of Substance. Erec was frozen to the spot, wound tight in rope from his shoulders to his feet. Bethany and Jam were bound up as well. Oscar and Jack were not, but stood frozen in the room.

Baskania's laughter echoed through the high-ceilinged room. He strolled through the doorway. This time his face was completely full of eyes, except for his mouth. Even his nose was replaced by eyes.

Anger filled Erec, clenching his insides. He'd fight to save his friends.

"Thank you, Oscar." Baskania patted Oscar on the head. "You've helped me once again."

A surge of rage poured through Erec. He opened his mouth to shout, but his anger spilled out with heat and flame in a more satisfying way. He struggled against the ropes around him with the claws that had sprung from his fingertips . . . fighting, tearing.

Baskania pointed a finger at Jam. Jam's head toppled over onto the ropes that bound him.

"Noooo! Not Jam! Leave him alone!" Erec shouted. Then he roared in fury. He could feel his tail thrashing behind him.

In a moment, Bethany was dead. Wolfboy was dead. Erec saw his eyes getting removed, then all went black.

He opened his eyes. The vision had faded away, and the room no longer looked green. He'd had a cloudy thought, and it told him that he had to get away from Oscar and Jack now if he wanted to keep what he had just seen from happening.

"Run!" he shouted at Jam. "Hide!" He looked at Bethany. "Follow me!"

Nobody moved. They just stared at him in shock. "Go, Wolfboy! Out of here. Back to your house," he shouted. Wolfboy put his head down and slowly walked out, tail between his legs.

Oscar said, "You're turning into a dragon."

Erec looked down at himself. His skin had a greenish cast and did look scaly, but it seemed to be fading fast.

Bethany had tears in her eyes. "That looked awful. Are you okay?"

She pointed toward the singed tablecloth. "You breathed fire. How did you do that?"

"I'll tell you later. Let's go." Erec grabbed Bethany's hand and pulled her into the hallway. Jam, Oscar, and Jack followed behind them.

"Go away!" Erec shouted at them over his shoulder. But the only one who listened to him was Jam. Erec had really just wanted Oscar and Jack to leave so that Baskania would stop following him.

Jam shouted, "Yes, sir! Here, sir." He tossed a silver disc at him, and Erec caught it. He tucked the Serving Tray into his backpack, then dashed as fast as he could up the hall. A moment later, though, he tripped over a rope that was floating at ankle length in the hallway and he crashed onto his hands.

Erec picked himself up. The others stopped around him.

In front of him, Balthazar Ugry stood gloating, a twisted smile on his face. "And what might you be doing now, running wild in the west wing? You might break something." He gestured at the suits of armor lining the hallway, each holding monstrous weapons, except for the one holding a teddy bear. That one shrank farther away when Erec looked at it. "I thought you didn't need babysitting."

Erec's voice was controlled yet strong. "We have to get out of here. I'm going on a quest. Stop tripping me up."

Ugry gazed at Oscar coldly. "I told you, Oscar Felix, you are not allowed to go on any quests with Erec, because of your unpleasant associations with the criminal Rosco Kroc." He pointed at him, muttering, and Oscar disappeared.

"What did you do with him?" Jack said, outraged.

"Put him back in his apprentice boarding house." Ugry sounded bored.

"Thanks!" Erec ran right past him. They didn't have any time to waste.

Unfortunately, Jack followed right behind. Erec had to get rid of him. If Jack saw where they went, he would tell Oscar, and then Baskania would know.

As Erec ran, he thought. Maybe he could lose Jack, tell him to meet them somewhere. The castle maze. And then Erec just wouldn't show up there.

A moment later, an unearthly howl echoed behind them. They could hear Baskania's voice thundering, "Block the Port-O-Door. Guard the castle entrance. Search the castle for Erec Rex. Piter's not here now to get in our way." After a moment he added, "And send someone to the entrance of the castle maze, and the center of the maze, now!"

Jack and Bethany followed Erec out of the west wing. "Look, Jack," Erec said, "I need to take Bethany into the maze. There is a place in the center of the maze that we can escape through. Meet us there in a few minutes, at the front, okay? I forgot something for Wolfboy. Bethany has to come show me where it is."

"I don't know," Jack said. "Didn't you just hear Baskania say for someone to go look for you in the maze? It would be crazy to go there."

"I know," Erec said, "except we have a sure way out from there. Just hide somewhere near it. Wait till you see me so nobody will catch you. We'll be there in a few minutes."

"Okay." Jack shrugged. "Listen, this is so strange. I don't know what's going on."

"Neither do we," Erec said, patting him on the shoulder. "Just meet us there."

Jack disappeared, and Erec shuddered thinking about what just happened. He had lied to Jack about where they were going, but it seemed like there was no way around it. Jack trusted Oscar. If he knew where Erec went it would just be a matter of time before he told Oscar everything.

When Baskania appeared in the castle, something odd started becoming clear to Erec. But an even stranger thing had just happened that really made him think. He would talk to Bethany about it and see what she thought.

He led her into the south wing. "This is our only chance of getting out of here. I thought about escaping this way when I found out Oscar was coming, even before I got that cloudy thought."

"Is that what that was?" Bethany shivered. "It looked awful. You were so . . . dragonlike."

"Yeah. Sorry." He took Bethany into the game room and flicked the shelf that had the water symbol up to the wall. The top of the pool table changed from a green, fuzzy surface to water. "I hope these backpacks are waterproof."

Bethany crossed her arms. "I don't get it, Erec. What's going on? Why did you tell Jack we were going to the maze? So we're not really meeting him there? You don't trust Jack now?"

It was time to try to explain to her what had just happened, but it would not be easy. Erec wished he understood it better himself. He leaned on the edge of the table near the water. "Listen, Bethany, and listen good. Our lives depend on it. You know what I saw in my cloudy thought?"

Bethany shook her head.

"I saw you and Jam getting killed by Baskania while he thanked Oscar for helping him again. Baskania knows everything Oscar knows. Everything. And Jack, whether he knows it or not, is helping. Jack tells things to Oscar."

Bethany was gripping her arms tight, shaking.

"Something really scary just happened out there," he said. "I realized that if Jack knew we were going here, to the game room, he might tell Oscar. So I couldn't let him know. Then I got a thought. I decided to tell Jack something else—that we were going to the maze, that we had a secret way out through the maze. And guess what?"

Bethany looked pale and just stared at him.

Erec nodded. "After I decided to tell Jack about the maze, I heard Baskania yell for someone to get to the entrance of the maze and the center of the maze to look for us."

"That's creepy." Bethany was shaking. "I thought I knew those guys. I just can't believe it." Her voice quivered. "But how could Baskania know about the maze if you hadn't even told Jack yet, just from you thinking it? Could it have been a coincidence?"

"Some coincidence. I think once I decided to say it, somehow that changed the course things were going to take. Like as soon as it was set that Oscar would at some time know where we were, then Baskania knew it right away."

Both of them thought about that. What could be the connection?

They didn't have much time. They looked into the water in the pool table.

"Where does it go?" Bethany asked.

"I don't know. A lot of places." He wondered if he could find his way back into Al's Well. He doubted it. At the time, the water in the tunnels had pushed him right to the castle. Would it push him somewhere else this time?

Bethany dragged her fingers through the water. "How will we breathe?"

Erec pointed to his wrist. "Our Instagills. Remember?"

She smiled. "I almost forgot. Haven't used them in a while."

They both slid into the water, then Erec took a breath, grabbed Bethany's wrist, and plunged down the water tunnel.

THE SEARCH FOR TRUTH

CHAPTER SEVEN

A Dragon in the Jungle

A T FIRST BETHANY kicked and flailed so hard that her arm slipped out of Erec's grasp. But he didn't need to worry. Soon they were both floating gently downstream through a wide tunnel filled with water. Passageways shot off from theirs, and they swam randomly down odd forks with no idea where they were heading. Their soaked clothing and backpacks weighed them down, but they weren't cold at all. Erec felt great.

Bethany held up her palms with a grin. Little feathery gills opened and shut in her hands. "Which way?" she asked, pointing at a large fork ahead. The words bubbled from her mouth, but Erec could hear her clearly, a side effect of the Instagills.

Erec shrugged and pointed to the left. It was easy to swim anywhere. Unlike before, when it seemed the Fates had decided to deposit him at the castle, Erec found the water pulled him in any direction he began to swim. If he wanted to go back where he had come from, after a few kicks the current would reverse. He and Bethany played around with it awhile, and they found they could even go in opposite directions past each other, each with their own current pulling them.

"This is so cool!" Bethany bubbled.

"I just wish we knew the way to Greece," Erec said.

As they swam, the tunnel grew wider until it was more like a cavern. Then, around a corner, appeared a huge round opening, about twenty-five feet across. The tunnel leading from it was much larger than the others. A sign glittering above its entrance read ASHONA.

"Look!" Bethany pointed. "We could go see Queen Posey!"

Erec shook his head and swam away from the entrance to Ashona. "We have to find the Oracle and a medium somehow. We can't get sidetracked."

After swimming for what seemed like hours, Erec wondered if they would ever see land again. At last he followed Bethany into a small tunnel that led up toward a spot of light. The spot quickly grew, and their heads soon popped above the surface in a cold lake. Both of them gasped for air.

The lake was surrounded by mountains. Birds twittered in the air, but no people or animals were in sight. Blue pine and silver fir trees added hints of color to the otherwise snowy woods.

As soon as Erec took a breath through his mouth, he felt cold. An icy wind hit his face, and his teeth started to chatter.

Bethany's skin looked blue. She said, "D-did you realize that we don't have d-dry clothes? It's January. I forgot, being in Alypium. The gold d-dome keeps it warm."

She was right. They would freeze when they got out of the water. It was already hard for Erec to speak through his clenched teeth. "We can't stay here. We'll freeze. Let's try to find somewhere warmer."

They dove back into the water. As soon as Erec's gills opened up, he felt warm again. "That was awful," he said. "We need to go someplace warm. Plus, I'm starving."

Bethany counted on her fingers, calculating. "I think we're traveling faster than it seems. Once we start to swim, the current really pushes us. Maybe we're near a coast."

"Yeah, but where?" They swam past more tunnels. "We better be heading south."

"I don't think we are, but I'm not sure," she said. "I think we're going east. Or west."

"That's reassuring."

"It might be okay." Bethany plunged left into a smaller tunnel. "We were in the mountains. If we just get past them it might be a lot warmer."

Erec followed her awhile, hoping she knew where she were going. He was beginning to feel tired and a little worried, and wondered how Bethany could stay so positive. She swung around and seemed to be able to read his expression. "Hey, just think—we're free. Nobody knows where we are. Baskania's probably still searching the maze for us. And getting lost in it."

Erec laughed, good humor restored. Even if they were cold awhile, they were free. And they had food waiting for them too. He mentally thanked Jam for throwing that silver platter to him.

He dove into a small tunnel that led upward, Bethany at his heels. Above him opened a circle of light. This time when their heads popped above the surface, the hot sun shone on their faces. They had surfaced near the edge of a huge lake surrounded by tropical teak forests and bamboo thickets. They swam until the water became shallow enough that they could walk.

Hot sunshine warmed Erec immediately, and his shirt began drying fast. "It must be over ninety degrees here," he said with a grin. "Don't know how we managed that one!"

"Look around," Bethany chirped. "No mountains. We must have gone pretty far."

"Where do you think we are?" he asked.

But there was no answer. Erec turned around to see Bethany standing in knee-deep water, her face pale.

"Bethany? You okay?"

She made a strange sound between a cough and a sputter, and pointed down into the lake. A knobby gray-green log drifted nearby. "Is that driftwood?" he asked, shielding his eyes from the sun.

But then it blinked. Was Erec imagining that? No, the log blinked again.

Then it yawned. Rows of sharp white teeth lined its mouth.

Bethany backed toward Erec, tripping and splashing in the water. She looked at Erec in terror. "It's a crocodile." Her voice shook. "A big one."

The crocodile swiveled, eyeing them. Erec stepped back in panic, his feet slowed by the water, and fell.

With a swish the crocodile's tail swung around so it faced them. It opened its huge mouth wide, flashing its teeth.

Suddenly, Erec's head spun. He felt his eyes turn in their sockets. Everything looked green. His dragon eyes were out. A lacy netting of Substance floated in the air, not the thick ropes he saw in Alypium and Otherness. This must be Upper Earth, he thought. He yanked Bethany behind him and took a step toward the crocodile.

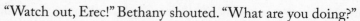

"Watch out, Erec!" Bethany shouted. "What are you doing?"

As he walked closer, he felt himself changing, growing. Soon his backpack felt too tight, so he shrugged it off, hoping Bethany would catch it. The buttons on his shirt popped. His skin felt funny, and when he glanced at his arm he saw scales.

Interesting, he thought. This was a cloudy thought, and he knew what he had to do. But he was not angry this time. And there was no vision or premonition. He wondered about that as he walked toward the crocodile, growing, claws sprouting from his hands. All fear had left him. Only a calm feeling remained in its place. Erec was not upset at the crocodile. It was only doing what its instincts told it to do. It was hungry and saw food.

The creature drew back as he got closer. Then it lunged at him.

Bethany screamed.

Before its giant mouth clamped on his neck, Erec breathed a stream of fire right into the crocodile's jaws. The animal jerked back in pain. A fierce surge of strength gripped Erec. He raised his claws, slashing down on the crocodile, breathing more fire on to its back. In seconds, the beast ducked under the water and swam away.

Erec was surprised. Breathing fire had filled him with a feeling of power, dominance. It felt good. He looked back at Bethany, who had picked up his backpack and was squeezing it with shaky arms. "It won't bother us again," Erec said.

Bethany stared at him in terror, not answering.

"What's wrong?" Erec splashed her, relaxed now.

A strangled squeal came from her throat. She pointed at Erec.

"What?" Erec spun around. "Is there another crocodile?" He couldn't see any.

Bethany shook her head. Her breathing sounded ragged. Finally she gasped, "You still look . . . funny."

Erec looked down at his reflection in the water and jumped in surprise. He was green, although it was hard to tell, since everything looked a shade of green through his dragon eyes. His chest was lined with scales. Torn clothing hung off him, and claws still jutted from his fingers. He wondered what his face looked like. Maybe it was best he didn't know.

"I won't hurt you." Erec held his hands up. "Sorry, Bethany." He knew he must look terrible. He strode to the shore and walked out. His shirt was already dry from the heat, and the cool water on his ragged pant legs felt good. Bethany followed him, though she looked uneasy.

Erec began to feel unsure too. What if he stayed like this forever? Would he always look like a freak? He'd never have any more friends. Everyone would be afraid of him. And would Alypium want him as their king then? Doubtful, he thought. They didn't even want him as king now. He sat under a tall broad-leafed tree and leaned against the trunk. "Time for a snack?" He realized he was starving.

Bethany nodded solemnly and took Jam's Serving Tray out of Erec's backpack. Several huge colorful butterflies floated past, and a golden-backed woodpecker tapped high over their heads.

"Look." Erec pointed at a huge ox wandering by with horns curling over its head. Bethany saw it and cringed, clinging close to the tree.

Erec laughed, feeling much better. "It won't hurt you. But I realized something. I figured out why I still look like this." Relief surged through him. He would not look like a dragon forever. He was sure of that now.

"Why?" Bethany's eyes darted to his. He could tell she was hopeful.

Erec pointed up into a tree. Slung over a sloping limb, one leg thrown over a smaller branch, a Bengal tiger lazed, black stripes cascading across its orange back. It was watching them.

Bethany froze in terror. She muttered, "Should we run?"

"Nah," Erec said. He sniffed, and rested his head back on his arms against the tree. He had to shift when he felt spines jutting from his neck and back grinding into the tree bark. "It'll come check us out in a few minutes and I'll scare it away. Then it'll leave us alone. I think we better wait to eat, though."

A smile snuck its way across Erec's face. It felt pretty good to know he could fight off a hungry crocodile and a huge tiger. There was no doubt in his mind what would happen. He wasn't seeing an image, like a movie in his head, like he had with his other recent cloudy thoughts. This time he just knew what would happen and what to do.

Bethany's lip quivered. She kept looking between Erec and the tiger. "There is no way you could fight that thing off."

"But I will." Knowing what would happen made him completely calm. Even better, a part of him was glad that Bethany was there to see how cool he was now, how strong. He began to whistle, thinking how impressed she would be.

In moments, the tiger scaled down the tree and approached them. Its huge shoulders and legs carved a swath through the tall grass. Its back swished and its tail flicked back and forth.

Bethany looked ashen, staring like a deer into headlights. The tiger, only a few feet away now, began to crouch.

But before it leaped, a huge roar erupted from Erec's chest. The tiger paused a moment. Erec sprang toward the tiger, flames shooting from his mouth. Fire shot into the tiger's face. It twisted its head back and forth, upset, and backed away from the flame. Then it turned and ran into the jungle.

Erec had known that was going to happen, but he was still surprised at how it felt. It seemed like every time he breathed fire, a strong emotion overcame him. Before it had been a sense of dominance and power over the crocodile, and the other times it had been anger. But this time it was a feeling of protectiveness for Bethany—shielding her, defending her from harm.

He turned to her with a smile, waiting to see her grateful face. But instead she was curled on the ground, tears drenching her cheeks. "Bethany? You okay?"

Bethany buried her face in her knees, which were squeezed to her chest. She didn't answer.

Erec sat next to her and patted her head, smoothing his fingers down her cheek. He could see his skin turning back to normal, his claws disappearing. "It's okay, Bethany. It's all over now." He kept his hand on her shoulder until she finally stopped shivering and fell asleep.

Erec fell asleep too, and he awoke starving. The sun was beginning to set. He shook Bethany. "Hey, wake up. Let's eat and see if we can find some kind of shelter around here."

Bethany opened her eyes. A big sigh escaped her when she saw her friend looking normal again. Erec picked up the Serving Tray. "I wonder how this thing works." He turned it over, rubbed it, and knocked on it. Nothing happened.

Bethany called out, like she was in a restaurant, "Give us some hamburgers."

In a flash, two huge, juicy hamburgers were sitting on the platter. Erec grabbed his and took a giant bite. "This is the best hamburger I've ever eaten," he said between gulps.

Bethany nodded, mouth full. "Give us some ketchup," she said. "And pickles." Little paper cups of ketchup and pickles appeared on the platter. They dumped them on what was left of the burgers.

Erec wanted to try. "Give us potato chips and scrambled eggs with cheese." The chips appeared in a paper bowl, and a pile of eggs with cheese appeared in another. Erec grabbed some of the eggs with his hand and scooped them into his mouth.

Bethany laughed. "What a barbarian. Give us forks," she said. And plastic forks appeared. They ate the eggs and chips, and Erec's hunger finally started to fade.

"Now, platter, I'd like a nectar fizz sundae." One popped onto the platter. "And a spoon," he added. "Bethany?"

"Me too. That looks good." Another appeared next to it. They dug in. After warm chocolate-chip cookies and milk they finally put the Serving Tray away.

"Thank you, Jam," Bethany sang out into the air.

Getting up, they walked aimlessly through the trees. While Bethany crunched over dried leaves and sticks, Erec moved soundlessly on them with his magic Sneakers. But they found no paths. "Shh . . ." Bethany stopped and pointed. "I think it's a hyena. Is it safe?" she whispered.

Erec saw what looked like a gray-brown dog with big pointed ears. It took a look at them and scrambled away. Erec felt a little nervous. "I guess it's okay. I'm not getting any more cloudy thoughts." He hoped he would get another one if he needed it. "At least I look normal now."

Bethany nodded. "You looked so freaky before." When Erec's face fell, she added, "I mean, not really that bad. I'm just not used to seeing you turn into a dragon."

"Where do you think we are?" he asked. The sun was getting lower in the sky, and there was no shelter in sight. At least it was still warm. "I wish I knew what to do. Anything. Just a direction to go." As he thought about it, doubts began to swarm into his mind.

"You know," he said, "I really don't know anything at all, do I? I don't know where I am. I don't know *who* I am. I'm supposed to be the next king, according to the scepters and that Lia Fail stone.

But I don't know why. I found out my birth mother is alive. But I have no clue who she is and why she left me. I found out my father is still alive. I don't even know where to look for him or why *he* left. Aoquesth said he was a great guy—little good that does me.

"And then I find out that awful memory of my father, that recurring dream, wasn't really my dad. Thanks a lot, Memory Mogul, for implanting that one in me. My luck, to get stuck with someone else's rotten memory of their dad. But is that all? No way. Because now I hear that there are two other kids around somewhere—I'm guessing they are kids—who are supposed to be the other two rulers of the Kingdoms of the Keepers along with me. And to make it worse, not only do I have no clue who they are, but King Piter does, and he won't tell me." A bitter laugh escaped him. "Well, I guess I should be glad they're around somewhere, so at least there is a chance that all three of us will be crowned, and Balor and his brothers won't get the thrones." He shook his head. "Like that will ever happen."

Bethany nodded. "Doesn't sound too likely. One of them is missing, and the other can't help and has to be protected? I wonder what King Piter meant about that."

Hearing King Piter's name made Erec scowl. "Face it," he said. "I have no clue about my father, my mother, or myself. I don't know where I am or what I'm doing." He looked into Bethany's eyes. "Maybe I should just go home."

"Only one problem," Bethany said. "Upper Earth is dying. The bees are disappearing, and the Substance is draining away. If we don't do something about it, there will be no 'home' soon."

Screeches resounded above them. A band of white monkeys with black ears and hands and scrunched black faces swung from the branches. One of them dropped Erec's Magiclight, which hit the ground with a thud in front of him. "What?" He picked it up. "How did they get this?" He turned it on to make sure it still worked, then put it away. But he saw that his backpack was unzipped. His bag of money was gone. Luckily the silver tray was still there.

He looked up at the branches. "Give me back my money!" he yelled up at them.

They just screeched back. It sounded like they were laughing.

"Too bad I can't turn into a dragon now," he said, shaking a fist at them.

Some of the monkeys shook their fists back at him. They swung around making that annoying laughing sound.

"Give it back, you dumb armpit-scratchers! Go pick bugs out of each other's noses and eat them!" he shouted. Bethany was starting to giggle.

One of the monkeys had opened the bag, and now they were passing coins to each other. They were amazingly good at not dropping any.

"Give those to me!" Erec shouted. One of the monkeys picked up a shiny gold ring coin and tossed it, hitting Erec on the head. "Ow!"

Erec tried to throw sticks at them, but none of them hit.

"Cut it out, Erec. They're cute."

"Real cute." Erec picked up the ring coin and put it in his pocket. "Little thieves." He threw a bigger stick and it hit a monkey in the arm. The monkey didn't look bothered by it.

"Erec!" Bethany looked mad. "Would you stop it? You could have hurt him."

"They stole all our money!" Erec kicked the dirt. What was wrong with her? "Why are you siding with the monkeys?"

She snapped back, "Because they're cute. Why do you have to be so selfish?"

It didn't seem to Erec that trying to get his money back from monkeys that had no use for it was selfish. But he felt guilty anyway.

And that just made him more upset. It didn't help that it was getting dark and he had no clue where they could sleep.

"Fine," he said. "Let's keep going. I give up." He walked in the direction they had been going, which was away from the lake. As far as he knew this path might take them into a thousand-mile forest. They might never get out.

Bethany waited a moment before following, then crunched after him, arms crossed. When Erec glanced back at her she called out, "We have food. We don't need money out here anyway."

After a few more minutes, Erec heard a loud clatter, which grew into a low roar, quickly coming closer. A wide, dusty truck with an open top rumbled into view. They ran toward it, waving their hands. A sign of civilization!

The truck skidded to a stop, and a dark-skinned man with straight black hair jumped through the door. He was about Erec's size and wore loose black pants and a white shirt embroidered with black swirls. The man ran at them, shouting something Erec could not understand, a rifle in his hands.

Bethany screamed as they turned and ran. The man chased them, yelling and pointing wildly, but it sounded like gibberish. He seemed furious.

Erec panicked. Now a man with a gun? Where were his cloudy thoughts? What would he do? The man raged, tearing after them.

Bethany tripped on a tree root. She flew a few feet in the air and landed on her stomach.

As much as Erec had been annoyed with her a second ago, he was now filled with fear. Standing in front of her, he turned to face the man. Maybe she could crawl away while he fought off this stranger. Erec grabbed a stick from the forest floor—the only thing he could find to defend himself.

But the man stopped when he got close to them. He continued

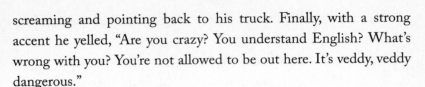

screaming and pointing back to his truck. Finally, with a strong accent he yelled, "Are you crazy? You understand English? What's wrong with you? You're not allowed to be out here. It's veddy, veddy dangerous."

Erec answered, "Who are you?"

"Look at you," the man said. "You're from England, no? Can't understand Marathi or Hindi? What are you doing out here? You want to get yourselves killed?" Erec could not place his accent.

Erec and Bethany stared at his rifle, afraid to answer. Finally the man looked at his own gun. "What, this? Don't worry about this. It's a tranquilizer gun, for the animals." He eyed the two kids more intently. "How did you get out here? You're not supposed to be here. Don't you know how dangerous this is?" Even though he had a strong accent, Erec could understand him perfectly.

Erec dropped the stick, exhausted and relieved. "We're lost. Can you help us?"

"I'll say you're lost." The man shook his head. "You're lucky I found you. I'm a guide here. I'm Rajiv. Just finished my last safari tour today." He gestured toward his truck with his gun. "Now get in the truck. What would you two do if I didn't find you here? Huh?"

They followed him to his truck and climbed in. Erec appreciated its comfort as he sank into the seat cushions.

"You were attacked." Rajiv pointed at Erec's torn clothing as it flapped around in the wind blowing through the open truck. Red scratches striped his chest. He nodded yes, not sure how else to explain.

They bounced over rocks and splashed through a stream, following a bumpy path through the jungle. Finally, they stopped at a group of buildings in a clearing.

"Where are we?" Erec asked.

"You don't know?" Rajiv stopped in front of a white house. "This is Tadoba National Park."

"And where is that?" asked Bethany.

"Near Chandrapur," the guide said. "You know that."

"We don't know," Erec said. "Where is Chandrapur?"

"East Maharashtra. You have to know that." He sounded annoyed.

"No, we don't know." Bethany persisted. "What country is this? Just tell us, please."

"India, of course." He threw up his hands. "Stop trying to distract me, you kids. I know what you're doing. You're going to have to tell me where you're from, no playing games. I'll figure out what to do with you tomorrow. I suppose you need a place to sleep?"

The house was one swash of bright color against another. Vivid fabrics hung from the ceilings and draped the lights, casting the rooms in glows of red and orange. A fire crackled in the front room fireplace, and soft couches cluttered the floor, woven with patterns of beautiful green, gold, and yellow silks. The wonderful smell of home cooking filled the air. Erec took a deep whiff. Indian food.

Two young kids were playing a game in front of the fire. Erec and Bethany watched them, unsure what to do.

"Welcome to our home," Rajiv said. "It will soon be a guest house for visitors to Tadoba Park. We stay in the basement, make the meals."

"It's lovely." Bethany looked around.

A woman rushed at Erec. She was wrapped in a colorful silk sari, the purple-and-red pattern melting into greens at the bottom. Her long black hair was pulled into a bun. "Oh, no." She was shaking her head with disapproval. "No, no, no."

Erec was about to excuse himself and leave the house, thinking that she must not like the looks of him. He could certainly understand why. But then the woman grabbed his wrist and yanked him into a bathroom. Bethany followed to watch. The woman unscrewed a bottle and doused a cotton ball with its contents. She dabbed it over the scrapes on Erec's chest.

"Ow." He winced. "That hurts."

"It will feel better soon." She tsked, shaking her head. "You'll need new clothing. I think you'll fit into Rajiv's. What attacked you?"

"A crocodile." Erec actually thought the scratches on his chest were probably from his own claws, but how could he explain that? The woman drew her breath in horror. She blotted Erec's chest again without thinking. Somehow, knowing a crocodile had attacked him made him need extra attention.

"And a tiger," Bethany added. She tilted her chin up with a hint of a smile.

Warmth filled Erec. He realized that she was proud that he was able to fend off the dangerous animals.

The woman looked confused. "And a tiger?" she repeated. Erec could tell she was deciding whether to believe them. He hoped Bethany didn't blurt out that he had breathed fire and scared it away.

"Well, the tiger didn't really attack us," he said. "It just came close."

The woman put her hand over her heart. "I don't even want to think about you kids out there in the preserve alone. Let me get you clothes and some food. Then we'll find your parents. I'm Sunita, by the way."

Sunita rushed off and brought back clothing for Erec. He changed into a white, long-sleeved collarless shirt, with embroidered stitching decorating the top. It hung below his knees. The white cotton pants were oddly shaped too, and seemed wide enough on top for three men to fit into, but they narrowed to fit his lower legs better. He pulled a drawstring at the top, gathering all the extra fabric into a big bunch. At least it was hidden under the long top. It felt like he was wearing pajamas, which actually was what Sunita said the pants were called, even though they were not meant for sleeping in.

Bethany laughed when she saw him and he felt his face get hot. "Hey, you look pretty good in that thing," she said.

Hearing that made him feel much better, even though he guessed she was just trying to cheer him up. They sat with the kids in front of the fire. "My name's Shreena," the little girl said. She pointed at Erec's amulet. "I like your necklace. This is my brother Sunil. What are your names?" Erec noticed Sunil wore a smaller version of his outfit. Shreena's shirt was shorter and pink.

"I'm Bethany, and this is Erec." Bethany smiled at the kids. "What are you playing?"

"Poker." Shreena batted big eyes at them. "Want to join?"

"Maybe later," Sunita said, appearing with large silver plates loaded with steaming rice and different foods. It smelled delicious. "Let them eat first."

Bethany looked at her plate in wonder. "What is all this? It smells so good." She tasted a little steamed pancake.

"That's patodi," Sunita said. "And those are varhadi prawns. And rice. The crunchy bread is dhapoda, it's like papad. And the soft bread is chapati. That's a potato, cauliflower, and tomato bhaji." She looked excited at their interest. "Let me know if you like. I'll be cooking for English-speaking visitors soon. We haven't met any tourists yet."

Bethany tasted the prawns and her eyebrows shot up. "These are amazing! I've never had anything like this before. And both breads are so good."

"Use the bread to scoop the food," Sunita instructed.

In between bites, Bethany said, "I've never had Indian food before."

"You haven't?" Erec asked. "Why? Did you think you wouldn't like it?" Then he felt bad for asking. Most of Bethany's life had been spent with Earl Evirly, who had been posing as her uncle. He never gave her anything. There was no way he would have taken her to a restaurant.

"Oh, this is nice!" A familiar woman's voice filled the room. Erec glanced around but did not see anybody.

"Erec, I'm over here, on the chair." His eyes darted to the chair under the window. "No," the voice said, "on this side of the room, by the fireplace."

He jerked to see, almost spilling the food on his plate. Who knew him here? But nobody was there.

A laugh rang in the air. "It's me, Mom. You forget me already?"

Erec smiled with recognition. Of course. He had forgotten about his mother's Seeing Eyeglasses. "No, I didn't forget you."

"Looks like you're doing okay. How's the quest going?"

"I don't even know what the quest is yet. I'm in India." He held his plate of food up a bit. "Met a tiger today and a crocodile." Only silence followed, so he quickly added, "I'm fine. Nothing bad happened. Just scared them off."

He heard June sigh. "I see Bethany's with you. Did you take anyone else?"

"No. It's just the two of us this time. We have to get to the Oracle in Delphi, Greece. Not sure how we'll get there, though. Any ideas?"

June laughed. "Got any money for a plane ticket? I could call and arrange it for you."

"Our whole bag of it got stolen by monkeys." Erec grimaced. "And Alypium money probably wouldn't be good here, anyway."

"Gold, Erec, is good anywhere," June replied. "As long as you know the right people. Speaking of that, who are these people? Did you meet them in India?"

"I just met them," he said. "They're really nice." He smiled at Rajiv and Sunita. Then he noticed they were staring at him, shocked. "Uh . . . I better go, okay?"

"Sure, sweetie. I'll check on you again in a few days. I'm trying not to bother you too much. Bye, honey."

"Bye." Erec's voice was soft as he gazed around the room. Everybody was looking at him. Usually Bethany could think of something to say to explain things, but even she was speechless.

Rajiv asked, "And who were you talking to, boy? I didn't see anybody there."

Erec was silent. What possible explanation could he give for what had just happened? How stupid was he? Why couldn't he have just not answered his mother? He hadn't even thought about how that must have looked.

And why hadn't June realized? Maybe she'd just assumed anyone with Erec would know what was going on with him.

"Um . . ." Erec stared at the stunned faces around the room. His heart sunk. These nice people would not want some freak staying in their house. And he was a freak. Breathing fire. Sprouting scales. Talking to an invisible mother. He had no place on Upper Earth anymore. It had been his home, but no longer.

Rajiv stood. "You just talked to someone here that we can't see. Don't deny it." He poked a finger toward Erec with each word. "We can tell with our own eyes."

"I'm sorry, I . . ." Erec put his plate down on the couch. "I should go."

Bethany looked worried. "He just . . . does that sometimes. He's sorry," she said. "He won't do it again. Erec's a good kid, really."

"I'm sure he is." Rajiv smiled thoughtfully. "But see? He said he wants to go." Rajiv rubbed his hands together. "I know what is happening. He is being led somewhere by the unseen. And I'm sure I know where he wants to go."

Erec couldn't believe his ears. What was Rajiv talking about?

"Where?" Bethany asked.

"To see Swami Parvananda. That is the only possible explanation." He sat down, satisfied. "A boy appears, attacked by a crocodile and a tiger but unharmed, does not know what brought him here, and he is talking to spirits." Now he was looking at his wife. "He is being led by the gods, maybe Ganesha, to somewhere. And the only place here where that would be is to Swami Parvananda. Our yogi guru. His presence sometimes calls people to him."

Sunita, Shreena, and Sunil sat and stared at Erec and Bethany like they were a television show. Maybe they were waiting to see the next crazy thing Erec might do. He was tempted to jump up and shout, "Boo!" but that would confirm whatever it was they were thinking, so he stayed quiet.

"And where are your parents?" Sunita asked. "Do they know where you are?"

"My parents are dead," Bethany said.

"I don't know who my parents are," Erec added. He did not feel like talking about his adoptive mother in New Jersey, especially as he might end up explaining that he had just been talking to her.

Rajiv nodded forcefully. "See? Of course. It all fits." He pounded his fist into his palm. "I'll take them in the morning to see the Swami."

CHAPTER EIGHT

Swami Parvananda

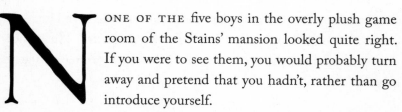

NONE OF THE five boys in the overly plush game room of the Stains' mansion looked quite right. If you were to see them, you would probably turn away and pretend that you hadn't, rather than go introduce yourself.

Dollick Stain was odd without question. Wooly white hair covered his head and ran down the sides of his cheeks like a beard gone wild, sprouting all over his neck and chest, despite the fact that he was only thirteen. Pointy white ears poking through his tight white curls, plus his thin face, only made him look more like a sheep.

Damon Stain had striking steel-blue eyes, as his brothers did, but his seemed a bit out of focus. On his head sat the floppy gray hat he always wore, sticking out at an odd angle from his head. Under it he had what looked like an oversize dog bone growing from the top of his head.

The third Stain triplet, Balor, had the windswept black hair of his brother Damon. He was the only one who had a chance of looking normal. Unfortunately, the wild glint in his eyes and his manic expression took care of that possibility.

The other two boys did not do much to inspire confidence, either. Tall, blond, and gangly, Ward Gamin was smirking and dressed far too warmly in an oversize coat that flapped around him oddly. Rock Rayson was blond and beefy, and had the habit of flexing his arm muscles whenever someone looked at him. Today he looked surly.

"Go sit on a Hydra pie," Rock snarled at Balor. "I don't care what you say. My dad said I'd be one of the three kings. Hecate Jekyll promised him."

"And where is she now?" Balor laughed. Damon joined in with a goofy guffaw until Balor slapped him on his head. "Baskania promised us we'd be the next kings. The Stain triplets. Can't beat that."

"But I'm the one who won all those contests with you guys," Rock whined. "Dollick just hung out and . . . grazed or whatever he does. This is the thanks I get?"

"You'll get your thanks when I'm all-powerful." Balor stifled a grin. "You'll be high up in the food chain."

"You didn't actually think they were going to let you rule," Ward's eyes mocked Rock. "The Stains will be lucky if they even get to touch the scepters once the Shadow Prince gets his hands on them."

"Shut up," Balor sneered. "Nobody's taking my scepter away from me. Not even Baskania, the great Shadow Prince." He stuck his chin in the air. "Plus, why do you think he chose us anyway?"

"Uhh . . ." Ward scratched his head with a sarcastic look. "Great question, actually."

Balor rolled his eyes. "It's because we're superior, doofus. Our father is Mauvis Stain, one of the greatest sorcerers on the planet, and we've inherited his abilities."

"Yeah, right." Ward pointed a thumb at Damon, who was kissing and cuddling a rubber pizza that he'd been carrying. "Bunch a' brainiacs."

Rock bunched his fists up. "This is garbage. You'd never let *me* talk like that to you." He glared at Balor.

Balor Stain cocked his fist back at him. "That's because you never have anything interesting to say."

A tall figure materialized in front of the boys. Two eyes were on each of his ears which, at the moment, were larger than normal to fit them, and more eyes covered his hands. He held up a finger to quiet them while he watched something.

Baskania turned around, gazing through his many eyes. As soon as he faced away, Damon began jumping up and down, scratching his armpits like a monkey.

"Stop it, bonehead." Balor batted him with the rubber pizza. "He's got eyes in the back of his head."

Sure enough, several dark eyes peered through his black shiny hair, looking wildly about. Luckily for Damon, they were occupied seeing things far away.

Baskania swung about again. "I have news for you boys. I want you to be on the alert for something."

He looked down his nose at Ward and Rock. "Having friends over? Show some respect and kneel before the future kings and emperor." Ward's and Rock's faces clenched in pain as a force slammed them onto their knees, then smashed their faces on the floor, arms stretched out in front of them. "Much better," Baskania sneered. The two boys lifted their heads, but remained stuck on their knees.

Baskania tapped his chin thoughtfully. "It has come to light recently that Erec Rex's friend Bethany Cleary, Ruth's daughter, has a secret. One that she doesn't want me to know. She almost told this secret to Oscar Felix a while ago. If she had, of course my informant would have reported it to me right away. But, unfortunately, he waited awhile to tell me that she had a secret at all, not realizing the urgency of the matter. I would like to have learned about it earlier."

He cleared his throat, a look of disgust on his face. "If I had found out about this secret before, I would have captured Bethany when I saw her last at the Labor Society and found out what it was. I'm very disappointed that I lost that opportunity. However, I will find her and learn what she is hiding one way or another. As soon as Oscar next sees either her or Erec Rex, I will be there, rest assured."

Dollick bleated, "*Baaa*-ut I thought you went to capture Erec Rex and his friends in the Castle Alypium when Oscar found out they were there and King Piter was gone. *Baaa*."

Baskania's many eyes narrowed to slits. "Do not speak in front of me ever again, you wooly simpleton. They escaped somehow before I could find them." A few of his eyes gazed out a window, and the rest remained glaring at Dollick. "I should have killed Erec Rex immediately when I saw him last," he mused. "Little good he did pulling that torn quest out of Al's Well. I'm not too worried, though. He managed to get away from me a few times now, but his luck won't last."

He focused on the crew in front of him. "I want you five boys to watch for Bethany Cleary, and Erec Rex, too. I've taken too much time dealing with him. He was so pathetic and weak last summer, he wasn't a threat. But now he has two dragon eyes, which I would greatly like to own. I need to capture him before he and his amulet grow any stronger."

Baskania snapped a finger and two large men appeared. They picked Rock and Ward off the floor, their knees still bent. "Time for you boys to donate to the cause," he snickered. The men carried Rock and Ward down the stairs and out the Stains' door.

Balor felt his hands shaking. Damon didn't get it yet, but Balor knew what Rock and Ward would be donating—an eye each that Baskania would add to his internal collection. He would use them to see through their remaining eyes and keep tabs on them, just like all of his others when he brought them to the surface of his face or arms.

"Don't worry," Baskania sneered. "I'm letting you three scared babies keep your eyes a little longer. I'll get them soon enough. For now you can content yourselves with the thought of your friends' eyes being ripped from their sockets. . . ." He went on with a gruesome, detailed description, seeming to delight in the torture he was causing them.

The minute Baskania disappeared, Balor rushed to the bathroom to throw up.

"It is said," Rajiv shouted back from the front of the van, "that Swami Parvananda hasn't taken a bite to eat in over thirty years. He only has to drink water every few days."

"Wow," Bethany said. "That's hard to believe."

"But true," said Rajiv, pointing at the air. "Nobody knows how old he is. Maybe over one hundred. He sees everything. He just sits and meditates every day. He'll know why you were called to him."

Erec was getting used to Rajiv's accent. Last night he had slept well in the guest house. Sunita had served them things called poha and upma in the morning, made out of rice, vegetables, and chilies.

They tasted good but were not Erec's idea of breakfast. So, after eating bits of them, he and Bethany conjured up banana chocolate-chip pancakes with Jam's Serving Tray.

The bumpy gravel-and-dirt path in Tadoba National Park soon turned into a small paved street. They drove awhile through the jungle, Rajiv's tranquilizer gun leaning next to him in case of an animal attack. On the way through the woods, Rajiv pointed out a sloth bear in the hills, a blue bull crossing a stream, and some white monkeys swinging in trees. They looked just like the ones that had stolen Erec's money. "Those are leaf monkeys," he said. "Harmless, simple creatures."

Erec sneered at them. "Harmless, simple, and rich."

As they turned off of the dirt road from the preserve, Rajiv pulled onto the left side of the street to Chandrapur. A car sped in their direction, whizzing by on their right. Bethany grabbed the bars that served as windows on the jeep and screamed.

Erec's heart pounded, but Rajiv stayed on the left side of the road. "What's wrong with you two?" Rajiv asked. "Never been in a car before?"

Bethany flushed. "Do you all drive on the wrong side of the road here?"

"No, we drive on the correct side of the road. I thought you did too, in England."

"We're from America," Erec said.

"America," Rajiv repeated, impressed. "You really *did* get lost."

The road snaked through hills and woods and eventually grew more crowded. As they neared Chandrapur, they shared the road with buses packed with people, sitting on top and hanging off the sides.

The colors and smells of India seemed to permeate the landscape. Rajiv pointed out a Brahma cow milling around by the road. Big baskets of brightly colored spices in front of shops mixed their scents with a herd of goats and fumes from auto rickshaws, little open-air vehicles that served as taxis.

Rajiv swung off the main street onto a dirt road that led away from the city. After passing some houses and fields, they drove another half hour until they reached a barren hilly area. Rajiv stopped the truck.

"You must be quiet when you enter the Swami's cave," he explained.

"He lives in a cave?" Erec asked.

"Of course." Rajiv sighed impatiently. "He's a yogi master. A guru. He's given up the physical world and all earthly things. His time is spent in the higher realm. I think he can show you what you need."

Bethany's eyes twinkled. "Erec," she whispered. "The yogi is a medium! We need a medium to go to the Oracle with us. Maybe this Swami could do it."

Erec smiled. Why hadn't he thought of that? A medium was exactly what they needed. Now they were getting somewhere.

Rajiv continued. "There are rules. When you go in, you bow low so your head almost touches the floor. Then you must say 'Adesh, adesh.' It means, 'I will do as you command.' You must say this. Practice."

They practiced saying "Adesh, adesh" a few times. "Can we go in now?" Erec asked.

"Patience!" Rajiv commanded. "Now, the yogi might not notice you for a while. He may be deep in meditation. This yogi is known to enter meditation and stay there for a week at a time. So if he does not answer when you say 'Adesh, adesh,' just wait. If you have been called to him for a purpose, he will respond soon. But never, never approach and touch him if he is in a trance."

"Would something happen to him?" Bethany asked.

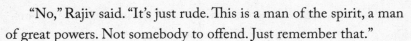

"No," Rajiv said. "It's just rude. This is a man of the spirit, a man of great powers. Not somebody to offend. Just remember that."

Bethany and Erec nodded. They headed toward a large hill with a path winding up its side. It led to a large gap in the stone.

"I will wait here," Rajiv said, looking up at the cave nervously. "It would not be proper for me to watch."

"It's okay if you want to come," Erec said. It looked like Rajiv was curious to see the yogi guru.

Rajiv bit his lip in thought. "No. It's not right for me to go. I'll wait by the truck."

Erec and Bethany climbed the path up the hill to the cave entrance. The small opening led into a wide, round cavern of white rock that was lit by the sunlight from outside. Another stream of light also shone into the small cavern from a side tunnel. When they peeked into that tunnel, they got a glimpse of an even larger room. Incandescent lights shone from inside. Erec glimpsed a figure, but then he darted away when he heard voices.

"Shh." He put a finger to his lips. "I think someone else is in there with him. Maybe we should wait."

Bethany leaned close to the doorway and tried to hear. "You're right. He's talking to someone. Listen."

Erec stepped closer. A thickly accented, sharp voice said, "You're dead now. I'll raise you."

He and Bethany looked at each other. "Did you hear that?" she whispered. "He's raising the dead. Like a séance."

Erec wasn't sure whether he wanted to go in and watch or get out of there right away. Then he heard the voice again.

"Oh, believe me. I have you," the voice said. "There won't be a stitch of you left when I'm done. You're fading out now. You're fading." The voice grew louder, shouting, "You're fading! I'll raise you now. I'll raise you!"

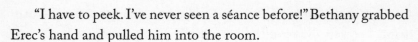

"I have to peek. I've never seen a séance before!" Bethany grabbed Erec's hand and pulled him into the room.

On a red silk pillow sat a small man with a long white beard. A big white sheet was wrapped around him like a dress, and a small white sheet was folded on top of his head, looking like a cross between a turban and an unmade bed. Next to him sat a bag of potato chips and an open can of soda pop. He held a cell phone up to one ear and tapped a computer keyboard in front of him. Erec could see that he was playing poker online.

Swami Parvananda nodded at Erec and Bethany as if to say, *Just a minute.* Then he shouted into the phone, "You're fading again. I can't hear a thing. Did you say you folded? You didn't? I can't hear! Oh, well." He hung up the phone and looked at Erec and Bethany. "Always works when I'm losing. Can I help you?"

Bethany giggled, and Erec felt ridiculous for thinking the guru had been raising the dead, when he was just raising his friend at poker. The guru popped a few chips into his mouth. So much for him not having eaten in over thirty years, Erec thought. And for giving up earthly possessions, too. His laptop computer looked like the latest model.

"Um, don't you *know* why I'm here?" Erec asked.

"Erec!" Bethany shot him her "that's rude" look.

"Let me guess," Swami Parvananda's sharp voice intoned. "You're two rich kids from America who came here on a holiday and want to meet the mystic they heard lives in the cave. To get your fortunes read. Right?" He yawned.

"Uh . . . no." Erec crossed his arms. This guy didn't seem so special to him. Since when did living in a cave and wearing a sheet make you know things? This "mystic" didn't seem to know anything. "I guess you really can't help us," Erec said, "seeing as how you can't see what's under your own nose."

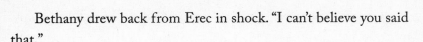

Bethany drew back from Erec in shock. "I can't believe you said that."

Swami Parvananda pointed a thumb at Erec and said, "Anything can come out of the mouth of a monkey."

Erec wasn't sure why this guy upset him so much, but something about the guru made him angry. "We came all the way out here because you were supposed to be some great guru who knows everything. And here you are playing poker and eating potato chips."

"What would you prefer I was doing? Raising the dead?" His lips twitched like he was trying not to smile. As if he knew.

Erec and Bethany exchanged glances. Could the Swami have heard them talking? It seemed unlikely. "I'm sorry," Erec said. "I don't know why I said that. We came here to see if you could help us. We're kind of on a quest."

"I know now. Sit down." The little man gestured to some flat rocks near his pillow. "Do you know why you got angry with me?"

Erec and Bethany sat before him. Erec shook his head.

"It's because you recognized me. You saw that I should know you, too. And when I didn't see who you were right away, you were upset."

Erec nodded out of politeness. He had no idea what the guru was talking about, but he was starting to feel much better.

"You don't understand yet," Swami Parvananda continued. "You have something inside you, something different from most people. You know things, like me, about . . . about what do you think?"

"Magic?" The word was out of Erec's mouth before he realized it.

Swami Parvananda tilted his head in thought. "That's an interesting way to put it, but I suppose it's true. Magic. Our earth. What it's made of."

"Do you mean the Substance?" Erec was eager to learn how much this mystic knew about magic. Maybe he could help them after all.

"I don't know what is 'substance.' I think you are talking about *prana*. In the East they call it 'Chi.' It's the energy that runs through the universe, that lets us all live. It flows through channels called the—"

"Aitherplanes," Erec blurted out.

"I was going to say the 'Nadis,' but maybe they are the same thing." The guru pursed his lips in thought. "Yes. I believe so."

"Have you noticed," Erec leaned forward, "that there is a problem lately with the . . . prana? Something's wrong with it?"

"Namaste," Swami Parvananda said. He pressed his palms together, fingers up, in front of his chest and bowed his head to Erec. "You are truly a seer, my friend."

"So you noticed it too?" Erec was amazed. "The Substance—I mean the prana—is leaking away, getting messed up?"

"I have, my friend. In fact, I was just chatting with my friend Swami Rictananda about it on a discussion board." He nodded toward his computer.

"Online?" Bethany asked. "Do mystics chat online now?"

"Why not?" the Swami said. "Easier than making a pilgrimage."

"Why do you think it's happening?" Erec asked. "What can we do? Upper Earth is going to die."

"Upper Earth?" The Swami wrinkled his nose in confusion. "Do you mean the north, or up in the mountains?"

"No, I just mean Earth."

Swami Parvananda sighed. "I wish I knew. We have all been meditating about it." He frowned at Erec. "I have a very funny feeling right now. If you don't mind, I'd like to do a palm reading for you." He looked at Bethany. "Maybe both of you."

They nodded, excited. A reading by a real psychic!

First Bethany sat close to Swami Parvananda. He took her palm and traced some lines on it with his finger. Then he held his hand over hers, not touching it, and closed his eyes. They sat there for a while.

Erec could see the Swami's eyes darting back and forth behind his closed lids. He wondered what the man was seeing. It felt good to watch someone else seeing things that nobody else could. So he was not the only one. Unfortunately, he could not control it like the Swami could. The things Erec saw with his cloudy thoughts descended on him on their own.

Soon Swami Parvananda opened his eyes. He held Bethany's hand and placed his other palm on top of it. Tears were in his eyes. "Never have I been so privileged." He bowed his head. "You, my dear, have the gift of sight. You don't know it yet. But someday you will be able to read into the future. It might have to do with math. And you have the heart to do the right thing with it when you do. My girl, you have made good choices so far with your friends and what to believe. Stick with your choices, even when your friends change their minds." He patted her hand, then nodded to Erec.

Erec and Bethany switched seats. When Swami Parvananda took his hand, Erec could feel a surge of energy through his skin. It was as if the Swami was electrified. He looked at Erec's palm, tracing the lines on it in deep concentration. Then he held his hand over Erec's and closed his eyes.

Images jumped through Erec's head as he sat. Growing up with June and his five adopted siblings. His old recurrent nightmare about his father, and then finding out from the Memory Mogul that the dream was really somebody else's memory. Meeting and then losing Aoquesth. His anger at his mother and then at King Piter for keeping things from him. Learning from an inquizzle that his birth mother was still alive.

And then cloudy thoughts. Dragon eyes. Turning into a dragon. As he watched the mystic's eyes dart beneath his closed lids,

Erec was sure he was seeing these same things. And then his mind went blank, just when he got the feeling that this man was seeing into his future.

Soon Swami Parvananda's eyes opened. He took Erec's hand in his. "My son." He looked both sad and kind. "It is you. You are the one."

Erec knew what he meant, but he needed to hear it. "The one to do what?"

The Swami nodded. "To fix the prana. Your Substance. If anyone can do it, it can only be you."

They sat quietly. The Swami was right. Erec wondered if he had known that all along, somehow. Or maybe just since he'd had both dragon eyes. They let him know things, deep down, that he wasn't even conscious of.

"Will I be able to do it? Will I fix the Substance?" Erec asked finally.

"Will you be able to?" Swami Parvananda said. "Yes. Will you? I don't know. I can see what's in you, but I can't see how you will use it. I can tell you it will not be easy."

Erec understood that. Somehow he knew it would be very, very difficult. It would go against his every fiber. He wondered, himself, what he would do.

"You have more powers than anyone I've heard of," the guru said. "They come from your eyes and that chain." He pointed at the Amulet of Virtues hanging around Erec's neck. "But you cannot control them yet. You must learn how, fast. If you let them go wild now, you may go wild."

Erec thought of how wild he had felt when he was a dragon, fighting the crocodile.

"You must learn to tame your powers, master them," the guru said.

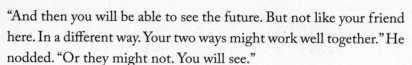

"And then you will be able to see the future. But not like your friend here. In a different way. Your two ways might work well together." He nodded. "Or they might not. You will see."

"I'm on a quest," Erec said. "Or, actually, I still need to find out what the quest is. The only part I heard was 'Get behind.' So King Piter told me to consult the Oracle in Delphi. But I found out that it won't work for just anyone. We need to find a medium to talk to the Fates. I was wondering if you might come with us."

The guru laughed. "I haven't left this cave in years." He nodded at his computer. "Don't have to, with this thing. My friends bring me what I need. But you don't need me with you anyway."

"How will I find a medium?" Erec asked.

Swami Parvananda giggled. "Look in a mirror."

CHAPTER NINE

The Little Dark Room

"M E?" EREC WAS dumbfounded at the Swami's statement. Sure, he saw snippets of the future with his cloudy thoughts, but he was no medium.

"Yes, you. You have everything you need. Just a little more learning, that's all."

"But how will I learn in time? Can you show me how to use my dragon eyes?" It did not seem odd to talk to this Upper Earth man about Oracles and dragon eyes. The Swami was not surprised at all.

"No, that I cannot," he said. "But you do know somebody who can. Somebody from your past, and your future. From what I saw in your mind, he's a good-looking chap. Nice, trim. No hair cluttering his head. Stylish clothing."

Erec could not think of a stylish bald man for the life of him. But Bethany smiled. "You're talking about the Hermit."

"But the Hermit's crazy," Erec said, drawing back. "He makes no sense at all."

"A very, very good sign." The Swami nodded.

"And how could I even find him in time?"

"Oh, I don't think that will be difficult," the Swami said. "I get the feeling he pops up when he is needed."

That was true. Erec remembered how the Hermit had appeared out of the blue right before his first two quests. And King Piter had said he had made the Hermit Erec's magic tutor.

"I think there is something else you will need from here," the guru said. "I will give it to you now."

They followed him into a small crevice in the rock at the edge of the cave. A wave of music surged to their ears. It sounded like a sea of tuning forks struck at the same time. The Swami pointed at rows of clear quartz crystals jutting from a table of rock. "These are the singing crystals," he said. "They will sing when they are in the presence of great prana—magic, as you call it."

The ringing was a lovely, relaxing sound, but it slowly faded. "They were singing because of you," the Swami said. "They detected magic within you. But they adjust and become quiet again. If you left for a while and came back, they would make noise again." He broke off a tall crystal the size of a celery stalk and handed it to Erec. "I'm not sure why, but I think you'll need this."

"Thank you." Erec put it in his backpack. The crystal rang in a loud, clear note, then quieted again. Probably because of the

Magiclight and Serving Tray in there, he realized.

Before they left, Erec pulled out the Serving Tray. "I see you still eat, contrary to popular belief. Do you want some lunch before we go?"

Curious, Swami Parvananda nodded. The three took turns naming items, watching them appear, then sampling them, desserts and main courses side-by-side. Seeing food magically appear in front of him did not throw the Swami off one bit. He named items they had never heard of, most of them delicious, and seemed just as happy trying blueberry waffles and tiramisu, although he avoided the meat dishes.

Bethany and Erec took a cue from Swami Parvananda and bowed low, like he did. Then they headed down the path.

"Do you think we should offer some food to Rajiv?" Bethany asked.

"I wish," Erec said. "I don't think he'd be as relaxed about magically appearing food, though."

"Couldn't we just tell him Swami Parvananda gave it to us?" she asked.

"And ruin his reputation for not eating in thirty years? I don't think so," Erec said. "Rajiv will be okay till we get back."

They hopped into the truck with smiles and waved at Rajiv in front. But Rajiv looked a little different from the way Erec remembered. Didn't Rajiv have hair?

"Hello, silly Erec." The Hermit swung around, black eyes twinkling. "Forget who I am already?"

Rajiv appeared from behind some trees and rushed over to them. "How was it? Did the Swami tell you what your path is, why you were called to him?" His eyes searched them for clues. "What was he like?"

"He was a true mystic," Bethany said. "You were right about him. And he really did help us."

"How? What did he say?"

Erec could not begin to explain, and Bethany was at a lack for words. But the Hermit said, "Songs unsung have the sweetest tunes."

"Yes, yes." Rajiv nodded and climbed into the driver's seat. "I hope you kids don't mind. This holy man was wandering nearby. I'm taking him back with us. It's good luck to give them food and shelter."

Erec had to admit, the Hermit fit right in here. Today the Hermit was wrapped in a big white towel with only his scrawny arms and the ends of his stick legs popping out. It almost looked like the Swami's outfit, except the Hermit's was terry cloth.

Their ride home was relaxing, and as soon as they walked in, Sunita presented them with huge plates of food. After stuffing themselves with the Swami, they were far too full to eat. They picked at it awhile, until Bethany said that meeting the Swami had messed with their stomachs. "I'm sure we'll feel better by dinner," she added.

The Hermit was inside when the two of them walked out of the house, but as they strolled down a path, there he was, sitting on a rock in front of them.

"How do you do that?" Bethany asked.

"Sit on a rock? It's easy." The Hermit giggled.

Erec noticed his accent was similar to Rajiv's, yet different somehow. Erec was glad to see him. If he could just learn to use his dragon eyes, he could become enough of a medium to use the Oracle and learn the rest of his quest. He began to explain, "We need a medium—"

"And I need a rare." The Hermit pointed at Erec. "And a well-done." He pointed at Bethany.

Erec rolled his eyes. How would he ever learn anything from this guy?

"I know what you need, Erec Rex, and I will help you get it. But first you must prove your faith in me. You must do as I say, without thinking, to show your complete trust, if you want me to teach you."

Did he have any alternative? "Okay." Erec waited.

"Follow me." The Hermit led them to a bridge over a deep brook. "You must walk across this bridge with your eyes shut. No peeking. To show your confidence in me. Only then can I teach you."

The bridge was made of narrow wood slats with no sides or railings. If Erec took a wrong step he'd plunge into the water. "Where do I start?"

"Right here." The Hermit led him to the middle of the bridge. "Close your eyes." He spun Erec in circles, until Erec had no idea which direction the bridge was going under his feet. "Okay, now walk."

"Straight ahead?" Erec asked. He wasn't sure about walking on the bridge without looking where he was going. It made him nervous knowing he could step wrong and fall right off.

"Straight ahead. Don't peek. You must trust me."

"Okay." Erec went forward a few steps, feeling the hard wood boards under his feet. He was cautious, unsteady, but kept moving. Then his foot plunged straight down, with nothing under it to catch him. He splashed, face-first, into the brook.

The Hermit was doubled over laughing when he climbed out. "Very good, Erec," he chortled. "You passed your test."

"But you didn't pass yours," Erec said, shaking off droplets of water like a dog. Bethany was laughing now too. "How am I supposed to trust you now?"

"That's your problem." The Hermit giggled. "I never said you wouldn't fall off."

"Not very confidence-inspiring." The water felt good in the heat so it was hard to be upset. Oh well, he thought. If falling off of a bridge was what it took to learn how to use his dragon eyes, that was a small price to pay.

The Hermit had Erec sit on a flat rock near a stream. The Hermit's legs were folded into a perfect lotus position. Erec's were sprawled in front of him. He was wearing another set of Rajiv's pajama bottoms and a top called a kurta. Bethany watched them from a grassy spot nearby, weaving a chain of wildflowers.

"Is reading the future with my dragon eyes like doing a dragon call or moving the Substance?" Both of those things Erec had done by concentrating on the love inside of him and sending it out through Aoquesth's eyes. He was getting pretty good at that.

"No." The Hermit slid a finger across the stone, drawing a picture in the dust. "When you call out to the dragons, and when you call out to the Substance, you are calling out. See? Now you will be calling in. Or crawling in, more like."

Erec waited in silence. He did not understand, but asking the Hermit questions did not always help.

"I will guide you," the Hermit said. He whipped the white terry-cloth turban off his head and spread it before him. "First, get out your Serving Tray."

Erec found Jam's tray and handed it to the Hermit. The Hermit produced a peeled orange, a soft-boiled egg, a bowl of pitted cherries, and three freshly baked chocolate chip cookies. He arranged them on the terry-cloth towel. "Now, when you use your dragon eyes for seeing into what will come, you are not throwing signals out through your eyes. You want to keep everything inside of you. It is like learning to work a movie projector. You must learn to go inside and be in control. Very different.

"Your eyes will show you the movie. You are in charge of the watching. You control the projector. Turn it on and off. Watch when you are ready. But can you control what you see?" The Hermit raised his eyebrows.

"No, I don't think so," Erec said. "I couldn't control what I saw with my cloudy thoughts. And Aoquesth could only see certain things too, when he looked into the future."

"Wrong answer." The Hermit slapped the rock. "Try again."

"Okay. I can control what I see?"

"Wrong answer," the Hermit said. "Try again."

"There are no other answers," Erec said.

"Wrong again. The answer is you can, and you cannot, control what you see. You cannot control it because you must sit and watch what your eyes choose to show you. And you *do* control it because they are your eyes. Somewhere inside, it is you making the choice of what to show yourself. You are not aware of it, but you show yourself what you need to see the most."

It all sounded wonderful, but Erec still had no clue how to do it. He looked at the food spread before him. It would have looked more appealing were it not sitting on something that had been wrapped around the Hermit's bald head.

"Okay, now we start," the Hermit instructed. "It is a kind of meditation. Close your eyes and follow where I take you."

Erec closed his eyes. The hot sun filtered through the leaves above, its warmth relaxing him. Every now and then a soft breeze drifted by. He heard the Hermit say, "You are sitting on a rock, resting in your body. Relaxing. Every inch of you fills yourself up completely." Erec visualized what the Hermit was saying. It was easy because it was true.

"Now," the Hermit continued, "you will go inside yourself more. Go in deeper. Picture moving out of your fingers and toes, leaving them, and going into a box inside your head. It is a dark room in there, but comfortable. You move easily. There is plenty of room for you. You are still inside yourself, but now just in one spot. In this room."

Maybe because the Hermit's voice was so soothing and the hot sun so peaceful, Erec found it easy to picture doing just what the

Hermit had said. He felt that he was deep within himself, safe in a dark room.

"Now go in again," said the Hermit, "through another door in that room into a smaller one, and then again into an even smaller one. They are deeper and deeper inside of you. All these rooms are comfortable, plenty big for you to go into. It feels good to be there."

Erec imagined going into two more rooms inside of each other. It was like entering doorways in a series of nesting boxes. He focused, and in his mind he was secure and protected in a warm, dark room in his mind.

"Now, in this room you see something. Two windows hang in front of you, but their shades are pulled down. No light is coming in. If you wanted, you could pull a cord that hangs between them and open the shades. But not yet. You are happy here now. There is another thing in the room too. It is a small box on a table. Go up to the box. Touch it."

Erec imagined walking up to a box on a table. He put his hands on it. It felt mysterious, exciting.

"Good," the Hermit said. "This box holds your future. Everything you want and do not want to know is in this box. What will happen to Alypium, to Upper Earth. If you will become king. When you will die. It is all inside."

The box seemed to pulse under Erec's hands. It held an enormous amount of energy. He was thrilled to touch it, be near it, but was afraid to see what was inside.

The Hermit's voice echoed through the dark room. "This box is your movie projector. Pull the cord to open the shades and concentrate on the box. It will show you something. Try it."

A chill raced through Erec. He grasped the cord and it felt warm and silky in his grip. Then he pulled.

The window shades flew open. Everything he saw through the windows was green. Fat ropes of Substance hung in the air. Then . . .

Screaming. Terror. Blasting noise. Fear. Explosion.

He yanked the cord back and the shades slammed down.

Erec took a while to return to normal. He felt like he was running in a panic through dark rooms, searching for the way out. Finally, when he realized he was sitting on a rock in the sun, exhaustion hit him. It was all he could do to open his eyes.

"Cool!" Bethany squealed. "Green light shined out through your dragon eyes! Did you see the future?"

Erec shook his head. "Not really. At least I hope not." He remembered how green light had shone through Patchouli's eyes and Aoquesth's eyes when they were reading the future. So this is what they had gone through? No wonder Aoquesth had been exhausted afterward. Patchouli hadn't been. She must have been a tower of strength.

"Oh." Bethany looked disappointed. "It looked like something was happening."

"It was weird." Erec wasn't sure how to explain. "I did see something, but I couldn't tell what it was. There was a lot of noise and a big explosion. Something really bad was happening, I know that."

The Hermit nodded. "You did very well. But in order to see more, you must conquer your fears of the future. Next time don't run away."

Erec noticed that the food on the terry-cloth towel was gone. "What happened to the food?" he asked.

"I ate it."

"Why? Did it have something to do with my dragon eyes?"

"No," the Hermit said. "I was hungry."

It was easy for the Hermit to sit in the sun, munch on snacks, and talk about Erec conquering his fears. But if he had felt what Erec had when he looked through those windows, he might have run away too.

Over the next few days, Erec worked with the Hermit on using his dragon eyes. He got used to going into the dark rooms in his mind, looked forward to it even. But every time he looked through the windows at what his dragon eyes were showing him, he was filled with terror. One time he made himself keep the shades open and watch a little longer. But all he saw was people screaming and concrete flying. Chaos. It was like a confusing nightmare. After watching a minute and not understanding what he was seeing, he pulled the shades down and left the room.

The Hermit was patient but insisted that he just needed to conquer his fear.

"But I looked for a while, and it was a confusing mess. And it wasn't good, either. I don't think watching longer would have helped."

"Maybe watching calmer would. Pretend you're at the movies with a tub of popcorn."

Yeah, right, Erec thought. Great flick.

Rajiv and Sunita started thanking Erec and Bethany more and bowing to them lower and more frequently. One evening, after many bows, Rajiv said, "We cannot ever repay you for this. You are bringing great luck upon us by staying here."

"We are?" Bethany asked. "Why is that?"

Rajiv pressed his palms together and dipped his head up and down. "You two were led to Swami Parvananda by the great powers of the universe. Now a holy man has been brought to you. We can see him working with you. I have seen you. You walk across a pile of sticks without making any noise. And you are letting us keep you in our house while you are here. That will bring us very good luck. We will be opening our guest house for tourists in a few weeks, and we can use that luck."

Erec hoped that Rajiv and his family got all the luck they needed. And he hoped he would have some luck of his own soon seeing the future with his dragon eyes.

"How long do I have to do this before I can talk to the Fates through the Oracle?" Erec asked the Hermit as they sat on their usual perch by the stream.

"Well, we could go now. I can see into the future, you know, so I could be the medium for you." The Hermit's eyes twinkled.

"What?" Erec blinked. "Why didn't you tell me that before? I told you I needed a medium."

"And I told you I needed a rare and a well-done. Remember? But you weren't so concerned about that then. Who do you think went with King Piter when he needed to go to the Oracle in the past? I did. Well, his AdviSeers Ruth and Balthazar did too, sometimes." The Hermit folded his arms and legs into tangled twists in front of him and sank into meditation.

Erec tapped on the Hermit's shoulder until he opened his eyes.

"What is it?" the Hermit asked. "You know how to practice on your own now."

Erec's eyes narrowed. "If you can be the medium for us, let's go now. I need to find out what this next quest is."

The Hermit's eyes crinkled. "Patience, young man. Patience. Are you really sure you want to run off on another quest before you know what your eyes are trying to show you? Try to do a quest when you're not in control of yourself? If you are in such a hurry, then learn this more quickly. Also, the Oracle will work better for you if you are the medium, not me. It will answer you directly then, and that is always best. Trust me, you need to learn to use your eyes better first."

Erec squirmed. The problem was, he didn't actually *want* to see what his eyes were showing him. It was just too terrible. That's when he realized that the Hermit was right. He really was afraid to see. And he would have to face his fear. No matter how bad the thing was, it was in his own future. If he didn't know what was coming, how could he ever fix it?

That was it! Warmth flushed through Erec's face. He could stop whatever the awful thing was that would happen. Aoquesth had told him the future could be changed. Patchouli had even changed it to let Erec save Bethany in time. So Erec could change it too. He would find out what awful thing was happening in the future, learn all about it, and figure out how to stop it from happening.

Once Erec realized that he had control over it, he was excited to get back in, open the shades, and let the box go. Show me your worst, he thought. And then watch out.

CHAPTER TEN

The Oracle

EREC LAY ON his stomach on the warm rock, as he had seen Aoquesth and Patchouli do. He closed his eyes and listened to the rush of the stream. A stray breeze rustled the broad teak leaves.

Then he focused. Soon he was entering the small room in his head, then the smaller one, than the smallest one inside of the rest. The rooms were inviting, comfortable. But unlike before, he couldn't wait to see what the box had to show him.

He found the small table and touched the thing on it that held the visions of his future. How lucky he was that he knew how to work it! It felt alive, pulsing, strong.

It was time. He focused on the box, took a deep breath. Then he opened the shades on the two windows and watched.

There were screams, terror. But this time, instead of running in fear and averting his eyes, Erec relaxed. He focused on the windows like he was watching a movie. People were scrambling in all directions. There was a loud blasting noise, then a louder boom. It looked like something huge was crumbling around them.

The image he saw through the windows looked like a camera panning across a scene. Like eyes scanning a crowd. Erec remembered the windows were eyes—his eyes. And that was when he noticed that he could control them.

If Erec turned his eyes to the left, he found he was still looking out the windows, but the view from the windows swung to the left. He could move his eyes up, down, in any direction, and make the windows show him what was happening in those places.

Fear still surged through him as he took in the scene. He realized it was the fear that he felt in the future, when the explosion was happening. But another strange feeling was mixed with the fear. It was a good feeling. Surges of power. He was strong, invincible, even though he was terrified.

A building was collapsing—he could see that now—and people were fleeing from it. He just could not tell where it was. Destruction wreaked havoc everywhere he looked.

When he was finally satisfied that he had seen all that he could, he pulled the cord to shut the shades and left the room.

When he opened his eyes to the light of day, he was exhausted. He glimpsed up at the Hermit grinning at him, then fell asleep.

* * *

Erec awoke alone, still on the rock by the stream. He had just had the dream again, the nightmare he always had about his father. It didn't bother him as much anymore, now that he knew that it was not his real father, just a fake memory of somebody else's father. The memory chip he had been given when he was little. Still, the guy in the dream was so familiar and creepy.

Bethany was tossing clothes into her backpack in the guest house. "We're leaving now!" she said with a grin. "The Hermit is taking us to the Oracle! And Sunita gave us both extra clothes."

Sunita walked in with a huge basket brimming with food. "Please. From us. Tell me anything else you need."

They thanked her, but she stopped them. "No, no, no. Thank *you*. And please come back anytime."

Erec was a little stunned when they found the Hermit waiting outside for them. "Does this mean I'm a medium now?"

"Yes." The Hermit nodded. "You are no longer rare. You are medium like me." He giggled, and Erec had to smile.

"But how will we get to Delphi?" Bethany asked. "Greece is so far away from central India."

"The same way I got here. Through the Castle Alypium Port-O-Door."

"What?" Erec said, filled with relief that they had a way to get around easily. "Where is it?"

"In the tool shed." The Hermit thumbed toward the small shack. "Ready to go?"

They thanked Rajiv and Sunita one more time and said good-bye to Shreena and Sunil. Then they followed the Hermit into the tool shed.

"You realize how strange this will look to Rajiv and Sunita?" Bethany asked. "We say good-bye, walk into their tool shed, and vanish?"

"That is good," the Hermit said. "This will bring them more luck."

"How could that be?" Erec asked.

"Because they will believe that something special happened. If they believe they are lucky, then they will do things to make themselves lucky."

Erec hoped that was true, because Rajiv and Sunita deserved it.

The Hermit punched the code numbers into the wooden Port-O-Door and turned its gold doorknob. They followed him into the vestibule and shut the door. On the other side was a door that, if they opened it, would lead straight back into the castle. But that was not where they were going.

A screen was divided into four colored squares: a white ALYPIUM section, a blue one saying ASHONA, a red one saying AORTH, and a yellow square labeled OTHERNESS. Erec looked fondly at that square, remembering his Cyclops, Hydra, and Valkyrie friends in Otherness, especially Tina.

Under the four big sections, the Hermit's finger tapped a thin orange stripe marked OTHER. A world map popped onto the screen. The Hermit poked the European continent, which grew larger, then larger again as he tapped near the Aegean Sea. A map of Greece blossomed before them. If Greece was a tadpole with its tail waving to the north, he touched again somewhere near its mouth, just north of Athens.

A map of Delphi sprang before them. The Hermit's hand glided past the Delphi Museum, a library, several resorts, and a lot of green space, then pushed a spot titled the Temple of Apollo, right next to Mount Parnassus. A detailed map appeared. It was an overhead sketch showing the Temple of Apollo on the side of the mountain, with the Oracle nearby.

The Hermit chose a crevice in the mountainside surrounded by trees. "This is the best place, right here. Good not to walk out into plain view. And it's close, so we don't have to pay to get in. It's earlier in Greece than in India, so it's still open to the public." It had not occurred to Erec that a mystical place like this might have tourists wandering around and an admission fee. He somehow had imagined they would be alone.

The screen said LOCK, and Erec heard the doorknob click. They opened the door out of the side of a hill that led down to a lush valley. No houses were in sight. A falcon swooped overhead, and a warbler's whoop tumbled through the sky. From their perch they could gaze down on fields and olive groves—a completely different look from Tadoba Park in India, but just as beautiful.

As they walked uphill, a spectacular sight appeared before them. Ancient ruins covered a plateau. Statues, altars, columns, and remains of stone walls decorated with ornate carvings stood as they had thousands of years ago. Erec and Bethany followed the Hermit through the ruins, tourists wandering around them. Something scuffled in the bushes behind Erec, but when he turned around nothing was there. He figured it must have been an animal.

"This path is called the Sacred Way," the Hermit said. Erec could see why. Spectacular sun-bleached columns lined the path, remains of Ancient Greece. Of course the Hermit was familiar with this place. He had been here many times with King Piter. "And this was the Treasury of Athens." The Hermit pointed at an impressive stone monument lined with columns in front. "It was where the ancient Greeks left money and treasures for Apollo."

What was left of the Temple of Apollo made Erec feel tiny. Six humongous stone columns still stood, ripples carved along their edges. Ancient foundation stones lay nearby, remainders of the huge temple. It must have once looked spectacular, with breathtaking mountains around it and hawks soaring overhead. Even now it looked otherworldly—maybe what Mount Olympus was supposed to be like.

When they followed the Hermit to the "theater," Erec heard more scuffling behind him. Was somebody trailing them?

The Hermit did not seem to notice. He pointed out how five thousand people could sit in the theater, a perfectly preserved horseshoe of stone seats built into the hillside around a center stage. Erec had never seen him in tour-guide mode before. It wasn't like the Hermit, he thought.

"Is the Oracle in the Temple of Apollo?" Bethany asked.

"No." The Hermit pointed the way they had come. "It's that way. Near the mountainside. Most people think it's part of the Temple, but the real Oracle is not." He looked around. "We can go there now."

As they walked down the path, this time Erec was sure somebody was behind him, following. The Hermit seemed to know it too. He did not turn around, but instead of going straight to the Oracle, he turned to show them another sight. Erec wondered if the scuffling sound might partly explain their guided tour. He glanced at Bethany, but she did not seem to notice anything unusual.

Soon there was another movement behind them and another. But when Erec looked, there was nobody there. It sounded like the noises were coming from more than one place. Were there several people hiding around them?

Who would know they were here? Then the answer hit him. Everyone. Jack knew they were headed to see the Oracle. He must have told Oscar, so Baskania would have people waiting. They would alert him when Erec arrived.

Erec grabbed Bethany's wrist. "They're here."

She froze.

The Hermit pointed toward the massive ancient stadium, stone seats around its huge dirt enclosure. He said loudly, "This was for the chariot races."

"What are we going to do?" Erec whispered.

The Hermit winked at him. "I've been watching. You have two followers so far. Maybe more soon. There was a third, but he didn't recognize you. I think he was looking for someone to go right to the Oracle. He was thrown off by our little walk around." He glanced over Erec's shoulder. "By the looks of these two, you can still talk to the Oracle. Better hurry, before we gain more company."

He led them to the edge of the mountainside, through some trees. A stream splashed by, hurrying away from the split in the rock where it burst into the light. "The Oracle is here, in the Castalian Spring. These waters connect to the home of the three Fates, like Al's Well and Ed's Well. But the properties of the Oracle will let you talk to the Fates from here."

He led them to the edge of a steep rise in the mountain. A still pond formed at the side of the stream. Near the edge of the pond sat a small stone well. As they approached it, the singing crystal in Erec's backpack began to chime, and then it quieted. The three of them looked over the circular wall into the water below.

"Why would there be a well by a stream?" Bethany asked. "Aren't wells made so people can get water?"

"Not this well." The Hermit laughed. "This is the Oracle. It was made for chatting."

The water in the well looked deep. Erec had the feeling that it led straight to the center of the earth. "I heard some tourists say that the Oracle is in the sanctuary of the temple."

"Good thing they think that," the Hermit said. "Keeps them away from here so we can do our business."

"I can talk to the Fates here?" Erec asked.

"You can now that you are a seer."

Erec had not thought of himself as a seer before. It was Bethany who was supposed to learn how to do that. He thought he saw her face twitch with disappointment, but maybe that was just him feeling guilty.

The Hermit explained, "If you had not learned to use your dragon eyes, I would have to ask the Fates your questions for you. They would see you when I stepped away, and answer to you. But they would not hear you then if you had more to ask. This way will be far easier."

"Can I talk to them now?" Erec heard more rustling behind him, and now in some nearby bushes in front of him too.

"First you must go into the little dark room in your head and open the shades. Look into the well. When the light from your dragon eyes shines in, the Fates will know you are here."

Erec nodded. He had practiced that enough. He leaned over the side of the well, which was as high as his waist, and looked in. Then he closed his eyes.

His imagination took over. He saw himself entering the small pitch-black room in his mind. A warm, comforting feeling spread through him. Then he passed through the next door and the next. There on the table was the small box. A ripple of fear stole over him before he pulled the shades open. He knew what he was going to see would not be pleasant. If only he could figure out what was happening, what building was exploding in the future, he could stop it. He knew that. But how?

Then it hit him. He was at the Oracle. He would ask the Fates! Surely they would know what terrible thing he was seeing.

With greater confidence, he opened the shades covering the windows. Before his eyes, people were screaming, running. Chunks of a building were falling, shattering all around him. Terror surged through him, along with another feeling. A strange confidence, pleasure, control. Power. It filled him with energy.

Erec turned his eyes one way, then the other, looking all around the scene. When he felt he had seen enough for the Fates to get an idea of it, he stepped out of the dark rooms and opened his eyes.

As usual, he felt his eyes swivel in his head, so he knew his dragon eyes had been out. It took a moment to adjust to the brightness outside. He was tired, but excited to talk to the Fates. Now he had two things to ask them: what the rest of his third quest was and what the horrible vision was that he was seeing in his future.

Then Erec smiled. Why stop there? There were so many other things he wanted to know about himself, things that were mysteries to him. He couldn't wait to find out everything.

Below him the water was changing. It began to swirl into a whirlpool of amazing colors, metallic shades, pastels, dusky ones. For a moment the water bubbled up like it was boiling, and then the surface became glassy smooth and dark, so that Erec could see his reflection.

What would the Fates sound like? Erec braced himself. Their voices were probably bone-chilling, inhuman, ghastly. The Hermit gestured him toward the water, and he leaned closer. "Fates? This is Erec Rex. I have a few questions for you."

Silence was his only answer, and for a moment Erec felt ridiculous talking into well water. But then he heard giggling and shrieking. It sounded like he had channeled into a slumber party. Maybe he had gotten the wrong number.

"It's Erec!" one of them shouted, sounding more like a crazed fan than a supernatural being who ruled over the fates of humans.

"Eeeeeek!" they all screamed, laughing.

"We were *so* expecting you," a voice giggled. "Too bad you can't pop over and, like, hang with us for a while." She sounded like a Valley girl, yet older and more earthy at the same time. In fact, the Fates managed to come across as extremely young and amazingly old at the same time. The only thing that wasn't quite human was the immense energy in their voices. Erec heard giggling, along with sounds of ice rattling and clinking glasses.

"I was wondering if you could tell me what the rest of my third quest is," he said. "It got broken off in Al's Well."

"Well, like, du-uh!" one of the Fates burst out. Erec could just imagine her rolling her eyes and painting her nails. "I mean, like, who do you think broke it? Unh!"

Another said, "We wanted you to come chat with us, Erec. And you didn't really, like, *want* to get the whole quest right then. I mean, did you?"

She was right. Balor would have found out what it was. And if Erec had not had to stick his hand back into Al's Well to look for the rest of the quest, he would never have escaped. "Can you tell me what the whole quest is now?" he asked.

Bursts of laughter issued from the well. A few of the Fates started to talk, but dissolved into fits of giggles. Finally one of them choked out, "G-get . . . be-hind." They all started laughing so hard that even Erec could not help but smile.

"What is it?" he said. "Get behind what?"

"That's it!" one said with glee, chortling, "Get . . . be . . . behind! Oh, yeah," she said with a giggle, "and set it free."

"Get behind and set it free?" Erec repeated, confused. "That's my quest?"

"Yes!" The three of them screamed, laughing anew as if it was the best joke they had ever heard. He heard more glasses clinking. Someone said, "Pour me another Cosmos Ripple, Decima."

"Oeww-kay." Erec glanced at the Hermit, who nodded sagely, as if this were a grave discussion. "So I have to get behind and set it free."

More hysterics broke out when he said it. It seemed best to move on and worry about the strange quest later. In fact, he thought, this might be a good reason to step out and not do the quest after all. Nobody would be able to figure out what it meant.

"I have another question," he said. "When I look into my future, I keep seeing a building exploding and people running away in fear. What's happening?"

The laughter calmed down, and after a few sniffs one of them said. "You will, like, totally figure that out soon. That's the Castle Alypium exploding, kid." Her voice warbled, "It's like mega-awesome. We love it, don't we, girls?"

There was a chorus of "Oh, yeah"s and "So rad"s.

The Castle Alypium exploding? Erec choked. And they loved it? How could they? He had felt the terror there. Then again, the Fates might not care much about human lives. They saw birth and death on a much bigger scale. But Erec would figure out what would happen to the castle. And he would stop it.

After some more movement in the bushes, a wiry boy with reddish hair rushed toward him—Oscar Felix. Erec flushed with anger as soon as he saw him. "Now you're following us, Oscar? Spying on us for Baskania? So you can tell him what we're up to? Just get away from me. I'm not letting you ruin things again."

Oscar's face was red. "Erec, please believe me. I've never talked to Baskania. He was lying. Really. That's why I came out here. Ask . . . ask that thing for me. Okay?"

Erec looked into the well. Why not? "Is Oscar Felix letting Baskania know where we are?"

A Fate said, "Well, like, *duh*. I mean, you already know that. Why are you asking us?"

Erec glared at Oscar.

"No! It's not true. They're wrong!" Oscar said.

Bethany frowned. "Erec, could you ask the Fates if Oscar is lying, if he knows that he is talking to Baskania?"

Erec leaned into the well. "Does Oscar know he is talking to Baskania?"

The Fates began shouting "Yes" and "No" until they were lost in laughter again. Oscar stared into the well, stunned. "There he is, girls. Unh! Fine!"

One of them talked insultingly slow. "I'll put it re-al-ly simp-ly so he un-der-stands. Okay? Rosco is telling Baskania everything Oscar knows."

"Rosco? Can he read my mind?" Oscar's face bunched up like he was about to cry. "I'll get 'im. I will. Just wait. He's dead. I'll get 'im."

"How does Rosco know what Oscar is thinking?" Bethany asked. "Did he put a spell on him? Plant something on Oscar so he knows his thoughts?"

"Rosco ruined *everything*," Oscar said. "I can't go on the quests. Now my friends can't be with me. And I bet my dad died because of our fighting. That wouldn't have happened if Rosco hadn't turned out to be a criminal."

Bethany patted his back. "Don't even think that. There is no way your father died just because you were arguing with him. That's you feeling guilty."

Oscar jutted his chin up. "All right then. Ask the well, Erec. Ask it. I want to know why my dad died."

"I don't know if that's a good idea." Erec did not want to upset him even more.

Oscar shook like he was about to explode. "Do it. I have to know. If you were ever my friend, then do this for me."

There was more rustling in the bushes behind them. Erec looked around, but whoever was there stayed hidden. He asked the well, "How did Oscar's father die?"

"He killed him." The Fate's voice sounded upset.

All eyes fell on Oscar. Oscar looked around, terrified. "I did not! I didn't. They're lying! That's crazy."

Erec turned toward the well. "Who killed him?" He was afraid to hear the answer.

It sounded like one of them said, "Oscar." But then they all heard it loud and clear. "Rosco killed him. He used a magic spell to make him stop breathing."

Oscar sank to the ground, crying. "Rosco did it," he said. "Rosco." He buried his face in his arms, sobbing. Then he rolled on the ground, pounding his feet and fists into it. Erec heard him say between hiccups, ". . . if it's the last thing I do. I'm having my revenge."

Bethany sat by Oscar and rubbed his back. There was more rustling behind Erec. He had more questions for the Oracle, and had to ask them fast. The Fates' chatter was fading, as if they were losing interest in him. "Wait," he called, "I have another question."

The voice of one of the Fates tinkled like a bell. "Your girlfriend better, like, jump in this well right now, before we talk any more. I mean, if you even like her at all. Or she'll be toast."

"What?" Erec looked at Bethany in shock. That didn't make any sense. Why did she have to go into the well?

Bethany didn't look excited about jumping in either. "Huh? Ask them why."

But the Hermit pushed her to the edge. "Don't argue. These three know what will happen, remember? Get in. There you go."

Bethany took a look at Oscar, then she put two and two together. Someone nasty would arrive soon. She jumped into the well with a splash and disappeared. Erec was glad she had Instagills. He leaned over the well again. "Could you tell me, quick, who my father is?"

A hand on his shoulder jerked him backward, and he fell onto the ground. Balor Stain shoved past him and looked into the well. "All right. I've waited long enough, 'got behind' him like I was supposed to. Stupid quest. Now it's my turn to ask some questions."

The Fates could see Balor but not hear him, Erec knew, since he was not a medium. So they seemed to think that Erec's question had been for Balor. "Look!" they screeched. "It's Balor Stain! Can you believe it? And he wants to know who his father is." They giggled.

"I do not," Balor said. "I know my father."

"This will be *so* funny," a Fate said. "He has no clue. Who gets to tell him?"

Erec dusted himself off and came closer. Everyone stared at the well, mesmerized.

"I'll do it!" the voice of one of the Fates rang out. "Balor, you and your brothers, Damon and Dollick Stain, were born on April twentieth, almost fourteen years ago, in Alypium. You were triplets, cloned from Thanatos Argus Baskania, who is your real father, then given to Mauvis and Perdita Stain to raise. I mean, like, Balor, didn't you notice something was weird about you guys?"

Erec stared at Balor in shock. He did look like Baskania, now that she mentioned it. Just much younger, with black hair and only two eyes. Balor looked like he was working something out in his head.

"Why does Damon have a bone coming out of his head, and Dollick look like a sheep, then?" Erec asked the well.

The Fates giggled. "They really, like, screwed up the cloning job. Thanatos Baskania had just eaten lamb for dinner. And when they took the laser slice from him to clone Dollick, part of the slice went through Baskania's stomach and got some lamb in it. And the slice for Damon got too big a piece of Baskania's thigh bone. So it messed his head up. That Vulcan cloning thing was pretty new then, and it still had bugs."

"Yeah," another said, "eeew. It was so gross. The bugs were, like, all over it."

A shadow fell over the well. The Fates screamed, "Eek!" and "Eeew!"

Erec looked up to see many eyes gazing back at him from one face.

CHAPTER ELEVEN

Snail Mail from Oscar

O SCAR!" BASKANIA CRIED. "Thank you again, so much, for alerting me that your friend is here. You will be well rewarded, I assure you. In fact," he raised his chin and grinned smugly under his many darting eyes, "someday I will place you at my side, put my full trust in our friendship."

Oscar spat in the grass but seemed afraid to say more.

Then Baskania turned to Balor, seething. "Are you happy now, fool? I sent you to do one thing. 'Get behind' Erec. It was your last chance to do something right. And instead you run up and ask the Fates who your real father is?" He sneered. "That was for me to decide *if* and when to tell you."

Balor looked stunned, like he was not absorbing what Baskania, his father, was saying. Erec knew that Baskania's attention would turn to him before too long. There was only one way out, and he needed to try to escape before Baskania noticed it too.

"Oscar." Erec nudged him with his foot. He nodded toward the bushes and whispered, "Go. Don't look at me." Oscar must have understood, for in a moment he was gone.

Baskania did not seem to care that Oscar had left. He looked at Erec and rubbed his hands together.

In a single motion Erec dove into the well. A second later Bethany was swimming beside him, their Instagills open again.

The Fates must have been helping him, for a strong current sucked them away, fast. The water felt both boiling hot and freezing cold, but it quickly turned to a normal temperature.

"Look!" Bethany screamed. Two thick ropes spiraled through the water toward them like snakes. Erec was sure Baskania had sent them. He kicked faster to get away, but one of the ropes was gaining on him. He knew it would wind tightly around him and drag him back to the Oracle.

"This way!" Bethany took a sharp turn into a small tunnel to the bottom of a lake. The ropes jerked behind them, spinning closer.

Then Erec heard a voice. "All right. Like, fine." "Fine" sounded like "fi-yun." It was one of the Fates. "We'll, like, fix it. Just this one time, since we were having such a fun chat. Don't count on us again, all right, kiddies?"

Out of nowhere two snapping turtles appeared in front of Baskania's ropes. The ropes sprang at the surprised reptiles and bound them tightly, dragging them away.

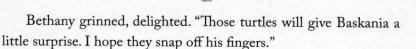

Bethany grinned, delighted. "Those turtles will give Baskania a little surprise. I hope they snap off his fingers."

"Or at least one of his eyes."

The image made both of them burst out laughing.

They waded out of the lake and sat drying in the sun under a stand of tall trees. A village stood in the distance, and cars rumbled far away. "At least we're not deep in a jungle this time," Erec said.

"I just can't believe that Balor Stain and his brothers are Baskania's sons," Bethany said.

"Clones," added Erec. It gave him a chill.

"I don't think Balor liked it either," she said. "Imagine finding out Baskania was your dad."

Erec would not have wanted that shock. "But you'd think Balor would love it," he said. "He was so proud to be the son of the 'great sorcerer Mauvis Stain.' Now his dad is even more powerful and evil. How perfect."

"I bet he'll like it once he gets used to it," Bethany agreed.

"Funny, he'll turn fourteen on April twentieth. He's just two days younger than me," Erec said.

Bethany considered that. "Interesting. I'll bet Baskania planned on Balor, Damon, and Dollick taking over the Kingdoms of the Keepers all the way back when he cloned them."

"And here I show up, trying to take the throne away from them." Erec nodded. "No wonder he hates me. I just wish I knew why I am supposed to be destined to rule here. It doesn't make sense. And also who those other kids are who are supposed to rule with me. Why did we get picked?" He wished he had more time to ask the Oracle questions. He could have spent days there, just finding things out.

What had he really learned at the Oracle, anyway? He'd heard a lot more about the Stain brothers than himself. He learned that Rosco had some tap into Oscar's mind and had killed Oscar's father. But what about the things he really needed to know? That terrible explosion in his future was the Castle Alypium blowing up. But he still had no idea when it would happen, or why, or how to stop it. And what he had found out about the rest of his quest was useless. "Get behind and set it free"? What could that possibly mean?

Erec took the Serving Tray out of his backpack, and they ate pizza, macaroni and cheese, chocolate bars, four types of chips, five kinds of cookies, French fries, and, in an effort by Bethany to be healthy, an orange.

But when they finished, they both felt a sense of loss. "Should we walk to those houses over there and see where we are?" Bethany asked.

"I guess." Erec shrugged. "I don't know what else to do. We'll have to find a place to sleep soon." They started walking. "I just wish the Hermit was here. Maybe he could help."

"I do too," a voice sounded right behind them. "If we could only find him, things would be so much better."

They spun around to see the Hermit strolling along, clicking his tongue in disappointment. Below the Hermit's long robes, feathers sprung from the back of his shoes like odd wings.

"Hey!" Erec shouted. Bethany threw her arms around him, then quickly pulled them away, not fully comfortable with him yet.

"What should we do?" Erec asked the Hermit. "I have no clue what that quest means. 'Get behind and set it free'?"

The Hermit giggled, then doubled over laughing. It seemed that he had the same sense of humor that the Fates did. "Oh, it's precious." He gasped. "Get be-hind. Oh . . ." He sank to the ground laughing, tears of mirth rolling down his face, and pounded the ground in delight.

Bethany and Erec waited expectantly until he calmed down.

"I know where you need to go. So perfect. So beautiful." He chuckled. "I can't tell you what to do there. That is up to you. But I know where you must go to find out. Tonight you can sleep on this nice patch of leaves. We will leave in the morning for Ceryneia."

"Where is Ceryneia?" asked Bethany.

"In Otherness," said the Hermit. "Much farther south than where you were before. It's right on the border of Otherness and northern Thailand, close to where the Ping River springs from the Chiang Dao Mountains. Not too far from the Upper Earth city Chiang Mai."

"Otherness is in Thailand?" Erec tried to remember what Jam had told him about Otherness. It ran through many countries and was filled with creatures that had been exiled first from Upper Earth and then from the Kingdoms of the Keepers. Jam had said a big section of Otherness ran through remote parts of Russia and China, and a bunch of other countries. Upper Earth people stayed away from those areas because they were hard to reach and untamed. They were also kept away by the spells and force fields that Baskania had put around Otherness.

The Hermit said, "There are parts of Otherness in most countries, some more than others. Ceryneia is a beautiful part of Otherness, just like Thailand is a beautiful part of Upper Earth."

Erec wished that his quest was more clear. His second quest had also been vague: "You must stop the monsters in Lerna." He'd had no idea who the monsters had been. In fact, he'd had it all wrong. But at least it had told him where to go. "Remember my first quest?" he asked. "It told me to open Patchouli's eggs in Nemea. You can't get more specific than that. I wonder why this one barely said anything."

"Maybe it had to be this way," Bethany said. "The Fates probably knew that the Hermit would figure it out. If it had been specific, then Balor and Baskania would know where to go too. Balor probably heard what the Fates told you at the Oracle."

She had a good point. Balor knew the whole quest now too, but he probably was as clueless as Erec would have been—as Erec was about everything else. The other important problems he had to solve still loomed over him. Who would blow up the Castle Alypium, and when? Plus, how could he help fix the Substance before things got worse on Upper Earth and all the bees disappeared? He wasn't sure if life would end on Upper Earth first because of the Substance draining out, or if the plants would disappear without bees to pollinate them, and there would be no oxygen left.

If only he knew his father, it would all be so much better. He wished that he had just that simple pleasure. Someone from here who could help him. Having a father was something most people didn't think twice about. Couldn't he have that one small thing?

The Hermit, almost as if he knew something Erec did not, crossed his arms, looked at the sky, and started to whistle.

After breakfast from the Serving Tray the next morning, Erec and Bethany followed the Hermit through the castle Port-O-Door and into the vestibule. After tapping the yellow square marked OTHERNESS, a map appeared on the screen. The Hermit touched the spot labeled CERYNEIA at the southern end, right near the border. He chose an unlabeled section and the door clicked.

Their Port-O-Door turned out to have lodged itself in the wide trunk of a jackfruit tree. The massive fruits with green, pebbled skin hung over their heads, some of the darker ones bigger than Erec could reach his arms around. They stepped into the sunlight of a perfect day. Dense bamboo thickets clustered nearby. Bright red orange blossoms with banana-shaped petals hung from tall coral tree branches. A few of the ripe jackfruits lying on the ground smelled of rotting onions, but even this did not mar the effect of the gorgeous scenery before them.

Erec and Bethany walked in awe, the Hermit trailing behind them. Narrow streams trickling through the mountains dropped off breathtaking waterfalls. Yet Erec was soon thinking about his quest. "'Get behind and set it free.' What could that mean? I'm guessing something is stuck under a big rock. I need to get behind the rock and push it out of the way to set the thing free."

"I don't know," Bethany said. "I was thinking you would have to get behind someone's idea. You know, support them. And with you backing them, you can set their idea free."

"Baskania seemed to think that Balor had to get behind me or get behind in the search." Erec tripped over a heavy jackfruit. "That couldn't be it, could it? I don't want to go find Balor and get behind him."

"I doubt Balor has anything to do with it," Bethany said. "Or the Fates wouldn't have made it so he doesn't even know where we are."

Erec agreed. "Maybe a big animal is stuck somewhere. If I get behind it I can find a way to set it free." He felt better about the quest now. The Hermit had taken him to the right place at least. Setting something free didn't sound nearly as bad as the battle in Otherness that had been his second quest.

Around a corner, a small village was nestled in the mountain. People worked on terraced fields cut into the hillside. The Hermit said that they were paddies, where farmers grew rice.

Bethany began to skip down the path, and Erec sped up to join her. It was exciting to be with her here in Asia, whether it was Otherness or Upper Earth. The people in the rice paddies looked human from a distance, but when Erec got closer he saw most of them had four or more arms. Several had extra legs as well. He counted sixteen arms and four legs on one of the men.

"Look," Bethany whispered. "They move so gracefully, like they're gliding."

Both the men and women had straight, long, black hair, but the women had pinned their hair up with lotus blossoms. A few of them appeared male in half of their bodies and female in the other half. Some had third eyes on their foreheads. Odd as they looked, they were beautiful and mesmerizing.

"What are they?" Erec asked.

"They have no name," the Hermit said. "Or they go by many names. They are very powerful. They once mingled with people, long ago, but now they choose to live in Otherness."

Erec could have watched them work all day, but the Hermit urged them along. "There is a human who lives here. He might be able to help you with your quest."

They walked up a dirt path into the village. A few of the elegant, many-limbed beings drifted in and out of the buildings and down the streets, but none of them paid attention to Erec and Bethany. Their houses looked welcoming, full of soft fabrics and vibrant colors.

A ranch house, much plainer than the rest, stood on the edge of town. A chubby man sat on the front stoop gazing at the mountains. He had only two arms and two legs, and definitely did not look as graceful as the others in the village. Scraggly gray hair fell on the sides of his face, circling his mostly bald head.

"I'll be watching," the Hermit said. But when Erec turned around, he was gone.

When the kids approached, a delighted smile lit the man's face. He wore a dark brown sackcloth tied around his waist with a rope, similar to Swami Parvananda's garb. His skin was far lighter, though, and covered with warts. When Erec got closer, he could see that the man had a glass eye, like Erec once had. It looked cloudy and old, though, like it needed changing.

"What brings you kids round here?" His voice sounded so goofy it made Erec wonder if he was crazy. But his one eye twinkled, and he seemed nice enough. "You just here to visit? Or are youse on the run?"

Erec wondered if he should tell him about his quest but decided to find out more first. "Just visiting," he said. "What's your name?"

"Call me Artie," the man said, his voice bouncing all over the place. "I just likes to live here with these nice people in Otherness. They's so pretty. Youse pretty too," he said, pointing at Bethany. "Not youse so much." He pointed at Erec. "Youse okay, but youse ain't pretty."

"Uh, thanks," Erec said. "So, anything interesting going on around here?"

"Oh," Artie's lips formed a small *O*. "Everything heres is interesting. It's really pretty here. Kinda like youse." He pointed at Bethany again, and her face turned pink. "Youse can make yourself at home here." He smiled. "Just wander yerselves around my place if ya wants. But if ya do, watch out fer me behind." He cackled. "It bites!" When Artie said it, it sounded like "bee-hind."

Erec and Bethany sent each other stunned looks.

Then Artie began cackling. "My behind is gonna get you. It's gonna bite you."

Bethany took a step back.

A serious look came over Artie's face. "My behind is a bee-utiful bee-hind, and nobody can touch it but me."

Erec looked back, hoping to see the Hermit somewhere. If he had ever thought the Hermit was crazy, he seemed totally normal after meeting Artie. Could the Hermit have brought them here for a joke? Erec wouldn't put it past him.

But Artie still seemed preoccupied with his bottom. "Where is it?" he asked, looking around. "Where did my behind go?"

"Uuh . . ." Erec pointed. "Aren't you sitting on it?"

"I am?" Artie jumped up, his dark robe wobbling with his fat belly. He turned around and looked at the step where he had been sitting, then he laughed. "I'm not sitting on anything!"

Yeah, not anymore, Erec thought. This guy was something else.

"What, youse wanna see my bee-hind? Is that it? Youse wanna see it? Pet it or something?"

Erec stepped back, horrified. "No!"

"That's good." Artie nodded. "Cuz nobody is allowed to pet it but me. But I'll show it to you. Come here. I'll show you my hinds quarters."

Erec started walking away, but Bethany stopped him, a funny look in her eye. "What was your quest, Erec?"

"Get behind . . ." Erec stopped, struck by the same thought she'd had. "No way." He shook his head.

"Didn't the Hermit bring you right here?" she asked. "How many times has Artie said 'behind'? That's the exact word from your quest."

"The Hermit brought *us* right here. If you want to go take a look at old Artie's warty bottom, go help yourself. But leave me out of it."

"Erec." Bethany's voice dropped a few pitches lower. "You are here on a quest. Get in there and get behind Artie's behind. Maybe something is stuck in it."

Erec felt so disgusted he almost gagged. What kind of a quest was this anyway?

He took a step toward Artie, who looked jolly as ever. If this was not really his quest, the Hermit was going to pay, big-time.

"Come on." Artie walked around his house toward the back. What, he couldn't show Erec his nasty tush right here? This was worse than Erec had thought.

Erec swung around to Bethany. "You are coming with me. If you are helping me on this quest, you come along. Understood?"

A nauseated look swept over her face. "Fine. Ugh."

The two of them followed Artie into his backyard. He walked up to a small barn and waved the kids inside.

Erec stopped. "No, I don't think I'm going in there," he said. "You can show us your behind out here, if you have to. Only if it's really important."

Artie looked crestfallen. "You'll want to see my bee-hind, really. She's a beautiful one." Bethany gave Erec a stern look, prompting him to stop arguing. "But she's in there," Artie added.

Bethany and Erec looked at each other, confused. They hesitated at the door, then plunged in.

Artie waved them over. In a pen stood a small red deer. Swarming around it were masses of honeybees. The deer did not seem to mind the bees at all. In fact, it looked completely comfortable surrounded by them. The bees were not attacking it in any way. A few buzzed away and some new ones flew in from outside as they watched.

Bethany's eyes were wide. "Erec. It's a bee-hind. A *hind* is a deer."

Then the answer clicked in Erec's head. Get behind and set it free. Could that mean this bee-hind? He tried to remember how it was spelled on the quest paper, then he realized that he hadn't actually seen it written. The Fates would have spelled it the normal way, to fool Baskania. They had said "bee-hind" in the same way Artie did. Maybe this was the thing he had to set free.

He opened the latch on its pen and swung the door open, but the hind did not run out. In front of Artie's stunned face, Erec reached in to grab it and run. The bee-hind bit his hand, hard. And a few bees stung him too.

Artie shook his head. "I told yas. Youse can't pet it. Only I can pet my bee-hind. I told youse it would bite you. Come on, let's fix that cut."

* * *

As Artie cleaned the gashes in Erec's hand and put a bandage on him, he said, "My bee-hind and me is best friends. I protect her and she protects me. We is really good together."

"How long have you lived here?" Bethany asked.

"As long as I can remember." Artie settled into a chair. "My son, Kyron, lives here too. He's a trapper and a dragon slayer. He'll be back tonight, if you want to meet him."

A dragon slayer? That didn't appeal to Erec at all. "Well, maybe we'll just find somewhere else to stay."

"I wouldn't advise that," Artie said. "You don't want to go talk to those other people, you know, thems ones with all the arms and legs. They's nice if you don't bother 'em. But youse don't want to bother 'em."

After being bitten by Artie's bee-hind, Erec believed Artie's warnings. "Is there anywhere else to sleep out there?"

Artie shook his head. "I wouldn't do that. There's a terrible beast that comes out at nights. It's a manticore. I wouldn't want to be out there alone. Our house is protected by my bee-hind."

Erec still couldn't stop thinking of the other meaning of the word *behind* and it started to make him laugh. Bethany was fighting back the giggles as well, but when they looked at each other, both of them burst into a fit of laughter.

"What's so funny, youse?" Artie asked.

But they couldn't tell him. "We better stay here with you, then." Erec coughed his chuckles away. "Thanks, Artie."

"I wish I knew where the Hermit was." Erec munched a slice of pepperoni pizza. "Maybe he could make sense of things."

Bethany ate an egg sandwich with ketchup, hot off the Serving Tray. "He's never around during your quests, though, so I guess that means this is probably your quest. To set that bee-hind free."

Erec ordered up a cloud cream sundae. "Yeah, the only problem is, it doesn't want to go free. It's Artie's best friend. You heard him."

Bethany agreed. "And, the hind is protecting Artie and his son from that dangerous manticore thing that lives here."

"I guess Baskania has no clue what the bee-hind is," Erec said. "Good thing the Hermit knew about it."

"He got it right away. I guess that's why he and the Fates were laughing so hard. They knew what it would sound like." Bethany smiled at the memory.

"I still don't get why I have to set it free, though, if it doesn't want to go anywhere."

Bethany popped a chocolate truffle into her mouth. "Maybe Artie's son, Kyron, will help us understand."

A rock in front of Erec's feet started growing larger before him, swirls of green and yellow spinning through it. "Look," he said, edging away from it. But when two tiny eyes popped out and looked up at him on long stalks, he immediately knew what it was. His name was written on the side of the snail's shell. "Someone sent me snail mail. I wonder if it's Tina." He picked up the creature and slid a piece of paper out.

But the letter wasn't pink or frilly, scented or covered with hearts. No, not from Tina, he decided. He opened it up.

Hey Erec,

You probably hate me now. I can't say I blame you, I'd hate me too. But I really didn't do anything. I hope you believe me. I would never betray you like that.

I just want you to know that I'm going into hiding so nobody can use me to track you down. I guess if Rosco can read my mind he'll know where I am. But I won't try to come after you again. It's my fault that Baskania found you at the Oracle. I know that now.

I've decided that I have a quest too. I'm going to find Rosco, and when he's not expecting it I'm going to pay him back for everything he's done to me, including killing my father. I can't even live a normal life now because of him. I know it will be hard to do because he can read my thoughts. So I'm still working it all out.

I hope you can write me back, but I understand if you can't trust me. If you do write, please don't say where you are or tell me anything you don't want Rosco and Baskania to know.

Your friend (believe it or not),

Oscar

Erec's heart sank. Poor Oscar. He could not imagine how terrible he must feel.

Bethany said, "Let's write him back. We have to tell him to stop planning his revenge on Rosco. He's just going to get hurt. He should move on and try to forget about it."

"Move on?" Erec asked. "How can he move on? He's living in hiding now. His dad is dead. I'd feel the same way if I were him."

"Erec! Things won't get any better for Oscar if he goes on some manhunt for Rosco. It's just dumb."

"I don't know," Erec said. "Maybe they would get better for him. If he got Rosco off his back he'd at least have a life again. He wouldn't be connected to Baskania, have someone reading his mind all the time."

"Got Rosco off his back?" Bethany crossed her arms. "How would that ever happen? He'd have to kill him, probably. You think that is okay?"

"Rosco killing Oscar's dad was not okay," Erec said. "Rosco ruining Oscar's life, tying him to Baskania, and trying to get us killed was not okay. Oscar is just trying to get free from this prison he's in. I hope he doesn't have to kill Rosco to do that."

"You hope?" Bethany shook her head. "This whole thing is ridiculous. Oscar can't get caught up in this. It will ruin his life."

"That's already happened. What does he have now? What's left of his life?"

"Just because he can't be friends with us anymore doesn't mean he has no life," Bethany said. "He can go do anything else."

"And know that whatever it is, the man who killed his father will know where he is going and what he is thinking at all times. And anything he does might help Baskania, who wants to destroy life as we know it."

They walked on rocks by the stream until they both felt better. "Are you going to write him back?" Bethany asked.

"I don't know," Erec said. "I need to find out if the snails are traceable. If Oscar gets one from us, Rosco will know it. He'll take the snail from Oscar in a second and figure out where we sent it from." He thought about it. "I wish I could write him back, but I can't take that risk. What if Baskania showed up here in a few minutes? That's the way it happens."

"It just seems so mean not to answer him." Bethany's back straightened. "I have an idea! We can get in the Port-O-Door and send his snail from somewhere else! That'll throw them off track."

"Awesome!" Erec grinned. "I know the perfect place to send Balor and Baskania next."

They found some paper in Artie's house, and Erec wrote:

Dear Oscar,

I want you to know you are still my friend, even though I can't talk to you. I don't blame you for how you feel about Rosco, but Bethany made me promise to say that you should forget about him and move on. Whatever you do, we are both behind you.

I think we are making progress with our third quest. I can't tell you about it in detail, but it is very dangerous. Let's just say we have to go inside somewhere and spend the night next to a terrible creature, and hope it gives us something after.

Let us know how things are going, and say hi to Jack for us.

Your friend,

Erec (and Bethany)

They walked down the hillside to the jackfruit tree where the Hermit had put the Port-O-Door, but they could not find it there.

"Looking for something?" a familiar voice asked. They glanced up to see the Hermit in the tree, swinging his feet and munching jackfruit.

"Hey," Erec called to him. "We need the Port-O-Door to send Oscar a snail mail back."

The Hermit swung down from the branch and held out his hand like a butler. "Hermit delivery, at your service. I'll take it in the Port-O-Door and send the snail from wherever you want. I moved it a few trees down."

Erec gave him the snail with the letter to Oscar. "Can you send this from the dragon reserve in Nemea? Maybe drop it in front of a dragon's cave?"

"With pleasure." The Hermit bowed.

"Hermit," Erec asked, "is snail mail traceable?"

"Completely." The Hermit grinned and disappeared.

CHAPTER TWELVE
The Manticore

A S THE SUN set over the purple-shadowed mountains, a trumpetlike howl blasted through the still air. Artie rushed out to find them.

"Youse best get inside my house, lest you want to be eaten," he explained. "That noise is the manticore. It'll shred youse to pieces."

They followed him in. "What's the manticore like?" Bethany asked.

"Terrible creature," Artie said. "It's a huge golden lion. But its tail is spiny and spiked, and its face looks almost human—except for its rows of sharp teeth it has, alls ready to eat yas up. Related to the sphinx, it is. It would shred yas as soon as look at yas."

Erec did not know a sphinx was a real creature, but after all he'd seen, it didn't surprise him. Artie went into the kitchen to fix dinner. Before long the door flew open and a young man walked inside. Kyron, Artie's son, stood over six foot three. His soft blue eyes and kind smile radiated through the room. He smoothed back his dark hair, regarding Bethany and Erec with wide eyes. "Visitors? And what brings you here?"

Erec was surprised. He had expected Kyron to be short and jolly like Artie, if not bald and goofy. But Kyron sounded as sharp as he looked.

"We're just . . . wandering in Otherness," Erec explained.

Kyron unstrapped his leather belt, and Erec saw a silver knife hanging in a holster. "Odd place to be wandering." He stared at Erec, waiting for a better explanation.

Erec could not think of one. Saying something like, "I'm here to set free your father's best friend, the bee-hind that's protecting the two of you," just didn't seem like a good idea. He looked at Bethany.

As usual, she came up with an excuse. "We're kind of hiding," she said. "There's a really nasty guy that's been looking for us. He almost caught us, but we escaped into a well. We have Instagills." She pointed at her hand.

Erec flashed her a thank-you glance, and Kyron walked over to inspect their Instagills. "Those are awesome," he said. "Who were you running from?"

"Some jerk called Baskania," Erec said. There didn't seem to be a reason not to tell the truth. Kyron had probably never heard of him anyway.

But Kyron's face grew solemn. "Thanatos Baskania?" he asked angrily.

Bethany and Erec traded looks. What was going on?

Kyron explained. "Baskania ruined our lives. He's the reason we've been hiding out here since I was a kid." He sat down and leaned back into the couch. "He pretty much destroyed us. So I know what you're going through."

Bethany and Erec sat near Kyron. "What happened?" Bethany asked.

Kyron's fists clenched. "My father used to work for Baskania, a long time ago. I know it probably sounds bad to you, since you know what Baskania's like. But he had my dad fooled. Had a lot of people fooled—still does, I bet. But when my dad saw for himself what was going on, he decided to quit."

Erec immediately thought of Artie's glass eye. Well, that explained that. He had probably given an eye to Baskania. But Artie didn't seem like the evil-henchman type. Specifically, he didn't seem bright enough.

Kyron continued, "So one day, about ten years ago, Baskania called on my dad to lure Balthazar Ugry away from the Castle Alypium. Baskania said he had a surprise for Ugry. My father, you wouldn't know it now, but he was super smart. He could figure things out real fast. And it wasn't easy to devise a plan to get Ugry to leave the castle, either. Ugry was one of the AdviSeers for King Piter, and he watched the castle like a hawk."

Erec nodded, not inclined to talk about his own experience with Balthazar Ugry quite yet.

"So my dad came up with this elaborate plan to lure Ugry out of the castle," Kyron said. "And it worked, of course. But then—" He flung a hand in the air, burning at the memory. "He found out what Baskania's plan really was. He wanted to get Ugry out of the way so he could kill the royal triplets and the queen. I mean, Baskania didn't come right out and say it. But my dad was smart, like I said. And," he lowered his voice, even though his father was not in the room, "he never forgave himself for it. For what happened to Ugry. And for what happened to everyone at the castle, too."

Artie walked in, whistling. "Dinner's ready, youse peoples! Come and eat it gone!"

Erec and Bethany pretended to eat the leathery meat in front of them, all the while thinking of what they could be ordering up from their Serving Tray. Erec felt bad for Kyron and Artie, stuck out here, hunted by Baskania. It didn't seem right not to share with them. He said, "You know, we have something that makes food for us. Would you like to see it?"

He took out the Serving Tray, and for the next hour the four of them dreamed up wild and delicious things to eat. Finally, after Erec finished a pancake filled with chocolate honey drops and topped with cinnamon cloud cream, chocolate sauce, honeycomb sprinkles, and spun-sugar birds, watermelon ice rimming the edge of his plate, he noticed everyone was looking a little sick.

"I think I overdid it," Bethany said, holding her stomach. Plates of half-eaten spaghetti, omelets, and desserts were spread around her.

While Artie was cleaning up, Erec asked Kyron to sit with them. A fire danced in the fireplace nearby. "You said your dad used to be really smart," Erec said. "What happened . . . I mean, what were you talking about?"

Kyron tensed up. "He was a genius. He was the only man to ever get an eye back from Baskania. Ever."

Erec was impressed. Kyron pointed up at a jar on the mantel with a round object floating inside. "Still has it."

Erec saw Bethany cringe. It didn't bother him, though. He'd had enough experience with eyes in jars that it seemed perfectly normal.

Kyron said, "And nobody quits working for Baskania, either, and lives to tell about it. Dad wanted his eye back, and he got it. Tricked Baskania completely. Made him think he was making some improvement to it and would give it back to him. But once he got his eye back, we escaped Alypium. Dad thought we were home free. . . ." He paused. Erec and Bethany waited. "Well, Baskania was furious. He set this manticore on us. It's like a lion monster. It always knows where we are, and it comes out every night. Howls like a trumpet. Don't know if you've heard it."

Both Erec and Bethany nodded to show they had.

"Dad knew the one thing that would ward off a manticore is a special kind of deer that's like the king of the bees. Called a bee-hind. There's only one in the world, and it was hard to find. We spent every day searching for it, on the run, and every night fighting off the manticore. I can't count the number of times we nearly died." He chuckled, picking up his silver blade. "At least I got good with a knife. Works well for me now."

A shiver ran through Erec when he remembered that Kyron was a trapper and dragon slayer.

"So we finally found the bee-hind, and we settled out here, in the wilds of Otherness. It was hard to find the right spot. Dad knew the manticore would follow us, and it would hunt whoever else was around if it couldn't get him. He didn't want to move to a place where it would hurt his new neighbors. So this area was perfect. The folks that live around here, the ones with all the arms and legs, aren't bothered by a manticore, that's for sure. They're amazing."

"They looked amazing," Bethany agreed. "I couldn't believe how beautiful and elegant they all were."

Kyron nodded. "Just don't talk to them, though. If you bother them, you're toast. But they're good neighbors. Stay out of our business. And the manticore is no match for them. So this worked out well." He hesitated. "Except for what happened to Dad. I guess Baskania must have known his manticore didn't find its prey. So he sent something else my dad's way."

Kyron scowled as he went on. "It was a death spell, and it had his name written on it, by magic, so it couldn't miss. But my dad was so smart he still managed to live. He dodged it first, then he grabbed a glass dish and held it in front of him. The spell still went through it and got him, but its magic was weakened by the glass. Dad got sick, really sick, but I nursed him back to health. He never was the same, though, after that."

They fell silent, listening to the crackling fire. It didn't seem fair, Erec thought. Artie had fought against Baskania when he found out what he was doing. He was smart and cared about others enough to find a spot out here where the manticore wouldn't hurt anyone else. And now Erec was supposed to take his bee-hind away? And let the manticore kill him? Well, he just wouldn't do it. That was that.

That night, Erec awoke to the sound of a loud trumpet. When it blared again, though, he could hear a whining gurgle at the end of its blast. It was the howl of the manticore, and it sounded close. He sat up in the sleeping bag Kyron had given him and walked to the window of Kyron's room.

The awful beast was pacing back and forth outside. It was built like a large lion, except for its odd, spiky tail. Its face, however, sent chills through him. Within its mane was a cross between the face of a lion and that of a brutish giant. Its big, wide forehead hung over its deep-set feline eyes. The most human feature was its broad, upturned nose, and under that was a wide red-lipped mouth set with rows and rows of sharp, pointy teeth.

It stopped pacing and turned to stare at Erec. Chills flooded down his back as the beast's bloodthirsty eyes bored into him. Its brow lowered, and then it blasted another trumpetlike howl.

Kyron sat up in his bed and glanced around. When he saw Erec, he sprang to his feet, then caught his breath. "Ugh, you scared me. Not used to seeing anyone in here."

"Did you hear that thing howl?" Erec asked.

Kyron rubbed his eyes, yawning. "I hear it howl every night of my life. I can usually sleep through it now, but it took a long time after we got the bee-hind before I learned to relax enough. Before that we just slept during the day, when we could, and fought and hid all night."

"How could that cute little deer keep the manticore away?" Erec asked.

"Just watch," Kyron said. "It still tries to attack us at least once every night. Sounds like it's riled up enough now that this will be it. Did it see you?"

Erec nodded, peeking out the window. The manticore was pawing the ground and hunching its back. It bared its teeth at Erec, scratching long claws in the air toward him. Then it reared up and charged.

There was no way Kyron's thin bedroom window could keep the manticore out. As it sprang toward him, Erec cowered and ducked back. But right as the creature was in midair, claws forward and jaws wide, it seemed to hit something. Its paws twisted over each other and its legs shot up, almost like it was caught in an invisible net.

The bee-hind casually strolled toward the beast. Erec thought the manticore would gobble it up, but instead it pulled away from the little hind as if deathly afraid. Then, while the manticore was still tangled in the air, a mass of bees swarmed from the cloud around the deer and attacked it, stinging with abandon. The creature howled a few more trumpet notes until it finally slid to the ground and slunk away.

"So that happens every night?" Erec asked, astonished.

Kyron nodded, falling back to sleep. But it took Erec a while to calm down after what he'd seen. There was no way he was going to take their bee-hind away from them.

The next morning Erec and Bethany sat overlooking the rice terraces. Watching the beautiful many-armed people working there was mesmerizing.

"I hope they don't mind us staring," Bethany said. "I wouldn't want to find out the hard way."

"I think it's okay. We're pretty far away from them."

"Are you thinking what I am about the bee-hind?" Bethany asked.

"Probably," Erec said. "That taking it away from Artie would be a crime?"

Bethany leaned back on her hands. "Yeah, that too. But I was also thinking about the missing bees. You know, like King Piter was talking about. Do you think the bee-hind might have something to do with that?"

The idea hit Erec like a spear. He felt his heart sinking, because he had the terrible feeling that she was right.

Erec walked by the bee-hind's stall a few times. The little deer gazed up at him with big black eyes through the crowd of bees swarming around it.

He thought he had made the decision to let Artie keep the hind, but if this was really the reason that the Substance was messed up all over the world, then he had to do something. But how could he do that to Artie?

Maybe if he just made a small attempt, then he could walk away and say that he tried. It was his quest, anyway. So he opened the stall door. As he suspected, the hind had no interest in going anywhere. When he started to reach in, it almost bit him before he yanked his hand away. And then he felt guilty for even trying to set it free, knowing what it meant to Artie and Kyron.

But what if it meant more to the rest of the world? The realization was settling upon him that it just might. The bees of the world were disappearing. What if the captive bee-hind was causing the problem?

He tried to think about something else. Maybe he should use his dragon eyes to see into the future. At least he might figure out how to keep the Castle Alypium from exploding.

He sat on a patch of soft grass under a teak tree and relaxed. Soon he was entering the small room in his mind, shrouded in darkness. Then the smaller room within, and finally the smallest room, deep inside. There was the box, and the shaded windows.

Erec ran his hand over the warm box. If only he could figure out its secrets. He steadied himself, then opened the shades and looked out into his future.

Fear coursed through him again, along with the overwhelming surges of power he had felt before. Screams of panic filled the air. Loud cracks echoed from chunks of building splitting apart. People were running in every direction. Erec turned his eyes all around, trying to catch a clue he might have missed, but nothing stood out. Frustrated, he decided to get closer to the windows. Maybe he could see more that way.

But when he took a step forward, the scene from the windows changed. It moved forward as well. This was something new. Erec realized that if he stepped to the right or left, the image he saw shifted to the right or left as well. Soon Erec was walking all around the small room, turning his eyes left and right. He found he could walk clear around the exploding castle.

The noise was nearly deafening. Shattered window glass and crystal from chandeliers sprayed through the air. Plush furniture fragments jutted from under piles of stone. He strode farther, noticing that the dark room he walked in changed shape so that he didn't run into a wall. Around a corner he saw the six huge stone statues of monsters standing in front of the castle. He had never paid much attention to them before, but now he noticed that one of them was a Cyclops. Cracks raced through the stone statues like hot rod spider webs, making the stone unstable. The statues began to move as if they had come to life, but they were falling apart.

Then Erec heard a familiar voice. He turned to see Balor Stain, holding a bronze whistle on a chain around his neck. Balor's eyes were wild with glee. "Check it out," he said, smirking.

Behind him stood Damon Stain, goofy gray stocking cap covering his bone head, and white, fleecy Dollick Stain. Seeing the three poorly made clones of Baskania made Erec shudder. So they were the ones behind this? Of course. Their gleeful expressions gave him no doubt. But why was Balor holding that whistle? Had he used it somehow to help him destroy the castle?

Balor liked to blow things up. He had nearly killed Bethany and a few other kids when he exploded the Under Mine during King Pluto's contest last summer. And he had a reason for wanting to blow up the castle, too. He hated King Piter, and he wanted to clear the way for him and his brothers to be kings.

Erec seethed with anger. He had to stop Balor. Who knew how many people would be hurt or killed otherwise? If only he had a way to see further back with his dragon eyes. If he could follow Balor back in time, before the castle exploded, he could figure out how to stop him.

When Erec opened his eyes to the bright daylight, he was exhausted. Bethany was doing math calculations nearby for relaxation, and he was too tired to even call out to her. But while he rested, an idea perched in his mind, lightly at first, then soon digging its claws in. He knew a way he could find out more about the bee-hind.

He dragged himself up and walked back to the stables. The bee-hind looked up at him innocently. Even though the bees were not bothering Erec, their loud buzzing and swarming made him antsy.

Erec wanted to view the bee-hind through his dragon eyes. Maybe that would give him a clue, especially since the hind might be connected to a problem with the Substance. He knew two ways to bring his dragon eyes out, but going into the dark room in his mind would only show him the future. So he used the other method, the same way he made them come out for the dragon call.

Erec focused on the love inside of him. His love for the world, his friends, his family, Aoquesth, and even himself. As he closed his eyes and concentrated, his eyes turned around in his head. He had gotten much better at controlling them.

But something was wrong. He could not see anything at all through his dragon eyes. Everything was white. As he stared harder, he saw it was a kind of lumpy white, with shaded bits here and there. But the hind and the barn were nowhere in sight. Erec could not even see himself.

He relaxed, and when his regular eyes came back out, everything looked normal again. But it didn't make sense. What was wrong with him? Had his dragon eyes lost their vision?

Bethany was lying on her stomach under a tree munching a peach, still doing math problems. She looked perfectly content. Erec plopped down by her side. "I can't see with my dragon eyes anymore." He told her what had happened.

"Why don't you try it again, out here?" she suggested.

That seemed like a good idea. Erec concentrated again and felt his eyes moving in his head. When he opened them this time, the air was full of huge chunks of white. He could see only bits of Bethany, bits of the sky and the trees around him. When he turned away from the house and the barn, he could see more.

He realized he was looking at the Substance. There was more of it than he had ever seen, jutting in huge columns and trunks like a giant maze in the air. He turned back toward the barn, and everything around it was white.

Erec broke his focus and let his eyes drift back to normal. "Bethany," he said. "This isn't good. That bee-hind is messing with the Substance like crazy. A ton of it is collecting around the hind. I think the reason I couldn't see in there is because the barn is totally stuffed with it."

He thought the problem through more. "I'll bet that's what the bee-hind uses to trap the manticore. He must be catching it in a net of Substance." He could also see why his quest was to free that thing. "Maybe this is the reason the bees are vanishing, and why bees are attracted to the hind. Maybe this is why Upper Earth is going to lose its Substance and die."

Bethany's eyes widened. "Do you think this is the whole problem with the Substance that King Piter has been trying to solve? Why the Substance is upset, why we all feel the sadness when we first go into the Kingdoms of the Keepers? It's all getting messed up by the bee-hind being here?"

Erec bit his lip. The idea was too immense to think about.

Erec and Bethany were tasting as many pie slices as they could dream up from the Serving Tray while they watched the many-armed people in the rice paddies. From their movements, it looked like farming was an art form for them, more than work.

"I don't think I can do it," Erec said, falling onto his back on the grass. "I can't do this to Artie and Kyron."

"I know," Bethany said softly, looking down at him. "I don't think you have much choice, though. What will happen to Upper Earth if that bee-hind stays chained up here?"

"It's not exactly chained up," he said. "It got out really easily last night when the manticore came by the house." Erec felt his stomach churn when he thought of the rows of teeth that creature had. "The bee-hind is already free to go. That's the thing. It wants to stay here. I don't know how I could make it leave, anyway."

"Maybe if you found out what Artie did to catch it?"

Erec closed his eyes. "Maybe. But I don't want to know. Even if I found out, I couldn't do it. I can't let Artie and Kyron get eaten by that manticore. Or have to stay up, running and fighting it, every night of their life." He sighed. "I bet old Artie couldn't even fight it off anymore, after that spell Baskania knocked him out with. The bee-hind is the only thing that can help them." He squinted at her. "You didn't see that manticore."

Bethany plopped on her back next to him. "I know. It's just . . . there is the rest of the whole world to think of too, you know."

Erec knew, but he did not want to think about it.

That night, Kyron returned with a wild boar slung over his shoulder. They ate from the Serving Tray, which let Kyron save the boar for trade when he went across the boundary into the Upper Earth city of Chiang Mai, Thailand. While Artie was cleaning up, Erec and Bethany sat with Kyron in front of the fire.

"How old were you when you moved here?" Bethany asked.

"I was nine." Kyron stared into the dancing flames.

Erec felt awful thinking of Kyron as a little boy, spending every night fighting off a terrible monster. Now Erec was supposed to make that happen again, for the rest of Kyron's life? He wanted to ask about Kyron's mother, but he had a bad feeling she might have been lost to the manticore, and he couldn't take finding that out.

So he tried to change the subject. "I hear you hunt dragons. Why do you do that? They're such beautiful creatures."

Kyron shrugged. "Everything's beautiful. They come in at a great price."

Erec didn't understand. "But they're smart, too. You shouldn't kill them—"

Bethany shot Erec a look and steered the subject right back again. "So how did your dad figure out that the bee-hind could help him?" she asked.

"He was really smart," Kyron said. "He knew a lot about animals."

Artie had walked into the room and was bouncing on his toes with a grin. "Yup, I knew lots and lots."

"All right, Dad." Kyron grinned. "You're still not so bad."

"And lots," Artie added, pointing.

"What did he do to make the bee-hind his friend?" Bethany asked Kyron.

Don't tell us, Erec thought. I don't want to know.

Kyron shrugged. "I don't remember. Complicated stuff, I think."

Artie bounced on his toes with pride. "I remember," he said. "It was easy. I was just the only one who could figures it out. I was so smarts. I had to tell it what the things were that I felt bad about. Like what I did to Balthazar Ugry." Tears filled his eyes thinking about it. "And what happened to the queen and her three babies because of what I did." He sniffed and wiped his cheeks. "So when you tell my bee-hind what youse feel bad about, it becomes your friend and will do what you want."

Kyron put his face into his hands. "Oh, Dad! You're not supposed to tell anybody about that." He got up and put his arm around his father to cheer him up. Then he looked at Erec. "Please don't repeat to anyone what you heard. If this gets out and someone takes that hind from us, we're dead."

Erec's face dropped. Now he had to make an impossible decision. "Kyron, is there anything that can kill the manticore?"

"Nothing," Kyron said.

"Not even a dragon?" A ray of hope lit in Erec. He could become a dragon, at least partly.

"Not even close. The manticore is a magical beast. It eats dragons all the time. Believe me, we've checked every option. My dad would have found something to kill it, if it was possible."

A magical beast?

A crazy idea popped into Erec's head. It wasn't perfect, he knew, but there was one thing he just might try.

CHAPTER THIRTEEN
The Virtue of Caring

TEARS DRIPPED DOWN Bethany's cheeks when they walked to the stable the next morning. "We can't do this to them. You heard Kyron last night. It's just wrong. I don't care what happens to the rest of the world."

Erec's eyes met hers. "But you do, Bethany. Think of all the Upper Earth kids out there who won't survive unless we fix the Substance. And all the animals."

"So, what do we do then? Free the bee-hind and just take off? Leave poor Artie and Kyron to their fate, and try not to think what we've done to them every day for the rest of our lives?"

"No," Erec said firmly. "You go ahead with the Hermit. I'm going to stay. I think I might be able to fix things for them."

Bethany grabbed his shoulders. "No way, Erec. You're not dying because of this. You're just doing what you have to here because of your quest. Don't do something stupid because you feel guilty."

He tried to ignore what she said. "I have to try something."

"What? You heard Kyron. Manticores eat dragons. And you're not even a full-fledged dragon. You'd never stand a chance."

Erec did not want to tell her his plan. He was afraid she would point out how crazy it was, and he didn't want to lose his nerve. So instead he approached the bee-hind's stall. It gazed up at him with its huge brown eyes. "Hind, I want to tell you some things I feel terrible about. First, I made a friend, Tina, feel really bad because I told her she looked ugly. I was holding the truth scroll, which made me tell the truth about what I thought. But I shouldn't have been thinking like that anyway. It was wrong, and it hurt her.

"And also, I've been too interested in making people like me. For a moment, before I decided to fight for the Hydras and Valkyries in Lerna, I considered going over to Baskania's side because I wanted the people of Alypium to think I was a hero." He filled with shame when he saw Bethany looking at him. But his confession was too important to stop. Painful or not, this was his quest.

"And I'm about to do something really terrible because I think I have to. I'm about to risk the lives of two wonderful people who have been helping me. If it goes wrong, which it probably will, then I'll never forgive myself."

The hind was staring at him now. Erec opened its stall, and it walked over to him, rubbing its head against Erec's hand. The bees swarmed around both of them now, but they did not harm Erec.

Erec crouched down before he lost his nerve. "Bee-hind, I want you to go free. You're collecting a lot of the Substance around you. I want you to go wild again and spread the Substance around like it's supposed to be. Make it so all the honeybees come back and can live in Upper Earth again."

The little deer rubbed its face against his hand one more time, then bounded out the door. Erec hung his head in shame, and Bethany sank to the floor in tears.

"Should we tell Artie?" Bethany asked. "I think he needs to get prepared."

Something bothered Erec. He noticed that his Amulet of Virtues looked the same. No new segments were glowing. Hadn't he completed his quest? Was releasing the bee-hind the right thing to do? He sure hoped so.

"You go ahead and find the Hermit," Erec said. "I'll meet you back at the castle. I'm going to wait and talk to Kyron tonight. The least I can do is tell him about this face-to-face."

Bethany stopped in her tracks. "Oh, really? And how will you get to the castle if I've already left with the Hermit in the Port-O-Door?" She swung around and gave him a hard look. "You're not planning on coming back, are you?"

Erec said quietly, "If I find a way out of this, which I think I might, then I'll figure out how to get back."

"You might never find your way back from here," she said, getting upset. "This is crazy. I'm waiting for you. We're going together as soon as you're ready."

There was no way Erec would let Bethany risk her life alongside him in what he planned to do that night. It was bad enough that he had put Artie's and Kyron's lives on the line. But it was obvious she would not leave him there willingly. At least not on purpose. He would have to trick her into leaving, then.

"All right," Erec said. "You can stay. But can you do me a favor? Just find the Hermit and tell him that he has to take something really valuable back to King Piter for me." He pulled the Serving Tray out of his backpack. "Tell the Hermit I don't want King Piter's favorite thing to get damaged."

Bethany eyed the tray. "I didn't know this was King Piter's. I thought Jam gave it to you."

"Now you know."

Bethany was suspicious. "What's so important about this tray, anyway? Are you just trying to get rid of me? I'm not leaving you out here alone to face that thing. If you risk your life, you're risking mine, too. So maybe you'll want to just rethink your plan."

Erec smiled, then gave her a hug. He hoped it would not be his last one. "Just do this one thing for me. You can come back when you're done, okay?"

She grabbed the tray and went down the dirt path to find the Hermit. Erec sighed with relief. The Hermit would appear when he was needed, as usual. And when Bethany gave him the message—to bring back King Piter's favorite thing to him safely—the Hermit would understand and take Bethany.

He felt sad but resigned as he walked back to Artie's house. If only another segment had lit up on his amulet then he'd know he had done the right thing. But, as it was, at least he would defend Artie and Kyron to his death.

Erec lay on his stomach in the hot sun, focusing on a blade of grass in the middle of a circle of sticks he had pounded into the ground. He had just marked the grass leaf with a tiny dot. He knew what he had

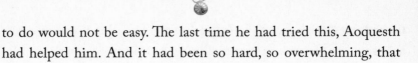

to do would not be easy. The last time he had tried this, Aoquesth had helped him. And it had been so hard, so overwhelming, that Erec ended up with a white streak in his hair from doing it. But it was the only hope he had.

He thought awhile about Aoquesth. The dragon had given his life for him. Erec would have died in the battle in Lerna. So it was only right that Erec risk his life to make things right for Artie and Kyron. Maybe he would make it. But, either way, he didn't want to think about that very much.

He focused intently on the dot on the grass blade. He brought his dragon eyes forward, as Aoquesth had taught him, by concentrating on love. Love for the world, the Substance, the bee-hind, and Bethany. Thinking about Bethany did the trick this time. He might never see her again. His eyes turned, and everything became green. Thick ropes of Substance hung in the air, but they looked normal now. Now that the bee-hind had left, the huge white clumps of Substance had dispersed.

He kept concentrating on the dot. He had to really see it. He had to know, personally, every thread of Substance in and around that spot.

At first nothing happened. He stared harder, squinting. It still just looked like a dot. How had he done it before? He tried to remember.

Then he could hear Aoquesth's voice, as if he were standing right next to him. "Love, Erec." That was all it took. Through his dragon eyes he poured out every drop of love that made up his life. He knew it might be over soon too, which made it all the more powerful.

And what he saw, what the Substance did for him, was unspeakably beautiful. It showed itself, unfolded, blossomed so that every hidden fragment within that spot became its own artwork, its own poem. This time Erec could see why the Substance carried magic. It was because the Substance *was* magic. And it was love. Love, magic, and life wove together interchangeably into this one tiny spot before his eyes. Layers upon layers of magic unfolded before him until he was overwhelmed by the infinity present within each tiny space in the world.

He knew what he had to do. He asked the Substance to change for him. To separate, to make a hole. Tear itself for him so that he could try to save two people he cared about. So that he could right his wrong. He knew it was not as good a reason as the last time he had asked the Substance to do this. That time he had been saving the last baby dragons in the world from Baskania. Now he was saving two friends.

But he asked with every ounce of his heart. And he could feel it say yes.

He pushed with his vision, moving threads, clearing space. Every white bead of Substance had to be moved away from the center of the dot. Then the gap needed to be bigger. Much bigger.

Erec had no idea how much time went by. But while he was changing the Substance, making a rift in it, he saw and felt each of the fragments that hung before him. And he heard them cry when the rip was made.

Every time he did something to help, it seemed another thing got hurt.

Finally, he collapsed on the ground, finished. He made a note where the tear in the Substance was, and then blackness overcame him.

It was getting dark when Kyron shook him on the shoulder. "Are you crazy, sleeping out here? It'll be dark soon. You better get inside before the manticore comes."

Erec staggered to his feet. He followed Kyron in, dreading what he would have to tell him.

But he was stunned to find Bethany sitting on the couch, a

solemn look on her face. "What are you doing here?" Anger surged through him. "Didn't the Hermit take you away?"

Bethany crossed her arms. "I'm not stupid, Erec. I understood that coded message you wanted me to send to the Hermit. So I didn't even try to find him. I said I'd be here with you, so here I am."

Erec paced, furious that despite his plans she was now in danger. "But it doesn't help—you being here," he spat out. "It makes it worse. Just . . . go. Run."

Kyron thought that was curious advice. "I don't know what's going on with you two, but she better not run anywhere now. It's getting dark out."

Erec picked up a pillow and threw it at her. "Great. Now you'll probably die too. That really makes things better."

Bethany hugged her arms, managing to look both scared and rejected. "I'm supposed to help you with your quest. Whatever happens. You might need me."

It didn't make sense to argue now. They were running out of time. Erec turned to Kyron. "Listen, your bee-hind is gone. The manticore is going to burst in here tonight. But I have a plan—"

"*What?*" Kyron ran out the door, then reappeared in a minute, frantic. "Where is it? What did you do with it?" He clenched his fists, panicked.

"I had to let it go." At that moment Erec realized that Kyron might kill him before the manticore did. "It was all me, my choice. Bethany had nothing to do with it," he added quickly.

Kyron picked Erec up and threw him roughly against a wall. His voice was choked with tears. "Why did we trust you? My dad will never survive this time. He doesn't have the wits."

Artie walked into the room. "What's going on with youse boys?"

Nobody had the heart to answer him.

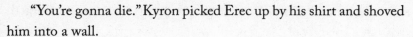

"You're gonna die." Kyron picked Erec up by his shirt and shoved him into a wall.

"Look." Erec's voice was clear and firm, ignoring the sting of pain. "I had to do it. It was messing up all the Substance in the whole world by being stuck here. People and all of Upper Earth were going to die."

With a snort, Kyron shoved Erec away and walked to the window. His voice was hard. "We don't have long. I'm taking my dad up a tree. That'll confuse the thing for a while, at least. I'd suggest you two come up with a plan."

"I already have a plan," Erec said. "But it's risky. And I need your help."

Kyron glared at him, but Erec came over to the window. Looking out with him, he started whispering.

Erec and Kyron waited at the window. Erec had taken his Sneakers off because they would interfere with what he needed to do.

Bethany threw her arms around Erec's neck and buried her face in his shoulder. "Don't go out there."

"It's our only chance."

"Oh!" A woman's voice echoed through the room. Erec recognized his mother's voice. She was checking on him with her glasses. "Is that Bethany hugging you?" she asked, knowing full well that it was.

"Um, yeah. It's not what you think. I mean, she was upset, but she's okay. I'm kinda busy now." Bethany stepped away. Erec did not want to frighten his mother, tell her that he was about to risk his life and may never see her again. But he did add, "Mom, I love you."

"Aww. That's sweet, honey. I love you, too. I'll talk to you later, then. Didn't mean to bother you."

"It's okay, Mom. Bye."

Bethany sniffed and stepped back with Artie, who was bewildered but at least quiet. Then Erec heard a trumpetlike howl and saw a swish of a spiked tail.

He ran outside, shouting. "Hungry, manticore? Want some dinner?"

The winter night was chilly, but Erec barely felt it. A low growl sounded nearby. He could hear something scratching the ground. Hopefully the manticore would not know that the bee-hind was gone, so it wouldn't head straight for the house.

"C'mon, kitty, kitty." Erec kicked some dirt, running into the lawn. "Here, ugly kitty. Come and get me."

The manticore appeared between some shrubs. It eyed Erec, drool seeping from between its teeth.

Erec backed toward the circle of sticks he had pounded into the ground, marking the hole he'd made in the Substance. A small jackfruit lay by his feet. He slung it at the creature but missed.

The manticore darted its eyes back and forth between Erec and the house, as if deciding which to attack first. Erec threw a stick at it, which grazed its shoulder, then he backed away. Flaring its nostrils, the beast rocked back then pounced toward Erec. It was over him in a flash, faster than he had expected.

Erec stumbled back toward the hole he had made in the Substance. Just as the manticore's claws sank into him, he toppled backward. Grabbing the manticore's mane, he fell into the hole.

Suddenly, the world was all chaos and confusion. Black-and-white specks swirled, completely lacking color and form. It was the whirlwind of nothingness inside the Nevervarld—the realm of no magic beyond the borders of the Substance. Nothing could live here except for dragons, and they could only live a short time.

All he could think about or remember were the rushes of flecks whirling in and around him. There had been flowers here, hadn't there? Did he need to get them for something? He couldn't

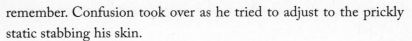

remember. Confusion took over as he tried to adjust to the prickly static stabbing his skin.

Then he became aware of another presence in the Neververld. It was the manticore. Erec could sense it, the only other living thing he could detect. It looked blindingly bright in the strange mixed static.

It was good the manticore was here. Erec remembered that now. He was glad that it had fallen in here after him. Now Bethany would be safe. Other details seemed more distant, other people that might have been involved. They were in another universe, somewhere, that Erec had once known.

He could hear the manticore's thoughts as it died. *What's happening? Where is my prey?* The body of the beast glimmered like a fading rainbow in the swirl of specks, then it began to turn gray. It could not live more than a few moments in here, Erec knew. He was sad now. A living thing was dying. Why was that happening again?

Strange forms were taking shape nearby. The sparks were hurting more as they crackled on his arms and face. Each one left him more tired and confused.

Then a familiar voice sounded. Was it around him or just in his head? *Thank you,* it said. *Yummm.*

He was glad that someone was happy. He had a vague feeling he was finished now. All he had to do was rest. The black-and-white sparkles were in him and around him. They made him so tired.

The voice said, *You are not dead. I see why. You are the human with the dragon parts—and you are more dragon now than before. But you will still die here before long. Leave now or rest with us forever.*

Erec was confused which was the right answer. He had no idea what to do.

But then he saw it, gleaming like a beacon in the swirling gray. A hand. It was alive, like he was. Bethany.

With every ounce of energy he had, he willed himself toward

the hand. Soon he grasped it, and it pulled him through a hole into a painfully bright place.

Kyron and Bethany were standing over him. Then he had to close his eyes. Their faces, as well as the twinkling stars, glowed so bright he felt blinded. Loud noises pummeled him, even though he was vaguely aware that they were distant jungle sounds.

Then, blaringly loud, he heard Kyron whisper, "Well, well. Look at you. I'll never kill another dragon again."

After drifting in the lifeless void of the Nevervarld, even the touch of the ground under him was too much to bear. His mind could not handle the overload, so he did the only thing he could and fell asleep.

Erec awoke on a couch in Artie's house. The table was covered with foods that everyone had conjured from the Serving Tray, but they had all waited for him to wake before they ate. He rubbed his eyes and sat up, still aching all over.

"Look." Bethany rushed over, picking up Erec's amulet. "Another one is glowing now. You did it!"

A third segment of the Amulet of Virtues now shone a glittering cream color. Erec peered at the black symbol on it. He wished Aoquesth was here to tell him what it meant.

Then he had a thought. For a moment he concentrated, looking mainly at Bethany. When his dragon eyes were out, he could read the symbol easily. "Caring." Well, he thought, there was no arguing that he had cared.

Kyron's face beamed with joy. "How can we ever repay you? Other than never hunting dragons again. After seeing the way you looked coming out of that hole from the Nevervarld, I'll never look at them the same," he said. Erec had no idea that he had transformed in there. "We're free now." Kyron grinned. "Dad and I can go anywhere."

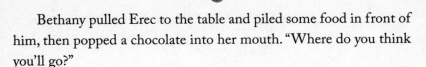

Bethany pulled Erec to the table and piled some food in front of him, then popped a chocolate into her mouth. "Where do you think you'll go?"

"I don't know." Kyron laughed. "Maybe we'll just stay here. But at least we have the choice." He sat down. "I guess I should thank you for fixing things for Upper Earth, too. I mean, easy to say now that we're okay and all." He looked embarrassed. "But remember, if you ever need us, we'll be there for you. One hundred percent."

CHAPTER FOURTEEN

King Stain

T HE NEXT MORNING Erec and Bethany found the Hermit. He led them through the mountains, past the streams and waterfalls, palm trees and bamboo thickets, then by the beautiful many-limbed people on their terraced rice paddies. The Hermit had put the Port-O-Door into a huge, umbrella-shaped cassia tree.

Walking from the tropics of southern Otherness into the Castle Alypium made Erec catch his breath. It seemed strange to cross such a huge space in a few steps. The west wing was cool and quiet, full of luxurious pillows and intricate tapestries. "We better lie low," Erec said. "Jack and Oscar can't know we're back."

Bethany nodded. The Hermit walked with them to the west wing dining hall. When Jam saw them, he dropped the tray of food he was carrying on a table and rushed over. "Is young sir okay?" He bowed, dusting Erec off.

"Yeah. Good to be back, though. Hey, thanks for the Serving Tray."

He reached into his backpack to get it, but Jam held up a hand. "Not at all. Please keep it, young sir. You may need it again."

Erec put it back, thanking Jam. "It's like a traveling restaurant."

But Jam looked worried. "Are you sure you are safe here, young sir? Might Baskania pop in again for another surprise visit?"

"I don't know," Erec said. "I don't think he will, though. Probably the only reason he came into the castle before is that he knew, through Oscar, that I was here and King Piter was gone."

Bethany added, "Baskania probably thinks we're off in Otherness somewhere, doing a quest. He wouldn't know to look for us here now, unless Oscar saw us. So we have to make sure he doesn't."

"Is King Piter around?" Erec asked. He could not wait to tell him that he had fixed the problem with the Substance.

"I think he's in his throne room," Jam said.

Indeed, King Piter sat atop his huge throne at the far end of the immense room. His scepter lay in the groove that was made for it in the arm of the chair. Erec found it hard to keep from staring at the scepter as he came close.

Balthazar Ugry was kneeling before the king, speaking to him. Erec heard him say, "I hope you give this your full consideration, your highness. It is of the utmost importance that we contain him. Now." He glared at Erec, giving him an icy chill. Then he drifted away, leaving the king with a troubled look.

Erec unlocked his gaze from the king's scepter and said, "We have great news. For the third quest, we had to find and set free the bee-hind in Otherness. It was locking up all the Substance there. So maybe the Substance problem is fixed now."

He waited for the king to jump up and celebrate. But the king just tilted his head. "I am aware. It was a great deed you did. And it will make the Substance more stable on Upper Earth, give them another ten years at least."

Only ten years? Erec could not believe it. "You mean it's not permanently fixed?"

"I'm afraid not." King Piter smiled sadly. "Don't be mistaken. What you did, freeing the hind, was extremely helpful. It gives us so much more time to solve the problem. If I can just figure out what the problem is. But we were in grave danger before. Thank you, Erec."

"Wait," Erec said. "If you knew about the bee-hind, why didn't you go free it?"

The king's hand touched his scepter, then pulled away. Erec found he was acutely aware of every movement the king made around it. "I didn't know about it until now, or I would have. Or at least I would have tried. I'm not sure I could have done as good a job as you did."

Erec noticed the king sounded resigned or defeated. He wondered why.

"Hermit," the king said, pursing his lips, "can I have a word?"

"Of course." The Hermit tilted his head. "You can have as many words as you like."

Erec appreciated that the Hermit was not afraid of the king at all. He never felt a need to treat him differently because of his station.

The king beckoned him closer. "In private, I mean."

"No need for that," the Hermit lilted. "We're all family here, right?"

Everybody eyed each other. Erec did not feel like family with anyone other than Bethany, and even she was not exactly the same as family. The king finally gave in. "All right, then. Balthazar warned me that there may be a problem soon with the castle. And he said Erec—" The king turned his attention to Erec.

"No problems," the Hermit said. "Erec will take care of it. He's already working on fixing it, aren't you, Erec?"

"I am," he agreed. "I've had visions about it with my dragon eyes. I'm going to figure out how to keep it from happening." He thought a moment. "But if you want to help me, you can."

The king laughed with relief. "No, you go ahead. It sounds like this is something entirely different than what I was worried about. Besides, you don't want me to take care of it. If I listened to Balthazar and took you away somewhere . . ." He shook his head. "If the Hermit says you will take care of it somehow, then I'll believe him." He looked relieved. "I didn't know you were aware of the problem."

The Hermit looked pleased. He spun around on one foot, then stopped like an oddly posed statue. "I remember what happened. Like it was yesterday." Then he winked at Erec. On the way out the door he whispered in Erec's ear, "I was the only one here who believed you."

Erec could only shake his head. What was the Hermit talking about now?

Wolfboy was so excited to see his master, he kept knocking Erec down faster than he could stand. Erec pulled his hooded sweatshirt far over his head, and he and Bethany walked their pets into the agora. They avoided Paisley Park, just in case Jack or Oscar were around. Oscar had said in his letter that he would stay in hiding, but it seemed best to play it safe. Anyway, they just wanted to get nectar fizz sodas and look at the magic shops.

Music pulsed up the street with the deep thump of bass drums. In the distance, the Alypium marching band approached. Seeing it made Erec shiver. It reminded him of the last time he had heard this marching band, when it had accompanied the Alypium army as it set out to fight against him and the Hydras and Valkyries in Otherness. And the time before that, when it had paraded through Alypium, riling everyone up to fight.

This experience was not much better. A magic carpet hovered in the air somewhere between the trombones and the cowbells. Around the carpet marchers held signs saying LONG LIVE KING BALOR; BALOR, DAMON, AND DOLLICK FOREVER; DAMON'S OUR SHAMAN; LET'S FROLIC WITH DOLLICK; and BALOR HAS VALOR. The crowds chanted, "King Stain, King Stain," again and again.

Sitting astride the carpet, waving regally at their fans with smug looks on their faces, were Balor, Damon, and Dollick Stain. Balor had some reddish scars on his face, and his arm was in a sling. As they rode closer, Erec saw that Balor kept lifting his sling, as if he were showing it off to the crowd.

"'Damon's our shaman'?" Erec looked at Bethany with disgust. "Do they know what they're saying?"

"Maybe compared to the brainiac who came up with those slogans, Damon might be a shaman."

"Doubtful." Erec pulled his hood farther over his face, then he pointed at the Stain brothers. "Look! Around their necks!" Amulets, just like his, sparkled on chains on each of the Stain boys' chests. Erec looked down at his own, then back at theirs. From where he stood they looked identical, except the Stains' were shinier.

He could not believe it. "Excuse me." He tapped the arm of a short-haired blond woman who was waving and clapping as the parade passed. "Could you tell me what's going on?"

The woman looked surprised. "You don't know? It's been publicized everywhere. All of the problems about who will be the next king have been solved." She was excited. "The Stain triplets won four quests already, so that Erec Rex kid just dropped out. He knew he couldn't compete. Now we only have to wait for them to finish the quests, and we'll get new kings! They say it won't take long."

Erec's jaw dropped. "Erec Rex dropped out of the race, did he?"

The woman bounced on her toes. "High time, too. He was really messing things up. For a while people worried the Fates might be getting old and confused."

Old and confused? Amazing. This woman had obviously never spoken to the young, bubbly-sounding and amazingly intuitive Fates. He clenched his jaw. "Didn't you all hear after that battle in Otherness that Erec Rex was on your side . . . our side? I thought he showed everyone the Archives of Alithea and—"

"The archives of what?" The woman looked confused. "I have no clue what you're talking about. I did hear there was a problem with Erec Rex at the Monster Bash in Otherness in the fall. He got on the side of the monsters or something."

Erec nearly choked. How could the people in Alypium not know what had happened in Otherness? The solders in the Alypium army knew. Why hadn't they told everyone that Erec was one of the good guys? Then he thought a moment. The army was under control of President Inkle. President Inkle was under Baskania's power.

"How does everyone know Erec Rex quit?" he asked. "And that Balor is winning?"

She shrugged. "It's all over the news. President Inkle announced it first. And King Pluto had a ceremony in Cliff Arena the other night. As soon as Balor recovered from his quest."

"Recovered?" Erec said, interested. "He was actually injured? What happened?"

The woman ran a hand through her short blond hair. "You don't know anything, do you? His last quest, number four, was to sneak into the cave of a real dragon in Nemea and spend the night with it!

He did it, but he got real beat up. He was in Alypium Hospital for a while."

Erec smirked. So, Baskania and Balor had fallen for his trick. Balor had spent the night with a dragon after the Hermit sent Erec's snail mail to Oscar from Nemea, in front of a dragon cave. And now they were pretending it was a real quest.

"And those amulets they have?" Erec wrapped his jacket around him, making sure his own was hidden.

"Yeah." The woman nodded. "They each have an Amulet of Virtues. Pretty cool. Soon they'll get the scepters, too."

"You know," Erec said, crossing his arms, "the Stain triplets are Baskania's clones. They're faking their way through these quests." Bethany shot him a warning look, but he ignored her. "You know what would happen if those three got the scepters? They would give them to Baskania." For a moment he thought he saw a little steam escape with his breath, even though it was warm out. He hoped his dragon side wasn't going to make an appearance.

"And . . . ?" The woman looked at him expectantly, like she saw nothing wrong with what he'd said.

Erec was about to continue when Bethany pulled him away. "What are you thinking? Do you want a mob after you again here?"

"No."

She was right. Arguing with one stranger here wouldn't change anything. They went to Cloud Nine, their favorite cloud-cream shop, and got extra large nectar fizz sodas.

Erec had mixed feelings about figuring out how to save the Castle Alypium from Balor's explosion. On one hand, he was proud that King Piter and the Hermit had put their confidence in him. But on the other, it worried him. What if he didn't figure it out? Would the king step in at the end and help him?

The king had made that strange comment about sending him away somewhere. Had Ugry really suggested that? What was that about? It must have been a mistake somehow.

Erec racked his brain to remember what Ugry had been whispering to King Piter when they'd walked into the throne room. Then he remembered. He said, "It is of the utmost importance that we contain him." Contain who? Balor Stain? Surely he couldn't have been talking about Erec.

Well, Erec didn't want to let everyone down, so he decided to explore more in the future with his dragon eyes. He had to get to the bottom of this.

On his bed, in his quiet room in the west wing, Erec closed his eyes. He pictured himself walking into the small room, and then the two smaller, darker rooms within it. It was a peaceful feeling, and even though he wasn't sitting in the sun by a brook, he relaxed. The box on the table thrummed with warmth and energy. It held all of his secrets, if he could only unlock it. He readied himself for the onslaught of emotion and drew open the shades on the two windows.

There he was again, in the middle of the chaos. He was not even sure if all the fear that surged through him was his own or a collection of the panic that surrounded him. Again, he felt the same feeling of wild power. He moved his eyes around to change the view from his two windows, and walked through the room, directing his movement around the castle.

Balor Stain stood just where he had before, smirking and holding his bronze whistle. What had he done with it? If there were only a way to step back in time from here and find out.

He walked farther and saw the huge stone statues crumbling in front of the castle again, moving as if of their own accord. Everything appeared as it had before. Erec thought hard. There had to be a way to find out more. He turned back to the castle. Maybe he could go inside. The castle entrance had caved in but he was only there in spirit and could not be harmed.

He walked to the castle, closed his eyes, and continued straight, then looked around to see that he had, indeed, walked into what was left of the falling palace. Huge spires and walls crashed around him through the caved-in ceiling. Erec was surprised to see glowing sheets of bronze light whipping this way and that. As one of them drew close, he saw it had eyes that burned like red coals. The darting bronze figures whooped and hollered with glee as they helped with the destruction, spinning chunks of foundation and flooring through the air.

Bronze ghosts. The last time Erec had seen them was in the Under Mine, the last thing that Balor Stain had exploded. He at least was relieved that only broken glass and chunks of concrete, and no people, were visible through the dust clouds.

Discouraged, he walked back outside, then around to where he had started. That's when he got a shock.

Standing where he had originally started, he saw himself.

For a moment he thought it was a shadow demon that looked exactly like him. But he quickly realized that he was looking at himself in the future. That explained why this was the spot he started from each time he opened the shades. It was odd looking into his own face. His eyes looked glazed, staring at the castle falling down.

Then he saw what was in his hand. And why he had been feeling that mad rush of power.

He was holding a scepter.

Erec sat with Bethany in the castle gardens. "I'll be too late," he said. "I could see that I'll manage to get the scepter to stop Balor, but I must not get it in time."

"I wonder how you'll get the scepter," Bethany said. "I guess the more you learn now, then the next time things might be different. Maybe you will get there in time. The future is changeable, remember?"

"I know. I think that the reason I even have the scepter at all then is because of what I've found out so far. I bet it's because I'll figure out what to do. I just need to do it faster, I guess."

He was worried that the castle was still crashing down in his vision, but glad to see things were heading in the right direction. He'd have the scepter in his hands! "Maybe I could just fix the castle again after it gets crushed. Put everything back how it was." That was it! He relaxed. Things would be fine after all.

Then another feeling overtook him. Hunger for the scepter. And he'd have it! Even the little hints when he looked into the future of how it would feel in his hands, the power it would bring him, had been enough to make him crave it more. He wanted it. Needed it now. What amazing things he could do with it! No more Balor, Baskania, or anyone who had gotten in his way . . .

A cold wave of revulsion hit him. Look how it was affecting him already. He had to face reality. Holding the scepter again was the worst thing that could happen. He knew what the thing did to him. He would never let it go after that. This was exactly what he had been afraid of, why he had not wanted to compete to become king. And now it was going to happen soon! He would *have* to find another way to stop Balor. No question.

A swirl of green and orange appeared in the dirt before them. As it grew larger, two stemlike eyes popped out and looked at him. It was a snail, and it bore his name.

Erec picked it up and pulled a letter out.

Erec,
I can never even begin to express how sorry I am. I wish I had never written you before. This is all my fault. I said that I hoped you'd write back.

If you are still alive (I hope), then please find it in your heart to forgive me.

I just didn't know. I thought if you wrote to me, but you did not say where you were, then nobody would find out. But right after I read your letter from Nemea, a group of sorcerers appeared and snatched it from me. And guess who was there? Rosco Kroc. My worst enemy. I can't believe he'd show his face after all he's done to me. Rosco grabbed the letter. He just pointed at me and tore it from my hands using magic. Then one of them put it through a tracer and they knew you were in Nemea, right in front of some dragon cave.

So it's my fault that Balor Stain even found out about that quest and won it. And when I heard you "dropped out" I figured I knew what happened. Every day I hope and pray you are at least alive. If you are captured somewhere, some day I will find you and set you free. If I ever learn that they killed you because of my stupidity than I will find whoever did it and get revenge for you.

I guess I don't need to stay in hiding anymore, to keep away from you. You won't be running into me by accident, wherever you are. But I may take cover a little longer until I figure out how to find and capture Rosco.

I guess I can't help you now, if you are alive. And please don't write back, for your safety. But I'll always be on your side.

Your friend,

Oscar

Erec read the letter twice. Poor Oscar. "I wish we could let him know we're okay. And that he still has to keep away from us."

A twinkle lit up in Bethany's eyes. "I think there's a way. . . ."

CHAPTER FIFTEEN

Ugry's Advice

O N T H E I R W A Y back into the castle, a voice rang out, "Hey, Bethany! Erec! You're back!" Jack Hare ran up to them with a grin, waving. "When did you guys get here? I was just coming to check in and see if anyone's heard from you."

Bethany and Erec looked at each other in a panic. "Jack . . ." Bethany's voice shook. "You found us."

Baskania was nowhere in sight . . . yet. Erec wondered if he would appear in a minute.

"Listen, Jack." Erec grabbed Jack's shirt. "This is extremely important. Can I trust you?"

"Of course." Jack nodded. "Shoot." He dusted Erec's hands off.

"You *cannot* tell Oscar you've seen us here. Do not mention us to him at all. Is this clear?"

Jack sighed. "Not that again. Listen, I'm telling you, I know Oscar. He's a good kid."

Bethany swung around. "Jack. There are things you don't know. We are trying to tell you. Oscar understands what's going on. He doesn't want to know where we are. His mind is getting read by Rosco. It's not Oscar's fault. They're using him to hunt us down."

They showed Jack the letter Oscar had written, and he let out a low whistle. "I can't believe Rosco is doing that to him," he said. "This is so unfair. Oscar's dad just died, and now he has to deal with this?"

"Guess how Oscar's dad died?" Bethany said. "Rosco killed him."

Jack's eyes widened. "No way."

Erec nodded. "Oscar says he's going to get revenge on Rosco. I'm sure he couldn't do it, even if he tried. He's not nearly powerful enough, plus Rosco can read his mind. But that's all he can think about."

"Do you understand now?" Bethany asked him. "Can we be sure you won't breathe a word to Oscar that we're here? Because if you ever do, Baskania will be here in one minute."

"No way." Jack looked bewildered. "I'll never tell him. Oscar's been gone anyway, since right after you guys disappeared. I've been worried about him, and you, too."

"If you want to come with us," Bethany said, "we're going to send Oscar a message."

"Wait." Jack put a hand up. "I thought he can't know where you two are."

"He can't." Bethany smiled.

Dear Oscar,
Bethany and I just had to write you back and let you know we are

THE SEARCH FOR TRUTH

alive and well. Baskania has not captured us. We realize now that we shouldn't have let on that we had to sleep in the dragon's cave for the quest. Luckily, by the time Balor got there we were gone. This time we'll be much more careful.

The quest we are doing now is very strange. We have to spend time in the coldest place on the planet. And then, right after, we have to do something really dangerous in the hottest place on the planet. (Or should I say, "in" the planet.) It's exciting but scary, and it might keep us away for a while.

Of course, I won't tell you where we are or where we are heading, so don't worry if anyone sees this letter. I just wanted you to know that we are fine, we are still your friends, and that you better still stay in hiding, and try to keep away from us, until this problem with Rosco is solved.

Erec

Jack, Bethany, and Erec laughed and high-fived on the way to the Port-O-Door. In moments, the annoyed-looking snail was tossed into the arctic snow of the South Pole.

This was perfect. Nothing like sending Baskania and his followers on a search to the freezing tundra and then to some insanely hot places. Erec flipped his pen in the air and caught it, picturing Baskania and the Stains freezing, teeth chattering in Antarctica, and then boiling hot. He started thinking about all the worst places in the world they could go. Soon he was whistling while he walked.

Jack joined them for dinner in the west wing dining hall that night. When King Piter showed up holding his scepter, Erec had a harder time taking his eyes off it. Seeing the scepter and feeling its power when he looked into the future with his dragon eyes was giving him even more of a taste for it now. For a while he had thought its grasp on him was finally weakening. But not anymore.

Could knowing his future, alone, change his future? he wondered.

The king seemed troubled and kept looking at Erec with a puzzled expression.

"Is everything okay?" Bethany asked him. "Are you worried about the Substance?"

He stroked his beard. "Maybe I've been too worried about the Substance. Things are happening right here, and I need to be more aware of them."

Erec nodded. "Like the parades in Alypium for the Stain brothers, and the lies going around that they're winning all the quests."

The king nodded. "My plants in Alypium told me about that. There's not much we can do about it, though. They can pretend whatever they want. But the scepters shouldn't go to them if they fake doing the quests."

Erec hoped the king was right. He had been able to use the scepters, though, before he finished any quests. He looked at the scepter again, hungrily. The king slid it to the other side of his chair, out of Erec's view.

"I'm concerned about the castle," he said to Erec. "Balthazar Ugry, my AdviSeer, spoke to me again. He seems to think we'd all be much safer if you were locked up somewhere out of harm's way."

"What?" Erec didn't understand. "How would that make everyone safer?"

Then he remembered that Ugry had told the king that "it was of the utmost importance that we contain him." So Ugry had been talking about *him*? That was ridiculous. "I'm not going to hurt anyone. I'm working to try to stop Balor Stain from blowing up the castle."

"Balor Stain? That's who is behind this?" The king was relieved. "Look, Balthazar has me a little concerned. Can you tell me what you've been seeing in the future?"

"Yes. I've been walking around the castle from different angles, trying to figure out what happened. And I saw Balor Stain laughing and holding his bronze whistle. He's the one that blew up the Under Mine during the contests last summer." Erec decided not to mention seeing himself holding a scepter. But he was going to make sure that changed, anyway. He knew he shouldn't have one.

King Piter tapped his chin. "I think I know what Balor's using that bronze whistle for. They can be made to call bronze ghosts."

Erec dropped his fork. "There were bronze ghosts there. Tons of them, tearing the castle apart. Balor must have called them. He always has that whistle around his neck. It would explain the bronze ghosts that were there when he exploded the Under Mine, too."

The king was smiling now, relaxed. "Balor Stain, huh? And I thought . . ." He shook his head. "Well, I suppose I can leave it to you to prevent, if the Hermit thinks that's a good idea. I'll be around to help if there's a problem."

He was amazed that the king seemed happier the more they talked about it. Erec certainly felt more upset. "So, you're not going to lock me up somewhere, then?" he asked.

"No. I think that would be an overreaction, especially based on what you're seeing and the Hermit's confidence in you. I'll reassure Balthazar that it will be okay. Just let me know if you find out anything else." King Piter waved his hand airily. "You have quests to do, young man. I'm going to figure out a way to get you to Al's Well to draw your next one."

As Erec listened to the king, he remained acutely aware of the scepter at his side. He had the feeling that the king was hiding something from him again. Why had he been about to imprison him "somewhere safe" a minute ago, and now he was fine letting him do another quest?

Erec felt angrier the more he thought about it. He was risking his life doing quests that he didn't want to do just to protect Alypium from Baskania, and the king wouldn't even be straight with him.

There were too many things he had wanted to know for too long, and he was sure the king had all the answers. It must be stubbornness that he wouldn't tell things to Erec. Or maybe he just thought Erec was a baby. Neither answer was good enough. The more he thought about it, the worse he felt. For a moment he considered grabbing the scepter and making the king talk, but then he realized that was not a wise thing to do.

But there was nothing wrong with bringing it up. He cleared his throat. "King Piter? I think it's time that you answered a few questions for me."

The king looked concerned. "Yes, Erec?"

"I want to know, for starters, who my father is. Aoquesth told me my father was a good man, but nobody will tell me more. I want to meet him. I think he's still alive." His voice took on a more urgent tone. "And I want to know if he has anything to do with why I'm supposed to be the next king."

King Piter's brow furrowed. "Erec, I know you must be curious. But you need to take my word for it that you cannot know this yet."

Erec took a sharp breath. "Why do I have to take your word for it? I am ready to know now, okay? No matter who my father is. Even if it's someone awful, like Baskania." He thought about the Stain triplets. At least they knew.

"No, Erec, you are not ready yet." The king gazed into the distance, lost in his thoughts. "Not yet."

"But I *am* ready. I've managed three quests now, and each has gotten harder. I risked my life . . ." He held his breath, trying to slow down. "So something as simple as this is not a big deal. I assure you."

"It is a big deal, Erec." The king closed his eyes. "You must trust me."

"Trust you?" Erec heard his voice rising. "What about you trusting me? You were about to lock me up a minute ago."

"Really, Erec, I'm sorry." King Piter's lips were drawn into a tight line.

Erec stood. "Well, I'm going to search for the truth, and I'll find out. With or without you. I don't need you to tell me. There are other ways."

"Then I *will* have to lock you up!" the king roared, slamming his hand on the table. Everyone jumped.

King Piter stood and glared down at Erec. "You're not giving me a choice. I told you that you weren't ready yet. Erec, *I'm* not ready for you to know yet either. It would be dangerous now, terrible, if you knew. More has to be done first."

Bethany looked like she was about to cry. She ran around the table and stood between the king and Erec, not sure what else to do.

Seeing how shocked everyone was, the king began to calm down. He patted Bethany's head. "Promise me that you won't try to find out, Erec. You don't even *want* to know. Please. I beg you."

Erec knew he had pushed the issue too far. "Okay, sorry."

Bethany and the king sat down, and everyone stared at their plates awkwardly.

"What *was* that?" Erec paced. "It's ridiculous that he can't tell me such a small thing."

"You might as well forget about it," Bethany said. "You promised him you'd forget about it. He said that you wouldn't even want to know."

"Of course I want to know. And I didn't promise anything. I just agreed so he wouldn't lock me up." Erec kicked a pillow, then sat down in the living room in Bethany's mansion.

Jack was entertaining himself by producing cake slices on the

Serving Tray. "Erec didn't have much choice, did he? He kind of had to promise that to the king so he didn't get thrown in jail."

After a knock on the door, Jam Crinklecut stuck his head in. "May I come in, modom?" He carried a tray of fresh brownies which the kids helped themselves to, even though they had just finished eating cake. "I'm sending word to young sir from the king that he has arranged for you to meet with Janus and go to Al's Well to collect your fourth quest."

"He did?" Erec handed a brownie to Jam, who took it with a bow.

"He did, young sir. He inquired and found that the Fates are indeed ready for you. You are to show up tomorrow at noon at the Labor Society, and Janus will let you through."

"Thanks, Jam." Erec wasn't sure he was ready for another quest after that last one. "Maybe I should just hang out here and figure out how to stop Balor from blowing up the castle, instead."

Bethany glared at him. "Don't even think about it."

Janus peeked out when Erec tapped on the door. His bony knees were knocking together under his shaggy tunic. He looked pale, dark bags layered under his eyes. "C-come in." He stepped back to let Erec, Jack, and Bethany in the room and quickly locked the door behind them.

All of them looked around the shop furtively, waiting for Baskania to pop into view. After a few minutes it seemed that they might be safe.

Janus, his long matted gray hair and beard covered with dust, still looked nervous. "I'm not happy with this arrangement," he said. "Someone's going to find out. And it'll be my job, or worse."

"Did anything bad happen to you last time with Baskania?"

"No." As he shook his head, dust flew off like water from a sprinkler. "I told him that John Arrete and Gog Magnon touched something they shouldn't have, and it froze them. He was suspicious that I made it happen, but Arrete remembered I told them to leave it alone. Baskania said I need to report to him if I see you again. If he finds out that I'm sneaking you in . . ." He wrung his hands together.

"We won't tell, Janus," Bethany said. "If anyone realizes that Erec went to Al's Well again, we'll say we snuck him in ourselves, without your help."

That made Janus relax a bit. He pulled out the quill pen and notepad. "I suppose I don't have to say it, but only those may come in here, blah, blah, blah." He pushed the paper forward, his voice a harsh whisper. "Now, sign it and get going. Take the elevator straight down and out the back. Try to stay hidden."

Erec signed his name on the pad and the words cut deep into the paper. Soon, light beamed from them into the room. Erec slipped easily through the membrane on the doorway and into the gleaming towers of the Labor Society building. He hiked his jacket hood over his head and walked, head hung down, straight to the elevator banks. People wearing business suits and checking their watches bustled around him. Nobody seemed to notice him.

People mingled near the elevator bank, but Erec was the only one who hopped on a glass elevator down to the basement. When he stepped off, he darted out the back door.

He knew the way across the grassy field to the hillside. After passing the tombstone that bore the name Jack, he climbed the path up to Al's Well.

Al was standing outside the stone wall, waiting. He hitched his pants up. "Ya better get dis done fast, kid," he said. "Dem Harpies been flying around here every day, keeping watch. Look." Al pointed, and Erec saw what looked like a big bird in the distance. "Come on."

Erec followed Al into the enclosure. The usual stench hit him, and he coughed until he caught his breath. He wondered if he'd ever get used to it. Flies buzzed around him and he batted them away. Before him was the closed shower curtain ring. "Go on, fast," Al said, waving his plunger toward Erec. "You think dis smells bad, you should check out Ed's Well. Ed's my brother." He pulled a cord and the white curtains swung open, revealing Al's Well, which looked exactly like a shiny white toilet. A row of servants fell to their knees and bowed their heads to the grass, arms before them.

Al motioned Erec forward, and he knelt before the porcelain commode. Green steam from the toilet bowl swirled around his face. After a glance up at Al, he plunged his arm into the liquid filling the wide latrinelike hole.

The mist was cold, and the water had the strange sensation of freezing and burning at the same time, painlessly. Erec was glad he wasn't swimming in it this time. He fished around awhile, hoping that something would go wrong and no paper would be there. What would it be this time? What danger would he encounter?

A warm paper alighted upon his fingers and he grabbed it. He pulled it out, but waited a moment before looking. Was it too late to throw it back in?

Al said softly, "I'd look now, kid. Not a great idea to hang out here."

Erec examined the dripping paper. "Take the Twrch Trwyth from Olwen Cullwich and seal the five Awen." He flung the paper toward Al, bewildered. "Huh? It doesn't make sense."

"It will," Al said gravely. He shook his head. "I didn't think dose things were real." He looked at the paper and gave Erec's shoulder a pat. "Wow. Well, good luck, kid." He didn't sound confident, not one bit.

Erec read it again. "The Twrch Trwyth? Is that like a Truth Torch?"

A chilling shriek shot through the air, making him jump. Then, in a second, the paper in his hand was swept up by the claw of a Harpy.

CHAPTER SIXTEEN
The Twrch Trwyth

THE HARPY'S BIRDLIKE black eyes glared at Erec from under her thick black eyebrows. Sleek black hair was yanked into a bun so tight, it looked like her face was stretched back from her beak of a nose. Long black wings flapped around her vulture body. Her thin black lips curled as she spoke. "You're in for it now, Erec Rex." She screeched and flapped away, taking Erec's quest with her.

Erec ran after her, reaching and jumping helplessly. Then he dropped his hands and hung his head. "Al, I don't remember what it said."

Al was digging in his pockets. After pulling out a flashlight, wrenches, hammers, and a frilly pink handbag ("Theirs," he said, looking embarrassed and tossing it down the toilet bowl), he dug out a pencil and paper. "I remember. Let's see," he wrote as he spoke. "'Take the Twrch Trwyth from Olwen Cullwich and seal the five Awen.' There." He handed it to Erec. "That should do it."

Erec looked at him in awe. "How did you remember that? It looks like you even got the spelling right."

"I'd hope so," Al said. "Everyone knows about the Twrch Trwyth and the Awen. Not hard to remember that. Now why don't you shoo on out of here before that Harpy tells the others where you are. A few of them together could carry you off."

Erec thanked Al and darted through the Labor Society into the shop where Bethany and Jack waited. "We gotta get to the castle, fast," he said.

The three of them ran back, trying to stay under trees to keep from being spotted overhead. When they made it into Bethany's mansion attached to the Castle Alypium, they slammed the door and fell onto the couches, panting.

"I've never heard of it," Bethany said. They sprawled on beanbags under the huge chandelier in her study that was lined with packed bookshelves. Jam was already there with trays of lunch and desserts.

Jack was puzzled. "I thought the Twrch Trwyth was some old story about a magical wild boar. But I've never heard of Olwen Cullwich or the five Awen."

"Al said everybody knows about them. Maybe I'll have to go back there and ask Al about it." That idea didn't appeal to him. It seemed the least safe place he could go. "A wild boar? So now am I supposed to go find a wild boar somewhere? Maybe someone has it locked up, like the bee-hind."

He handed the paper to the butler. "Jam, do you know what any of this means? It's my next quest."

Jam took the paper with a white-gloved hand. He raised it to his eyes with pinched lips and a serious expression, but as soon as he read it he began to cough and choke. "But, young sir, this is ridiculous. The Twrch Trwyth? The five Awen? It's all make-believe."

"You've heard of them?" Erec motioned for Jam to sit with them. The butler looked at the couch, which was all the way across the room, then genteelly lowered himself onto a beanbag chair and folded his hands on his lap. "I'll tell you what I know," he said with his British accent, "but I never thought any of it was true.

"Living in the Castle Alypium, I've heard a lot of legends. One was about a wild boar called the Twrch Trwyth. Twrch used to mean boar, in an old Celtic language. But Trwyth—nobody knows anymore what that meant. Maybe it was the boar's name. Maybe it was something the boar owned. But the word sounds a lot like 'truth,' and I wonder if that is what it might have meant then, too.

"The Trwyth Boar, as he was also called, modom and sirs, was supposedly alive many hundreds of years before I was born. They say he once had been a great king of Ireland who had made the Fates angry, so they turned him into a beast. But he became the king of wild boars and was noble and proud as such. He stayed just as regal and kept company with some of the kings of Ireland, Scotland, and Wales. Even King Arthur was acquainted with him, they say.

"The Trwyth Boar had an odd habit of carrying a comb and scissors locked into the tuft of hair between his ears. It was said that was the easiest place for him to keep them, and he wanted them with him at all times. For these were not an ordinary comb and scissors, of course. They held great magic. The golden comb would show its bearer the ultimate truth of anything that he or she saw, letting its carrier always know what to do and who to trust. And the magical scissors could fashion anything into anything else. Like a dress made of money, or a house made of leaves. A few snips and the wished-for thing assembled itself."

Erec perked up when he heard that. He would love to find that comb and scissors. They sounded as good as the Serving Tray, maybe even better.

Jam continued, "Of course, it was only a matter of time before someone decided they had to have the Trwyth Boar's comb and scissors for their own. Soon, the boar was no longer able to consort with kings. He spent the rest of his life on the run. But no matter how powerful the hunter, how clever or persistent, the Trwyth Boar was always able to escape. The boar lived a very long time, as things with magical powers often do. Many hunters wasted their whole lives searching for him and chasing him. And most of these hunters met with terrible, untimely deaths.

"Until finally, there was a great hunter named Cullwich. He had fallen in love with the daughter of a giant, even though he knew the giant would never agree to their marriage. But the giant surprised him. 'Find the Twrch Trwyth,' he said, 'and bring me its comb and scissors. Then you may have my daughter's hand in marriage.'

"For many years Cullwich hunted the boar. It was terribly difficult. The boar was not only smarter than most men, but it also had the help of its magical comb and scissors. However, unlike the other hunters, Cullwich was not searching for the Trwyth Boar because of greed. He was searching out of love. This gave him some unique abilities as well. And the Trwyth Boar could see he was a good man and did not want to harm him.

"Finally, Cullwich caught the Trwyth Boar and took its comb and scissors. Some say it was Cullwich's heart that led him along the right path. Others say that the boar was tired of running and finally gave it up willingly, because he liked Cullwich better than the other hunters. But, in either case, Cullwich got the golden comb and magical scissors. And he snipped off some of the boar's hair to carry them in."

"Did he give them to the giant?" Bethany asked, perched so far forward she was about to topple out of her beanbag chair.

"It took a while for Cullwich to return to the giant," Jam said. "And when he did, he saw the situation in a new light. He was carrying the comb, so he could look into the hearts of the giant and his daughter. He realized that the giant was evil. He would cause great destruction if he had the comb and scissors. So he knew he could not give it to him."

"What about the girl?" Bethany asked.

"Ah, yes. The girl. Well, Cullwich still liked what he saw. She was pure of heart and loved him, too. So he gave her a choice between him and her father. It was up to her. She chose to be with Cullwich. So Cullwich used the scissors to cut up the giant's cave while he slept, and it fashioned itself into a prison. And the two set off to find the Boar again."

"Why did they want to find it?" Jack asked.

"That was how Cullwich was. He no longer needed the magical instruments so he decided to return them. Many people would have used them for power or greed, but not him."

Erec's ears reddened, and he felt ashamed, knowing he would have kept the magical things for himself. "Did they find him?"

"Yes, but it took a long while," Jam said, "and by this time, without his magic, the Trwyth Boar was dying. He no longer wanted them back, said it was too late for him. But Cullwich was a smart chap. He was afraid the comb and scissors might fall into the wrong hands. So he took them to a powerful druid sorcerer, someone like Vulcan himself, and had them shrunk down, with the lock of the Boar's hair, to a tiny size and placed into a small vial that he would wear on a chain around his neck. He wanted the vial to be shaped like the Twrch Trwyth, to honor the boar."

Jam saw that his audience was smiling, and he held up a hand. "But this is where the story gets strange. They say the druid recognized, when he was working on the vial, that the powers coming from the small objects were too strong. They had grown much greater when he shrunk them. When they were close together in the vial, the scissors' and comb's powers combined to make a new thing altogether. What he was making was fast becoming the most powerful object that ever existed.

"The druid walked around his workshop, amazed. Everything he brought the vial near glowed, its magic doubled, tripled. That was when he invented a plan. He would keep the vial for himself, tie it to the five Awen, and rule the universe."

"What are the Awen?" Erec asked. He had forgotten, until he heard that word, that this had to do with his fourth quest. Now it felt ridiculous. He had to find this Trwyth Boar himself? It was dead, Jam had said. And finding that old vial didn't sound any easier.

"The Awen," Jam said, folding his fingers together, "are five of the greatest mysteries of the world, with some of the heaviest known magic. They are located along what is called the Path of Wonder. Awen is an old druidic word, which I believe means 'mystery, enlightenment, inspiration.' It also meant 'great poetry,' which they believed carried vast magic as well."

Jam thrummed his fingers on his knees. "So this druid saw how the vial's power had increased beyond imagination and how it made all other magical things near it grow tremendously in strength. He was greedy and decided that he would use this to make himself more powerful than anything that had ever existed. The druid was brilliant, and was able to fit the boar-shaped vial with five openings, each of which would only respond to the magical signals of one of the five Awen—the greatest magical things he knew. When all five Awen were plugged into it, each of their powers would grow intensely to form a magical shield that would let him control the world. He would set out along the Path of Wonder, he decided, find the Awen, and become all-powerful."

And this is what I am supposed to do? Erec thought.

"Well," Jam said, "needless to say, the plan did not work out as he wished. He collected the Awen, but after he plugged just a few of them into the boar vial, its power overcame him, killing him instantly. His wife did not want the vial around, as you can imagine, and she returned it to Cullwich. They say he wore it around his neck until just before he died, then passed it down to his eldest daughter, who passed it to her son." Jam shrugged. "So that's the story. But it's all make-believe."

Erec looked at the paper in his hand. *Take the Twrch Trwyth from Olwen Cullwich and seal the five Awen.* He wasn't so sure.

King Piter's eyebrows slowly rose in the west wing dining hall that night. "You are joking, I am sure."

Erec pitched the paper toward him, and the king read it. "I can't believe this. It's impossible." His brow darkened with anger. "I'm going to have a word with the Fates, if they think this is funny. I mean, our quests were tough. For one of them I had to build this castle by magic. Each of us built our own. But this . . ."

Erec was impressed that the king had built this castle himself. He still could not do any magic with his remote except move small things a short distance. And he might not even be able to do that anymore, as it had been so long since he had practiced. He wished he had time to spend with the Hermit to learn. He was sure the Hermit would be a far better teacher than Pimster Peebles had been. At least that was one good decision King Piter had made.

The king stared at the paper and scratched his chin. "This just can't be. Hermit?" he called, although the Hermit was not in the room. "Can I trouble you for a moment?"

Suddenly the Hermit was sitting in the chair next to the king's, wearing a small loincloth and a huge grin. "You may continue to trouble me for a while yet." He laughed at his own joke.

The king pushed the paper toward him. "Erec drew this from Al's Well. It can't be right, can it?"

The Hermit glanced at the paper, unimpressed. "If he drew it, he blew it." He chortled, finding himself funny as usual, and soon was clutching his sides.

"If he found it, he'll pound it. If he picked it, he'll lick it." The Hermit then stuck a thin finger into his nose, picked something out, and put his tongue on it, all the time laughing as if it were a great joke.

"Eew."

"Yuck." Erec, Bethany, and Jack all doubled over, both disgusted and laughing.

Bethany held her palms out in front of her face as if she were trying to not see more. She whispered to Erec, "Ugh! That's the first thing I've seen him eat."

Jack made a loud spluttering noise.

The king frowned, ignoring them all. "Listen, how many people have tried to do this, to take the Twrch Trwyth from Olwen Cullwich and seal the five Awen? They've all died."

That made Erec stop laughing. "Huh?"

"Yes." The king was not pleased. "Many sorcerers, far more powerful than you, have lost their lives in this pursuit. And they spent years preparing first. Decades." He turned sadly to the Hermit. "How can we let him do this?"

"Let him?" the Hermit asked. "The choice is his. But he has something those sorcerers did not have."

"Oh, really?" King Piter asked.

The Hermit nodded. "The right reasons."

"He does?" Bethany asked, chiming in. "That sounds like the story of the Twrch Trwyth. Only Cullwich could capture the boar because he was doing it for the right reasons."

"Easy enough to say," King Piter scoffed. "But Erec not only has to find the Trwyth Boar vial, he must connect it to the five most powerful objects in the world, and survive what happens when their powers all amplify."

It didn't sound encouraging, Erec thought. He would have to be a fool to attempt that.

"What are the right reasons?" Bethany asked. "Just to do it because the quest told him to? Is that enough?"

"There is more, of course." The Hermit gazed at Erec. "You know those girls, the Fates. Always something up their sleeves. There is a reason they want you to find this vial and connect it to the five Awen."

They all waited for the Hermit to go on. Instead he began to whistle contentedly.

"Well?" Bethany asked. "What is the reason?"

King Piter covered his face with his hand and shook his head. "It would fix the Substance. *If* you survived, which is doubtful."

The Hermit nodded. "Oooh, nothing big. Just that. Setting the Substance permanently, so it won't leak away anymore. So Upper Earth won't die in ten years. But no pressure." He twiddled his thumbs. "You do whatever you think is right."

"Wait a minute!" Erec felt tricked. "I thought the last thing I did, freeing the bee-hind, fixed the Substance for Upper Earth."

"It did." The Hermit nodded. "For about ten years. The king told you—"

"I know." Erec gestured toward the king. "But he is going to fix it by then, I thought."

The king shrugged. "I'll certainly try. I've been trying for centuries."

That didn't inspire Erec's confidence. "Well...well..." He thought about the idea from all angles. "Why did the Fates want me to bother freeing the bee-hind before I did this? Wouldn't that have been a waste of time since this will fix things more?"

"Not really." The Hermit examined his hands. "That was easier. Good to do that first, in case you fail at this quest."

That sent a chill through Erec. He might fail? He really might die? That wasn't what he wanted to hear.

"Also," the Hermit added, "if you succeed at freezing the Substance where it is, better that the bee-hind is loose, spreading it around where it needs to go. Good that it's not frozen all clumped up like that."

The king shook his head. "This is still impossible. He's supposed to get the Twrch Trwyth from Olwen Cullwich? Olwen doesn't have it anymore. Remember? After having his life threatened *several* times, he destroyed it."

The Hermit grinned. "I guess that will be Erec's problem."

The king relaxed, seeming content that Erec could never find the Twrch Trwyth vial so he wouldn't be in such terrible danger.

Erec asked the king, "Do you know Olwen Cullwich?"

"Yes. A very good man. Olwen is a scientist, a sorcerer, and he was a viceroy in my court. A long time ago he wore the Twrch Trwyth around his neck. His mother passed it on to him to protect. It had been in their family for generations. He kept it secret, of course. You would not find a wiser and gentler person than Olwen." He chuckled. "I'll never forget the pie incident."

The Hermit joined in laughing.

"What pie incident?" asked Bethany.

"Olwen loved pies. We had a celebration for his birthday one year, and Hecate Jekyll, our head chef then, baked twelve kinds of pies in his honor. You should have seen the look on Olwen's face when he found out." The king's gaze misted over, reliving old times. "But we never expected what would happen." Deep belly laughs erupted from the king. "We had a clown at the celebration. And the next thing you know, Olwen had a pie in his face. A cherry one, I think, was the first one."

"The first?" Jack raised his eyebrows.

"Yes. Olwen froze a moment in shock, then he decided to get even. He picked up some kind of cream pie and aimed it at the clown, but that clown just batted the pie right back into Olwen's face. It got ridiculous, Olwen picked up another, but he was so sticky that it slipped to the ground. I think he stepped in that one. And when he picked up a blueberry pie—I remember blueberry getting all over the whipped cream—he slipped on the pie on the ground and got the blueberry pie in his own face. I don't know how many pies he went through trying to get that clown back. Maybe all of them. But the clown ended up clean as a whistle. And poor Olwen was covered, head to toe." He chortled.

The talk of pie was making Erec hungry for one. "But what did he do with the Twrch Trwyth?"

The king grew solemn. "A day or two after the pie incident, something else happened to Olwen. He almost lost his life. He was captured by a rogue sorcerer who tried to make him talk. . . ." He paused. "It wasn't pleasant. And Olwen barely survived. He knew keeping the Twrch Trwyth was a great responsibility. It could not fall into the wrong hands. But there was also no good that would come from keeping it. The only reasonable thing was to get rid of it. So he did that, many years ago."

The king's forehead wrinkled in thought. "This whole thing with the Twrch Trwyth is crazy, though. It's gone. I don't know what will happen with the scepters if you cannot complete all of your quests. That didn't happen when we were going through this process. I guess we'll just have to see how it plays out." He shrugged. "Nothing is the same this time, especially since you are doing the quests alone."

That reminded Erec of the two other people that could have been helping him. He certainly could use the assistance.

"So, he might not be able to complete the quest? Are you saying this is impossible?" Bethany asked.

The king nodded. "I'm afraid so. Even if Olwen did have the Twrch Trwyth vial, how would Erec ever get the five Awen? Are they just going to unlodge themselves for him?"

"Yes," the Hermit said. "That's exactly what they will do. He owns their master."

Everyone turned to him in shock. "I do?" Erec asked.

"In your backpack," the Hermit said. "You have one of the singing crystals."

So the crystal that the Swami had given him controlled the Awen somehow?

King Piter leaned back in surprise.

"Erec must make this choice himself," the Hermit said. "He knows what he is facing, his odds. But only he can secure the Substance to save Upper Earth."

Erec nodded. No problem. He just had to do what no powerful sorcerer had ever done before—and somehow not die in the process.

Erec pulled up his hooded sweatshirt, and Bethany and Jack wore hats so they would be harder to spot by flying Harpies. Olwen Cullwich lived in Alypium. They decided to pay him a visit sooner rather than later. Baskania knew what this quest was now, too. No doubt the Harpy had showed the paper to him. If the Twrch Trwyth still existed, Baskania would want it for himself.

"I can't think of Olwen Cullwich now without thinking about twelve pies in his face and all over him," Erec said.

"He sounds like a nice guy," said Bethany. "I bet he'll help us if he knows where the Trwyth Boar vial is."

"He's gotta know," Erec said. "I mean, that's what my quest is. To get the Twrch Trwyth from Olwen Cullwich. Not to find it somewhere else."

Jack nodded. "This guy is a scientist who was in the king's court. He's going to want to help you save the Substance, I'm sure."

They kept their heads down on their way to the street where Olwen Cullwich lived. The sun had set, and Erec was glad it was dark outside.

"There it is!" Bethany pointed. Light shone from all of the rooms in the small home. When they grew nearer, voices rang through an open window downstairs.

"Maybe we better check it out first," Erec said. They crept in front of the house and peeked in.

Standing near the window was Thanatos Baskania, his black cape flowing. Erec could see two open eyes on his forehead, one on his cheek, and one on his chin. A man and woman nearby him, each wearing an eye patch, were tearing books off shelves, dumping out drawers.

The man who must have been Olwen Cullwich was motionless at the far end of the room, facing them. His well-combed gray hair and neat clothing made him look just as Erec had pictured him. He seemed familiar, as if Erec had known him long ago. But his bright blue eyes were wide with fear. He stood in an odd position, which made Erec sure that Baskania had frozen him to the spot.

But he was still able to talk. "I'm telling you, I don't have it. I haven't had it for years. Your . . . pals will find that out when they're done ransacking my house."

Erec, Bethany, and Jack wedged themselves into a row of hedges in front of the house where they could still see and hear through the window.

Baskania sighed. "Dear Olwen, you don't understand. I happen to have evidence. It was decreed by the Fates that you give the vial to somebody. Now I just need to make sure that it will be me. If you want to keep your house neat and tidy, just tell me where it is, and we'll call this search party off. Simple. Or we can do it the hard way."

Erec couldn't believe it. Why had he waited to come here? Now Baskania would get the Trwyth Boar. Not that Olwen Cullwich would want to give it to him, he was sure. He hoped that Olwen could think of a way to fend off Baskania until Erec could talk to him alone.

Then Erec realized that he was probably lucky that he had arrived now, shrouded in darkness. This house would be watched around the clock when Baskania was not here. They would be waiting for Erec to show up so they could catch him.

Other people with eye patches poured into the room. "We can't find anything," one of them said in a deep voice. "We used the magic detectors and found a few other choice objects that we took apart and searched. But no vial."

"Then look again." Baskania glowered. "Tear the walls apart."

Olwen spoke through gritted teeth. "It's . . . not . . . here. How can I make you understand that?"

Baskania tilted his head as though he was considering this possibility. "Well, now that you put it that way, I do know ways you can help me understand better." He pointed a finger and a small puff of dark smoke flew from it.

Olwen screamed in pain. "Aaaannh! Stop. Stop. Please. I'll tell you anything. Please, make it stop!"

Baskania lifted his finger and blew on it like it was a match. Olwen's head drooped. "So you're ready to talk?"

Olwen nodded.

"Good." Baskania looked thoughtful, then he pointed again and a white puff of smoke shot from his finger. "This will ensure that when you do speak, everything that you say will be true." He smiled. "Now, when did you first get the Trwyth Boar?"

Olwen spoke slowly. "It was passed down to me from my mother, from her father, from many generations back. My mother gave it to me to guard when I was thirty-five."

"Very good." Baskania smiled, like a teacher helping a slow pupil. "I'm sure this is a prize I will very much like having. Now, where do you keep it, Olwen?"

"I *don't.* I no longer have the Twrch Trwyth."

"Hmmm. It seems the truth spell was not strong enough for you." He shot another white puff from his finger. "Or do you need the other kind of persuasion again?"

"No!" Olwen shouted. "I'm talking. What do you want to know?"

"Where is the vial?"

"I don't have it. I swear. I got rid of it. Too many people were after me for it. It was too dangerous for me to keep. And I had no use for it other than to guard it. It's gone."

Baskania tapped his chin. "You don't say. Well, then, let's hear it. Who did you give it to? Not that they could have it. I know it's on you, somewhere. But I'd like to hear your story anyway."

"I couldn't give it to anyone," Olwen said. "It was far too powerful. My father warned me that there was nobody I could trust with it. I had to get rid of it another way."

"Ahh. Now we're getting somewhere. What other way did you choose?"

Olwen mumbled something and looked away.

"What is that? I'm sorry, you'll need to speak clearer. That is, if you want to live."

Olwen eyed him darkly. "I swallowed it. I researched the best way to dispose of it before I decided. It was recommended as a way to cover up its magic, so it might not be found again someday in the future. I

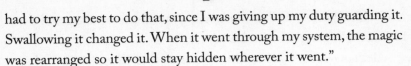

had to try my best to do that, since I was giving up my duty guarding it. Swallowing it changed it. When it went through my system, the magic was rearranged so it would stay hidden wherever it went."

Baskania regarded him with an odd expression. "You swallowed it." He was quiet a moment. "This can only mean one thing. But just to be safe, we will wait until the search party is finished."

People trickled in and out as the room was slowly chipped away. Baskania stood quietly, and Olwen gazed around, still paralyzed. Finally, it was decided that the vial was not in the house.

Baskania nodded. "You may all go now. Leave Olwen here with me."

Erec trembled as Baskania's one-eyed followers poured from the house. He shrunk farther back into the bushes with his friends.

Baskania spoke again. "Olwen, I'm afraid there is only one answer. If you swallowed the Twrch Trwyth"—he counted on one finger— "and we know that you still have it"—he counted on another—"then that means it is still inside you." He ticked off a third finger and sighed. "Such a shame."

"That's ridiculous." Olwen sounded desperate. "It's absurd. I swallowed it over eight years ago after eating a slice of pie. That pie isn't still in me, either."

"Tsk, tsk, tsk." Baskania shook his head. "Sometimes we live to pay the price for our poor decisions. Well, regardless, I am going to find the Trwyth Boar. I think I'll help you a little, though, keep you alive as long as possible, in case you have more to say to me." He raised both hands, curved as if they were claws, and streaks of green light shot from them into Olwen. "That should do it."

Olwen looked crazed. "What are you doing?"

"Just finishing the search," Baskania said. In front of their eyes, he made a motion and Olwen Cullwich ripped, his left half splitting from his right half, straight down the middle. The man, amazingly, was still

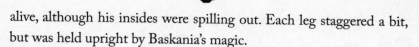

alive, although his insides were spilling out. Each leg staggered a bit, but was held upright by Baskania's magic.

Bethany opened her mouth to scream, and Erec clamped a hand over it. "Shhh." He covered her eyes with his other hand, but she pushed him away.

Each half of Olwen was looking down at himself in shock. "What did you do to me?" When he spoke, both sides of his mouth moved at the same time, but his tongue was split so he sounded garbled.

Baskania stepped closer to inspect both sides of him. "No luck yet." He made another motion, and now both halves of Olwen were split front to back. Each arm and leg were cleaved in two so he was four long strips. The front halves tripped forward a bit, and all four parts of him wavered unsteadily.

Unbelievably, Olwen was still talking. Erec could not understand him anymore, nor did he want to. Jack threw up in the bushes, and Erec almost joined him. Tears flowed down Bethany's face. When Erec saw her, his eyes brimmed over as well.

Baskania casually looked through Olwen's body, then split him again and again. Soon he was shredded into tiny pieces all over his floor. Erec only hoped that Olwen was no longer alive.

"Oh, well. It's not here," Baskania said. "I suppose you were right, then." He snapped his fingers and disappeared.

CHAPTER SEVENTEEN

Ghost Ship to Avalon

IT TOOK MOST of the night for the three of them to calm down. Jam was in and out of Bethany's mansion with hot compresses, trays of steaming milk, and hugs. Erec gagged on the milk and had to run to the bathroom, choking. Jack had a glazed look, as if he'd decided to take a vacation from reality. All three of them took turns crying and comforting each other.

"I guess that settles it," Erec said. "The Fates were wrong.

There will be no fourth quest. Substance or no Substance." They all decided to sleep on Bethany's beanbags. None of them wanted to be alone.

In the morning Erec felt groggy and stiff, with the sense that he'd had a terrible nightmare. After a while he realized that it had been real. The three decided to take a walk in the castle gardens for a change of scenery. Normally Erec loved the perfect, warm weather Alypium had because of its golden dome, even in the middle of winter. But now it all felt wrong. He'd had enough here. Going further with the quest did not seem possible, or even remotely desirable.

"I've got it," he said. "We have a Port-O-Door. Let's take a trip somewhere fun. Jack's never been to Upper Earth. You'd love it there, Jack. We'll go somewhere relaxing and take a vacation."

"Great idea." Bethany perked up. "We could use a break. Somewhere warm. It's cold in North America now."

"Maybe we could go to an island in the Caribbean," Erec said. "Or Hawaii. I've always wanted to go there."

"I've heard of Hawaii," Jack said. "Something about ancient kings and magic totems."

"Forget all that," Erec said. "We're going to see the nonmagical part of Hawaii. Beaches, tourists, and luaus. I want to go scuba diving and climb a volcano."

"Hey! What about Tahiti?" Bethany hopped on her toes, excited. "That could be great."

"We'll do both!" Erec and Bethany high-fived each other.

Then Bethany's smile dropped. "Problem. What hotel will let us in—three kids without an adult? We'd get hassled the whole way."

Erec thought a moment then stuck a finger in the air. And with one word, they were all grinning again. "Jam."

"Yeah! He'll definitely come with us!" Bethany relaxed.

"Everyone will think we're a bunch of rich kids with our butler taking care of us."

"We *are* a bunch of rich kids," Erec said. "Don't forget the bags of gold, silver, and bronze coins we have. And you're living in a mansion here, remember? Now all we have to do is decide what we want to take with us. Who knows? Maybe we won't ever come back."

"We've *got* to take the Serving Tray," Bethany said. "And your Sneakers, in case we want to sneak anywhere."

"And Wolfboy," Erec added, "and Cutie Pie."

"Of course."

Jack thought a moment. "Maybe your mom could give you her glasses. Then we could stay as long as we wanted and check in with our families."

Erec thought about his mother a moment. How could she object to this after he'd already been all over the world? It would be a piece of cake after risking his life so many times. And Jam would be there to keep an eye on them. That would seal it.

"Of course you'll want to take a few bathing suits and towels," said a voice under them, making them jump. The Hermit was sitting cross-legged in a cluster of giant daisies, their huge multicolored tops spinning up and landing around his face. A large one covered his lap. Erec couldn't tell, but he hoped the Hermit was wearing something under the daisy. "And a good book or two. Nice to read by the beach." He nodded. "You could stay a long time. A good ten years at least, until the world ended and Upper Earth died off. You'd all be about twenty-four then. Too bad time ends up going faster than you think."

Erec scowled. He didn't want to hear it. "That's going to be someone else's problem. I'm through with it."

The Hermit nodded. "It will be someone else's problem. Everyone else's problem. Too bad none of them will be able to solve it."

"I can't either." Erec pointed at himself, breathing harder. "It's over."

"It sounds like it is over," the Hermit agreed. "For everyone."

"Hermit!" Erec punched his palm. "What can I do? You know what happened, I'm sure. Baskania searched Olwen Cullwich's house, and . . ." He couldn't say it. "He's gone now, anyway, if I ever had a chance to get that Twrch Trwyth from him. Even Baskania's given up."

The Hermit put a finger to his lips. "Hmm. Who do you trust more, Baskania or the Fates? You know how our three girls work. How your cloudy thoughts work. Do you trust them? Did you doubt when your cloudy thought told you that Bethany would tell Oscar her secret, and Baskania would find it out if you didn't stop her?"

"No. But that was different," Erec said. "I knew that. I don't know this."

"You decide who to trust. Up to you!" The Hermit pretended to think hard. "So, you can trust Baskania, enjoy your vacation, and try to make the next ten years good ones, or you can trust the three Fates and do your quest. It's dangerous. No guarantee you will succeed or survive. You might be better off in Hawaii."

Erec kicked a rock in frustration. It spun through the air and knocked the top off of a wide blue daisy with a yellow center, and sent it whirling into the air. Then he growled, "All right. Fine! I'll do it. At least whatever part of it I can. But afterward, it's Hawaii."

There was another reason Erec could not go to Hawaii, when he thought about it. Balor Stain was going to blow up the Castle Alypium, and he still had not figured out how to stop him. It was time he gave it another try. He sat on his bed in the west wing and closed his eyes.

Soon he was entering the small, dark room in his mind, and

THE SEARCH FOR TRUTH

the two smaller, darker ones within it. Inside he again saw the box on the table, the part of him that knew everything his future had to hold. If only he could choose what it showed him. He wanted to see what would happen with this crazy, impossible quest. Then again, the Hermit had said he *was* choosing what to show himself. A different part of him was. If only he could make those two parts of himself meet and talk.

He ran his hand over the box, feeling the life pulse within it. Then, bracing himself, he opened the shades on the windows of his dragon eyes.

He was there again. Castle crashing down. People screaming and running. This time, before he rounded the corner, he turned back to look where he had come from. There he saw himself again, transfixed, holding the scepter.

He could feel the scepter's power streaming through his body, shooting from his fingers and toes. He could do anything at all that he wanted. The scepter pulled him closer. Soon he stood right next to the future version of himself, admiring the gleaming gold in his hand. He raised a finger to touch it, but it fell right through. The scepter, like everything here, was a mirage.

It was frustrating being so close to the scepter yet so far. He managed to pull himself away and walked around the corner to find Balor Stain.

There Balor stood, holding his bronze whistle and laughing. How could he rewind time? Find out what had happened before this moment? He walked up to Balor and passed a hand through him, not able to feel a thing. "You menace," he said to Balor's image. "I'll figure this out, one way or another."

Then he closed his eyes and concentrated. *Move back time. Push it further.* He knew it was all in the box. He just had to show it where to go. *Think. Back. See back . . .*

It was working. Everything was a blur, but he could feel that time was going where he wanted. Backward.

Balor was laughing and pointing to the castle. Damon and Dollick were behind him. "Look," he said. "It's crumbling."

The castle begin to crash down. A massive spire trembled, then tipped, falling through a roof.

Balor's face lit with delight. "I love it! Hey, I know, guys." He turned to his brothers. "Just the thing to help this along." He picked up his bronze whistle and blew it.

Suddenly, swarms of bronze wraiths flew through the air. One hovered in front of Balor, red eyes burning.

"In there," Balor said, pointing. "Go to it!"

The bronze ghosts sailed into the castle. Balor watched, laughing, still holding his whistle.

This was where Erec had first seen him. There would be nothing new from here. But, just in case, Erec stayed a while longer and watched the castle cave in. When it was nearly gone, and he couldn't take it anymore, he pulled the shades on the windows and left the small room in his head.

So, Balor really had called the bronze ghosts there. King Piter had been right about his whistle. Now if Erec could figure out how to change the future, not just watch it, he'd be set. But he comforted himself with the knowledge that he would be there, at least, with the scepter. He would use it afterward to fix whatever bad thing happened to the castle. No problem.

Erec looked in his backpack for the singing crystal that Swami Parvananda had given him in India. The Swami had said he knew Erec would need it. He felt guilty remembering that. He had

THE SEARCH FOR TRUTH

wanted to walk away from his quest too easily, give up too fast.

He picked up the tall, clear crystal. If this was the master of the five Awen, he might as well go on the Path of Wonder and find them. The crystal wasn't so difficult to get, so maybe the Awen wouldn't be either. How he would ever find the Twrch Trwyth, though, was beyond him.

Jack and Bethany were eating lunch in the west wing dining hall. Erec waved to them. "Listen, I've made a decision. I'm going to try to find the five Awen. If you guys could help me learn about them first, I'd really appreciate it. But I'd like to go on this quest with Jam, I think, if you two don't mind."

Jack and Bethany shrugged, but neither of them looked happy. "Why is that?" Jack asked. "I haven't gone with you since your first quest. And I already took the time off with my tutor."

"I don't know," Erec said. "Just seems like a good idea." He didn't want to bring up the real reason for his decision. He had put them—Bethany especially—in enough danger. After she appeared in Artie's house the night when the manticore could have shredded them all to bits, he was through jeopardizing her life.

Bethany's lip pushed out, but she didn't say anything. The three of them walked to the library tower in silence. Finally, she said what was on her mind. "Are you sure you even want me to go to the library with you? Since you're that sick of me?"

"That's not it," Erec protested. "Really. I just—"

"Don't want to hang out with me anymore. I know."

"No! I wish you could go. But—"

Her chin crinkled. "No biggie. I guess I just had us pegged as better friends than we really are."

"Look." Erec gave up pretending. "I do want you to come. But it drives me nuts to put you in danger. Please, just this time, wait here for me. I almost lost you in Otherness."

"And I almost lost you. What's the difference? I'll be fine, Erec." She had perked up considerably.

"The difference is that I have to go, and you don't."

"This sounds familiar," she said with a hint of a smile. "Isn't that what you said to me when we first met? You said you had to go through the sidewalk, into the unknown, and I didn't. It was too dangerous for me to risk it." She paused. "But remember what I said? I'm going with you. That was the deal. You needed my help to get in. And I'm glad I did come. Imagine if I was still stuck there with nasty Earl Evirly."

Just like back then, Erec worried about what would happen to her, but he also didn't like the idea of going alone without her. But this time he would stay firm. It wasn't the same. "No, Bethany. I'm glad you were with me before. But this might be more risky. If something happened to you I'd never forgive myself."

Carol Esperpento, the librarian, sat at her desk. She lifted her squinting eyes to them over the narrow granny glasses that jutted out far from the sides of her face. She pointed at the third floor after they asked where they might find books about the Awen. "The books must stay here," she warned sternly.

On the third floor, they found books about the Awen in the sections "The Great Magic of Upper Earth," "History Mysteries," and "The Awen of Celtic Poetry."

Jack pulled a book off the shelf called *Ah, When? When Were the Awen Discovered, and How You Can Discover Them Too.*

"Look at this." Bethany laughed, pointing at a book called *Get Your Stinkin' Awen Away from Me.* She took *The Total Loser's Guide to Capturing the Awen and Not Losing Your Mind* and *How the Five Awen Ruined My Life* off the shelf and sat down. Erec picked up a book called *Aptly Named? Awen: Beauties or Beasts.*

"Hey, Erec," Jack said. "Bad news, bud. Looks like these Awen

are kind of bad luck charms. At least that's what they seem like."
He read some more.

"I don't know," Bethany said. "Here it says they hold really powerful magical spells made by an ancient druid. But they're stuck where they are. It's really hard to collect them. . . ." She ran her finger down the page. "Oh, wait. Unless you have a singing crystal. It finds them like a metal detector and draws them in."

"Yeah." Erec saw the same thing in his book. It looked like bringing back the Awen would be easy with the singing crystal. "It says the crystal is the master of the Awen. Cool."

Jack pointed. "The druid who created the Awen was called Bile. He did it by capturing huge amounts of power and putting them in really small packages. But the things caused a lot of damage. I mean a *lot* of damage. His whole land was ruined. So he made this Path of Wonder, a magic passageway that led to some of the most beautiful places on Earth, and he spread the Awen through it." He frowned. "That way each of those spots had some of the problems, but they weren't all in his place, piled on top of one another."

"Why didn't he just destroy them?" Bethany asked.

"Probably too greedy," Erec said. "Seems like all these old sorcerers were. Maybe he wanted to use them for something."

"Or maybe he couldn't destroy them," Jack added.

They read for a while longer before Bethany said, "Erec, you've got no choice about taking us with you. It's impossible otherwise. The only people who have succeeded have been in groups, the larger the better."

Erec found that same information in several places, then he dropped his head into his hands. This was not the news he wanted. He was going to have to take along a bunch of people to help him. If he put Bethany in danger another time he'd never forgive himself. But then again, the Awen had been collected before. It was not deadly, he hoped. At least it was possible, unlike getting the Twrch Trwyth from Olwen Cullwich or hooking the Awen to it. Maybe it wouldn't be too dangerous after all.

"The druid dumped the first Awen on an island called Avalon, near England," Bethany read. "And the Path of Wonder starts there."

"No problem, then," Erec said. "We'll just have to find Avalon."

Jam fitted them all with backpacks, slipping the Serving Tray into Erec's. "I do wish I could come help you, young sir."

Erec studied him a moment. "You are coming, Jam. That is, if you're sure you're up for more danger."

Jam's eyes lit up. At the same time, Bethany and Jack looked uneasy.

"Are you getting rid of one of us?" Bethany asked.

"No. We're all going together."

"I thought you couldn't do that," Jack said. "You can only have two other people on your quest."

Erec said with confidence, "This isn't my quest yet. I'm sure of it. It's just getting things ready for my quest. I could have ten people help me with this. So far I've really done the quests alone, anyway. At least the parts that mattered, that made the Amulet of Virtues light up." He thought a moment. "Well, except for the second quest. Aoquesth did that one with me."

He grimaced. "It's all messed up now, anyway. King Piter's triplets were really supposed to do these quests, if only they were alive. I still don't get why I was chosen. And where those other two are who should be helping. I can't be in charge of all three kingdoms myself."

"Well, if you get one throne, and Balor and Damon Stain take the other two," Bethany said, "then try and get Alypium if you can."

Jack laughed. "If Damon Stain becomes king of Aorth, I'm moving for sure."

A silence settled over them as they thought about the Stains taking over. "Why am I doing this?" Erec asked. "Even if I do become king, the other two thrones are open for the taking. I don't see how that will help anything."

"Well," Bethany said, "we'll just have to find the other two rightful rulers . . . wherever they are."

The idea was wonderful, having two other people to shoulder his burden. But it also sounded impossible. It was easier to think about the task at hand. "It seems like the more people helping with the Awen the better. It's a shame Oscar can't come. Think Melody would want to join us?"

Melody Avery had been Bethany's roommate during the contests in Alypium last summer. Bethany was still friends with her, and she lived in the apprentice boardinghouse in Alypium. Bethany's eyes lit up. "That would be great! I'll go find her. She'll be in Paisley Park now with her tutor." Then her eyes narrowed. "You better not be trying to lose me. Leave without me and you're dead, buster."

Erec held his hands up in protest, then Bethany took off. "So?" he said to Jam and Jack. "Ready to leave without her?"

They looked at him quizzically, and he smirked. "Just kidding," he said.

Bethany and Melody met Erec, Jam, and Jack in a sitting room near the west wing Port-O-Door. Melody smiled shyly, her tight black curls draping around her dark brown face. "I swore her to secrecy," Bethany said. "She won't tell Oscar or anyone else that you're here or where we're going. Her tutor gave her time off, and nobody else will know."

"Thanks for asking me, guys," Melody said. "I'm ready for some adventure."

"Cool." Erec nodded.

Jam handed Melody her own backpack and put one on himself. Then he passed out winter parkas, scarves, and gloves to everyone. Typical Jam, Erec thought. Prepared for everything. They crowded into the vestibule of the Port-O-Door and searched the Upper Earth map of Great Britain for Avalon.

"Cardiff, Oxford, Birmingham, Sheffield. I don't see an Avalon here," Jack said.

"It's an island," Jam said, scanning the ocean. "But I can't find it on this."

"You won't find it on the map," a bouncy voice piped up behind them. The Hermit was dressed in a thick down coat that went down to his sandaled feet, and his head was topped with a red stocking cap. Erec had not seen him enter the vestibule. Everybody scooted aside and let him through to the map. He touched a spot on the Isle of Man, a small island nestled among Northern Ireland, the North of England, and Scotland. Then he moved their Port-O-Door to a small secluded spot in the north of the island, past the town of Cranstal.

Cold air blasted them as they walked out onto a rocky beach. Their Port-O-Door had shrunk to fit into a boulder near the base of some cliffs that hung overhead. In the distance, icicles sparkled on the naked tree branches in a nearby glen. Beyond, on a heath, the purple moor grass, heathers, and gorse tossing in the wind had turned gray from the cold. A skylark twittered and a seagull swooped by, impervious to the cold.

The ocean before them swelled and sank against the rocks in a fierce rhythm, roaring like a tyrant as it came in. The dusky gray sky seemed immense. Erec shivered under his parka. It had been a while since he had experienced cold weather, and it actually seemed nice, at least with the stark ocean before him.

The Hermit motioned for them to follow him to the water's

edge. He closed his eyes and held a long stick in front of him with both hands. An eerie melody spilled from his lips over the roar of the waves. "*Am gáeth tar na bhfarraige. Am tuile os chinn maighe. Am dord na daíthbhe.* I am a wind across the sea. I am a flood across the plain. I am the roar of the tides." His voice rang starkly among the pounding waves. The melody sounded foreign, something from an alien world. He paused, and waves drizzled the noise of a thousand tiny, tinkling shells.

The Hermit struck another haunting chord. "*Óig dar mhuir, mile laoch líonfas ler. Barca breaga bruigfidid.* Let these youths float across your ocean, thy thousand heroes fill your sea. Bring your magic ships to moor."

In the distance, a hazy image appeared. It resembled a boat and a cloud at the same time. Erec thought it was the sea mist, but as it approached it looked like a ghost ship. Wispy figures manned the deck and brought the vessel onto the pebbled beach without a sound.

Erec and his friends followed the Hermit up a plank of blurred wood. Although Erec could see the water right through it, the boat felt firm beneath his feet. Everybody was quiet and somber as the boat left the shore. Cold mist shrouded their faces as they sped away. Soon they could not see the island they came from, only swirls of white and the sea below. The figures steering their vessel were as hard to make out up close as they had been from shore. Erec chose not to look at the—they just made him nervous.

Bethany wrapped her arms tightly around herself, shivering, and Jam's teeth chattered. Only the Hermit looked confident and serene.

Soon a wooded island loomed into view. It was gorgeous, with lush ferns and tangled arbors beyond the small sandy beach. They headed down the plank onto the shore. Erec turned to wave thanks, but the boat had vanished.

"Is this Avalon?" Erec asked.

"It is." The Hermit nodded. "You will want to find the druids' cave in the center of the island. They will help you find your way."

"You're not coming with us?" Jack asked.

"Yes, of course," the Hermit answered with a grin, perfectly aware that his answer could be taken either way.

"Do you mean—?" Jack swung around to ask him, but the Hermit had vanished.

CHAPTER EIGHTEEN
The Singing Crystal

BETHANY SAID, "THAT'S just the way he is. He'll be
around when we need him."

They trudged through thickets, shoving their
way through ice-covered heather, bilberry, and
gorse. After pushing through a stand of prickly
pines, they found themselves in a forest of massive oak trees. Gray
sky peeked through the bare branches as they walked in silence,
scarves around their faces. While everyone else's feet sank into

the dead leaves and small patches of snow, Erec's Sneakers did not make a single footprint.

As the group walked toward the center of the small island, Erec began to feel irate. He could not put a finger on why, but for some reason he was annoyed with everyone. Bethany shot him a foul-tempered glance. How dare she! Erec raged inside. He went out of his way to let her come here, and this was how she repaid him? By being snooty? Even Jam wore a look of long-suffering annoyance. Erec rolled his eyes. Why did he bother with these jokers? He should have come alone, like he'd planned. Or, even better, not even bothered with this stupid quest. How come it always had to be him dealing with everything? What did he get out of it?

Soon they found a cave entrance in the side of a steep hill. After sneering at his freezing friends, Erec walked right in. Why bother knocking, he thought. After coming all this way, whoever was here had better see him, and now. The group pushed their way in after him, jostling one another and trading dirty looks.

A boy wearing a long gray robe over a floor-length brown tunic appeared with a huge oak staff in his hand. He looked like he was about sixteen. Soft brown hair tumbled around his face, but his bright blue eyes were narrow slits. "America. Alypium. Aorth." He scanned the crowd. "Who said you could barge into my home? You think it's a tourist trap? Get your ugly mugs out of here and go back home." He pointed out of the cave with a scowl.

Rage overtook Erec, making him forget he had been annoyed with his friends. All his frustration spilled out onto this rude boy. "This is the thanks we get? We came all the way out here to do something good, to help people. Something important. Not that you would understand anything about that, living in some cave."

"Out!" the boy shouted. "That's it. Out of here. Now." He started herding them out the door with his staff.

But a boy with sandy blond hair rushed into the room at the front of the cave, screaming at him. "You idiot! Is this how you treat our guests? You never do anything right. Can't you be nice for once?" He hopped on his feet, fists clenched, looking ready to spring.

This shifted the brown-haired boy's concentration away from Erec and his friends. He threw his staff to the floor. "That's it, Dagda. I'm not taking any more of your garbage. You don't know your own head from a can of rotten potatoes." He shoved Dagda, hard, and the two fell to the floor, tumbling over each other, fighting.

As their fists flew, it took everything that Erec had not to join in kicking or pounding one or the other of the boys. He didn't even know who he was siding with, they both made him so angry. Jam was clenching his fists too, and Jack looked fierce.

Bethany ran over and kicked the blond boy in his side. "Get up!" she shrieked. "You nasty jerks, treating each other like this when we're standing here. We've come a very long way, and we don't need this."

The two boys rose and looked down at her menacingly, clenching their fists. "Who are you to come into our home, shout at us, and kick me?" Dagda, the blond boy, said.

Erec stepped in front of Bethany. "If you have something to say to her, you better say it to me." He wanted to fight these rude strangers, even though it occurred to him it wasn't the right thing to do.

"Gladly." The dark-haired boy raised a fist.

But then a girl's voice shouted from the cave entrance. "Look at you, Lugh. Nasty as ever." A beautiful girl stood, hands on hips, her gleaming long red hair blowing in the wind.

The boys looked at her bitterly. Even Erec felt angry at her, although he was not sure why. "We sent you away, Brigid," Lugh, the dark-haired boy, said. "You're not welcome here anymore."

"You sent Dagda away last week, and now look at him." Brigid pointed at the blond boy.

Everyone turned to look at Dagda, who faced the crowd, seething like a cornered animal. He pointed at Erec's group. "Let's get rid of them first, then we'll talk about it."

"No," Brigid said. "I want to hear why they came." She glared at Dagda, then looked at Erec as if challenging him to come up with something good.

Erec tried to collect himself before speaking. This was going terribly. He would try to explain that they were supposed to get the help of the druids to find the Awen. And then he would tell them that if they were the druids, he was terribly disappointed and would give up now rather than have to deal with them one more minute. . . . No, that wasn't right.

Then Erec's mother's voice echoed through the cave. "Hi, sweetie! Just checking up on you, dear. Everything okay?"

Nobody but Erec could hear her, so they all looked at him, surprised, when he shouted, "You again? Just leave me alone! I can't get two things done here without you bothering me." He fumed. "After how miserable you made my life, changing my looks, not telling me who my father is, or anything about my birth mother, and making all my old friends forget I existed, you think you'd cut me a break. But no, you just keep right on messing me up."

June's voice was shaky. "Sorry, then. If that's how you feel, I'll talk to you another time."

"It is how I feel. Go away."

Everyone snarled at Erec, but Bethany waved it off. "Ignore him," she said. "He's an idiot."

Jam finally provided the introductions. Each word sounded controlled and difficult. "We just need to find the Awen and take them away from you." Even though Jam tried his best, his words came out sounding negative. Erec waited for them to start fighting with Jam.

But the three kids in the cave looked stunned. Lugh dropped to the ground and hugged his knees to his chest. Brigid approached and looked at them curiously. "You'll take them?"

Erec glared at her. Why was she looking at him like he was some specimen? "Steal them from you," he corrected. He wanted to make her angry, for some reason.

But instead she backed up, as if afraid, and hugged herself against the cave wall.

"They can't do it," Dagda spat. "Look at 'em. Bunch a' idiots."

"Shut up, Dagda," Brigid whispered harshly. "Not now." Then she pointed down the tunnel that led deeper into the cave. "Get away, Dagda, Lugh. You'll ruin it. Go. Let me help them."

"Shut up, Brigid," Lugh said. "Don't tell me what to do."

They started to fight again, but Jam snarled, "We need to take your Awen away from you. Will you *find* it within yourselves to help us?"

Lugh stood and began to wildly wave his arms in circles, what looked like a desperate pantomime. Erec was annoyed, but Lugh and Brigid fell quiet. "Backward," he finally said. "Opposites. It's *not* okay to talk in opposites, that's *not* the way this will work. Get it?"

"Duh," Erec said. "Then don't talk in opposites. Why would you want to anyway?" He turned to his friends to laugh at Lugh for being so stupid. But his friends only threw him back mean looks, which made him feel worse.

"*You're* being stupid, Erec." Bethany said. "He's trying to give us a clue. If you had half a brain cell, you'd figure that out."

Lugh smirked at Erec and continued. "You are not Erec." He pointed at Erec. "This is not a cave." He gestured around the cave.

Okay, Erec thought. I got it. Let's get on with this dumb game.

But Lugh seemed less annoying as he spoke. "You are *not* welcome here, and we do not want to help you. We absolutely don't want you to take the Awen, and we won't show you where the Path of Wonder is. If you choose to get the Awen, we will make it as difficult as we can, and will certainly not reward you."

So, they wanted to help. That calmed Erec down a bit. Everyone looked more relaxed.

"Why do you have to talk in opposites?" Erec asked. "Are you stupid or something?" He wasn't sure why he threw that last bit in, except that it seemed to be the case.

A room full of angry eyes shot at Erec. The response he got filled him with rage. How dare they judge him like that?

With obvious effort, Lugh continued, speaking again in opposites. "I do *not* talk in opposites, because it does not help communicate here. If I did speak in opposites, everybody would be very angry with me." He took a breath, concentrating. "The Awen here is weak. It did not put a curse on us. The Awen on Avalon is not called 'Harmony.' It did not destroy our harmony.

"We cannot trick it for a while by speaking in opposites. Otherwise the Awen makes us helpful and nice."

His voice calmed Erec, like a warm blanket on a cold day. Why had he sounded so shrill before?

Bethany took a stab at it. "My name is not Bethany Cleary. We are not here to take your Awen. We don't want it." She looked satisfied. Erec was glad she sounded like herself again, and he wanted to give her a hug.

"Why don't you always talk in opposites then?" Jack asked. "Not smart enough?"

It took all of Erec's control not to pounce on Jack and fight him. Why did he bring Jack along, anyway? How stupid could he be not to speak in opposites, and rile everyone up?

"Do not talk in opposites," Jam instructed him, "or we will not ignore you."

Lugh said, "We *can* talk in opposites all the time. It is possible." He shook his head. "We do not save it for important things." He motioned to the cave floor and they sat in a circle. "But you can easily get the Awen. It is simple. How will you not do it?"

Erec thought a moment. Was Lugh saying that it would be too hard for them? He reached into his backpack and pulled out the singing crystal.

Lugh, Brigid, and Dagda grinned. Erec could feel the room lighten.

"That is not a singing crystal." Dagda pointed. "You will not be able to collect the Awen with that."

Brigid looked concerned. "Other people have not come with singing crystals and not taken the Awen. But the Awen never came back each time. And we want the Awen to return back here, and along the Path of Wonder where they do not lie now. It is very easy to keep the Awen from coming back here again."

So, Erec thought, it was hard to keep the Awen from returning to where they started, even if they collected them with the singing crystal. "How can we not keep the Awen away from you forever?" he asked.

"I know." Brigid shrugged.

Erec thought he might have the answer. The reason people had taken the Awen in the past, he supposed, was to hook it to the Twrch Trwyth and become all-powerful. They all had died in the process. But he was only doing it to complete his quest. So this time might be different. If he could do what he was supposed to do and live through it, the Awen could stay locked into the Twrch Trwyth forever to hold the Substance together on earth.

But who was he kidding? How could he do it if everyone else had failed? Most of them had been powerful sorcerers, and he could barely do any magic at all. Plus, the Twrch Trwyth was long gone.

"I know, too," he said. "It's easy. I won't try, though. I won't give it my best shot." A new thought came to him. "But there is not a chance that I'll have luck. The Fates are against me."

The kids brightened at this news. "We won't tell you the way, then," Brigid said. "The Path of Wonder is short. You must collect the Awen here first, and get them as you go out there, not as you come back."

Dagda nodded, tossing his blond hair over his shoulder. "Take them as you go, not on your way back," he agreed. "They are very easy to hold, so you want to carry them for as long as possible. And you want to keep as many of them with you as you can at the same time."

Brigid said, "Don't find where they are on your way out along the Path of Wonder. They are easy to find, so learn where they are at the last minute."

Bethany concentrated, getting the negatives straight in her mind. "We will not go. Should we not go now or not wait?"

"Don't go now," Lugh said. "You want to stay here. It will help you to be here."

Erec agreed with that statement. Being here was terrible. He could not wait to leave.

Brigid leaned forward. Her green eyes looked serious. She pointed around the room. "Be careless. The Awen are easy to carry. Each one will not impart on you its blessing. And when you hold it, the Awen will not have a much stronger effect on you."

The idea of holding one of these things sounded awful. "You must have no clue where your Awen is here on the island?" he asked.

"We don't," Lugh agreed. "Don't follow me. I can't show you now."

With that backward invitation, they set off. They trooped after Lugh about ten minutes, breaking frozen branches along their way. Erec's crystal began to hum like a tuning fork as they neared a bubbling stream. Lugh pointed down at a large rock. "It's not under there. Don't remember where we are."

They all looked around, taking note of the scenery. Jam pulled a paper from one of the pockets of his formal black coat and jotted a note.

"Don't lift the rock," Brigid said, pointing. "So you can't see what the Awen looks like."

Erec took a deep breath and tilted the rock upward. His crystal rang in a grand sounding chord. Under the stone was a many-sided ball that glistened red. Black symbols were printed on each of its many faces.

"It's not a dodecahedron," Brigid said. "It does not have twelve sides. Not a magical number."

Erec recalled the twelve segments on his amulet and nodded.

"Touch it," Brigid commanded. Slow on the uptake, Jack reached a finger toward it, but she slapped him away with a stern look.

"Oops," Jack said.

They walked back to the cave, Erec noting the way they had come. Lugh said, "Do not get this Awen at the end of your journey. Now I will not show you where the Path of Wonder ends." He motioned them to follow him to another cave entrance farther in the woods. This was much smaller, a hole they would have to crawl through.

"Where will this not take us?" Bethany asked.

"It does not go to an ugly island in the South Pacific that has a name," said Brigid. "Then you will not go to Geirangerfjord in Sunnmøre, Norway, the Great Wall in China, and the Andes mountains, which are not in Peru, and not in that order."

"Are people happy and content in these places?" Bethany asked. "Do they not speak in opposites?"

Lugh had to consider that question. "The other places each do not have their own problems from the Awen placed there."

Brigid said, "This is not the order of the Awen." She ticked off her fingers. "Not the Awen of Harmony, not the Awen of Knowledge, not the Awen of Creation, not the Awen of Sight, and not the Awen of Beauty. They all have the same blessings."

Lugh pointed at Erec's backpack. "Do not get your crystal out now. When you do not go through the next exit, you will not be affected by the Awen of Knowledge. You will not lose your knowledge. Do not follow your crystal. Do not remember to follow your crystal. Do not tell yourselves to do that now, again and again." He pointed around the group. "None of you."

Erec wondered what losing his knowledge meant. But he held his crystal and concentrated. *Follow this. Follow the crystal. Follow the crystal.*

The others stared at the crystal, deep in thought. Then they thanked Lugh and his friends, "No thanks to any of you." "No thanks." And they climbed, one by one, through the small tunnel.

The tunnel was long and rocky, and it hurt Erec's knees. But even though he was sore, he felt incredibly better. "Hey, everyone!" he called behind him. "All okay now?"

A chorus of yeahs and cheers erupted through the tunnel. Erec thought his own mood was even lighter than usual, probably because of how great it felt to have left the Awen of Harmony behind them. "Remember everyone," he said, "follow the crystal. I don't know what the next Awen will do to us, but—" Words fell away from his mouth as the tunnel exit approached. The landscape was beautiful.

He stopped and sat in the hole of the tunnel exit, unaware that he was blocking everyone's way. Beautiful smells from bright and pretty flowers filled the air. A waterfall cascaded down a mountainside. Before him spread a sandy beach. The weather was hot so he dropped his parka in the sand.

His friends pushed out behind him, and soon a pile of coats formed on the ground. They all gazed at the beauty around them. A long while later, Erec felt hungry. "I want food."

"So do I," a few others agreed. But they all looked around, unsure what to do about it.

"I want a hamburger," Erec said. Then he smelled a hamburger. The scent made him hungry. It was coming from his backpack. He opened it, and a hamburger sat on a silver tray. He grabbed the hamburger and started eating it.

"I want a hamburger," Jack said. He looked in Erec's backpack and saw one on a tray and grabbed it.

"I want one too," Bethany, Melody, and Jam each repeated, and each, in turn, found a burger waiting for them, although they had no idea why.

After eating, Jam said, "I think we're supposed to be doing something."

All of them agreed, but none could figure out what it was. Their surroundings were beautiful, but Erec could not put a finger on why. He looked in his backpack again and saw the crystal.

"Wait a minute," he said. "Follow the crystal." He grinned, holding it up.

"Follow the crystal!" There were joyous shouts of agreement, but nobody seemed to know what to do next. Erec concentrated as much as he could, which was difficult. The crystal. Follow it. What did that mean?

As he held the crystal, it made a humming sound. Then he felt it pull him toward the small tunnel opening next to them. He walked forward, holding it, and climbed into the tunnel.

After crawling a little ways in he sat down. What had happened? His usual thoughts crowded into his mind again. The Awen of Knowledge had made them forget the simplest things. They were lucky that the Serving Tray had given them food, or they might have sat there and starved to death.

He was supposed to follow his crystal to find the Awen on that tropical island, and then the next passage along the Path of Wonder. It seemed impossible. For starters, the crystal had led him back here, where he had come from. It was probably just as attracted to the Awen they had left as the one they would find next. Maybe if he jumped out far from the cave entrance and started walking with it, then it might take him to the next one. It seemed the only way.

But he had to get his friends to follow him and take their coats and backpacks, too. With intense resolve, he put the words in his head. "Get coats and backpacks. Follow me. Get coats and backpacks. Follow me."

He hurried through the tunnel and took a few steps away from it. "Get coats and backpacks. Follow me. Get coats and backpacks. Follow me. Get coats and backpacks. Follow me."

He was not sure why he was saying it, but his friends rose to their feet and looked at him in wonder. They picked up the coats and backpacks around them, a few grabbing two, and others taking some from one another. Then they trudged behind Erec.

"Get coats and backpacks. Follow me." Erec repeated it like a chant, walking, or rather, being pulled by the crystal he was holding. The others behind him continued to trade coats and backpacks and walk after Erec like lemmings.

"Get coats and backpacks. Follow me." The crystal in his hand hummed, led him forward. They walked across the beach and behind a huge waterfall. The water sparkled as it tumbled down before them, splashing mist on their faces.

"Get coats and backpacks. Follow me." The crystal pulled him to a pile of pebbles, and it made a clear ringing sound. It pointed at a yellow ball with writing on it, but he did not know how to read.

Should he pick it up? No, nothing was telling him to. He didn't know what to do now. Except keep chanting. "Get coats and backpacks. Follow me."

Behind the shiny yellow ball was a hole in the wall of rock. Erec had gone into a hole like that before. He held his crystal toward it and felt a tiny tug. "Get coats and backpacks. Follow me."

His followers traded their coats and backpacks again, then climbed after him into the hole.

CHAPTER NINETEEN

A Proposal

AFTER CRAWLING A few yards through the rocky
tunnel, Erec's head cleared. He stopped, and the
others did as well. "We better talk now, in here,"
he said. "I don't know what it'll be like the next
place we go."

Everyone tried to sit up as best they could. Jam pulled a
notepad from his pocket. "I wrote down the places we're going
and the order of the Awen."

Bethany smiled. "Always prepared. Thanks, Jam."

"I wasn't prepared for that Awen of Knowledge. Truly sorry, modom."

"That was pretty powerful magic," Erec said. "I'd be shocked if you could have done much about that."

Jack looked down at his stomach. "Did I eat a hamburger?"

Erec bit his lip. Jack must have forgotten he was a vegetarian.

Jam read from his list. "The places—Avalon, where we started. Then an unnamed island in the South Pacific."

"I know why it doesn't have a name," Jack said. "Nobody there could think to name it."

"I don't think anyone could survive there," Melody said. "They'd forget how to get food and water."

"I didn't see any animals there," Bethany agreed.

"Next we will be in Geirangerfjord in Sunnmøre, Norway," Jam said. "It's cold there. Thank you for making us take our coats, Erec."

Erec laughed. "After I was back on the island, I didn't even know what I was saying. I guess the trick was to put a phrase in my head and just keep repeating it out loud. You guys did whatever I said."

"It's funny," Jack said. "I had no idea what else to do. I was just glad you had a clue."

"We'll have to remember that trick on the way back," Melody said.

Erec thought about that. The way back. They would have to pick up the Awen of Knowledge and find their way back to the other cave. How in the world would they do that?

"This is going to be rough," Bethany said. "Remember Brigid said the Awen would have a much stronger effect on us when we're carrying them."

There was silence as they each thought how difficult it would be. "Where do we go after Norway?" Erec asked.

Jam read, "The Great Wall of China—I've always wanted to see that—then the Andes Mountains."

"What are they?" Jack asked.

"The Great Wall runs through China," Erec said, "a country in Upper Earth. It's supposed to be beautiful, but it's really long. Like a thousand miles or something."

"Four thousand one hundred and sixty miles," Bethany recited. "Six thousand five hundred kilometers." Then she glanced around shyly. "Sorry, I tend to remember numbers."

"I don't remember why it was built," Erec said.

"Why, to protect the ancient empire," Jam said. "And the Andes Mountains run through the west side of South America. We will be in Peru, home of the ancient Incas. A lot of magic still exists there, I heard."

"Wait a minute." Bethany frowned. "So there *is* magic on Upper Earth. Avalon is in Upper Earth—because we got there from the Upper Earth map in the Port-O-Door. All the places where the Awen are have magic. At least they have the Awen, and it sounds like they have other magic too."

Erec remembered the Pro and Contest, the second contest in Alypium last summer. A man in one of the movies thought remote areas in Upper Earth still had magic. Well, he was right.

Erec thought about what they would face next. They had to be prepared this time. "What is the next Awen, Jam?" he asked.

He looked at his list. "Harmony and Knowledge are behind us. Next is Creation, then Sight and Beauty."

"Creation?" Melody said. "I wonder what that one will do."

"Doesn't sound good," Bethany said. "If Harmony caused us to feel the opposite of harmony—"

"Discord," Jam added.

"Yes, discord," Bethany said. "And Knowledge made us have the opposite . . . made us forget everything. Then Creation—"

"Causes destruction," Erec said.

It looked dark when they peered out the hole, so they decided to sleep inside of the tunnel. It seemed safer to approach this next Awen well-rested, and they were unsure what would befall them when they stepped out into the Norwegian fjords. Erec asked the Serving Tray to produce huge marshmallows for each of them to use as pillows, and they managed to get comfortable in their downy parkas on the rock. Jack asked him for another marshmallow pillow after he ended up eating his. "Sorry," he explained. "I was hungry."

When light flooded into the tunnel the next morning, they woke one another and sat up.

"Any ideas before we climb out?" Erec asked.

"Well, we shouldn't lose our minds this time," Bethany said. "And we should be able to get along together. I guess we'll see what destruction does to us."

When they climbed out of the cave, the group was so overwhelmed with the devastating beauty before them they almost did forget everything else. But this time Erec felt completely himself, just like he had in the tunnel, with all his thoughts focused on what came next. It was a great feeling after being near the last two Awen.

They were standing on a small plateau at the edge of a huge forest that ran up the side of a steep hill. Pines and bare-branched, massive spruce trees grew in scattered stands nearby. The sky was the kind of blue that made Erec's heart sing. On the other side of their path, a stark cliff dropped straight into a fjord, a fat water inlet that rolled in from the sea. Across the winding Geirangerfjord, more mountains shot high into the air like tall slices of chocolate cake topped with spruce tree sprinkles.

"So this is Norway," Bethany said in awe.

"Geirangerfjord. In Sunnmøre." Jam nodded, gazing around, stupefied by his surroundings.

Bethany pointed down to the water. "So that's a fjord?"

"I believe it is, modom. They were carved out by glaciers aeons ago."

They pulled their parkas around them. It was freezing, but it didn't feel too bad with the scarves and hats that Jam had put in their backpacks.

"Everyone okay so far?" Erec asked.

Everybody felt fine. Erec took out his singing crystal. "Show us the way." At first the crystal pulled him back toward the tunnel that they had come from, so he walked with it in a new direction. Then he felt another tug, pulling him down a dirt path.

As they trooped in single file, Erec felt a rumbling in the ground. Startled, he looked around. "Do you feel that?"

"Yeah," Melody said. "Is it a glacier coming?"

They didn't see any glaciers in the fjord. "I hope it's not an earthquake," Bethany said.

The rumbling soon turned into shaking as they tramped down the path. Large chunks of earth started breaking off from where they were walking and tumbled down the cliff below.

"Aagh!" Melody screamed, clutching at the tall grasses growing by the path. The ground had broken away from under her, leaving her dangling with one foot on the path and the other waving over a gap.

Jam swung his backpack toward her, keeping his arm through one of the straps. "Grab it, modom."

Melody let go of the grasses with one hand and latched her arm around the other strap. Jam swung her onto the path next to him.

She had tears in her eyes. "Thank you, Jam."

He was embarrassed. "Of course, modom."

The farther they ventured down the path, the more rifts appeared in it. Soon the path disappeared completely, leaving only jagged dirt islands hovering on the remains of the slope. They hopped from one to the next, careful of slipping. Erec's singing crystal continued to pull them farther into what was quickly becoming a treacherous passage. Small tables of earth were perched on dirt pedestals high in the air, and none of them seemed stable.

A low rumble grew louder, and the small patch Erec stood on began to shake. "Watch out!" Bethany shouted, pointing up. A huge boulder was bouncing down the steep hill above them. Jam yelped, then leaped over a rift onto the cracked dirt where Erec stood. The boulder smashed right where Jam had been, taking the entire piece of cliff down with it.

Shaken by the near miss, they moved slower, stepping carefully over yawning crevices and chasms. Far below, the fjords washed away all evidence of the destruction from above.

"This was a good place to put the Awen of Creation," Bethany said. "At least there aren't people out here for it to hurt."

"'Cept for us," Jack muttered.

Finally, the singing crystal led Erec to an immense cave that looked like it had been blown out of the side of the cliff. The wide, round cave had a roof and walls, but it had no floor, only the sea channels racing about a mile below them. In the center stood a small round perch, just big enough to support several people. Some kind of bird's nest rested in its center.

The perch was supported only by an arm of earth reaching from the cliff side below. A single, scraggly footpath led from where they stood to the center perch. It was a thin wedge of dirt atop a narrow ledge.

Erec's crystal pulled him toward the center. "Stay here," he said. "I don't know if this will support all of us. Let me just make sure the Awen is in there."

He took a few steps out on the path, then felt something shaking under his feet. He hurried forward, but the dirt under him was turning. He tripped, grabbing the earth to break his fall and straddled it under him. A large chunk fell away behind him. He scrambled onto the center perch and waved at the group facing him across the divide, showing them he was okay.

The singing crystal rang a brilliant note. In a huge abandoned nest rested a black dodecahedron. Sunlight gleamed off its many sides, making the black carved markings on them barely visible.

Taking this thing out of here would not be easy. Erec backed away fast, then carefully trod down the thin dirt path to cross the ravine. As soon as he stepped over a new break in the path, a loud crack sounded, then another. Huge chunks of earth fell away before and behind him. He crawled across what was left of the trail, hopping over the gaps.

When he neared the end, eight hands were reaching for him. He let them drag him onto solid ground. When he looked back, the thin trail of dirt had fallen away, leaving just wedges, like stepping-stones.

Erec held the crystal out, ignoring its pull back to where he had come from. After walking awhile he felt a new tug. Soon, before them opened another small stone tunnel.

When they were all safely inside the passageway, they rested against its stone walls. "That was terrible," Melody said. "I think that was the worst of all."

"I'm not sure," Jam said. "The Awen of Knowledge put us in just as much danger. The only difference is that we were not aware of it at the time." He drummed his fingers, thinking ahead as always. "We're going to need some rope when we go back there. A lot of rope, I think."

"What's next?" Jack sounded uncertain, still shaken by all the avalanches. "I can't wait to hear."

"The Awen of Sight," Jam said. "At the Great Wall of China."

"I've always wanted to see the Great Wall of China," Bethany said, excited. "Even though the last Awen was terrible, the fjords were amazing."

"I'm not sure you'll get to see the Great Wall," Erec said. "Considering the Awen of Sight is there. I can imagine we won't see much."

"Maybe it's just our insight that will be damaged. Or our foresight," Melody said.

"We'll just have to see," Jam said. "But I say we take out the Serving Tray and have some lunch before going on."

They passed the tray around, sharing what amounted to a feast, then put it back into Erec's backpack. After crawling through the tunnel, they stepped out into a dense fog. Mists whirled around them. They unzipped their parkas, feeling too warm. Erec took his off, but the wind quickly chilled him and he put it back on again. It seemed to be under fifty degrees, but much warmer than Norway had been.

A lone ginkgo tree towered over them, but beyond that, all was blurred. Erec took his singing crystal out and let it tug him forward. "Follow me," he called.

The group wound in a tight trail down a grassy hill. Soon, a huge dark shadow hovered before them. Erec wasn't sure if it was the Great Wall of China itself or some castle or fortress. It might have been a giant storm cloud that reached down to the ground. Hearing chattering voices, he steered closer and could make out human forms walking through the mist.

He called out to them, "Hello? We're visitors here. Is the Great Wall of China here?"

There was no response. As Erec walked closer to them, the mists closed around him, making it harder to see. Only when he was practically on top of them could he make out who they were.

Three hunched old figures walked slowly, batting long canes against the ground in front of them. Two were women and one was a man who had short gray hair poking from under his cap. They were toothless and wrinkled, and they stood still, peering back and forth in the fog with closed eyes.

One of the women started to speak in hushed tones. Erec could not understand a word of the language she spoke, but he had the feeling she was wondering about the noise he made.

"Hello?" he said quietly, standing at her side.

She jumped back in terror, eyes still shut.

"Do you, by chance, have some rope, modom?" Jam asked her.

The woman gaped around her, eyes shut, confused.

"She's blind," Bethany said. "They all are."

"And they can't understand English, it seems," Jam said. "I think we best leave them alone. We're frightening them."

Erec let his crystal pull him toward the towering shadow, and his friends followed. "I hope when we get this Awen out of here, they'll be able to see again."

"I wonder why we can see here and they can't," Jack said.

"Maybe we'd become like that too, after a while." Erec said. The singing crystal pulled him farther until the darkness morphed into a humongous stone wall. Wedges of earth and mortar cemented the stones in place. It towered over twenty feet tall, but more impressive, it blended as far as they could see into the mist around them.

"This must be it." The crystal pulled him to a crack in a stone. Erec tugged at it, and a rock came out in his hand. A beautiful chord rang from his singing crystal. Under the rock rested another dodecahedron, a few inches in diameter like the others. This one seemed to glow an eerie blue, though Erec could not be sure. When he looked at it, his vision fuzzed.

He placed the rock back and let the crystal pull him farther. "Stay with me," he called. Each of them held the shirt of the person who walked in front of them. Erec took the lead. Soon they reached the small entrance of a rocky tunnel cut into the side of a grassy hill.

After a brief rest in the tunnel, they climbed out onto a perch in the mountains. It was hot, so they all dropped their coats by the tunnel entrance. Bethany pointed out that it was summer in the southern hemisphere now. Erec was glad to be able to see what was happening around him again.

"Where are we, Jam?"

"The Andes Mountains in Peru."

Something seemed odd, although Erec could not put a finger on it at first. He knew that Bile, the powerful old druid who had invented the Awen, had designed the Path of Wonder to pass through his favorite places. But something about this place did not seem as majestic as the others.

Erec checked off a list in his mind. Craggy brown mountains reaching for the sky? Yes. Bright blue overhead with fluffy white clouds? Yup. Wooded hillsides, a condor swooping in the sky, snow-capped ridges above, and tropical forests in valleys below? Uh-huh. Well, then, what was wrong?

A bright orange bird perched on a rock, staring at them, its head tilted. Something was also wrong with this parrot, or whatever it was. It just looked . . .

Ugly. The bird looked hideous. The whole setting was somehow plain and disappointing. "I don't get it," Erec said. "I thought the Andes mountains were supposed to be beautiful."

"I'm sure they are," Jam said. "Just not in this spot. The Awen of Beauty is close by. It wouldn't affect the whole mountain range."

When Erec looked farther in the distance, he could see that the mountains were, indeed, beautiful. But everything close by looked unappealing. Well, he thought, if this was the only problem they would have with this Awen, he could handle that. This one must be the easiest to deal with.

Erec let his singing crystal lead him along a path carved into the mountainside. It felt good walking on solid ground without worrying about crashing into fjords a mile underfoot. He looked back to make sure everyone was okay, then tripped and stumbled when he caught sight of them. His friends looked terrible. Erec stopped and swung around, concerned.

"Are you all okay?" It didn't seem so. Bethany's cheeks and forehead swelled with blotchy red marks and sores. Her hair hung oddly, the left half drooping into her face. Jam looked sick, his skin pallid. Dark circles ringed his sunken eyes. Jack looked red and shiny. His skin seemed drawn tightly over his face, and his lips bulged like sausages. Melody's skin was covered with strange growths, and her features had changed so that she looked like a male wrestler.

What was happening to them? Erec wondered. Were they allergic to something?

A horrified expression bloomed on Bethany's distorted face. She squealed, "What is wrong with you? You look awful. Are you sick?"

Erec touched his face. It felt normal. "You all look pretty bad too." They all looked at one another, screeching and jumping. "Hey, guys." Erec was glad at least his voice sounded normal. "Let's try to keep our eyes on the path so we don't have to see each other too much. It's just the Awen of Beauty. No big deal." He turned around, glad to be facing forward with everyone else behind him.

Soon they approached a village. Small circular homes with round stone walls were topped with thatched roofs of dried grasses. People spinning wool, husking beans, chewing on sugarcane, and tethering unkempt llamas outside their homes stopped what they were doing. Crowding around Erec and his friends, they pointed, laughing, but Erec could not understand their language.

Erec was sure they were giggling at how awful he and his friends looked. But then he got a better view of the villagers. Most of them were shorter than he was. The men wore colorful ponchos with bright geometric designs, and the women wore bright loose skirts and blouses. Beads and pendants hung around their necks. Yet they were so badly put together they were difficult to look at. Their skin seemed to hang off their frames at odd angles. Noses bulged sideways, black teeth jutted forward, scars and warts covered most visible skin. Each was so unpleasant to look at that Erec had to keep shifting his gaze from one to the next.

"Hi," he announced. "We're traveling through, on a quest for something hidden near here. Have you heard of the Awen?" He wondered if the villagers had any idea why they all looked the way that they did.

The villagers seemed not to understand, but they crowded around Erec and his friends, reaching out craggy hands and touching them. Erec began to feel uncomfortable in the crowd and stepped away, pushing a few hands aside.

Some of the villagers pulled a man from one of the houses and shoved him forward toward Erec. The man looked just as awful as the others in the village.

He shook Erec's hand. "I Hakan. I Englis." It took some thought for Erec to decipher from his heavy accent that he was saying he spoke English. "I from Ollantaytambo, near Urubamba. We talk Quechua. I know English from tourist in Ollantaytambo."

Erec was fairly sure that this village would not get many tourists. Tour guides would probably want people to come away thinking how beautiful the Andes were. Not only were the people here difficult to look at, but the village was stark and unappealing.

Hakan nodded his head a few times. "You eat?"

"Um, okay." Erec wasn't looking forward to whatever food they produced, but he did not want to be rude.

Shouts in Quechua resulted in people running in different directions, excited. Soon Erec and his friends were presented with steaming bowls of quinoa laden with potatoes, beans, and corn. It looked terrible, but it actually tasted delicious. Erec found that if he closed his eyes when he was eating, it was a truly wonderful experience.

Hakan explained that this village had a curse. They had offended Pachamama, the Earth Mother spirit, and she had taken their beauty away from them. Hakan said that he once looked nice, but after spending time with the villagers here, he too had been affected. He still managed to fall in love and settle down. "Love deeper than looks." He pointed at Erec and said it again.

They thanked the people and talked about moving on. Erec would be glad to take the Awen of Beauty away from this place. Soon they might experience life differently, see the mountains around them as they were meant to be seen.

Jam paused. "Do you kind people have some rope we might take with us?"

Erec was glad that Jam had remembered to ask. He was sure that some rope would come in handy when they were back in Norway with the Awen of Creation. It was strange, here in the summer heat in Peru, to think that he had just been in freezing Norway.

Hakan spoke in Quechua to the villagers. Soon they were shouting, giggling, and slapping each other on the backs. Hakan turned to Erec with a grin. "We have rope. You can have. But trade. Rope for you."

"Rope for me?" Erec repeated, shaking his head to show he did not understand.

Hakan pointed at a girl who stood under a thatched roof of one of the nearby homes. "That Chinpukilla. She like you lot. She need marry now. Want you marry."

Erec choked. Never mind the fact that Chinpukilla looked like a cross between Godzilla and a slimy giant slug. Never mind that he would sooner kiss Tina, his many-eyed Hydra friend, than this human. Regardless of all that, Erec was not in the market to get married. He was a bit young. And staying here, or carting his new wife around with him, was not an option.

"I . . . don't think so." He put his hands up in front of him. "I mean, no offense, but—"

"Chinpukilla love Rec. She never see so beautiful man ever."

Bethany made a gagging sound near Erec.

"Thanks for the vote of confidence, Bethany," he said.

"Not like any of us look good now," she said.

It was true. Erec knew he must look terrible. But compared to these people, living near the Awen of Beauty for their whole lives, he probably looked like a movie star.

A man walked forward with a stern look, calling out something in Quechua. Hakan said, "This Qhawana. He Chinpukilla father. You new father."

"Not so fast," Erec said. "I can't get married. I'm sorry."

Hakan spoke to Qhawana and then said to Erec, "We give you rope, three llama, and new house. Okay?"

"No!"

Hakan and Qhawana had a quiet conversation. Erec was glad he could not understand them. Then Hakan said, "Rope, four llama, house, and corn patch. Final offer."

"Think hard, Erec," Bethany said.

Jack laughed. "Drive a harder bargain, dude. Maybe you can get them to throw in a little money, too. Hey, that's an idea. Maybe we could trade you for the rope, some money, and some more of that great stew. Sounds like a fair trade to me."

"Shut up."

Hakan looked like he was considering Jack's words. Erec said, "I'm not getting married. Sorry. Could you give us the rope anyway? We're trying to take this Awen away and help you out."

"Awen?" Hakan looked confused. "No marry, no rope."

Jam bowed to Hakan. "Sir, we will think about your kind offer. We must go now on our errand. When we come back we will discuss it."

After they left, Jam said, "They have rope. Now we just need a plan to get it from them."

"But first, the Awen of Beauty," Erec said. They followed the singing crystal around the mountainside into an area that looked even uglier than what they had just seen. "It must be this way."

CHAPTER TWENTY
The Awen of Creation

NASTY STEEL-GRAY ROCK jutted up on either side of the barren path. Erec tried not to look at his friends; their features were becoming coarser and more disturbing. He knew he must look awful as well, but at least he felt fine.

The singing crystal's pull grew stronger, leading him to a small hole in a rocky ledge under an orchid tree. The tree was in bloom, but its flowers looked like droopy red welts. Erec felt sick looking at it.

Right inside the hole sat a shining green dodecahedron. Black symbols gleamed from its twelve faces. Although the chord ringing from his singing crystal sounded clear and beautiful, the Awen itself looked nasty.

Fear gripped Erec for a moment. He had yet to touch one of the Awen. Would it permanently affect him? Well, there wasn't much choice, and he'd come a long way. He reached in and grabbed it, but it would not move from its spot.

Erec remembered that Lugh had said removing the Awen was almost impossible without the singing crystal. He had called the crystal the master of the Awen. So Erec touched his crystal to the Awen of Beauty. That did the trick. The green twelve-sided object rose from its crevice, lifted by the tip of the crystal into the air, and then dropped into Erec's hand.

Erec felt a rush of satisfaction. He had done it! This quest was possible after all. Soon all of these cursed places would be fixed again.

He spun around with a grin. Melody looked at him and screamed, and Bethany gagged and fainted. Jack, after one glance at Erec, retched several times into the grass. All of them looked even worse than before, so Erec figured he must too.

Jam turned away, a hand out as if to ward off the sight of Erec. His voice shook. "Are you okay, young sir?"

"I'm fine," Erec said. "I look that bad?"

Jam nodded, facing away. "Put the Awen in your backpack, if you please. Maybe that will help."

Erec dropped the green glowing dodecahedron into his backpack. "Any better?"

After a quick glimpse, Jack said "no" and threw up again.

"How bad can I look?" Erec asked. It seemed impossible to look bad enough to cause the reactions his friends were having.

Melody's hand sheltered her face from him. "Let's just say the new you features a lot of pus, bones, and bugs."

Erec's hands flew to his face without thinking. What he touched felt nothing like a face at all. But at least it didn't hurt him. "I'll walk ahead of you so you won't have to see me."

"Don't look at his back, either," he heard Bethany say, choking.

As they followed Erec's footsteps up the path, Erec's mom's voice echoed around him. "Listen, Erec. I'm really upset ab—" She gasped, then screamed. After some sputtering, Erec heard nothing else.

"Mom?" There was no answer. She must have taken the glasses off.

Then her voice reappeared and she gagged, crying. "What happened to you? Oh, Erec!"

He stopped and covered his face. "Don't look at me, Mom. Just listen to my voice. I'm fine. I just look bad because I picked up this Awen. It will go away. I promise." He thought back to the last time they had talked, and he said, "I'm really sorry about what I said to you before. There was another Awen there making everyone angry. I didn't mean any of it."

Erec heard her breathing hard. She spoke slowly, "Well, I'm glad you're not mad. Are you sure you're not hurt?"

"I'm fine. Just forget what you saw here. It's not real. Okay? I'll talk to you later."

She murmured something and then was gone.

Jam said, "I think getting the rope may be easier than we thought. Do you agree, Erec? Maybe young Chinpukilla will be less inclined to marry you now."

Erec laughed. "I'll tell her I agree to the wedding. See what she thinks."

When they got to the village, Erec paused and let the others go ahead of him. He heard Jam explain to Hakan how much they needed the rope and how Erec had agreed to marry Chinpukilla.

"But I warn you," Jam said. "Your curse here is not affecting him well at all."

When Erec walked into the village, people ran away, screaming. Chinpukilla put her hand over her mouth and ran off like she was being hounded by dogs.

Sweating, Hakan said to Jam, "You must take him away. He will bring greater curse. He not stay here."

Jam looked like he was considering the suggestion. "Are you sure Chinpukilla will get over it?"

Chinpukilla was now shrieking to the mountains.

"Yes, yes." Hakan nodded. "Take him away."

Jam scratched his chin. "Hmm . . . I suppose we could, if you give us a lot of rope."

"Yes. Rope." Hakan rushed into the village. Soon everyone was carrying coils of rope out to them. "Please, take." Erec and his friends grabbed as much as they could carry and then headed toward the tunnel.

"Thank you," Jam said as he left. "I think your Earth Mother spirit will forgive you for doing such a good deed."

The singing crystal pulled Erec ahead toward the rocky tunnel leading back to the Great Wall of China. He grabbed his parka and climbed in first, facing away from everyone else, and hanging his hood over his head to shield himself from their view.

Still, groans echoed in the tunnel behind him. "I think we all look a lot worse now," Bethany said. "I mean, nothing near as bad as Erec." Then after a pause she called ahead, "Sorry, Erec."

"It's okay," he said. "Just as long as it goes away eventually."

They passed around the Serving Tray, but this time they did not share the food it produced with each other. All of them ate with their eyes closed, which was the only way they could enjoy their meal. The Awen of Beauty made their food look bad, and looking at each other was enough to turn their stomachs.

"Maybe we should talk with our eyes closed too," Melody said, relieved.

"Great idea," Bethany agreed. "Hey, Melody, could I ask you a favor?"

Suddenly, Erec remembered what Melody's gift was. He knew what Bethany was about to ask her for, and he fully approved.

"Yeah?" Melody asked.

"Could you play us something? This trip has been a little intense. And we don't know what tomorrow holds. It would be so nice and relaxing. If you don't mind, I mean."

Everyone born in the Kingdoms of the Keepers had a magical gift. Erec's gift was his cloudy thoughts, and Bethany's was her mathematical ability. Jack could talk to animals, and Jam was always prepared. Melody's gift was exceptional. She could produce the most beautiful music Erec had ever heard.

Soon, a mesmerizing, gorgeous refrain filled the tunnel. Erec immediately relaxed. The visual horrors of the day were washed away. He snuck a glance and saw one of Melody's legs sawing over the other like a bow across a violin and her arms and fingers waving through the air. He looked away quickly so nobody would see his face, and also because she appeared grotesque with the Awen of Beauty nearby. But with his eyes closed, the music was sweet and perfect. The sounds of violins, oboes, harps, and bells swelled together in perfect harmony. Erec remembered that she could make sounds from even the flutter of her eyelids.

After the concert they all felt considerably better. "Thank goodness the Awen still lets us hear beauty in music," Jam said.

Bethany yawned. "I think we should get some sleep. Tomorrow's going to be rough, I think."

"I wish we could see what people back in the village look like now that we took their Awen of Beauty away," Jack said. "They're probably celebrating."

"And thankful that they sent all their bad luck away with Erec," Bethany said.

They made themselves comfortable on their down parkas, and Erec asked the Serving Tray for big marshmallow pillows for everybody again. One glimpse at the pillows made him disgusted. They were full of gloppy green goo, but they felt comfortable. When he closed his eyes he fell fast asleep.

Erec awoke the next morning to shrieks and shouts. Someone had awakened and screamed upon seeing the others, which had set off a chain reaction. He glanced back to see what was going on, but then everyone's screams turned into sounds of full-fledged terror and gagging.

"Sorry." He looked the other way, putting his hood over his head. "At least where we're going next we won't see each other so well."

"That's a relief," he heard Jack say behind him.

Erec remembered the way to the crevice in the Great Wall, even though the singing crystal was pulling him there anyway. He was glad the mists blocked everything, including his face, from view. It wasn't far. Soon, the immense shadow of the Great Wall of China loomed before him.

"I really hope I can see this someday when the fog is gone," he said. "I'm sure it's amazing."

"It must be," Bethany said, "if that druid guy, Bile, picked this spot for his precious Awen."

Erec jiggled the rock, and again a piece came out in his hand just as his singing crystal struck a chord. Behind it was a hazy blue glow. If he squinted at it he could see that it had sides, another dodecahedron. He pulled it, but it did not budge from where it was wedged. Then Erec remembered and touched his crystal to it. The blurry blue object rose in the air at the crystal's tip. He brought it over his hand and let it fall.

All went black. There was not even the hint of shape or color around him. Erec froze. "Guys? You okay?"

"Yeah, sure," he heard Jack say. "'Cept my vision just got worse when you pulled that thing out. Hard to tell for sure through the fog, but the wall looks like a big blur."

"I can't see anything," Erec said, still frozen. "It's solid black."

He could hear discussion around him. Some voices seemed nearer than others. Jam sounded close. "If young sir cannot see holding the Awen of Sight, I will gladly be the one to carry it."

"Thanks, Jam. But I'm okay." Right now, swamped in complete blackness, Erec just wanted to see a glimpse of what was around him again. But he dragged everyone here along with him. It was only right that he should have to bear the burdens of the Awen.

A strange noise came from nearby. It gave Erec the chills, not knowing what it was. Then he heard Jack say, choking, "I can't handle this. Don't walk over here, guys. I just threw up again. I mean, you'd think it would be better not being able to see you as well. But it's worse. I just got a glimpse of Erec, and it was like this distorted, rotting, worm infested corpse-thing coming at me through the mist."

"Time for me to enter a beauty contest, sounds like." Erec said. "Maybe I should compete against Baskania."

"Yeah, you win, hands down." Bethany's voice was choked. "Sorry. I see what Jack's saying. Problem is, it's so hard to see, I can't stop looking at you by accident. Not like looking at anybody here is fantastic now."

Jack sounded annoyed. "It's not fair for you to carry the Awen of Sight, Erec. You're the worst one to look at. Someone else should get to have it. It would be a relief to be blinded if it means I don't have to see you again."

A spurt of laughter popped from Erec's mouth at the idea that he looked so bad his friends might fight over who got to be blinded near him. Unfortunately, the sudden laugh must have made everyone glance his way because he heard more screams, moans, and throwing up.

"I'm happy to give this to someone else," Erec said. "You want it, Jack?"

There was a pause. "You sure nobody else wants it?" Jack's voice said. "I'm happy to take it."

"Go ahead," everyone murmured.

Jam unzipped Jack's backpack and put Erec's hand over its large pocket.

"Now drop it, young sir," Jam said.

The minute that the blue dodecahedron left his hand, vision sprang back to Erec's eyes. But he did not have quite the vision he'd had before. He could see what the others were describing. Even though he was right next to the Great Wall, the stones were blurred and distorted. Jam's red, puffy face seemed to pop out in odd blurs through the mist. It was a frightening effect, and he could imagine how bad looking at himself must have been.

Jack stood still. "I can't see anything."

"Yeah, I know," Erec said. "It's pitch-black when you're carrying that thing. We'll have to lead you out of here."

"Yeah," Jack said. "But it's still a relief that I'm not going to see Erec's face again." He gagged, remembering it. "Hey, no offense, Erec, but could someone else lead me out of here?"

"I think this is a good time to use the rope," Jam said. "We'll need it for sure in Norway, with the earth cracking away under our feet, especially since we can't see well anymore."

That's right, Erec thought. He would have to climb over a crumbling abyss to pick up the Awen of Creation without being able to see well. Chances were, the entire cavern would crumble into the sea a mile below after he picked the thing up. He wasn't sure how they would use the rope, but they definitely needed a plan.

Jam, as usual, proved amazingly helpful. He laid out the ropes and knotted the longest two segments together. With his eyes closed, Jam handed one end of the rope to Erec. "Wrap this twice around your chest, under your arms, and I'll knot it securely at your back." He then measured out four feet of rope and told Bethany to wrap the next coils around herself the same way. After knotting her back, he did the same with himself, allowing another four feet of rope before handing the next part to Jack. "This puts you right between me and Melody," he told Jack. "Erec is way up front, far away from you."

Erec knew this lineup was meant to comfort Jack, and he couldn't get over the strangeness of looking bad enough to inspire that kind of comment. Jam measured out a few more feet and handed the end of the rope to Melody to wrap around herself a few times. He tied some extra knots around Melody's and Erec's rope ends.

"Now, young sir, you will be our leader with your crystal. Jack, I'll keep the rope taut for you to grip. If you need to grab my shoulder it's okay."

Jack held the rope in one hand and Jam's shoulder in the other, taking cautious steps since he could not see what lay underfoot. Blinding mists swirled around them. Erec wished he had a rope to clutch as well. But at least the crystal was pulling him.

After a few steps Erec felt a harsh jerk from the rope, almost pulling him over. Then he heard Bethany's voice. "Sorry, I tripped. I'm okay."

Then Jam called, "If we're in Geirangerfjord and the ground drops out under one of us, it will be best if we can keep the rope taut. That is, if we can all remain standing and not knock each other over. Maybe if we walk slowly on the same count."

This was difficult, but they took turns slowly calling out "left, right, left," until they got used to the rhythm. When someone tripped, the others braced themselves to stay standing. And the ones who did trip didn't fall as far that way. After a while they got better at walking half-blinded without yanking each other down.

The ginkgo tree near the grassy hill looked like a looming monster with sharp claw branches against the gray mist. Erec climbed into the rocky tunnel, and the mist followed them in.

They passed around the Serving Tray in the tunnel. Everyone was unusually quiet. "You all right, Jack?" Erec asked. "We can trade off carrying that Awen of Sight if you want."

"I'm okay," Jack said. "Getting used to it. No use switching now that we're learning how to walk around like this. I'll just get better at it. No, looks like I'm blind and you're ugly for the duration."

"I'm going to be destructive, too," Erec said. "Soon enough. Any ideas on how I can get that next Awen, Jam?"

"I've been mulling over our options, young sir. I actually arranged us in this order for a reason."

Erec smiled. "Glad we have one person who's prepared here. What are you thinking, Jam?"

"Well, it seems when you climbed over the ledge to get to the center of the cavern, where the Awen was, the path disintegrated. If you did it again, you'd surely be stranded in the center."

"And there's only one way down from there," Jack said.

"Thanks, Jack," Erec said. "That helps."

Jam cleared his throat. "Our being tied together like this gives us more . . . length. If one of us is in the middle of the cavern, another can be at the ledge, or near it. And if the ground breaks loose under someone, we can keep them up this way. We just have to move slowly and steadily."

"What if the ground breaks under two or three of us at the same time?" Bethany said nervously. Erec was sure she was calculating their odds.

"Let's not think about that, modom." He paused. "One more thing. I put Melody at the end because she is the lightest. If the ground crashes away under her, we can hold her up easiest, without her dragging us down after her. So she should be the one to lead the way across the path to the Awen of Creation. Erec, Bethany, and I will be on the other end, pulling her to safety."

"Thanks a lot," Jack said. "Am I a weakling now?"

"No," Jam pointed out, "but you are blinded. You will not be able to find a ledge to grasp for safety if necessary."

Jack muttered about being useless baggage, but Erec said, "No way. I can't let Melody go across that bridge first. It's not even a bridge anymore, it's just some crumbled stands of dirt. It's way too dangerous. It's nice enough for all of you to come help me like this, but I can't risk your lives any more."

"Chill out, Erec," Melody said. "Jam makes a lot of sense. I'll be tied with a rope to you all anyway. If I fall in anywhere, we all do."

"That's just it," Erec said. "I don't want you all to fall to your deaths. I'm going to untie myself and do it alone."

"That's impossible, Erec," Bethany said, exasperated. "You know it too. If you're alone in the middle of that cavern you'll be stuck out there forever. And once you pick up the Awen of Creation the whole place will crash in around you. You have to realize that."

Erec closed his eyes. Was there any other way? Then he perked up. "I know! I'll do a dragon call. Maybe Patchouli or one of the other dragons can help me fly across the cavern."

"Not possible, young sir. Dragons cannot come into Upper Earth, dragon call or no."

Erec could not think of what to do. How could he risk the lives of his friends?

"Listen, Erec," Jack said. "You're not the only one who is responsible here. We all need to help. Do you think any of us wants Upper Earth to be destroyed in ten years? This affects everyone."

"Jack is right," Melody said. "We're in this together. None of us are going to let you make a huge mess of things, trying it all on your own. We have a chance of making it work if we do it Jam's way, so that's what we should do."

Erec knew she was right, but it was hard for him to accept. "If we're going to stay tied together, why don't I climb out there first, at least. I have the singing crystal, anyway, so that makes sense."

"Like you can't hand it over to someone else?" Bethany said.

"But what if it doesn't work for other people?" Erec pointed out. "Who knows? It was given to me."

"The singing crystal is the master of the Awen, young sir," Jam said. "Not only for a specific owner, I believe. If you went first and fell in, which you would, we would have less strength at the front of the rope to pull ourselves to safety."

Erec thought about it. "Okay," he finally said. "Thanks, guys."

When they climbed out of the dark tunnel into Geirangerfjord, sunlight blasted Erec's face, making his eyes clench shut. But the mist poured out around them. This time he could not see the spectacular mountains nor the fjords rushing below. Even if the mist was not there, his vision still would have been distorted.

Erec passed the singing crystal to Melody. He was not ready for her shocked and disgusted reaction when she accidentally glanced at his face. "Ugh!" she screeched, almost dropping the crystal.

Erec twisted the rope around his chest so he was facing the other direction, at the end of the line. "Left. Right. Left. Right," they called out, taking slow, sure steps. When the dirt began to crumble around his feet, he stumbled. A chunk loosened below him and in a few minutes he heard a quiet splash. Wavering unsteadily, he grasped the cliff's edge, leaning back against the taut rope to help him stay upright.

A loud crash sounded from above, and at the last second he saw a huge boulder racing down the mountainside. "Duck!" Jam shouted. Everyone crouched as the massive rock bounced over their heads, whistling through the air as it flew by. The length of time before they heard it crash into the waves did not make anyone feel better.

Soon Erec heard a scream and a tug on the rope. He stopped.

"It's okay. I'm okay," Melody said, panting. "Almost fell straight down the cliff. I couldn't see where I was going. We're at the cavern."

Erec wished he could see more than white mist and occasional blurry glimpses of rock that must have been the far wall of the cavern. Jack was quiet, but Erec felt for him. He knew what the breaking path looked like, and now he'd have to cross it blinded.

Then he had an idea. "Why don't we put the two Awen down by the side of the cliff here. That way Jack can see for a while when we climb across the land bridge."

"Awesome." Jack grinned.

But Jam said, "Do you really want to take that risk? With the land crumbling beneath us, the Awen might drop into the fjords. And when we're rushing out, what if we can't find them?"

Jack was quiet a moment. "Would it be better if I untied and sat out here, then? That way I won't mess up and pull anyone down."

"I don't think so," Jam said. "We'll need a longer chain than just four people if things crumble. Plus, you wouldn't be able to protect yourself out here, blinded. The earth might crumble under you."

"Don't worry, Jack," Bethany said. "We're tied together. We won't let you fall." She sounded like she was trying to be brave.

"Just tap with your feet before you set them down," Jam said. "I'll direct you too. We'll all have to concentrate. The ground will be dropping beneath us as we go."

"Let's crawl out there," Erec suggested. They all agreed, dropping to their knees and feeling with their hands on the ground. It felt safer being closer to something solid. Erec could even make out a few distorted blades of grass.

"Step," Jam called to signal a move forward.

Erec felt a huge gap before him. It was only after he reached way ahead that he felt ground. "How did you get across this?" he called to Bethany.

"Feel to the right," she answered. "It's closer."

Sure enough, closer ground lay to his right. All of a sudden, Jack yelled out in terror and Erec felt the rope tug. "You okay?" he called.

"Yeah. I almost fell. . . ."

The five of them crawled a bit more when Melody yelled, "Stop! I'm there." They all held still. Erec could hear the singing crystal ring a chord. Fear raced through him. How fast would everything crumble when Melody picked up the Awen of Creation? Probably right away.

"Wait a minute," he called out. "Before you touch it, Melody, let's all turn around in our ropes and face the other way. That way we can be ready to go."

"Good thinking, young sir." They all twisted and faced back to the cliff edge. Jam said, "Open your backpack, Melody. As soon as you grab the Awen, drop it and the crystal straight into your backpack and zip it. That way you'll have both hands free for climbing."

"Okay," Melody said.

A tense moment passed before she shouted, "Got it! Let's go!"

"Step," Jam called urgently.

Erec grasped the land over the ledge to his right and sprang onto it.

"Unh!" He heard Bethany falling behind him.

An ear-splitting crack echoed through the canyon. Sickening crunches filled the air, rock grinding against rock. Reverberating thuds shook Erec's bones as he struggled forward. He glanced behind him but saw only mist.

A terrified scream burst through the air, and the rope grew tight around his chest. With a jerk it shot to his waist and pulled him backward. Struggling to keep his balance, he tugged the rope from his stomach, and worked it back up to his chest. Still, it was hard to pull. He wondered how many people were dangling. "Get on your knees, everyone," he shouted. "Or the ropes will slide off."

He could not tell what was happening behind him. But as he reached forward he fell awkwardly onto his face, overcome with dizziness. What was happening to him? He needed to concentrate or they would never get to safety. He couldn't lose Bethany, all his friends . . .

He struggled doggedly forward, nearly blind. As he reached for the next patch of grass he saw a rush of motion in his head. It was like a film playing backward, fast. Upper Earth dying. Baskania with scepters. What was happening? His mind spun and he felt like he was falling, clinging to the ground around him. The rope tugged him back and he fought it with all his might.

Then the movie in his head played forward. It was a cloudy thought. He wasn't sure whether to be relieved, though, when he saw what it showed him.

Everything was a green blur of mist with distorted Substance netting the air. They were falling, all of them, crashing into rocks on the cliff sides until the fjords rose to meet them. Some were dead already; the rest would be soon after the crash.

No! Erec raged. This would not happen. Fire shot from his mouth, singeing the ground around him.

The ground! He realized he could see it now with his dragon eyes out. Not as well as usual, but he could see where to go. But then his mind was back in the vision.

The rock wall of the cliff whizzed by as they dropped past. Water shot around them, hard as bricks because of the distance of their fall. He was sucked under, pulled down, his breath leaving him.

Fury surged through his being. This would not happen.

Then the instructions from his cloudy thought were crystal clear. *Grab here.* He dug his claws into a bed of dirt, tugging the rope behind him. *Leap there.* His anger gave him strength to fight. *Twist this way. Then jump onto that perch.*

Erec glanced behind him. With his dragon eyes he could see that Jack and Melody were dangling on the rope, Jack's feet kicking into Melody's face. Jam had a grip on some crumbling earth he'd happened to grab when Erec dragged him over it. And Bethany hung between them, the rope under her arms. Her legs flailed around in a panic.

The ground beneath them cracked, giving way faster than they could walk. The center of the cavern was demolished. It was up to him. He knew what he had to do now. And, odd as it was, it felt perfectly natural. A relief, in fact.

Pounce. **D**ig *into the dirt.*

And then . . .

Fly.

At that moment, Erec took to the air. He felt wings push out from his shoulder blades, tearing through his shirt, beating against the air. As they grew, they pushed the rope lower down his chest, and pushed at his backpack until he had to slide one arm out of it and carry it from the other. He sprang from his hind legs into the air, wincing from the strain of lifting the four behind him. The rope squeezed tight against his chest, which was growing larger. He flapped, pulling himself through the air to the cliff's edge.

When he landed, Bethany, Jam, Jack, and Melody crashed onto solid ground. But the earth caved in under Melody, leaving her hanging again.

He had no time to waste. Erec jumped, clinging with his claws, dragging his friends from spot to spot on the remaining land. He carried them another short distance, flying over the path they had originally followed, knowing just where to go. Soon he saw the rocky tunnel and dove inside.

After crawling a short distance he relaxed. He pulled a dazed and bruised Bethany in behind him.

She gasped when she saw him, and threw her hand up in front of her eyes. "Now you're ugly and have green dragon scales."

When she was safe, he reached around her to help Jam in. "Wait!" he shouted. "Help Jack up, but Melody can't come into the tunnel yet. She'll have to hang on to the rope until we know what we're doing."

Bethany protested. "We can't let her dangle out there. She needs a rest."

Jam shook his head. "Erec is right. The minute we pull her in here with the Awen of Creation, this tunnel will crumble."

They all rested against the rock wall to get their breath.

"I'm okay out here," Melody called in. "At least when I'm hanging in the air, things aren't caving in around me."

Erec could see landslides rushing past her, but Melody was close enough to the ravine's face to avoid them so far. The entire area would be a pile of rubble after this.

Erec felt his dragon eyes revolve back and his regular eyes come out, which meant that his vision was lost again in the mists. Yet his powers had saved them from an impossible situation. They had completed their third step.

The tunnel was filled only with the sounds of quiet breathing. Everyone was afraid to move an inch after what they had been through. Erec faced away from everyone so they wouldn't accidentally look at him.

A strange swirl of yellow and green appeared in the dust between two rocks. It was hard to see, but he was sure a pair of eyes were peeking at him.

"A snail!" He picked it up and pulled a letter out, holding it next to his face so he could read it.

Dear Erec,
Please, please stop writing me. I don't know if you are okay, but

*Rosco appeared again right after I read your letter, and Baskania was
with him. They took it from me, and it seemed like they knew exactly
where you were talking about. Rosco said something about the Fire Pit
volcanoes under Aorth and how that would be a likely place for a quest.
And Baskania knew just where the coldest place on the planet is. They
planned to find you, and then they vanished.*

*If you are still there, you have to be more careful. Sending me a letter
is like sending it straight to Baskania.*

*I am, and will always be, working and planning for the day when
Rosco no longer has his grip on me.*

    Your friend,
    Oscar

Erec read the letter aloud, and Bethany and Jack cheered. "We'll
have to send a few more letters," Erec said happily. "Lead them on a
wild-goose chase. But right now we need a plan to get out of here.
Once we get to the island, we'll all forget what to do. And with the
Awen of Creation with us, we'll just sit there as the land collapses
around us."

Bethany said, thinking aloud, "Last time, we all followed you
when you told us what to do. I still remember you saying, 'Get coats
and backpacks. Follow me,' like it was from another life."

"A simple chant won't be so easy this time," Erec said. "We have
to do several things. Get the crystal. Put it somewhere. Then follow
the crystal to the next tunnel. All the while the Awen of Creation
will be causing destruction around us."

"I've got an idea," Bethany said. "Those of us in the tunnel won't be
affected by the Awen of Knowledge until after we climb out. Melody,
Jack, and Jam can stay in the tunnel and shout out directions."

That seemed like a great idea until Jack said, "Better do it fast, though.
The tunnel will start caving in the minute Melody comes in here."

"I better take the singing crystal now," Erec decided. Melody fished it out of her backpack, and Jam passed it to Erec.

"One other problem," Jack said. "Who's going to hold this next Awen? If it makes us all forget what to do, I'm sure the person holding it won't be able to function at all."

"I'll do it," Bethany volunteered. "I haven't held one yet. And I'm right behind Erec, so he can help me if I need it."

Erec smiled when she said that. So Bethany trusted him the most. Even if turning into a dragon made him kind of a freak, it still was pretty cool what he was able to do. She was proud of him, he was sure, which, for some reason, seemed like the most important thing of all.

CHAPTER TWENTY-ONE
A Furious Butler

BALOR STAIN TREMBLED. Three rows of eyes crossed his father's forehead today. Balor could not help but wonder if he recognized Ward Gamin's or Rock Rayson's among them. Thankfully, he did not.

Candles flickered in the dark sanctuary hidden in the center of the Green House. Ward and Rock stood nearby, sporting identical black eye patches. Dollick was *baa*ing nervously, and Damon was tugging his brother's woolly hair for fun.

Damon said, "I still don't get it. Dad's not dad?"

"Shut up," Balor hissed. "The Shadow Prince is our father. We'll talk about it again later."

Damon looked at Balor quizzically, then approached Baskania with his hand out. "Can I have some money, Pop?"

"Fool," Baskania hissed, and Damon tumbled backward onto his bottom. "I see you two are recovering nicely," Baskania said, glowering at Ward and Rock. "Maybe, if you prove yourselves worthy, I'll take your other eyes one day, and you can join the blind followers at my headquarters."

Rock and Ward exchanged nervous glances with their remaining eyes. It was apparent they would rather be anywhere else.

"It seems the five of you have had no better luck than anyone else in locating Erec Rex or Bethany Cleary," Baskania said. "They may have gone into hiding. It is possible they are working on . . . Erec's next quest. He must have finished his third one, somehow. But the Harpy police gave me his fourth quest—that one is impossible. I saw for myself that Olwen Cullwich does not have what he is looking for." He snorted angrily. "What bothers me the most is that I don't know how he's doing it. How did he finish his third quest? What did he do?"

He stewed in a silence that all of the boys were afraid to break. Then he went on, "I need to find Bethany Cleary and learn her secret. I feel it will be quite important to me. We will have to find another way to draw her here. Find a weakness of hers. If we captured Erec, of course we could lure her in. What else does she care about? She has other friends, but it's best if we find something that will make her rush in without thinking. Can you boys think of anything?"

"She has a pink cat that tells her secrets," Balor said. "She calls it Cutie Pie." Balor remembered how that cat had once given him some nice cuts with its claws. He mused how he would love to see it taken away from Bethany.

Damon stroked an imaginary pizza in his hands. "Pizza pie. She loves pizza pie."

Baskania's face lit up. "Cutie Pie. Pizza pie. I think you boys have given me an excellent idea."

After their short rest, they were ready. They climbed as far into the tunnel as they could, stretching the rope taut, before Jack pulled Melody in. As soon as she entered, loud cracks resounded through the passageway. Melody screamed as they all raced ahead of the collapsing rock.

As Erec ran through the tunnel, he said over and over in his head, "Pick up the yellow thing with the crystal. Put it in Bethany's backpack. Pick up the yellow thing with the crystal. Put it in Bethany's backpack."

He and Bethany spilled out of the tunnel into the hot sun. Where was he again? He looked at Bethany, confused. She, too, seemed totally lost.

But words echoed through his head. "Pick up the yellow thing with the crystal. Put it in Bethany's backpack."

"Hurry!" Jack shouted.

The crystal in his hands was pulling him toward a shining yellow thing. "Pick up the yellow thing with the crystal." Okay. He pulled the yellow thing up on the end of the crystal. "Put it in Bethany's backpack." He put the crystal over her backpack, which was unzipped just enough for it to fit, and dropped the yellow thing inside. As soon as he did, she collapsed.

He smiled. He'd done a good thing, he knew. Now he could rest by the pretty waterfall.

Screams came from a dark tunnel nearby. He wondered what that was about. Then he felt a yank. Someone was pulling him into it and pushing Bethany out at the same time.

As soon as he was back in the tunnel, his head cleared. Bethany was slumped over her ropes outside, unable to do anything.

"Is Melody okay?" Jack sounded panicked. "She's not answering."

Jam was tugging on the rope. "I've got her. We have to move fast."

Erec nodded, thinking intently about what he would repeat: "Follow me. Follow the crystal."

The tunnel was disintegrating around them. Erec threw himself onto the sand behind the waterfall. Mist poured out of the tunnel with Jack, surrounding them.

"Follow me. Follow the crystal." Erec chanted the words until he realized that was something he could do. He marched forward, clutching the crystal before him. It was pulling him somewhere. Something was yanking on him the other way, though. Everything was blurry behind him. Someone was dragging on the ground, tied to him by a rope. It looked like a girl.

Should he pull the rope off? It seemed like a good idea. But the words in his head said to do something else. "Follow me. Follow the crystal." Okay. He followed the crystal, aware that others behind him and the dragging girl were doing the same.

Loud crashes and strange noises echoed around them. Huge waves smashed into the shore, but they were easier to hear than see. A tree fell somewhere, and he heard a cry. The sand under his feet felt wobbly, and the ground was shaking. But the crystal in his hand kept pulling him. Steadily, amidst the odd crashes and despite the tugging on his chest, he forged ahead. Soon he reached the entrance to a rocky cave.

The moment he crawled inside, his head cleared. He caught his breath and looked out the tunnel entrance. Although his vision was blurred by the mist, it looked like chaos out there. Bethany hung limply from the rope tied under her arms. Erec's heart went out to her.

He had to think. Once he pulled her into the tunnel, he'd forget everything again. Then he had a great idea. He reached around Bethany and pulled Jam into the tunnel with him, keeping her and her Awen of Knowledge out. Jam came to with a startled look. "What will we do now, young sir?"

"I had a thought. If we keep Bethany in the tunnel while we pick up the last Awen, then we'll know what we're doing when we're in Avalon. Maybe we should keep Jack in there with her. Then we'll be able to see better too."

"Smart idea, young sir. But Melody can't stay in the tunnel with them. It would cave in."

"I know," Erec said, thinking about that part. "We'll have to take her out with us. If there were only a way we could keep her safe. . . ."

Jam frowned, setting his mind to this problem. "She seemed best off hanging in midair."

Erec took his rope off, knowing they had to keep moving. "I'm going through the tunnel and out into Avalon. See if you can hear me when I shout in to you. I'll give you instructions so you'll know what to do after you pull Bethany in here."

He scrambled on his knees down the rocky tunnel, and out the other end into Avalon. But as soon as he set foot on the ground, he was instantly in a bad mood. Why did he have to do all this stuff, anyway? Why was he always saving the day for everyone else? He shouted into the tunnel, annoyed. "Can you hear me, fuzz brain? It's me. You know, the one who has to save your sorry hide all the time."

A faint echo laughed back. "I hear you loud and clear, kind sir."

"Go!" Erec screamed. "Hurry up. Pull Bethany in, you idiot. Pull Jack in, and Melody. And fast, stupid! Get your act in gear. Crawl down the tunnel. Now, you dumb fools! Before Melody ruins everything again with her rotten Awen of Creation. Speed it up."

Yelling felt good, and soon he saw Jam approach, dragging

Bethany behind him. The clueless look on Jam's face made him more upset. Crashes resounded behind them from Melody's Awen.

"Stop, fools!" Erec shouted at Jam. "Yes, you. Untie yourself. Loosen the rope and pull it apart." Erec was exasperated, having to explain to Jam how to untie the knots. "Now, you get out here."

Jam climbed out, and a look of frustration immediately overcame him. "You didn't need to snap at me, young sir."

Erec did not like Jam's tone when he said "young sir." He also didn't like how Jam avoided looking at him. This "ugly" bit was getting old. His friends were so weak, not being able to take a little change in his looks. He yelled into the tunnel for Jack to untie both himself and Bethany. After a lot of screaming on Erec's part, Jack managed to do so, even though he was blinded and confused.

Erec grabbed the rope around Melody and pulled. In a moment she crashed out of the tunnel, tumbling on top of him, then screaming in horror when she looked into his face.

"Stay there. Don't you move," Jam said to Jack. Bethany slumped against the wall of the tunnel, and Jack sat next to her, stupefied and content not to go anywhere. At least the tunnel was no longer caving in.

Melody jumped away from Erec, and the ground exploded under her feet. She tumbled into the pit she had created. "Look what you did, you ugly moron!" she shouted angrily. "Now what's going to happen to me?" She fell further into the pit as the ground collapsed under her. Rocks began to tumble on top of her. "Save me, you beast! What, did your brains melt away with your looks? You had to make me carry the most dangerous thing. Are you trying to kill me or something?"

Lugh, Brigid, and Dagda appeared with their long gray robes, ankle-length brown tunics, and huge oak staffs. After gagging from looking at Erec's face, blond-haired Dagda grabbed Melody's rope.

With help from Lugh, he climbed onto a tree limb and tied her so she was hanging from the rope secured under her arms.

The whole time Melody cursed and spat at them, furious. "Is this the best you can do? My luck, I'm surrounded by mental midgets. I'm supposed to keep hanging here while everyone else goes off to drink lemonade?"

"Do not speak in opposites," Lugh called up to her.

"I'm not, you freak," Melody shouted back, obviously knowing what he meant and not wanting to play along.

"Nobody speak in opposites," Lugh repeated, nodding at Erec.

The reminder calmed Erec a bit. "We do not need to get the Awen here now. We do not want your help." Tremors shook through the ground under them, but at least the world was not collapsing yet, with Melody dangling free.

Though Brigid averted her eyes from the horror of his face, Erec noticed she looked excited, even despite the negative feelings the Awen was casting out. Probably because they hoped to be rid of it soon. She said, "We are very upset with you. You did a terrible job so far. But you look fantastic. I hope you do not feel okay."

"I do not," Erec said. "I am not fine."

She nodded. "Has it been easy?"

"Very easy." Erec nodded. "We nearly lived several times." He looked around. "I did not think that druids were here. Are they not here?"

Brigid swallowed a laugh. "We are not druids," she said, pointing at herself and the two boys.

"You are not?" Erec was surprised. "I thought druids were . . . young. You look too old to be druids."

Lugh looked pleased. "We are much younger than we look. We cannot choose how we appear so we do not make ourselves look young."

"Why do you not stay here, in this place?" Jam asked. "Why do you leave?"

Lugh said, "We leave because this is not our home. Legend does not tell that someday one will not take the Awen away. So we do not wait for that day to come."

Dagda said, "When you do not bury the Awen in the Isle of Man, then do not come right back here, please. We do not have gifts for you."

Erec frowned. "Why would we not bury them?"

"The Awen will not stay where you bury them for three weeks. After that, they will not return to where you found them. Burying them will not keep them safe, and will not minimize their effects."

Erec nodded. He pulled his singing crystal out and let it lead him to the stream where they had originally seen the Awen of Harmony. Jam, Lugh, Brigid, and Dagda followed him, leaving Melody snarling, hanging from the branch.

The crystal pulled Erec to the large rock by the stream. He lifted it as the crystal struck a chord. The red dodecahedron with black symbols on its sides had a ruby aura around it.

"I should not carry this one," Jam said with a scowl. "It is not my turn."

Erec thought to prepare him. "It will not make you very angry, I think. Are you not sure?"

Jam shrugged. "I'm not sure. Don't give it to me. I can't handle it."

Lugh held a finger up. "Don't wait a minute." He returned with a large sheet made of sewn-together animal skins and nodded.

Jam unzipped the top of his backpack and Erec lowered the red dodecahedron into it. The instant it fell, Jam screamed in rage and attacked Erec. Erec jumped back in shock, trying to scramble away. Words could not form fast enough for Jam, so he grunted and hissed, kicked and spit. Erec rushed backward, but Jam fell on him, punching hard.

Lugh and Dagda wrestled Jam off Erec and held him down while he jerked furiously, sputtering in anger. Brigid straightened the sheet out on the ground, and the three, with Erec's help, managed to roll Jam in it. Soon he looked like a nasty cigar with a fire-red face for a tip. At least he was harmless now.

Lugh said, "Do not come with me. I will not call your boat for you."

Erec followed Lugh along the path toward the shore where they had come from. When they reached the sandy beach, Erec pulled his coat tighter around him.

Lugh faced the waves, holding his wooden staff before him. He chanted a haunting refrain. "*Am gáeth tar na bhfarraige. Am tuile os chinn maighe. Am dord na daíthbhe.* I am a wind across the sea. I am a flood across the plain. I am the roar of the tides." Erec recognized it as the same song that the Hermit had sung. It was beautiful and frightening, as if it were from another universe. As he paused, Erec could hear water rush over a thousand tiny tinkling shells. "*Óig dar mhuir, mile laoch líonfas ler. Barca breaga bruigfidid.* Let these youths float across your ocean, thy thousand heroes fill your sea. Bring your magic ships to moor."

Foggy wisps fluttered in the air, gradually forming into the hazy shape of a boat. Its vague edges churned like a cloud, and soon figures appeared—the wraithlike sailors who had taken them to Avalon. The ghost ship shimmered in the sunlight. Soon it slid onto shore, silent as the mist.

Lugh spoke to the ghosts in a strange tongue that Erec could not understand. They seemed to be nodding, but when Erec looked straight at them they were hard to see.

Lugh said, "They will not bring you back here after you bury the Awen. Let us not bring Jam onto the boat first."

They carried Jam, spitting and growling, into the ship. As soon as

Erec walked off the ghost ship he felt wonderful. He grinned, "It's over! The Awen of Harmony is leaving Avalon. It feels great here now!"

Lugh was prancing and spinning through the air, singing songs in a strange tongue. "You did it, Erec! You saved us!" Then his face grew sober. "At least for three weeks. Yet even three weeks of freedom will be pure bliss. I cannot wait to celebrate with you when you return."

"I hope it will be forever, not just a few weeks," Erec said. "Once I hook the Awen to the Twrch Trwyth—"

"The what?" Lugh looked a little disappointed. "That can't happen. It's been tried again and again. It's not impossible. I mean, it's impossible." He smiled faintly. "Sorry, it's hard to drop the opposite thing."

Erec said, "There is a small chance it might work this time. I have the Fates on my side." He did not tell Lugh that the Twrch Trwyth was missing, and he had no idea how to hook the Awen to it safely.

Dagda and Brigid were celebrating and hugging when they returned. "I've never felt this great!" Brigid sung.

"Who would be best to put on the boat next?" Erec asked. "I suppose Jack. He won't cause too much ruckus there."

The ground shook under the tree where Melody was tied. Branches fell around her. She called to Erec, "Hey, down there! Sorry about all I said before. Just got caught up by the Awen, I guess." She looked at Erec with a doleful expression, then immediately turned away in revulsion.

"You okay hanging like that?"

"Yeah," she said. "Better than causing avalanches and falling into pits."

Erec went to the tunnel and said to Jack, "Climb out now."

Jack did as he was told, leaving Bethany there asleep. Mist swirled after Jack into Avalon, and soon it was very hard to see. Jack perked up when he stepped out. "Where are we?" He felt around him until Lugh and Brigid grabbed his hands.

"We're in Avalon now," Erec said. "We've got all the Awen. Jam's in the boat. He's a mess now."

The druids led Jack into the ghost ship, and soon Avalon cleared again.

"Time to get Melody, I guess," Erec said.

Lugh shook his head. "I think it's best to put your other friend on the boat first. Melody will cause titanic waves. Once she is on board, you will want to cross fast."

They returned to the cave entrance. "How will I get her there?" Erec asked.

"Your crystal will lead you," said Brigid. "There are two Awen on that boat. It will pull you there."

Erec rehearsed in his mind, "Follow the crystal into the boat. Follow the crystal into the boat." He reached in and picked Bethany up, throwing her over his shoulder.

She was heavy, though, and he wondered if he should put her down. "Follow the crystal into the boat." What was that in his head? Something he should do. The crystal was in his hand, pulling him. There were no instructions about putting the heavy weight down, so he just followed the crystal.

Soon they came upon a sea of mist. The crystal pulled him into it. He started feeling awful. Angry. He couldn't see anything. He did not know what to do. This stunk. He threw down the heavy thing on his shoulder. Strange ghostlike hands shoved him out of the mist and down a plank.

Then his head cleared. He was standing on the shore, relieved he had managed to load Bethany onto the ship. With Lugh, Dagda, and Brigid, he went back for Melody. "You ready?" he called to her.

"Ready as ever," she said. Lugh climbed the tree and let her down. When she landed on the ground it started to cave in, but Erec and Dagda grabbed the rope and lifted her high, carrying her with their arms over their heads.

Dagda only tripped once over the shifting ground, but when Melody dropped, a tree fell right next to them. They swooped her back up and swung her onto the ship.

"Will she sink it?" Erec asked.

"The ghost ship won't be affected," Brigid explained. "But the water around it will. The sailors will do their best not to lose you on the way. And they will push you ashore when you get there."

Erec could not see anything through the mist except for a strange shape high in the air. Looking closer, he saw that the sailors had tied Melody up onto their mast.

"See you soon, I hope." Erec waved to them as he walked onto the ship. Where was he? He couldn't see and he felt terrible. Angry. He didn't know why, but everything was wrong. He caught glimpses of people here and there in the mist. They looked ugly and horrible. He hated them. Waves crashed overhead, soaking his clothing. He hated the waves, too. It was all their fault that he felt bad. Someone close by was raging and screaming. It was bad, very bad, and it would never end. He crossed his arms tight around his chest, wanting to fight someone.

Before long someone was pushing him. "Leave me alone!" he shouted. He stumbled onto a rocky shore and was clearheaded once more. Now he had to secure the Awen.

CHAPTER TWENTY-TWO

A Disturbing Vision

EREC SPLASHED WATER on his face, and in a moment of stillness between the waves, he caught a reflection of himself. He choked. How could his friends have managed to look at him all this time? His face looked like a rotting zombie out of a horror movie. Erec backed away, terrified. He had to find a place to bury the Awen fast.

The shoreline was rocky, and the ocean waves pounded against it relentlessly. Better not to bury them near the water, he decided. He walked toward a cliff, through a strip of icy grasses. Nearby he spotted a huge rock by a spiny furze shrub. That seemed like a good spot.

Erec found a stout stick, dusted the snow off it, and scraped the ground. He was going to lever it out of place. But the ground was hard and icy. As hard as he tried, he could not poke a hole into it. Finally, in frustration, he ran back to the ship. "Send Melody out," he called to the ghost sailors.

He could hear noises and Melody complaining, and then she stumbled down the plank toward him. A pit formed underneath her when she tripped on the shore. Waves crashed around them, and a stormy wind began to blow hard pebbles into their faces. He explained quickly what he needed her to do, and helped her to the spot by the rock, pulling her out of pits she was creating with each step. When she got to the rock, she kicked the frozen dirt a few times, and it soon crumbled under her into a hole.

"That's great, Melody," Erec said. "Now let me give you my Awen."

Melody opened her backpack. Erec pulled out his Awen of Beauty and placed it in her pack with the Awen of Creation. They dropped it into the hole and backed away.

Melody stamped her feet a few times, but nothing happened. Overjoyed, she threw her arms around Erec. "Thank goodness. Plus, you look so much better."

Neither of them would look normal, though, until they were away from the Awen. Wind whipped stones through the air at them, but Melody could now stand without the earth melting beneath her since she was no longer holding her Awen.

"Who should we get next?" she asked.

Erec thought about it. He could not get Jam until there were more people to help hold him down. And Erec wanted to put off bringing Bethany out as long as possible. "I guess Jack."

Erec called to the sailors to send Jack off the ship. Fog rolled out with him onto the beach, making it hard to see. "This way, Jack." Erec led him to the hole. He took the Awen of Sight out of Jack's backpack, and suddenly everything was black.

"Awesome, I can see again!" he heard Jack say. Then, with relief, "You look a lot better, bud. I mean, not great, but still . . ."

With a stick, Melody lifted the backpack from the hole and brought it to Erec. "Just drop it," she said. Erec let go, and the Awen of Sight joined the other two in the backpack. That helped a lot.

"Think we can handle Jam?" Erec asked them. He called to the sailors to send Jam out, and a snarling, rolled-up Jam slid down the plank. His face was red and sweaty. He growled, trying to reach Erec and bite him.

Erec almost lost his temper, but he said, "Don't speak in opposites, guys. Don't follow me."

They laid Jam down by the hole and unrolled him. As soon as he was loose, he dove at Jack, but the three of them wrestled him down. Melody lifted the backpack from the hole with the stick and laid it next to Jam's. Erec tilted the side of Jam's pack up and let the Awen roll into hers. Melody lowered it back into the hole. Jam collapsed, exhausted.

"Now we just need Bethany," Erec said, growing angry. He stopped himself. "We do not need Bethany. You three, do not go on the boat. Then do not give me instructions from there."

As soon as the others boarded the boat, Erec called, "Don't send Bethany out here."

Bethany slid down the plank, unconscious, into the mist. Erec felt angry at how helpless she was.

Someone yelled to him, "Take Bethany to the big rock." They kept yelling it over and over. He didn't like being told what to do. It wasn't nice. But he didn't know what else to do. He grabbed Bethany by the hair.

"Pull her by her arms," someone shouted. Why were they always yelling at him? He grabbed her arm and tugged her over to the rock. "Take the backpack from the hole," someone yelled. He made a face toward them. Fine. He could lift it out with a stick.

A girl's voice yelled, "Dump Bethany's backpack into the other one," again and again. So he did it.

"Drop it in the hole," someone shouted. He did, and then Bethany started to move.

She sat up, dazed. Then she made a face at Erec. "I don't like you."

"I don't like you, either," he said.

With his friends' directions, he covered up the backpack with dirt, then shoved the rock over it, angrily. Then he and Bethany followed their friends' calls back on to the ship. Grumbling, the two of them walked to the plank and climbed aboard.

Cheers echoed over the waves as the five congratulated one another. It felt so good to see again, be happy, and know what was going on, let alone feel safe and not look disgusting.

Erec had never felt happier than he did in Avalon that night. They had done it, taken the awful Awen away from those poor people. Even if he did not succeed, and the Awen returned in three weeks, he would have given his druid friends and the Peruvian villagers a needed break. They kept dancing, singing crazy songs, and jumping with joy.

"We want to give you gifts," Brigid smiled. Erec had not noticed how nice the druids looked, like storybook fairies come to life. They were kind and playful now that the Awen was gone. "We will read your spirits," she said, "and decide your gifts from that. It is a tradition that druids give fun gifts. We love jokes, you see. So they will be practical gifts, like practical jokes."

The three druids studied Erec and his friends, then disappeared into the tunnels in their cave. Erec heard hysterical laughter coming out. He was glad, because it must have been a long time since they had laughed like this. It reminded him of the Hermit, who was always laughing about something. Erec would need to find him soon.

When they returned, Brigid pulled out a tall black bag tied with a silver tassel. She announced, "This is for you, Erec, for all you did for us." She burst into a fit of giggles, and at that point Erec didn't care if the gift was a smelly sock. It was enough of a present just to see her so happy.

He was shocked when Brigid pulled three golden scepters out of the bag. For a minute, he froze. They looked just like the ones King Piter, Queen Posey, and King Pluto had. How did they know? He edged away from them, shaking his head. What would he do? The last thing he needed was a scepter, never mind three of them.

But something was different about these. He couldn't put a finger on it at first, but then he realized. He wasn't drawn to them. They just seemed like ornate gold posts that held no attraction for him at all. He was curious to look at them closer but did not want to make the mistake of touching one and getting sucked in by it.

Brigid's hand covered her mouth, and she was giggling despite her efforts. Dagda snickered. "These will be good for you to practice with." He picked one up and tossed it to Erec.

When it fell into his lap, Erec was stunned a moment, waiting. But nothing happened. He could feel no magic at all coming from it. It was refreshing in a way, seeing a scepter that did nothing. "Are they fake?" he asked.

"These are for you to get used to being around scepters without losing your mind." Lugh laughed.

"You can program them," Dagda explained. "If you put a hair or two from someone into a slot at the base, it will work for them."

"Cool," Erec said. "What can they do?"

"Try it sometime," Lugh said, laughing. "You'll see."

"Now Jam." Dagda handed him a shining silver tray. "This is a Serving Tray. But a different kind than the one you had. Try it out."

"Thank you, kind sir." Jam looked at it hesitantly. "Um, may I please have some ambrosia?"

"A sensible choice." Lugh laughed again.

On the silver platter appeared a bowl of something chunky, like ambrosia, but it had a terrible smell. When Erec looked closer, he saw it contained rusty, bent nails, rotten apple pieces, and crawling slugs.

"Oh!" Jam politely took the nasty food off the tray. He dusted the new tray off and put it in a pocket in his vest that fit it perfectly. "Thank you so much." He nodded as if greatly pleased.

Lugh handed a scroll to Jack. "For you, Jack, a treasure map. You like treasure, I'm sure."

Jack nodded. He unrolled the scroll and studied it. "This map leads from here to my parents' house in Aorth," he said. "Is there treasure in my house?"

The druids doubled over laughing. "Yes. Of course."

Jack thanked them, folded the paper, and put it in his pocket, smirking a bit at Erec as if he thought the druids were crazy.

"Now Bethany," Brigid said, dragging a big plastic bag over to her. "For you." She took out a big rock and set it by Bethany.

"Wow, thanks." Bethany patted the rock. "I've always wanted my own rock."

"This is a nice rock," Dagda said. "It screams when a rightful king is crowned, during a coronation, or when it first meets them, whenever you want."

"Like the Lia Fail?" Bethany looked it over. It did look a lot like the Lia Fail, which was placed at the side of King Piter's throne. That one definitely screamed when the rightful king arrived during a coronation.

"Exactly!" Lugh grinned. "Except this is a fake. You can program it to scream for whoever you want. There is a little microphone underneath it, and you tell it what to do. Have fun with it." Lugh fell over laughing.

"Oh, goody," Bethany said sarcastically. "This will be fun." She turned it over and saw a small "Made in Avalon" printed on it. Then she thought about it a while. "You know, there might be a time I can use this to surprise Balor Stain. Hmm ..."

"And Melody." Lugh sat next to her. "I really think you need this." He handed her a case. Inside was a shiny golden flute. "I'm sure you could learn to use it."

Melody regarded it in surprise. "Thanks." Everyone in the room knew that she had no need for instruments. She could produce any music she wanted without them.

"Try it," Lugh insisted.

So Melody picked it up and blew. Instead of music, a horrendous screech came from the thing. "Great." She shuddered and put it away quickly.

"Oh, almost forgot!" Dagda tossed a package wrapped in paper to Erec. "You have a dog, right? This is a gift for him."

The package smelled bad. Erec opened it and saw poop inside. "Ugh!" He threw it across the floor.

"Don't want it?" Dagda cracked up. "Lots of different kinds of animal droppings in there. Your dog would love it. You could set up a little showroom for him, like a hands-on museum."

"No," Brigid said with a laugh. "A nose-on museum."

"I think," Erec said, "I'll pass."

After an evening of celebrating, Lugh called the ghost ship for them, and the three druids thanked them profusely. "Come back anytime," they kept saying.

Brigid put a lifting spell on Bethany's fake Lia Fail so she could carry it easily. They hopped on the ghost ship and set sail over sparkling, calm waters. When the ship neared shore, they all looked uncomfortable, knowing what waited for them on the beach. But Erec spotted an open Port-O-Door on the side of a white cliff by the shore. The Hermit was inside, waving from the vestibule.

Erec returned to the small, dark rooms in his mind. His bed in the west wing felt so relaxing and quiet after all he had been through that the first two times he had tried to look into the future with his dragon eyes, he had fallen asleep. But now he was there, visualizing opening one door after another, until he was in the smallest room with the box on the table.

He needed to find out more. Before he had pushed time back to see what had happened earlier with Balor at the castle. He would just push it further now. The Hermit had confidence in him. Surely he would figure this out.

He opened the windows into the riot around the crumbling Castle Alypium. Again, he felt the fear, the rush of power. He stepped away and turned to see himself holding the scepter. Instantly, he was drawn to it, but his hands passed through it.

Not now. He dragged himself away. There were more important things to do. Of course, he thought, those fake scepters the druids had given him didn't help him resist the real one at all. Not that he had expected them to.

Balor stood as before, holding the bronze whistle in his hand. When Erec had backed time up, he had seen Balor blow the whistle to summon the bronze ghosts that were tearing the castle apart. Now he would go further back, find out how to stop this.

He closed his eyes and concentrated. *Go back. More. Further.* It was hard, like pedaling a bike up a cliff. But he could do it. *Move back. Pull time back . . .*

It looked like a slower version of his cloudy thoughts, a movie playing backward. But this time he could control it. He let it rewind until they were somewhere else, then he let go and watched.

The room sparkled with the light of a hundred candles. Their glittering reflections bounced off of the golden statues, urns, and antiques that artfully filled the room. Balor, Damon, and Dollick Stain looked nervous. Dollick was licking the white, wooly fur on his shoulder until Balor slapped his head. "Cut it out, lamb chop."

Tall, spindly President Washington Inkle stood nearby, anxiously biting his lips. The scabs around his mouth were worse than usual. Only a few strands of gray were left on his bald head, and he looked bent and shaky, like a noodle in the wind.

Behind a huge desk sat Thanatos Baskania. The circle of eyes rimming his face glanced disconcertingly in all directions. He leaned back in his velvet chair. His nose suddenly flattened, caving in. Skin grew over his mouth until his lower face became a flat plane. Then deep craters appeared in it, covering his cheeks, making his jaws wider, and eyes began to emerge from each pit. Soon his face was covered with eyes, looking everywhere, seeing things that were happening far away.

Baskania's hands jumped, and he clasped a small silver ball. It was in the form of an eye, with a coal center showing through a hole that was the pupil. The eyes on his face melted back into his flesh, leaving him with a sea of holes like a piece of swiss cheese. His skin stretched over them, swallowing them, and his nose and mouth erupted.

The Stain boys and President Inkle, unhappy witnesses to this morphing, jumped when a wild howl erupted from Baskania's throat. In a moment, Rosco Kroc appeared, scaly and green with a snoutlike face. He wiped his mouth, shaken from his own response howl which he had let loose before he appeared.

"You have news for me, Rosco?" Baskania tilted his head.

Rosco nodded. "Oscar found out. It's time. Now. Time for the Castle Alypium to come down." He rubbed his hands together.

"Well done." Baskania sounded delighted. "This is so much sooner than I expected. Such luck! What a wonderful surprise. I can always count on you, Rosco. Will you be attending the festivities?"

Rosco shook his head. "I've seen enough, Prince of Shadows. If I may take my leave." He bowed low. After Baskania thanked him, Rosco disappeared.

Baskania smiled at his triplet clones. "You hear that, boys? Run along and enjoy. I'll see you at the castle—that is, what's left of it."

The thick oak doors parted before Balor, Damon, and Dollick, and they ran through the Green House, across the streets of Alypium to the castle. Balor laughed and pointed. "Look," he said. "It's crumbling."

The castle had begun to crash down. A massive spire trembled, then tipped, falling through a roof.

Balor's face lit with delight. "I love it! Hey, I know, guys," he turned to his brothers. "Just the thing to help this along." He picked up his bronze whistle and blew it.

Suddenly, swarms of bronze wraiths flew through the air.

Erec pulled down the shades to stop the picture. What had Oscar found out? So the whole castle crumbling could be stopped by keeping Oscar from learning something? He would have to send Oscar a snail mail and warn him to keep his distance. Maybe that would take care of it.

There was something else he needed to see, though. Erec steadied himself and opened the shades on the windows one more time. People were running wild, screaming. He stepped away, then turned to see himself holding the scepter. How had he gotten it? Maybe it held another clue.

He closed his eyes. Push it back. More, into the past. He felt like

THE SEARCH FOR TRUTH

he was wrestling time itself. He gritted his teeth, concentrating, until the movie began to rewind. Slowly but steadily he forced it back until he was somewhere else. Then he relaxed to watch.

He was in the castle now, in the throne room.

"Erec, no!" King Piter was reaching to him, upset.

Erec held the king's scepter in his hand. Its power surged through him, making him invincible, perfect.

"Put it down, Erec," the king pleaded. "Give it back to me, son."

"Son"! How dare he call Erec that now? Now that he wanted something from him.

But Erec did not want to give the scepter back. It was taken care of. The king would get it back one of these days. It was time for Erec to enjoy it. He could make better use of it now. It was his turn, finally. And he would use it as he wished. He let the buzz of electricity take over his mind, washing away all other feelings.

The king pointed a finger. Erec knew he was working magic on him. Or trying to. But not this time. Erec was the strong one now. He tipped his scepter and the king disappeared. Give him a nice little visit with the druids in Avalon, Erec thought.

He strolled outside to the castle gardens, enjoying the immense electric energy of the scepter. Crackles snapped in some bushes behind him. When he turned he saw a flash of red hair, then heard footsteps running away. Oscar again! What was he doing here?

In a few minutes he heard a noise. Loud cracks and crashes echoed and the ground began to shake. He turned to see the Castle Alypium caving in before his eyes. He tilted the scepter and told it to clear everyone out from the castle so nobody would get hurt. Its power surges rocked him, dazed him.

He stood, gripped by fear and surges of power from the scepter, and watched the Castle Alypium fall apart.

Erec recognized this as the spot where he had originally seen himself. He shut the windows, left the room, and choked a sob.

Erec and Bethany sat on beanbag chairs in her mansion, the two Serving Trays before them. Jam had given Bethany his new one when she heard he was planning on throwing it out. "You never know," she said, "it may come in handy. If only I knew which one was the good one, I'd ask for a snack."

"Only one way to find out," Erec said. "Can I have a jelly doughnut?" he asked.

A sugared, jelly-filled doughnut appeared on one of the trays, and a black ball, oozing green slime and covered with worms, appeared on the other. "Ugh!" Bethany jumped back. "Get it away."

Erec picked up the tray by the edge and tossed the disgusting doughnut thing out a window, then wiped the tray clean with a paper towel. "Better put this one somewhere else." He handed it to Bethany, and she stashed it with the fake, programmable scepters and phony Lia Fail.

"Cheer up." Bethany handed him the doughnut, but he'd lost his appetite. "I'm sure you'll figure out a way to change things."

"I don't know, Bethany. The thing is, from what I can see in my future, I won't want to change things. It looks like I steal the scepter from King Piter, and it totally overcomes me, makes me power mad. It's my fault that the castle comes down. I send the king off to Avalon, Oscar catches wind that the king is gone and without his scepter, Baskania finds out, and it's all over."

"Yes, but you know all that now." Bethany poked her finger onto the silver Serving Tray. "That has to count for something. So you won't send King Piter away next time when it really happens."

Erec dropped his head into his hands. "I wish. But I could tell, when I was holding it, I wasn't thinking rationally. I was swept up by the scepter. Who knows if I'll really do it differently or not." Erec felt sick. Going into the dark room in his mind and seeing the scepter in his hands again and again was just making him want it more. Could that be why he finally lost it and stole the scepter from the king? Could this be a weird loop of fate, where something in the future happens only because he is looking into the future? Thinking made him feel worse. Maybe it was time he took a break from the small, dark room for a while.

Bethany pushed the platter away, no longer hungry. "Either way, Oscar is the key. Let's send him a letter. If we can make sure he stays away, then we might avoid the whole problem." She gave him a half smile. "Hey, I know what will happen now too. That has to help. I'll keep an eye out for Oscar and try to keep you away from King Piter's scepter."

They found paper and drafted a letter:

Dear Oscar,
What I am about to tell you is extremely important. You need to stay away from me. Something bad will happen if you see me. I know you've been really good about this, but you might accidentally run into me. So please change what you will do and make sure you don't follow me anywhere, or go where anyone at all could see you.
I hope this makes sense.
Your friend,
Erec

"Why didn't you tell him not to come to the castle?" Bethany asked.

"Then Baskania would know I'm in the castle now. I had to keep it vague." He thought a moment. "I guess we should send this snail from somewhere else so they don't know we're here. Want to come with me to the Port-O-Door?"

They studied the map of Otherness in the vestibule of the Port-O-Door. "This looks like a good spot." Erec pointed.

A grin broke out over Bethany's face. It was far away, an edge of Otherness that bordered with eastern Mongolia. It bore the name Cesspool Pits. She tapped that spot on the map, and when they heard a click, they opened the door.

Noxious stench filled the vestibule. This land in Otherness was aptly named. In front of them, a wasteland of oozing pits bubbled with grotesque shades of green and brown.

"Hurry!" Bethany held her nose, backing away. As Erec dropped the snail outside the door, its eyes swung toward him and shot him a dirty look before it sunk into the ground.

Cutie Pie, pink and fluffy as ever, bounded across the lawns of the castle and jumped in Bethany's lap by the fountains. Erec had never seen the pudgy cat running; she usually preferred to be carried. Bethany picked her up, amazed. "Cutie Pie?"

Cutie Pie rested a paw on her shoulder and cupped another in front of Bethany's ear. It had been a while since Erec had seen Cutie Pie telling her a secret. He wondered what it was about.

Bethany's jaw dropped, then a smirk lit her face. "How immature. You'd think they'd have something better to do." She put the cat down and said, "Sounds like the Stain boys are up to their usual tricks, picking on people. I don't know why this is so important to Cutie Pie, but she heard them talking about stealing pie and taking it with them to the Green House. Probably just the beginning of them strolling around, taking whatever they want from people." She shook her head.

Then a sly smile lit her face. "I can't stand to hear about them making everyone miserable. I've got an idea." She grinned. "Along the lines of writing letters to Oscar, and sending Team Dread on a wild goose chase. Maybe I'll make a pie and leave it out somewhere in Alypium for them. I can leave it near the Green House to make sure they get it."

"Make a pie?" Erec didn't understand. But then he remembered the new Serving Tray they got from the druids. "Think you can get that tray to make something that looks good on the outside?"

"Easy as pie." Bethany grinned.

Erec walked through the castle gardens, recreating his vision of the future in his mind. It was painful to think about. His worst nightmare was coming true, watching himself giving in to the scepter and ruining everything. This was why he hadn't wanted to do the quests to begin with. He never should have even started them.

The sun felt good on his back. He didn't want to look at the castle anymore or even be near it. The pressure was awful. So he walked past the maze and into the woods. After a while, he found the trickling brook where he had sat a long time ago, upset when he had first found out what the people of Alypium thought of him.

He thought he'd had problems then, but he'd had no idea what problems were. Big deal if people didn't like him. At least he wasn't about to destroy everything because he was too weak. He sat and threw sticks and pebbles into the water. The Hermit believed that Erec could take care of the castle problem. The Hermit also thought Erec would be able to find the Twrch Trwyth and do the fourth quest that the Fates had given him. Too bad the Hermit was goofy. Why had he ever listened to him?

Erec went over what he had seen in his head. He had stolen King Piter's scepter from him and used it against him, sending the king to Avalon. He had then walked into the castle gardens, all pleased with himself and power mad. Then he'd spotted Oscar running away.

A few minutes later the castle had started to collapse, and Erec had used his scepter to rescue whoever was inside of it.

Baskania had found out it was time for the castle to come down because of Oscar. Erec had seen that for himself. And Balor, Dollick, and Damon had run to watch, and Balor had called on the bronze ghosts to help.

Erec hung his head. All he could do was hope Oscar wouldn't show up after he got the letter. That and try his best to ... What? His best not to do every single thing he saw himself doing? Not to steal the scepter. Not to send the king to Avalon. Not to run outside. To go somewhere different so Oscar wouldn't see him?

He hoped he could and would do all of these things. The only problem was that he knew how he would feel and what would be going on in his head when he had the scepter, and none of it was rational. It was like hoping he would do the right thing when he knew he'd be insane.

When it became too painful to think about, he turned his thoughts to the fourth quest. At least he and his friends had done some good there. Even though he supposed the Awen would return to their original spots in a few weeks, Erec and his friends were giving the druids a real break, as well as the others whom the Awen had affected.

If there was just a way to keep the Awen from returning. He had to hook them to the Twrch Trwyth, but that was impossible. Erec wondered if maybe Olwen Cullwich had known where the thing was hidden before Baskania had torn him apart. What a brave man, if he had, keeping the secret hidden through all that.

Erec shuddered, remembering Olwen's demise. He missed Aoquesth. Maybe if Aoquesth were here he would have an answer to the problem. He knew so much.

Aoquesth. A thought popped into Erec's head. He had wondered, a while back, if there was a way to change things. If only he could go back and save Aoquesth, if he could figure out how to relive the battle in Otherness that was his second quest. He had almost forgotten the Novikov Time Bender in the castle basement. Maybe he could use it to change the past so Aoquesth could be alive now.

Water tumbled over the stones in the brook, spurting tiny fountains into the air. Erec stared at it, frozen.

Aoquesth. Time Bender. Olwen Cullwich. It all clicked.

Erec stood and ran to the catacombs under the castle. That was the answer. He was going back in time.

CHAPTER TWENTY-THREE

The Novikov Time Bender

OMER, THE GOLDEN ghost, hovered in the air before the Novikov Time Bender. He seemed to be smiling, although his features were hard to make out. "Welcome back, Erec Rex."

"Thanks." Erec hesitated. He didn't want to say anything to ruin his chances. "I would like to use the Novikov Time Bender, please. It's really important."

"I know you do," the ghost said, fluttering in the air. "And I know why."

"So . . . it's okay?"

"Your motivations are the best, Erec, no matter what your results may be. That is all that matters. Steering the future is up to you, not me, as long as you are driven by your heart."

Erec looked at the machine with apprehension. It did not help that it looked like a gold coffin with a glass front. "Can I see through it when I'm inside?"

"Yes, until you turn the dials. Then you will see only where you are in time. I can watch over you through the glass. Or when I look in the viewer." He pointed at a small television screen extending from the side of the Time Bender. "There I can see what is happening where you have gone."

"So you'll see on the screen what I'm doing, and through this glass case you'll just see me lying there?"

"Yes."

Going into the past seemed too easy. Erec had expected some resistance. "Will you let anyone know that I went?"

"Not if you don't want me to."

He heard his voice crack, and he realized he was afraid of going. "Do I need to take anything with me?"

"You won't be able to," the ghost said. "That was a problem with the first prototype. People went back naked because they could not take clothing with them. This new model will give you a version of what you are wearing now, made to fit you at any age you pick."

"And when I go back, will I know everything I know now?"

"You will. Except your body will look the same as it was at that time, of course."

Erec then asked a question that really bothered him. "What happens to the other version of me that was there then? What if I run into it?"

"That's the beauty of the Time Bender," the ghost said. "You can't run into yourself. You go into your body at that time. So there will be no other version of you there. Whatever you do when you go back will be all that you do then. Your old self evaporates from your body a while, then returns when you leave."

"Does it remember anything?" Erec asked. "Will the old me remember what the new me did after I leave?"

"No, the old you will have no idea. It will feel like a bit of amnesia, I'm afraid. That's why it is only recommended to use the Time Bender once. More times might cause a problem. Are you sure you want to do this?"

"Definitely." Erec gulped. He had his doubts, though. "Could I get stuck there?"

"That should not happen. Unless, of course, somebody keeps you from coming back to this room again. You have to get back here to return." The ghost stretched what looked like an arm, and the machine lowered so it was flat on the ground.

That put a time limit on his visit, for sure. Best to get this over with before he got too nervous. He pulled the handle on the glass front door of the Time Bender, climbed in, lay down, and shut the door over him. Three red dials hung against the side of the machine near his shoulder.

This was it, he thought. His chance to fix everything. If he succeeded, Aoquesth would be alive and well when he stepped out again. Not only that, but everything would be better. Everything.

Erec was not going back to the battle where Aoquesth had died. He wanted the Time Bender to take him back much further. Back before he ever had left Alypium, before he had his memory removed. He would find Olwen Cullwich and get the Twrch Trwyth. And while he was there, he would learn who his father and birth mother were.

And he would do one other thing too, which would change everything. If he was successful, Aoquesth would be alive again.

Erec had to think before he turned the top dial to a date. He was born on April 18, almost fourteen years ago. He could not remember anything before he was four years old, so that was probably the time his memory had been removed. But his mother had told him he was the wrong age for a long time, and it was hard to remember being that young anyway, so he couldn't be exact.

He needed to choose a date before the castle was turned on its side. That way he'd be able to get out of the catacombs and back in again when he was ready to leave. In the fall, King Piter had said the castle had been on its side for almost ten years. So Erec would go back a little while before then. That timing seemed perfect.

Erec wound the three dials—one each for the year, month, and day—to bring him back ten years and five months. It would be August 18, when Erec was three years and four months old.

When the last dial stopped on the number 18, the front of the glass clouded. A whirl of dust and specks blew by from right to left outside of the glass, making the box feel like the inside of a tornado. His arms twitched, aching. Then his whole body shook, twisted, flailed in the machine. Everything hurt. He felt dizzy, filled with strange sensations, a gurgling in his stomach that rose up to his throat.

His head tingled, but when he reached up, to where his head should have been, to rub it, it wasn't there. Instead his hands were on his shoulders. He had to stretch much higher to touch his head, which seemed to have grown enormous. Maybe that was what all the itching, stretching, and pinching was from. His body was getting distorted.

For a moment he panicked. What if something had gone wrong?

He remembered how awful he had looked holding the Awen of Beauty. What if this journey disfigured him permanently?

He took a breath, telling himself to relax. No matter how bad he was now, he assured himself that it would get fixed one way or another. He looked down at his hands and arms. They were small and spindly. In fact, his whole body was small and spindly, except for his stomach, which stuck out a bit, and his enormous head.

The glass front of the Novikov Time Bender cleared, and he could see the room and the golden ghost through it. Had it worked? Was he right back where he'd started, only deformed now? With some difficulty, Erec pushed the glass door open and sat up.

Homer gathered above him in the air like a golden storm cloud with facial features. "You made it, Erec. Good for you. How are you feeling?"

"I made it?" Erec's voice sounded high, and his words came slowly, like his mouth was stuffed with cotton balls. It was hard to even form the words, as if his mouth had its own ideas of what to do. "Am I back ten years?"

"You are," Homer said. "You might find it interesting to look in a mirror when you get a chance. There are plenty up in the west wing."

Erec was very interested, but he dreaded the idea too. He might see what he looked like before June, his adoptive mother, had changed his looks—if he wasn't too deformed now to tell. He'd never even seen a picture of himself at this age. It would be unnerving.

"Thank you," he garbled. It sounded like his mouth was ultraslow and full of food. At least his mind was moving at the normal speed.

He reached the golden doorknob and walked into the catacombs of the castle. They looked exactly as they did when Erec had walked down them a few minutes ago—which was over ten years later—except they seemed much taller and wider now that he was small. He knew where he was going, but he took twice as long to get there with his little footsteps.

He found himself much more aware of the floor, as he was closer to it. He had never really worried about seeing rats or mice down here before, but now they would be much bigger compared to him, and the thought frightened him. In fact, anyone he ran into would seem huge and able to scoop him up and do anything to him. He was pretty defenseless, he realized.

Climbing the stairway into the west wing was tiring. Each step seemed immense. He opened the door and darted into a shadow behind a suit of armor. Maids and butlers scurried about, cleaning and carrying trays. People in suits and long black cloaks whizzed down the hallway. Erec could not believe how huge they were. He had to lean his head back to see who was walking nearby.

Then Erec froze. Balthazar Ugry was there, right in front of him. It took Erec a minute to be sure it was him. Ugry looked exactly the same, yet different, somehow. Less frightening. More normal. But Erec could not place why.

He waited for Ugry and a few other people to walk by. Then, when nobody was looking, he darted behind a statue and stole down the hallway. There were a lot of sitting rooms with mirrors. He just had to find one that was empty.

Erec pushed the door shut so nobody would see him. An ornate mirror hung on the wall over a row of molding that was just over his head. It looked like it was three feet off the floor, and he guessed he was just over three feet tall. But even when he stood on his toes, his eyes just missed the mirror.

He pushed a soft, cushioned chair against the wall and climbed onto it, which took a little doing as the seat was about as high as his chest. But when he stood and looked at himself, he jumped. A tiny child was staring back at him. A stranger. Curly blond hair tumbled around his face like a girl's. But his face didn't look girlish, at least. It was wide, with round, pink cheeks and a pointy chin. Only his blue eyes looked relatively unchanged.

Again he had to stretch his arms all the way up to reach over the top of his head. Now, looking in the mirror, he realized it was not because his head was abnormally big. It was his arms that were small. He looked pretty much in proportion—for a tiny kid, at least. His clothes looked funny on him, the same red tee shirt and jeans, but at least they fit. At least he had clothes.

So, he nodded into the mirror, this was what he had to deal with. Could be worse. It was actually to his benefit to be little like this. When he was done spying around in the castle, he would stroll into the agora and wait for some nice person to come help him. Maybe walk into a shop and ask for a policeman, say he was lost. It would seem perfectly natural that he had no clue where he lived and just called his parents Mom and Dad. He knew his own name, Erec Rex, and the police should be able to find out where he lived from that alone. They would take him safely where he needed to go. Then, voilà—he would get to meet his father and birth mother.

A chill zipped through him. Out of habit, every time he thought about his father he remembered that terrible old dream, that awful memory of the father that had turned out not to be his. What would his real father be like? Aoquesth had said such great things about him. He hoped his father lived up to them. Either way, Erec could not wait to finally meet him.

And his birth mother, too. He had so many unanswered questions for her. Why would she leave him? What would happen to her? She might not know all the answers yet, of course. Those were things that would happen in her future. Maybe he could change them while he

THE SEARCH FOR TRUTH

was here. Who knew? Maybe he could rearrange things so that he was never adopted to begin with.

Then he felt guilty for thinking that. June was a better mother than he could ever imagine. He wasn't sure what he would do when he met his parents, if he would try to change his fate or not. Maybe when he spent time with them, the answers would all become clear.

But first he had to make a decision. He needed to do three things on this journey. First, meet his parents and find out what had happened to them. Second, find Olwen Cullwich and get the Twrch Trwyth. And third, there was something he had to do at the castle that would change everything, save everyone, and bring Aoquesth back. But should he meet his parents first and then come back to the castle? Or should he do the other two things while he was here?

The door flew open with a bang. An old woman in a maid's uniform clattered in with her equipment. She took one glance at Erec and marched over to him with a fierce expression.

"Hi." Erec smiled. He was about to launch into an explanation, but the maid grabbed him by the waist and flung him over her shoulder.

"Put me down." The words came out slow. He realized that he sounded like a three-year-old, despite his best efforts. The maid was marching him somewhere and did not seem to care one bit what he said. "Let me go. I'm going home." The words took too long and came out squeaky. The maid rounded a corner. Erec began to struggle, throwing himself around so she would lose her balance. But no matter how much he kicked and flailed, she was stronger and did not come close to dropping him.

Deeper into the west wing, Erec got nervous. Where was she taking him? They wouldn't punish a little kid for being here illegally, would they? Maybe she was going to find someone to take him home. That would work for him. He relaxed and waited.

The maid opened a door to a vast playroom and set him down. Toy shelves were everywhere, with massive toys on them. It took him a moment to remember that the toys were not massive; it was just that he was small. "I found this one in a parlor, way down by the hall of armor," the maid grunted, annoyed.

A young blond woman rushed to Erec and fell to her knees before him. "I was looking for you, sweetie! Where did you go, Prince Poo-Poo Head?"

Erec felt dizzy. What was this? Someone had been looking for him? And who was Prince Poo-Poo Head? It did not sound like a compliment. There must be some mistake. He looked around the room. Two other kids who looked about his size were playing nearby, both with blond curls like his. A girl was coloring in a book on a rug, with boxes of crayons and markers spread around her, and a boy was running around the room with his arms out, pretending he was flying.

The boy spotted him and ran right into him, knocking him over. Erec's shoulder hit the wood floor, which hurt, and the boy's shoe smashed into his face. "Crash!" the boy shouted. "Crash Prince Poo-Poo Head." Then he ran away, looking over his shoulder as if he expected Erec to chase after him.

Erec dusted himself off and looked at the woman. "I'm not Prince Poo-Poo Head," he managed to get out, slowly.

Before he could clarify further, the woman sat him on her knee. "You're not?" her voice sung. "You don't want to be Prince Poo-Poo Head anymore? Okay, then." She bounced him up and down. "Who will we be today?"

Erec pointed at himself. "I'm Erec Rex."

"I know, silly." She kissed his cheek. "Of course you are. So you don't want to be called Prince Poo-Poo Head, then? You just want me to call you Erec now?"

Erec nodded. How did she know him? He looked at the other two kids in the room, confused. "Who are you?"

"I'm Clio. You know me, silly. I was just sick last week. It hasn't been that long."

The boy ran toward him, head bent, as if to knock him over again. "Prince Poo-Poo Head," he growled as if he fancied himself a train engine.

Erec stepped behind Clio just in time and let the boy sail by. He said to her, "I want to go home."

She looked at him curiously. "This is your home, silly. Are you playing a game?"

Something was wrong. This was not his home. This was the castle. And those other two kids . . .

They looked like him.

No. Erec shook his head.

"What's wrong, sweetie? You look funny. Are you feeling okay?" Clio put a hand on his head.

Erec could not answer. This was impossible. He was here, in the castle, with—and looking just like—two other kids who also lived here. They looked like . . . Erec couldn't think the word.

But he had to. They looked like triplets.

Erec bit his lip. Clio hugged him and said, "Oh, sweetie. You look scared. I think something upset you when you got lost. Were you frightened out there?"

Erec nodded, just to get her to lay off a minute. He had to absorb all this information. He pointed at the little girl. "Is that my sister?"

"Yes," Clio said, "and that's your brother." She pointed to the boy. "And you are Erec, and I am Clio. Very good."

"We are triplets?"

Even though the word sounded garbled, like his mouth was full of food, Clio was impressed. "Very good! You are triplets.

That's the right word! You got it." She mussed his soft curls, proud of him.

Erec sat in disbelief, and she pulled him onto her giant lap. He was one of the triplets? But he thought that was impossible. The triplets would be . . . no, they would be his age. He'd just found out that he was a year older than he'd thought he was.

Maybe this wasn't real, he thought. Maybe this was just a dream. He looked up at Clio. "Pinch me," he said, although it sounded more like "Pitch me."

Clio understood him anyway. "Now, why would I do that, Prince Poo-Poo Head—I mean Erec? I wouldn't hurt you."

Erec slapped his own chubby cheeks until she stopped him. He certainly felt it. Did that mean he was really awake?

"Now stop that," Clio said. "I don't like to see you hurt yourself, sweets."

Erec looked at her. If this was not a dream, if he was really one of the royal triplets, he wanted proof. "I want my mom." The words came slow. He wanted to say, "I want to see my mom," but it would have been much more effort. Anyway, nobody expected him to speak well, the way he looked.

"Your mother is busy," Clio said. "But I'll see what I can do."

She went to the door and called for someone. Another woman appeared and they spoke awhile. She heard Clio say, "I have no idea how he got out. I was watching them the whole time, I promise. I asked a few people to search for him. Could you let everyone know he's okay?" She looked at Erec. "He wants his mom now. Normally I wouldn't interrupt her, but he seems pretty upset."

The woman disappeared and Clio sat down again with Erec. "Would you like a story?" She reached for a book.

"No, thanks." There was no way he was going to sit through a baby book now.

THE SEARCH FOR TRUTH

"That was so polite," Clio gushed.

Erec walked around the room, surveying its contents and avoiding the other boy's wild attempts to knock him down. His *brother's* attempts. He stared at the boy awhile in shock. He had a brother and a sister. Strangely, the girl looked familiar, which did not make sense. His memory of this time had been removed. But the more he looked her over, the less sure he was. Nobody he knew really resembled her at all.

He waited, hoping his birth mother would come in soon. He would finally get to meet her. So, she was the queen?

And his father was King Piter? That thought made him angry. It couldn't be. Surely, after all the time they had spent together, if King Piter were Erec's father, he would have said something by now.

What was it that the king had told him? Something like, "*I'm not ready for you to know who your father is yet.*" That was real nice. He didn't feel like dealing with a son. Gotta love it.

The door opened and a woman walked inside and looked around. "Erec? There you are." She swept brown hair back from her face, crouched down, arms spread wide to catch him when he ran to her.

But Erec just stared at her, bewildered. He knew exactly who this was. He could not believe he was seeing her here, now, at the castle. It was June, his adoptive mother, but she looked so young. June had said she used to work at the castle. He had forgotten. Was *she* his real mother? Was she the queen? Had nobody been straight with him?

"You're right," June said to Clio. "He's not his normal self." She tilted her head. "You okay, Prince Poo-Poo Head?"

"He wants to be called Erec now," Clio whispered.

Erec walked closer to his mother, torn between wanting a hug, some comfort and safety amid all his disturbing thoughts, and wanting to throw something at her for lying to him all those years. "Mom?"

June flushed. "Did you hear that?" she asked Clio. "He called me Mom. Poor thing's all mixed up. He's never done that before."

She sat on the floor. "Come here, Erec."

Erec walked to her, now completely confused. He let June put him on her lap. "I know you've had a bad afternoon. You got lost, didn't you? We asked for your mother to come see you, and she said she would be here soon." She hugged Erec, and the hug felt better than any he could remember. "It's okay, okay . . ." She rocked him back and forth. "You're safe now."

With June's big arms around him he finally relaxed. But, to his horror, the stress of learning that he was one of the royal triplets, the stress of going back in time, and the stress he had been through with the Awen and the manticore caught up with him. He choked, and then tears streamed down his cheeks. This was horrifying! He didn't cry like this anymore, in front of everyone.

Of course, June didn't think twice about it. She just kept rocking and patting him, which made it worse. Erec's tension poured out along with more tears. He buried his face in her shirt in shame. Maybe it was this stupid baby body that made crying so easy. Whatever it was, he didn't like it.

CHAPTER TWENTY-FOUR

Olwen Cullwich

THERE WAS A burst of scurrying, straightening, and dusting off of clothing. "Queen Hesti's coming!" a voice whispered loudly near the doorway. "And she's blond this afternoon. She'll be here any minute."

"Kids," Clio said sweetly, "your mother's here. Stand straight, now, and give her nice smiles."

Erec's nerves jumbled and he felt funny, almost sick. After all this time he would finally get to meet his birth mother. And she was a queen, no less. What would she be like? He had so much to ask her.

The door flew open, and a tall, beautiful woman walked inside. Her hair was a long, curly blond, like theirs was, and she had high cheekbones and green eyes so soft that they were almost gray. Erec gasped when he saw her. Maybe it was his height, but from where he stood, she looked like a powerful Amazon warrior.

Clio bowed. "Your majesty, your hair looks lovely today."

"Thank you, Clio." The queen walked over to the little girl and knelt down beside her. "What are you coloring, honey?"

The little girl pointed. "A flying pony."

"Zoom! Zoom!" Erec's brother whipped by her, almost knocking over his mother.

"Slow down there, tyke," Queen Hesti said. She turned to Erec. "What's wrong, little Poo-Poo Head? Did you get lost? Come here, honey."

Erec slowly walked to his mother, stunned. The queen exchanged looks with Clio, acknowledging that he was acting strange. He stood before her, looking into her eyes. So this was her. He couldn't believe it. She wrapped her arms around him, and he hugged her back with his little hands. It was strange, he had never seen her before, not that he could remember anyway. But this was his birth mother. And here she was hugging him. He was glad, but it still didn't feel the same as when June had hugged him before.

"Erec, do you want to spend some time with me today?" His mother smiled. "I'd like that."

"Yes." Erec searched her eyes. What should he ask first? He didn't know where to begin. "Do you love me?" He hated the way his voice squeaked.

The queen kissed him all over his face, which made him blush. "Of course I love you, sweetheart. You're my baby." She hugged him again.

But Erec pulled away this time. "Are you going to leave me?"

She looked concerned, tilting her head. "No, honey. Why are you asking that?" She looked at Clio accusingly. "What happened to him when he got lost?"

Clio wrung her hands. "I'm so sorry, your highness. I have no idea how he got out, but he wasn't gone long. One of the maids found him straightaway."

Erec didn't want to make Clio look bad. "I'm okay, really." "Really" sounded like "weally" when he said it, making him cringe.

The queen looked at him oddly. "Okay. Erec, you don't seem yourself. Why don't we go get a treat together, just you and me?"

"Treat! Treat!" his brother shouted, closing in.

Clio picked up his hand. "You're staying with me, Prince Muck-Muck. We're having a big old treat here, just for you."

Erec walked out of the playroom holding his mother's hand.

The cloud cream sundae tasted better than any Erec had ever had. His mother shared it with him, dipping her spoon into his bowl. That was fine, since it seemed three times the normal size, and he was filling up fast.

Erec was enjoying getting to know his birth mother, but he had so much he needed to ask her. "Is Dad King Piter?"

"Yes," she said patiently. "That's what other people call him. You just call him Daddy."

Now that he had confirmed that fact, Erec felt another rush of anger. King Piter really was his father, but he'd just never felt like telling him. Considering the number of times the question came up, it was practically the same as a lie.

But sitting next to his beautiful mother, his anger drained away. How would his life have been different if she had raised him? If he'd grown up knowing he was a prince? What would that have been like, rather than growing up with no money in a crowded house, moving every year?

It occurred to Erec that this woman, his mother, was still alive somewhere, in Erec's future! He knew he would have to find her when he went back. If only he could figure out why she'd left. Maybe then he could find a clue to where she was. "Is King Piter nice to you?"

The queen smushed his cheeks together. "Call him Daddy, honey. Of course he's nice to me. We love each other. And you have to be nice to people you love, right?"

"Will you ever leave me?"

"No." The queen ruffled his hair, looking concerned. "What happened when you got lost? Did you see something scary?"

"No." Erec shook his head.

It was time to try now. This was the third thing he had planned to do on his visit into the past. The most important thing he had to do here. More important than learning who his birth parents were, and even more than getting the Twrch Trwyth. After this everything would change.

Erec had to warn her and the king about what would happen to them so they could prevent it. It would stop the chain of events that would lead to all the problems. Erec would not end up doing quests alone. Aoquesth would not die protecting Erec. Everything would be different. He had to warn King Piter and Queen Hesti that the queen would be attacked, that the king would be bewitched and put the castle on its side, that their triplets would be killed. . . .

His breath caught again when he remembered. He was one of the triplets. So they weren't killed. Of course. That's why he was supposed to do the twelve quests, be the next king. Why he was the rightful ruler. King Piter should have told him.

He pointed at himself. "I'm thirteen. I—"

"No, honey, you're three," Queen Hesti corrected.

Erec wished he could speak faster. It took him so long to get words out. "I came back in time from ten years later. I'm thirteen."

The Queen stared at him in shock. Erec felt a rush of relief. He had finally gotten his message across. "I can't believe it," she said. "Can you say that again?"

It took him a while to get the words out, but he finally managed to repeat it.

She shook her head in disbelief. "Where did you learn to talk like this? That's amazing. These are such big boy words. 'Ten years later.'" She thought a moment. "You actually will be thirteen ten years from now! Did you know that? You are so smart." She kissed him. "I think we know what your magical gift is, Erec. We've been waiting to find out. You have the gift of brains, or an amazing speaking ability at least. This is wonderful."

It occurred to Erec that she was more excited about the words he was using than what he was actually saying. He tried again. "Someone will try to kill us. We should hide."

"This is fantastic," she said. "But don't talk about killing, sweetie. That's not a nice thing. I guess it will take you a while to figure out how to use your big words."

Erec sagged from the effort of trying to make her listen. "I really came back in a time machine. Hecate Jekyll is bad. She'll put King—Daddy—under a spell."

The queen pursed her lips in thought. "Maybe it's a storytelling gift." She kissed his forehead. "Whatever it is, I'm so happy for you."

Erec wanted to scream in frustration. She wasn't listening. "Olwen Cullwich," he said. "I want Olwen Cullwich."

His mother laughed. "You are full of surprises today, Prince Poo-Poo Head. You remember Olwen? That's pretty good you remember his name."

"Can I see him?" Erec felt his lower lip slide forward.

"No, Erec. He is a friend of Daddy's. We don't play with Daddy's friends, okay?"

As wonderful as it was to meet his mother, the exchange had been a disaster. No matter how hard he tried, she focused only on his great vocabulary but did not believe anything he said. He couldn't actually blame her. How convincing could he be, stammering out words like a baby?

Soon he was back with his brother, who would only refer to himself as "Prince Muck-Muck," and his sister, who preferred "Princess Pretty Pony." As exciting as it should have been to meet his siblings, they were far from interesting.

He had to find Olwen Cullwich. And, angry at him or not, he needed to talk to King Piter. He had to warn him about what would happen, just as he'd tried to warn his mother. Maybe he could make him listen.

"I want my daddy," he said to Clio.

"Your daddy is busy, sweetie," she answered. "He'll come say good night later."

But Erec did not want to wait for later, when King Piter would no doubt pop his head in and whisk off again. He needed to talk to him now. It would be harder to escape, he knew, with Clio on high alert. But he waited until she was in the bathroom with his sister and then snuck out the door.

Before anybody noticed, he shut it and dashed behind a plant. Making his way forward, he darted behind statues and doors, carefully waiting until the hallways were clear. Everything seemed immense now, but he still knew the way to King Piter's throne room. He hoped the king was there.

It was hard to pull one of the heavy throne-room doors open, but

Erec managed to slip through. At the other end of the room, King Piter sat on his throne. He looked just the same as Erec remembered, except his hair was brown, not white. Talking to him was another familiar figure, who looked identical now to how he did in the future: the Hermit.

At first Erec's heart leapt when he saw the Hermit. He would help him explain everything to the king. But then Erec remembered that the Hermit would also have no clue about what was going on with him. Ten years ago the Hermit only knew Erec as a tiny kid.

Erec ran across the room, which took a while. King Piter and the Hermit looked up at him with surprise.

The king said, "Erec? Is that you? What are you doing here, boy?"

Erec climbed up the Lia Fail next to King Piter's throne and said, "I have to talk to you, Dad."

Saying "Dad" to the king sounded strange. The king set Erec on his knee. "You shouldn't be running around out here, Erec."

"Dad, I came from the future." He wished his words were clearer, and that he could sound older.

The king's eyebrows shot up. "Did you hear that?" He turned to the Hermit, amazed. "He said 'the future.'" Then to Erec, "Those are awfully big words for such a little boy. Good job, son." The king looked proud.

The Hermit, on the other hand, seemed interested. "You came from the future, Erec?"

Finally, Erec thought, someone was listening. "Yes. I have to tell you. Bad guys are going to try to get us. Hecate Jekyll will put a spell on you. We have to go away for a year." Would that take care of the problem? Maybe it would just put it off. Erec had another idea. "Let us sleep in your room from now on. Then we'll be safe. And guard the door."

King Piter's mouth hung wide open. "You are incredible, Erec. It's like you got super smart overnight. Can your brother and sister talk like this now too?"

Erec wanted to shake him. "Listen to me. Let us sleep in your room."

"That's amazing," the king said, stunned. And then, as if part of it finally sunk in, he said, "Good try using those big words, son. That's my Erec. As soon as he can speak well, he's trying to con his way into sleeping in our room." He laughed.

Erec closed his eyes in frustration. The Hermit watched him carefully. Finally, Erec said, "I came through your Time Bender." If this didn't explain it, nothing would.

The king bent his head toward him in amazement. "My . . ." He glanced at the Hermit, then lowered his voice. "You must have overheard me talk about that with your mother. I'm going to have to be a lot more careful." He shook his head. "Erec, you must never mention that thing again. It's a secret, okay? Just forget you heard me use those words."

"I have a dragon eye," Erec said, pointing at his blue eye. "I got it ten years from now."

The king could not believe what he was hearing. "And we think you three never pay attention to us. You've heard me talk about dragon eyes too? I'm going to have to be much more careful around you."

Erec sizzled with anger. Same old King Piter, not listening to him, not trusting him. And not owning up to being his father later. He held back the urge to pound him with his tiny fists, which would do no good at all. At least he could make the king uncomfortable, though. "Time Bender," he said. "Time Bender. Time Bender. Novikov Time Bender."

The king grew more and more flustered each time Erec said it.

"Shhh!" He held his finger before his lips. "Erec. That is not to be talked about. Secret words, son. Okay? Secret."

Erec glared at him. "Time Bender."

The king dropped his head into his hand.

But the Hermit asked, "What if he really is from the future? Maybe you should let the triplets sleep in your room awhile."

"Easy for you to say," the king said. "Then the nursemaids will be in and out. Or I'll be up half the night taking them to the bathroom and getting them drinks. No, they are fine where they are. And Erec is not from the future," he added. "He's from the same place his brother and sister are from. I happen to have known them all a little while."

Erec's respect for the Hermit grew immensely at that moment. But at least he could make one more request. "Olwen Cullwich," he said. "I need Olwen Cullwich."

"Olwen?" The king laughed. "He's a viceroy in my court." His forehead wrinkled. "I can't imagine you've even met him. You really remember him?"

Erec nodded. "Can I talk to him?"

The king looked like he was losing interest in the conversation. "No, Erec. You cannot talk with grown-ups that you don't know. Olwen is not a friend of yours."

"I need Olwen." Erec felt tears coming and could not stop them from pouring from his eyes. Ugh! He was so angry at himself for losing it. This would ruin any credibility he had. That was, if he'd ever had any at all.

"Okay," the king said, clapping his hands. "Time to go to the nursery. Sorry, Hermit. I better take him back."

"Would you like me to?" the Hermit asked.

"Yes!" Erec shouted. "I want Hermit!"

The king looked unsure. "I don't think so. I'll put him back myself, thanks." He picked Erec up.

Erec grabbed the Hermit's nose—the only part of him he could reach. The Hermit gave him a knowing nod, like a respectful salute.

"Olwen Cullwich!" Erec shouted, before his father, King Piter, carried him away.

Clio was beyond apologetic when the king returned Erec to the playroom. "Maybe it's best if someone else takes over for a while," the king said sternly. Clio ran from the room in tears.

Erec felt terrible about Clio. But at least her replacement was June.

"Mom!" He ran to give her a hug when he saw her. June had a big smile and a squeeze for him but said, "Just call me June, Erec. Save 'Mom' for your mommy, okay?"

"Okay. Mom? I mean, June?"

"Yes, Prince Poo-Poo Head? I mean, Erec?"

"I want Olwen Cullwich. I need Olwen."

Every chance he got over the next day he asked for Olwen Cullwich. Everyone seemed to think it was amusing, and they took turns speculating why he was fixated on that name. Nobody thought he had a clue who Olwen really was. Erec felt like a talking monkey—interesting, but not capable of making sense to anyone.

Finally he gave up. He stood against one of the toy shelves, arms crossed, a bitter look on his cherub face. Everything was going wrong. He was here, in the very spot he lived when he was little, seeing everything he always wanted to know about. He now knew exactly who his father and birth mother were. He saw June in action—no more questions about what she used to do in Alypium. He was in the same city as Olwen Cullwich, who still had the Twrch Trwyth. Everything was in place for him to make a clean sweep and fix everything, but nobody would pay attention to him. He was helpless.

He kicked a small wooden duck into a pile of toy animals, sending them flying. That was it. He was not going to let other people stand in his way. It was time to take care of things himself. Even if it meant wandering through Alypium in a three-year-old body to find Olwen Cullwich.

He told June that he wanted a hat, and she found a floppy denim one for him to wear. Then he waved his brother over. "C'mere. What's your name again?"

"Prince Muck-Muck!" the blond boy shouted, running around like a maniac.

"What's your real name?"

"Prince Muck-Muck!" the boy shouted louder, raising a plastic sword over his head.

"All right, put that down." Erec said. "Come here, Prince Muck-Muck. You know that girl? Our sister? What's her name?"

"Princess Pretty Pony!" The boy sped to his sister, zoomed around her awhile, knocking her crayons over, then ran back.

"All right," Erec said, "I have a secret."

Prince Muck-Muck's eyes lit up. "Tell me."

Erec whispered in his ear. "Throw Princess Pretty Pony's crayons and markers all over. Very funny." He flashed him a smile.

Prince Muck-Muck looked delighted. He laughed and clapped his hands, jumping on his toes. "Mess, mess!" Then he spread his arms out and raced to his sister with a demonic face. "Mess, mess!" he shouted.

Erec didn't wait one second. As soon as Prince Muck-Muck began to destroy Princess Pretty Pony's work, making a mess, mess, June headed over to intervene, and Erec darted out the door.

Once he was out of the west wing, it was easier to move around. People seemed busier, talking in groups or heading somewhere in a hurry. He pulled his hat tight over his head to hide his blond curls. A few people threw him funny looks when he darted out the front doors of the castle, but they must have figured he was running to a parent, as he smiled so confidently.

The front of the castle looked the same as Erec remembered from ten years later. The six stone statues of monsters looked immense now that he was small. Seeing them reminded him of how they would crumble in the future, unless he figured out how to stop Oscar—and himself.

The agora had changed a lot, though. Cloud Nine, his favorite cloud-cream shop, was not there, nor was Tricksters, the magic shop where Mr. Peebles had bought him his first remote control. He figured out a system to get around on the streets. As soon as he saw someone staring with a concerned look, he would wave wildly and start to run toward some other passerby, as if he had just found the person he was looking for.

He got pretty far this way. Soon he found a police officer gazing wistfully into a store he did not recognize. When he got closer he saw that its sign read VULCAN. Large wooden feet stuck out from the building's foundation at each corner. Erec noticed they twitched every once in a while.

The only other time he had seen a Vulcan store, it had been prancing and running wild in Otherness. They were rarely seen in Alypium and Aorth. Erec was surprised to see it sitting nicely in a row with the other stores, letting people wander in and out, although he did notice its toe was beginning to tap impatiently.

He approached the police officer, not thinking about his age. "How long has this been here?" Hearing his own slow and squeaky voice instantly reminded him how young he appeared.

"Well, hello there, little guy." The officer smiled down at him. His dark brown hair trailed down into a mustache and beard that surrounded his friendly smile like a halo. A badge on his uniform read, "Mark McMac, PC." He looked around. "Who are you out here with?"

"You," Erec's little voice said. He knew that would generate some interest.

"Hmm . . ." The officer picked him up. "I think we better find out where you live. Somebody's probably missing you right now."

"What is PC?" Erec asked.

"Primo Creator. Just a side business I'm starting up."

Erec nodded. "Can you tell me something?" he squeaked out.

"Why, sure." The officer smiled. "Why don't you just call me Officer Mark. Or Mark, if that's too hard."

Erec repeated himself slowly, hoping this time to get an answer. "How long has this store been here?"

"This one?" Officer Mark pointed to the Vulcan shop. "Pretty sure it just got here today. It's been sitting a long time for one of its kind. If I wasn't on duty, I'd go in. But I can't risk it now. This thing might hop away at any minute. I could end up miles away if I'm not careful." He looked at Erec warningly. "Don't you go wandering in there, understand? Vulcan shops usually won't leave when there are people inside them. But if shoppers take too long, or if the store's been waiting awhile to go, forget it."

Mark gazed through the open door of the shop. "I've got some great ideas, young fellow. One of these days I'm going to talk to Heph Vulcan about them. You see," he smiled, "I could take or leave working for the police department. It's okay, I guess. But I'm an inventor. As soon as I get a few more ideas lined up, if I just can get Heph Vulcan's ear, I'll be set."

"What are you inventing?" Erec asked.

Officer Mark looked at Erec and hesitated, but he must have felt confident that telling a three-year-old was safe. And he looked like he was bursting to talk about it. "All kinds of things. Some of them are simple. I make a mean chocolate cheesecake. But other things I'm working on are pretty complicated, kid. You wouldn't understand. I've been to Upper Earth recently, and they're doing some pretty neat things with computers there. Computers are these things that let people—"

"I know what computers are," Erec said.

"Good!" Mark was impressed. "I'm creating a kind of magic computer that we can use here. But I'm not sure what to call it. It will let people talk to each other, like the e-mail on Upper Earth. I know it's complicated."

Erec said, haltingly, "Call it the MagicNet. On Upper Earth they have the Internet. You can make it the same. Do it so people can buy things through it and look up things. They could search for something, like a lion hair, and a bunch of screens will show vendors selling it. They can bid with one another for the sale. Or it could connect to a library to read the books there. Or hook to a school to talk to an expert in something." It was tedious getting the words out, but Erec enjoyed the amazement on Mark's face as he spoke. Then he remembered these ideas must seem completely new to him.

Mark was fascinated. "You've got some gift, kid. Those concepts are incredible. Wait a minute." He searched for a notepad and began scribbling, "Vendors on screens . . . bidding war . . . colleges and libraries . . ." He grinned at Erec. "You're amazing. I thought I had some good ideas before, but now I'm back to square one again before I even approach Vulcan. I know how I can make this work. This is wonderful. Thanks, kid!" He laughed. "The MagicNet. I like it. I will call it that, as a tribute to you." Mark scratched his chin. "What's your name, kid? I better get you home."

"Cullwich," Erec said. "My name is Erec Cullwich. My father is Olwen Cullwich, in Alypium."

Officer Mark gave a nod. "All right, young Mr. Cullwich. Let's find out where you live."

"There must be some mistake," Olwen Cullwich said in surprise. "I don't have a son."

He looked so much like he had the last time Erec had seen him, ten years later, with perfectly combed, neat hair, sharp clothing, and kind blue eyes. Only now his hair was auburn, with streaks of gray. Seeing him made Erec sad. He tried not to think about what would happen to Olwen in the future. Well, if he set things right here, maybe Olwen would have a chance.

Officer Mark looked suspicious. "This kid here says you're his dad." He peered past Olwen into the house. "Your wife around?"

"I'm not married," Olwen said.

This was when Mark turned his questioning gaze to Erec. "You sure this is your dad, kid?"

Erec nodded and reached for Olwen. "Dad," he called to him.

Olwen did not reach back. "I'm sorry. There must be some mistake."

Erec became worried. He could not afford to mess this up too. He said to Olwen, "The Twrch Trwyth. I'm here about the Trwyth Boar."

Olwen's face turned white as a sheet. He looked like he couldn't believe his ears. "Th-that's just a story. It's not true." He turned to Officer Mark for support. "Everyone knows that story isn't true."

The officer shrugged. "Yeah, it's some fairy tale. You read it to your kid?" He asked, frustrated. "Aren't you gonna take him?"

Erec reached toward Olwen again. "I came from the future to warn you. Let me come inside."

Mark patted Erec on the head. "This little guy is pretty smart. He's a great kid. You're lucky."

Olwen looked back and forth between the officer and Erec. "You want the Twrch Trwyth? How do I know you're not going to turn into something terrible in there and try to—"

"Try to what?" Mark asked. "He's just a kid. All kids are terrible sometimes. You want me to take him back to the station because he's been misbehaving?" He threw Olwen a reproving glance.

Erec leaned toward Olwen. "I won't hurt you, I promise." He laid a baby hand on Olwen's shoulder.

Officer Mark rolled his eyes. "Don't tell me you're afraid of your tiny son. What's wrong with you, guy? This is some bright kid you got here."

Erec whipped his hat off, letting his golden curls bounce around his face. "I'm your prince. Now let me in."

While Mark seemed to think that "prince" was Erec's nickname, Olwen recognized him in an instant. "O-okay. I'll take him, officer."

Once they were inside, Olwen Cullwich paced nervously while Erec sat on a tall chair and watched him. Finally Olwen brought out some cookies and milk.

Erec said, "This is very important. You need to give me the Twrch Trwyth. I'll take it to the future with me and hook it to the five Awen. I have them ready. We need it to fix the Substance."

Olwen gulped in shock. "I don't know what you're talking about. The Awen is a myth. A story. I'm sorry."

Erec tried to make his baby eyes look stern. "I know you have it, Olwen. There's no use pretending. I'm from the future. Something really bad will happen to you." He shuddered, thinking about it. "You have to get rid of it to protect yourself. I know people have already been bothering you for it. It's putting you in danger."

Olwen nodded in agreement, but the situation was still too odd for him to believe. "If you're really from the future, prove it. Tell me something that nobody else knows will happen."

Erec had to consider. He should have been prepared for this.

What had the king told him about Olwen, again? There was a story about his birthday party and twelve pies. . . .

"Is your birthday soon?" Erec asked.

"In three days." Olwen crossed his arms. "You could have found that out anywhere." He rubbed his head. "Do you realize how strange it is talking to a tiny kid like this? Could you change your shape to look like an adult, at least?"

"I wish. Too bad I'm stuck this way. Here's some proof. At your birthday party at the castle—"

"I'm having a party at the castle?"

"You will. The king is going to surprise you by having twelve kinds of pie since you like pie so much. But he hires a clown, and one thing leads to another, and you end up with most of the pies smashed all over you."

Olwen looked like he didn't buy it. "I suppose now that I know, I won't be inclined to start a food fight."

Erec shrugged. "Just do whatever you would have anyway. King Piter told me about the pies ten years from now. It stuck in his memory that long. We'll see, I guess. I wish I knew more things to prove I'm from the future. The only other thing I know isn't very pretty. It's what will happen to you if you don't do something different with the Twrch Trwyth."

Olwen walked Erec back to the Castle Alypium. Seeing it from the outside reminded Erec that he had to figure out how to save it, and soon. When Olwen dropped him off in the west wing, Erec said, "Find me on your birthday. I'll show you where to put the Trwyth Boar."

Erec spent the next three days talking about going to Olwen's birthday party. Everyone was amazed that he even knew about it. They were sure they had not mentioned it to him.

"Maybe I'll sneak you down," Clio whispered, "since you're so interested in him. I suppose it wouldn't hurt for you to meet the man. He'll probably be flattered."

If you only knew, Erec thought.

He also tried on a few more occasions to warn King Piter and Queen Hesti about what would happen in their future. Queen Hesti's hair was a different length and color each time Erec saw her—short and black, long and red. But she still looked just as beautiful, her grayish green eyes laughing and joyous. Even though it was obvious she loved Erec, she could not bring herself to believe a word he said with his stumbling baby voice.

Erec even told the king that he would put the castle on its side to protect the Time Bender. The king looked at him like he was a mixture of crazy and brilliant, but then just reminded him never to use the words "Time Bender" again.

Out of spite, Erec repeated, "Time Bender," a few times before the king left the nursery. Then, after he was gone, Erec felt sick. His stomach rumbled and shook, until he realized he was about to start sobbing. He fought it, but his toddler body could not control the dam of emotion that burst inside of him.

Tears covered his face as he crumpled onto the rug. He had come here to change things, to save Aoquesth. And he couldn't do anything. If only they would listen to him, everything would be different. Erec would not end up going on the quests alone, and Aoquesth would live. But nobody would pay attention. He tried and tried, but the best he could do was make them think he was trying to sleep in his parents' room.

If he could not save Aoquesth, this trip would be a failure.

It didn't seem to matter anymore that he might get the Trwyth Boar from Olwen Cullwich and save the Substance. Aoquesth had given his life for him, and he was powerless to change that.

* * *

After he reminded her all day long, Clio took Erec to the hall where the surprise birthday party for Olwen Cullwich was to be held. But she'd made him eat dinner first and get cleaned up for bed. Then she waited awhile so they wouldn't interrupt Olwen's dinner.

She walked in with Erec on her hip—he was getting used to being carried, and it certainly got him places faster—when he spotted Olwen at the head of the table. Blue smudges, red stains, chocolate, and whipped cream covered his hair, clothes, and the parts of his face he had not wiped clean.

When Olwen spotted Erec, his eyes widened. He excused himself and went straight to Erec.

"You remember my son?" King Piter chortled. "He's been talking about you a lot lately. For some reason he's been obsessed with you."

Olwen nodded, though he was trembling. "Can I speak with him a minute?"

"That would be nice. He'd love it," the king said. "And then if you want to change clothing I'll have one of the servants help you."

Erec turned to Clio. "Put me down."

"Okay," Clio said, amused. She said to Olwen, "Do you mind? I hate to interrupt your birthday."

"No, please," Olwen said. He crouched before Erec. "You were right about the pies," he said softly, "but I'm still not sure what that means. Maybe you heard your father talk about the clown. Maybe you talked to the clown about putting a pie in my face." He thought a moment. "I guess, though, it would be tough to predict the rest. I could have stopped myself from trying to get the clown back, but something about the way he looked at me just got me, and I let myself go. I don't know." He shook his head. "Do you have something else you could tell me to prove what you're saying? It's just hard to assume you're really from the future."

Erec tried to remember what else the king had said about Olwen.

"Wait. There was something. The king said soon after today you got captured by a sorcerer who did something bad to you, trying to get the Trwyth Boar. You barely survived. Keep an eye out. Be ready for him."

"Thanks." Olwen looked shaken. "Listen, I need to think about this longer, see what happens."

"Come with me," Erec said. "Let me show you something."

Olwen announced to the others that he would be back, that Erec wanted to take him somewhere. King Piter and Clio protested, saying that it was his party and he didn't have to take care of a child. But he waved them off and followed Erec out into the west wing.

After walking a ways, Erec said, "It would be quicker if you carry me. If you don't mind."

Olwen picked him up, and Erec directed him into the catacombs under the castle. "I'll show you how I got here." He knew that the king would have a fit if Olwen, or anybody else, found out about the Novikov Time Bender. But Erec didn't care what King Piter thought. Especially after finding out how the king basically had been rejecting him as his own son all this time. Plus, the castle would be on its side soon, and that would keep Erec from getting back to the Time Bender. He needed Olwen to understand now.

Homer floated in the room where the Time Bender was. "Hello, Erec," the ghost said. "You've brought a friend. Nice to meet you, Mr. Cullwich."

Olwen stumbled over his words. "I . . . you're a golden ghost. And . . . this—" He walked over to the Time Bender, surveying it from top to bottom. "Is this what I think it is?" He looked at the dials inside. "C-can . . . I use it to go forward? See the future?" Olwen ran a hand over the machine.

"It's a Time Bender," Homer said. "Erec used it to get here, into his three-year-old body, from ten years from now."

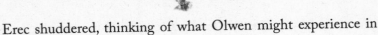

Erec shuddered, thinking of what Olwen might experience in the future.

"It's too dangerous," Homer told him. "You might go past the time when you are no longer alive, and then you would remain stuck there."

Erec did not want to tell Olwen that he knew when and how he would die. But maybe he could find a way to change that. "Olwen," he said, "someday Baskania will ask you if you know where the Twrch Trwyth is. Please do not tell him you swallowed it. Okay? It's really important."

Olwen turned pale. "How did you know ...? I was just researching how to get rid of it. And that was the way that was recommended to me."

"I know because I heard you tell Baskania in the future. Just ... don't say it to him, okay?"

Olwen nodded, absorbing all he'd been told. "I think I'm convinced. I was going to get rid of the thing anyway. It's too dangerous for me to keep. If you need it for one of your quests, Prince Erec, to fix the Substance with the Awen—if you can do that—I'll let you have it." He reached behind his neck, undid a clasp, and pulled a long chain from under his shirt. On it hung a glass vial in the shape of a fat pig. The top of the vial was soldered onto the chain. Erec could see tiny fragments of hairs in the vial, and a miniature comb and scissors.

Olwen handed it to Erec, but Erec did not take it. "We need to hide it here," he said. "Find a crack in the stone. Somewhere it can stay hidden for ten years and not be found accidentally."

Erec felt the Twrch Trwyth would be safe in the room where Homer kept watch. Olwen felt around the walls. "Here's a loose stone." He pulled it out. "Right in here might work. Will you be able to reach it?"

"I'll be a lot taller then," Erec pointed out. "Just do me a favor, okay? Please don't tell anyone you put this here. Especially Baskania, when he asks you later. Or he'll get it before I do and use it for all the wrong things."

"I know enough about Baskania to know that he should never get hold of this vial." Olwen studied the loose stone, then turned to Erec. "Will you remember where it is in ten years?"

"Sure. I'll be there to get it in two minutes."

Olwen looked surprised. "You're not going back upstairs? What will I tell your parents?"

Homer said, "You can say he went back to the nursery. That's where they will find him, when this Erec goes into his future again. And the little Erec won't remember one bit of this."

Erec took a deep breath. It was time to go back. If only he knew the small details of what would happen to his parents soon, like he did with Olwen, maybe he could convince them he was really from the future. But there was nothing he could think of.

"As long as you leave the Twrch Trwyth here, I'll go back now. Thank you." He reached a little hand up to shake Olwen's big one.

CHAPTER TWENTY-FIVE

King Piter's First Mistake

EREC'S BODY WENT through strange distortions, painful stretches, and yanks in the Time Bender. Dust clouds whizzed around the glass from left to right, making him dizzy. He was sore and tired when it cleared, and it took some effort to push the glass door open and sit up.

The loose stone where Olwen had hidden the Twrch Trwyth looked just as it had before.

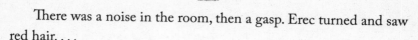

There was a noise in the room, then a gasp. Erec turned and saw red hair. . . .

Oscar was in the room with him.

Oscar looked as scared and shocked as he did. He almost fell over, backing away. "I'm sorry. I'm sorry. Sorry," he kept saying, wringing his hands. "I didn't think I'd see you here. Or I'd have never come. Sorry, Erec. I'm so, so sorry."

They both looked around, waiting for Baskania to materialize at any moment.

"I'll go," Oscar said, his face red and distorted, as if he were starting to cry. "Why are you here? Wait, don't tell me anything." He stopped. "Listen, Erec. I will *not* let Rosco tell about this. He can't." Oscar caught his breath. "It's not just saving you, which I would do no matter what, it's also the Time Bender. Baskania *cannot* find out about this. Imagine what he would do to the world? We'd all be dead, long ago, if he was to get his hands on this."

His face grew a deeper scarlet and he kicked a wall. He grunted, "I *can't*. I *won't*. Rosco, if you are hearing this, listen hard. I will end my life right now if you send Baskania here. I can't go on like this. If you ever felt a thing for me, this needs to stay *quiet*." He paced, pounding and kicking the stone wall until his hand was bleeding. Erec was frightened for him on top of being afraid that Baskania would show up. "Erec, I will not let Rosco tell this." He looked at Erec with pleading eyes.

Erec knew as well as he did that he had no real control over what would happen. "Why were you here at all, Oscar? Didn't you get my snail mail?"

"Yeah." Oscar nodded miserably. "But I had no idea you were in the castle now. Seems like you were always off doing quests all over the place. And even if you were, I never thought you'd be down here in this room. I was so careful when I snuck down here, so that nobody would see me. I kept my head down the whole time and stared at the floor so I wouldn't see anybody at all. I can't believe you were here in the Time Bender."

"But why did you come here?"

"I had to see it again." Oscar pointed at the machine. "I just had to. Can't explain. I've been thinking about it, that's all. I had some ideas I needed to talk to Homer about." He nodded toward the golden ghost.

"Look, we need to get out of here," Erec said. "Baskania might show up any minute."

"Okay. Sorry, Erec." Oscar looked miserable. "I'll stay far away now."

Erec felt terrible for him. "Look, let me know if I can help you with this Rosco thing. I'll do anything, okay? And we'll always be friends. Promise."

"Yeah, sure." Oscar sniffed and ran out of the room.

Erec looked both ways down the hall to make sure nobody was coming. Then he pulled the loose stone out of the wall. Olwen Cullwich's boar-shaped vial was right where he had placed it ten years ago. Erec removed it and slid the chain around his neck and tucked it inside his shirt, alongside his Amulet of Virtues.

Baskania still had not shown up, which surprised Erec. Had Rosco actually listened to Oscar's threats? His insistence?

Homer hovered in the air. "Good luck, Erec," he said. "I hope you succeed with your quest."

Erec thanked him and left while the coast was still clear.

There was still no sign of Baskania, or Oscar, as Erec walked back to the west wing. It was strange and wonderful seeing everything from a normal height again. He felt so much more confident in a teenage body instead of dealing with those spindly, tiny arms and legs, relatively huge head, and embarrassing voice.

His visit to the past could have gone better, but at least he had the Twrch Trwyth around his neck. The Hermit had been right again. And the Fates knew what they were talking about. Erec just had to realize that the Twrch Trwyth had been waiting for him all along, back in time. Thank goodness Olwen had left it there for him.

Erec grew sad as that thought came to him. Olwen was dead now. Erec remembered seeing him die. But hadn't going back in time changed how that turned out?

He thought so. Something was different now. Hadn't something awful happened to Olwen before? He remembered it, in a way, something terrible, gory, and upsetting. Something about Olwen being torn apart? But that memory was fading fast.

No, Olwen was not torn apart. Erec remembered hiding in the bushes with Bethany and Jack. He had been panicked that Baskania would make Olwen spill the beans about hiding the Twrch Trwyth. But before Baskania could ask him much, Olwen had popped something into his own mouth and had died immediately. He had taken his own life to protect Erec's secret. Baskania searched Olwen's house and didn't find anything, then gave up.

Erec could not believe how generous and noble Olwen had been. Erec had a vague feeling that things were different before he had gone back in time. Something awful and disgusting had happened to him before, Erec thought, but his memory of that quickly faded. Maybe Olwen's fate had changed after he went into the past. He guessed he'd never know. But there was one thing he knew he had not fixed. He still had not figured out how to save Aoquesth. Maybe it was impossible. But he would never give up.

Now Erec had another mission. Before he returned to the Isle of Man to try his luck at hooking the five Awen to the Twrch Trwyth, he had to talk to King Piter. His father.

* * *

The king was in his throne room with the Hermit. Erec walked in, stone-faced. "Can I have a moment, please?" he asked the Hermit. "With my father."

King Piter's eyes widened in fright. The Hermit, however, looked as casual as if Erec said this alarming truth every day. He patted Erec on the head as he left. "Have a good time, little Poo-Poo Head."

"So." Erec scowled at his father. "I guess I can't expect you to give me any satisfactory explanation why you abandoned me with June. And then, on top of it, why you never bothered to fess up that you were really my father—even though you knew I was trying to figure that out all this time."

He was seething, and he paused to catch his breath. "You have a lot to answer for. And I'm not leaving until I get all the details."

The king grabbed his scepter and looked around the room in fear. Erec looked too, wondering if Baskania had appeared, but he saw nobody. "Erec, I tried to explain. You are not ready to know this yet. I am not ready either."

It sounded to Erec like the same old song and dance. "You can keep saying that, again and again, but it's not going to take away what I already know. I just went back in time, with your Time Bender, to when I was three. I tried to warn you, by the way, of what was going to happen to you. Too bad you wouldn't listen to me."

"I know." The king nodded. He seemed a shadow of his normal self. Weak. Resigned. "I realized too late that I should have listened to you then. I am sorry, Erec. I've made some mistakes, but that was a big one. My second big one."

King Piter had once told Erec that he would make three mistakes, and so would Baskania. The Fates had predicted that, and by now Erec believed what the Fates said. So, letting himself get put under a spell by Hecate Jekyll was King Piter's second mistake. Now Erec knew that if the king had listened to him, he could have prevented it. And the king had said that he didn't know what his third mistake would be.

"So, what was your first mistake?" Erec asked.

"It was a big one." The king looked around again fearfully. Erec did not see anybody else with them. "I'll tell you in a minute. But first, please remember I never wanted to abandon you. I did not have a choice because of my first mistake. I love you, Erec. I always have."

"Just not enough to admit to me you are my father," Erec said bitterly. "I guess you were afraid I would take up too much of your precious time." His mouth twisted in disgust. "Funny, you had the time for Bethany. You let her think you were like a father to her."

"Bethany needed me," the king said. "Think about what she had before, with Earl." His eyes were moist.

"I needed you," Erec said fiercely. "My whole life I grew up thinking I had a horrible father from that memory replacement. But I still wanted to know who he was. To know something about where I came from, where I belonged. I wished for a father so hard and for so long. You don't know how much it meant to me. But here you were, alive and well, and not even bothering to send a postcard." Erec's voice caught. "I guess you were too busy trying to fix the Substance to even make one phone call."

The king rubbed his forehead furiously. "It's not like that, Erec. It is my fault you are feeling this way, my fault that I couldn't tell you a long time ago. But that's the way it worked out."

"Why?" Erec demanded.

"Give me a minute." The king took a breath. "You'll find out soon enough, anyway." He looked sick, wiping sweat off his forehead. Then he glanced up. "Here's one thing I might as well tell you. You know the memory replacement you got, the horrible father?" He paused while Erec nodded. "That was Bethany's memory."

Bethany's? Erec was confused. He thought Bethany's parents were supposed to be so great. "That was her father?"

"No, it was not her father. It was Earl Evirly."

Erec was stunned. Earl? The voice in his dream had sounded familiar after he'd met Earl. But he had never made the connection.

The king looked weary. "Just go to the Memory Mogul when you get a chance. He'll take the memory out for you. You don't need to carry that one around."

Erec noticed that the king was waving his scepter toward him. It was odd. The king never played around with it, and Erec knew why. He was smart to handle it as little as possible. But King Piter was definitely bouncing it toward him, even though Erec could not feel any magic coming from it.

The king observed the scepter in his hand. "Best I tell you now, Erec. My first mistake was a big one. Even bigger than not listening to you and letting myself get hypnotized for ten years." He sighed. "You had not only warned me, but months earlier I had a warning from the Oracle as well. The Fates told me that I would be gone soon, out of action. They were referring to my being bewitched by Hecate Jekyll, it turns out. But I thought they meant I was going to die.

"They said that my child would succeed me and fix what I could not fix. They may have been talking about the Substance. I still hope you will be able to fix that, Erec, when I could not." The king was shaking his scepter more as he spoke. "I thought I would die soon, that you three would take over for me. I wasn't happy about going, but I had no idea that things would turn out so badly in the castle. The Fates are not always forthcoming with all the information, I am afraid.

"So my first mistake was misinterpreting the warning that the Fates had given me, even before I ignored yours. Boy, did I get that wrong. I was convinced I was going to die. So, when Hecate Jekyll put me under her spell, in my last clear moments I was sure that was the end for me. Of course, if everything went her way and they crowned the Stain boys as kings at the coronation, she would have killed me soon after, I'm sure. They were just keeping me around to convince people that I was handing my throne down in an orderly, planned way.

"Hecate Jekyll cast her spell just five days after the awful night when intruders broke in and almost captured you. Your mother barely escaped with her life. I was still stunned by it, but I was figuring out ways to bring you back, protect you here. I was worried though, since I thought I would die soon and not be around to help you. Your dragon eye had been waiting for you here in the castle. But since my AdviSeers were all gone, and everything was a shambles, it did not seem safe here anymore—especially since I was sure I would not be around to watch it for long. Aoquesth agreed to guard it for you, luckily.

"You see, I did put one thing together. In those few days after you were almost kidnapped, I remembered everything that you had warned me about. You had said you came from the future, from ten years later. You said you got your dragon eye around then. Earlier than you should have, mind you. So I told Aoquesth when you would be showing up for it."

Erec gasped, putting it together in his mind. No wonder Aoquesth had known.

The king continued. "I was distraught. I felt helpless, trying to plan for you to come home, yet thinking I wouldn't live to protect you. So when I first felt Hecate Jekyll's spell sink in, after I sipped that cup of tea, I was sure I was dying. I decided to do two things while my scepter was still in my hand. First, I put the castle on its side, to hide the Time Bender from Baskania and other people who might use it for evil. They would destroy the world if they found it.

"And the other thing I did . . ." He waved the scepter more, gripped it tighter.

"Yes?"

The king sighed. "I had built this castle, Erec, with magic. It was my final quest. Posey and Pluto built theirs then as well. The old castle that Baskania had once put up was destroyed. We had to use our scepters to do the job, but that was okay, because at the moment we finished that quest we were the rulers, and able to use the scepters then anyway.

"When each of us built these castles, we used much more than just bricks, stone, and wood. A lot of magic went into these walls. Magic that is only attuned to me. This castle is a shield to me, a fortress. I am stronger in it, much more powerful. The magic of this castle responds only to me. That is why, when I was hypnotized for ten years, the castle rebelled and refused to let itself be cleaned. This castle is a part of me, in a sense.

"So I knew when my triplets would finish their quests, when it was time for them to take over as rulers, their final job would be to destroy the castles that exist and build new ones for themselves with their scepters. These new castles will be attuned to each of you, strengthening you, and serving nobody else but you."

The king hung his head, then he looked at Erec with sad eyes. "I was afraid. I thought I'd be long gone before you would become king of Alypium. That is where you are destined to rule, Erec. But what would happen if I were gone? Someone else would take over. You might get stolen, waylaid. There were evil plans floating about; that was obvious after what happened to you and my AdviSeers. So I conjured a quick but permanent spell, something to make sure that no matter who took over, you would end up ruling Alypium one day.

"I put an enchantment on the castle, so that no matter what, an hour after you found out that you were my son, it would self-destruct. And another spell on my scepter, so that at that same time, it would fly to you and become yours. So you must have gone back in time an hour ago?"

It seemed like ages ago that Erec had used the Time Bender to go back to his childhood. But while he was gone, no time must have passed here.

The king's words sank in slowly. "You put a curse on your castle?"

"Yes. A big mistake, as it turns out. At the time, June was keeping you safe in Upper Earth. And the plan was, until I could bring you back to the castle safely, that she would raise you as a normal child there. You would not know who you are, or your relation to me, so nobody would find you. We made that plan before I put a spell on the castle, but I also used my last second with my scepter to send June a final message reminding her not to tell you who you really were.

"But I also knew that someday you would discover that you were my son, because you came back in time to warn me. I couldn't give the castle to you when you were three, but I thought by age thirteen . . ."

The king shook his head. "It was crazy, on all accounts. If I'd had time to think it over, I'd have made the spell go into effect years after you found out. But I had only minutes and I was completely distraught—dying, I believed. I made the spell unchangeable, so I can't do anything to fix it. I had to, or someone would have figured a way to undo it, and I couldn't let that happen. So, there you have it."

The king looked sick. "The lengths I went to to keep you from finding this out were enormous. Spreading the word that you had died. I was always afraid that you would hear from someone that 'Rex' was my last name, so I made it taboo in the castle. Luckily, half the people in Alypium probably don't even know I have a last name."

"Why didn't you change my name?" Erec asked.

"There is a lot of power in your name. You needed to keep the name to keep the power." The scepter was now shaking wildly in the king's hand. Erec could now see his knuckles were white, gripping it. The king could barely hold on to it.

"This will fly to you soon," the king said. "You are not ready for it. I'm sorry, Erec. Try to give it back to me if you can."

That made Erec nervous. "If I can? What do you mean?"

The scepter was yanking itself loose from King Piter's grasp. "I know how the scepter affects you. It will be hard to let go this time, harder than it was before. You've used it too much already, long before you should have. The best chance you have now of learning to control it is to hand it right back over to me for safekeeping. Okay?"

A loud crack echoed through the room. Erec didn't see what caused it, but he knew what was happening. The castle foundation was starting to split. "We have to get out of here," he said. "It's going to come down any minute."

The king's scepter wrenched itself from his grasp. It flew at Erec, straight into his hand. Warm power flowed through it. It felt better in Erec's hand than ever before. His Twrch Trwyth vial grew warm against his chest. Was it making the scepter's power even stronger?

Tingles of energy raced through him. He could do anything. Horror wavered in the back of his mind. He knew that this massive strength was a terrible thing. It would distort him, make him power mad. But those thoughts were overwhelmed by an amazing surge of wonder, the feeling that everything was now fixed and fixable.

"G'day, mate!" The words of the scepter echoed in his head. "Pleased to be at your service again. Anything you'd like me to do right now for you?" Erec had almost forgotten that the scepters spoke to their owners, gave them advice. Queen Posey had told him that only their owners could hear them, except during the coronation ceremony, when everybody could hear what they said.

King Piter watched him, wary. "Give it back, now. Okay?"

Erec eyed the scepter, unsure what to do. A loud snap and a bang resounded through the throne room, and the floor shook. "Can I use it to fix the castle?"

"No," said the king. "Or I would have done that myself. Unfortunately, the spell I put on the castle is unchangeable. This castle will destroy itself now. Nothing can stop it. Now give me the scepter, Erec."

"But then there will be no castle here," Erec said. "Am I supposed to use the scepter to build a new one now?"

The scepter's voice said, "That's certainly possible, if you'd like."

Erec knew he was up to the job, especially since his Trwyth Boar vial was making the scepter stronger. Using it for such a big task made his mouth water.

"No!" The king looked frantic. "The amount of power and energy that would take is enormous. It would destroy you. Please, Erec. Wait for that. You can always do it later. But now it would completely overwhelm you. You would be just a shadow after that, lost like Pluto."

King Pluto. For the first time, Erec realized he was his uncle. "My own uncle sent me into Aoquesth's cave, knowing I could've been killed in there?"

The king nodded. "Pluto is a good man, somewhere underneath. But that part of him is lost. That is what the scepter, and Baskania, have done to him."

Erec stroked the scepter. It felt so good in his hands. So right. He would never make those mistakes, lose sight of good and evil. He wasn't as dumb and immature as the king seemed to think. "I'll tell you what," he said. "I'll use the scepter just a little longer, and then I'll give it back to you." He slid a finger down its side. "A little more time can't hurt. I don't want to give it up just yet. No, not yet."

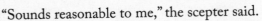

"Sounds reasonable to me," the scepter said.

"Erec," the king said, exasperated, "don't let it steer you." More loud bangs echoed around them, and the walls shook in deep ripples. "There is nothing you need it for now. Let me keep it for you, please."

"You just want it for yourself," Erec snapped. Then he drew back in alarm. What was he thinking? He became aware of the fear racing through him, and his misgivings, and he felt confused. "I thought I'd use it to help me put the five Awen on the Twrch Trwyth, to finish my quest and fix the Substance." That seemed like a good idea. Working with those Awen would be next to impossible otherwise.

"You can't use the scepter to do your quests, Erec," the king told him. "Your quests are for you to do, not the scepter to do. You need to learn from them, and grow."

"But how else can I connect the Awen to the Trwyth Boar vial? The Awen of Knowledge would make me forget what to do."

"Once you have the Twrch Trwyth vial, the Awen won't affect you as much as they did before," King Piter pointed out. "Nobody else can help you, though. Your friends would be helpless with all five Awen there." The king gazed at him with admiration. "So you got the five Awen . . . and the Twrch Trwyth? That's amazing. I thought the Trwyth vial was long gone."

"It was. Olwen Cullwich hid it for me in the castle when I went back in the Time Bender."

King Piter's brow wrinkled as he recalled something from the past. "Funny, I have a vague memory of you wanting to see Olwen way back then. Strange, I never thought much about it." He sighed. "Nobody else knows why I didn't want you to find out you were my son. I couldn't have word getting around about the castle destroying itself."

Balthazar Ugry soared into the room out of nowhere, a swish of black cloth through the air. "I *told* you, sire," he steamed. "He should have been locked up. Now look what he's done."

Ugry's icy stare and his smell chilled Erec to the core. Ugry pointed his carved wooden walking stick toward Erec. Waves of green light shot from its end. Erec watched, horrified, as the rays reached toward him, then bent in the air around him, circling him. He didn't feel anything, but they terrified him, still.

"It won't work, Balthazar," the king said sadly. "You can't do it."

Erec realized then that Ugry was trying to stop him with those rays, but he was too powerful for them. Smirking at Ugry, he shot a blast of rope toward him from the scepter, to tie him up. The rope shot straight through Ugry, though, and fell to the floor.

The king cleared his throat. "This is not helping, Balthazar. Please. I need to speak with Erec alone, not rile him up."

Ugry scowled, looking back and forth between Erec and the king, then swept from the room.

The king scratched his chin. It seemed like he was trying to calm Erec down, keep him talking. "I thought I was being so careful. Homer was guarding the Time Bender. One point I don't understand. I knew you had gone back in time to warn me, but I thought that would change, since I made sure you didn't know I was your father. I thought that would keep you from going into the past. It never connected that going back there would *let* you find out I was your father." He thought awhile. "I was sure you already knew you were my son when you went back. Why else would you have come to help me?"

Erec said, "I went back to warn you because I wanted to fix everything that happened starting then. And I found out who I was when I got there." The king looked smaller now, hunched in his throne. Erec remembered that he was five hundred years old. He would die soon without the scepter. Erec closed his eyes. He knew he was not ready for it yet. Let the king have it awhile longer.

But he felt so strong now, so incredible. What should he do?

Then it occurred to him. He would let himself have it just awhile longer. But he'd put a spell on it to make sure it would return to the king before long. He'd get the king out of here. Put him somewhere safe, close to where Erec was headed. That would make sure the scepter would go back to the king soon.

He closed his eyes and said aloud, "Stay with me, scepter, until we see King Piter next. Then fly back into his hands and work for him."

A surge of power tore through the scepter, streaming through Erec's body, blossoming from his fingertips. He felt like he was flying, on top of the world. Then the feeling ended.

"Erec, no!" King Piter was reaching to him, upset.

The power of the scepter surged through Erec, making him invincible, perfect.

"Put it down, Erec," the king pleaded. "Give it back to me, son."

"Son"! How dare he call Erec that now? Now that he wanted something from him.

But Erec did not want to give the scepter back. It was taken care of. The king would get it back, one of these days. It was time for Erec to enjoy it. He could make better use of it now. It was his turn, finally. And he would use it as he wished. He let the buzz of electricity take over his mind, washing away all other feelings.

The king pointed a finger. Erec knew he was working magic on him. Or trying to. But not this time. Erec was the strong one now. He tipped his scepter and the king disappeared. Give him a nice little visit with the druids in Avalon, Erec thought.

He strolled outside to the castle gardens, enjoying the immense electric energy of the scepter. Crackles snapped in some bushes behind him. When he turned he saw a flash of red hair, then heard footsteps running away. Oscar again! What was he doing here?

In a few minutes he heard a noise. Loud cracks and crashes echoed and the ground began to shake. He turned to see the Castle Alypium caving in before his eyes. He tilted the scepter and told it to clear everyone out from the castle so nobody would get hurt. Its power surges rocked him, dazed him.

He stood, gripped by fear and surges of power from the scepter, and watched the Castle Alypium fall apart.

CHAPTER TWENTY-SIX

The Battle Between Love and Hate

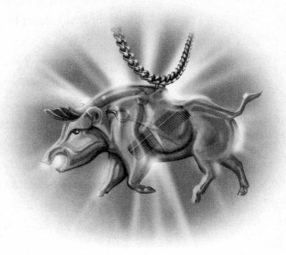

PEOPLE WERE RUNNING in every direction, screaming. Mass panic filled the air. People who had been in the castle were standing in awe outside, watching it implode. The noise of the splitting foundation and crashing towers was deafening. Several of the turrets were starting to shake and topple, crashing in through the roofs.

It was like déjà vu, standing here, feeling what he was feeling now. Erec had been here so many times in his mind, looking at his future in the little dark room. He was sure that someone else had been destroying the castle, when he was really to blame all along. He cringed as it caved in before his eyes.

So Oscar had been out here. Just like he had seen in his visions. Well, he knew why now. Oscar had been moving slow, hiding, and keeping his eyes down. It probably took him this long to get out of the castle from the catacombs.

Could Rosco not have told Baskania about the Time Bender? It seemed that was the case, as Baskania had never showed up. Did Oscar actually stop him somehow? Rosco had told Baskania, "It's time for the Castle Alypium to come down." He knew from Oscar that the castle was crumbling. But nothing about the Time Bender. Erec wondered why.

He knew that if he walked around the corner, he would see Balor Stain and his brothers. Balor would be holding his whistle, laughing with glee, just having loosed hordes of bronze ghosts to help finish the castle off.

The last person he wanted to see now was Balor. Or Baskania, who would be showing up soon. Thinking of him, Erec ran into the woods near the gardens and watched the castle tumble down under a stand of tall trees. With each step he bounced high into the air. His magic Sneakers were stronger now that he had the Twrch Trwyth, he realized.

Then a worry flashed into his head. Where was Bethany? She was probably safe. She couldn't be in the castle anymore. But she'd be upset and not know what was going on. With a tip of his scepter Bethany stood before him, staring around her in shock.

"Are you okay?" Erec asked.

"How did I get here?" She looked out at the collapsing castle, confused. "Look at that." They were quiet awhile, watching the destruction continue. "I don't understand anything today," she said.

"Maybe this is all a dream. I was finishing a new proof, a really big one, to tell me which foundation of math I should base the latest book I'm writing. And then the walls started to shake. I thought it was an earthquake. And then Jam appeared on a flying carpet!"

Her face was glowing, remembering her adventure. "He said the castle was caving in. He saved me and Cutie Pie. The carpet was really big, and I dumped all my important things, magic things, the druid's gifts, my money, and my math work on it. Then," she told him proudly, "we went to your room and grabbed your MagicLight, your money, and everything we could find before it all fell apart. Jam got Wolfboy out of his doghouse, so he's safe too. And he flew us far away. Then I appeared here with you." She stared at the castle as it crumbled before their eyes.

Erec noticed the six huge statues in front of the castle quivering, wiggling from the cracks running through them. Then he blinked. Maybe it was his imagination, or the angle he was watching from, but it looked like the statues were running, galloping away.

Bethany sounded dazed. "I just hope King Piter is okay. And you . . . thank goodness . . ." She gasped, noticing Erec's scepter. "What . . . what happened? How did you get that?"

"It's all going to be okay, Bethany. I got the Twrch Trwyth, and I'm going to the Isle of Man again to attach it to the Awen. King Piter is waiting for me in Avalon." He did not feel like going into the details of how the king had gotten there. Erec could imagine her disapproval. "I went back in the Time Bender, back to when I was three," he explained. "That's how I got the Trwyth Boar from Olwen Cullwich. And King Piter programmed the castle to collapse when I found out. . . . You'll never guess what I found out there."

Bethany looked dazed, like his words weren't fully sinking in amid the chaos around them. "What?"

"I'm one of the royal triplets. King Piter is my dad."

Bethany stared at him in horror. "But . . . no. That's not possible. He's—"

"I know," Erec said, scowling. "You'd think he'd have bothered to tell me by now. But I guess he couldn't, because his castle would collapse when I found out."

Bethany looked back at the castle falling to pieces. "You . . . you did this?" Her lower lip trembled. "You're King Piter's . . ." Her face flushed and she clenched her fists. "You ruined *everything*! I hate you!" Tears sprang to her eyes and she ran away.

Erec's head spun. It was so hard to think straight after all that had happened. Why did Bethany have to blame him? He was only trying his best. He didn't know the castle would collapse. She didn't have to get so mad at him.

Surges from the scepter raced through him, as well as waves of dread. He had to go to the Isle of Man and finish his quest. King Piter would get his scepter back, and everything would be fine again. Erec would clear things up with Bethany later. She'd forgive him for ruining the castle. She'd have to understand that it wasn't his fault really.

Then again, maybe he shouldn't go to the Isle of Man yet. Why give up the scepter so soon? He was getting used to its warmth, the great feeling that it gave him just to hold it. It seemed wrong to let that all go so soon. Think of all he could do with it now that he finally had it.

No! Erec thought, shuddering. He had to go to the Isle of Man immediately. It would be hard enough giving up the scepter as it was. He could feel the part of him that craved the scepter growing stronger. If he kept it longer it would take him over completely. He looked around. The Port-O-Door in the castle would be gone now. How would he get to the Isle of Man?

Of course. The scepter. The king said he couldn't use it for the quest, but getting there was not really part of his quest. He wondered if he should bring anyone with him. But, like King Piter said, nobody else could help him there. The Awen of Knowledge would make them unable to do anything.

Take me to the coast of the Isle of Man, where the Awen are buried, he thought. And, in a blink of an eye, he was there.

The cold wind made Erec shiver. He had forgotten to bring a coat. The energy rumbling through his hand from the scepter warmed him and reminded him how he could get one. Put a coat and hat on me. Make me warm, he thought.

The jolts of power surging through him made him feel invincible. He could feel the Twrch Trwyth vial tingling around his neck, strengthening the scepter's power. Yet at the same time he was depressed. And dazed. He definitely felt dazed. Fog rolled across the island, and it was hard to see through.

Erec knew the king would not approve of him using the scepter for transportation or to get a coat. But what business was it of his, anyway? This coat and hat felt great, and he was as warm as he had been in Alypium. Why was King Piter butting into his business anyway? What good had he ever done for Erec? What a lousy father.

Erec could not remember why he had come. But something around his neck felt warm. He pulled it out. It was the Twrch Trwyth on a chain around his neck. Then he remembered the Awen. That was why he was confused and grumpy. He probably didn't look so hot, either. But at least he could think now that he had the Trwyth Boar vial in his hand.

Mists twisted across the landscape, making it look surreal. Dangling icicles danced under bare tree branches in the wind, like sparkly fingers pointing at him. A huge cliff loomed over the edge of a grassy heath like an immense shadow. Tangles of heather shimmied in the fog with purple moor grasses, beckoning him forward. Seagulls screamed overhead, their calls like harsh laughter. *Aaa . . . aaa . . . aaa.*

He came upon the boulder near the spiky furze shrub. The Awen were hidden under there. Without warning, the ground rumbled. A huge rock tumbled down the nearby cliff. As he walked closer to the boulder, he felt more dazed and ill at ease, annoyed. Why was he here? Why couldn't he just go home and go to bed? Why were the Fates always lugging him here and there, running stupid errands? Let someone else do it for once.

A warm buzzing in his hand felt good, and something spoke to him. "Mate, you might want to take that boar vial out and hold it, clear your head a bit."

All right, he thought. Erec closed his hand around the vial and felt better. He just had to attach the Awen to this somehow. But how? Nobody had told him how it worked. He tried to remember what he did know. Let's see. Lots of people died trying this. That was the one thing he knew. Also, the Trwyth Boar vial made all the magic it hooked to far stronger.

Erec frowned. If the Twrch Trwyth made the Awen much stronger, what would happen to him when he hooked one up? He could see why people had died. How was he supposed to do it? Once the Awen of Knowledge became stronger, he wouldn't be able to function at all.

There was one easy solution. He was holding it in his hand. The scepter could do it for him easily. Who cared if King Piter said that he wasn't supposed to do his quests with it? He had it now, so why not use it? What was he even doing this for, anyway? To score some credit with the Fates? To look good to the Alypians?

No. The only reason was to fix the Substance, save Upper

Earth. And if using the scepter would be the easiest way, then good for him.

A scuffling noise made Erec turn around. He saw a shadow in the distance. A person was approaching. Another figure followed, but he could not make out who either of them were.

They were coming closer, headed straight for him. Erec crouched near a rock, scepter held out in front of him. He could use it to capture them. Anger filled him, and he became confused again until he touched the Twrch Trwyth, which was now quite warm.

The figures grew closer but were obscured by the haze. Erec wondered if they could see. As they approached, Erec felt a chill. He grasped the scepter more tightly.

But despite his grip, it jerked out of his hand and flew away into the mist.

A spike of cold filled him, along with a pang of longing. He had lost everything. Who were these people? Did they steal his scepter? He wouldn't be able to connect the Awen without it. What would he do now?

Erec hunched, frozen, as the two people came into view. Both of them wore dark scowls. The shorter one walked calmly toward Erec without a word. The other, tall, bent, and weary, held the scepter.

He still could not make out their faces. A glint of light reflected off the shorter one's head. Was it red hair? Oscar? All he could really tell was that whoever it was looked angry. The larger one started to bend the scepter toward Erec, then stopped. Erec could hear him talking out loud to the scepter, arguing.

It was hard to make out, but Erec could hear, ". . . don't like him. Want to make him go."

The smaller one trudged closer like a lone soldier in an angry gloom fighting a faceless enemy. Finally Erec could make out his features. Wiry, bald, and wrapped in a huge blanket, the Hermit looked like Erec had never seen him, muddled and upset. The taller man was none other than King Piter, covered in a down coat. He was discussing with his scepter how he hated everyone and just wanted to get rid of them.

Erec was glad the scepter had put a shred of doubt in the king's mind about sending him into the abyss. He rushed forward and pressed the king's hand onto the Trwyth Boar vial.

The king's eyes sharpened, and his mouth dropped open. "Erec!" He looked down at the magic vial. "So this is the Twrch Trwyth. Amazing. Wonderful job." Erec and the king held the vial between their two hands.

"Just wait until you let go of this vial," Erec said. "You'll think I'm doing a terrible job then. Anyway, I haven't done the hard part yet. The Awen are still under there. Why are you here?"

The Hermit was gazing at them with stupefied hatred.

King Piter said, "I had no choice, really. The Hermit told me this was where you would be. I had to get the scepter back from you before you really made a mess of things."

Shame and desire both raced through Erec. "I wasn't making a mess of anything. The scepter brought me here and gave me a warm coat. But I'm going to need it to hook the Awen up to the Twrch Trwyth. Everyone else died doing it, do you understand? I have to use the scepter and make it easy."

"No, Erec," the king said quietly. "The scepter is not an option here. If you manage to put the Awen together with the Trwyth Boar, that energy alone might be too much for you. If you used the scepter at the same time, your brain would probably boil out your ears."

"Really?" Erec longingly eyed the scepter, almost ready to take the risk. Then he shook his head, forcing himself out of its spell. "But how will I do this without it? Everyone else died."

The king closed his eyes, pained. "This is another reason I am not able to watch you on your quests, why I have assigned the Hermit to always be there with you for them, whether you know he is or not. It's too hard for me, as your father, to see you take this kind of risk. It is a hard decision to even let you do the quests at all. I'm putting a lot of trust in the Fates. My experience with them, and having done my own quests, reassures me. They would not tell you to do something you cannot do. It's only . . ."

"Only what?"

The king laid a hand on his shoulder. "There are no guarantees, either. The outcomes depend on you as well, Erec. Sometimes they depend on things you cannot control, things deep inside of you. It is possible that you could make a wrong decision here. The Fates know that you *can* succeed but not that you *will*."

Erec stared at the scepter, living proof that the Fates could offer no guarantees. If his father had not shown up, and the scepter hadn't flown to him, as Erec had programmed it to, he definitely would have used it with the Awen and would have been killed.

The king said, "Part of me wants to send you back to a safe room in the castle." He sighed. "I guess there is no castle now, though."

Erec's cheeks burned. "I'm sorry about that."

"Completely my fault. My mistake, remember?" King Piter smiled thinly. "Anyway, I want to send you somewhere safe, not let you do this. Try to hook the Awen up myself. But if the Fates did not ask me to do it, my chances would not be good. You are a wise young man, Erec. If anything is holding you back here, if you don't feel up to it, I will take you away from here and protect you. It's very hard for me to see you make this choice."

Erec thought about his father's offer. He had gotten this far. The Awen and the Twrch Trwyth were only a few feet apart. How could he walk away and let the Awen go back and make those places miserable again? And not stabilize the Substance for Upper Earth? Everyone there would die in ten years otherwise.

"I'll be fine. . . ." Erec was not sure whether to call him Dad or King Piter. Neither sounded right anymore.

Tears welled in the king's eyes and a half smile lit his face. "At least I won't know what's going on."

They both turned toward the pit where the Awen rested. The ground trembled beneath them, and a small avalanche bounded down the cliff nearby.

"Will you stay this time?" Erec asked. "I can have two other people with me, remember?"

"Of course I will," the king assured him. "Not that I'll be any help. But before I let go of this vial, I am instructing my scepter not to let me do anything bad to Erec or the Hermit, or do anything to harm this quest. No spinning you into space. . . ." He laughed. "Sorry about that. I forgot who you were, just didn't like you much for some reason."

"I know. Thanks . . . Dad." It felt good saying that, maybe even more so because there was a chance that he might not see him again. He gave his father a quick hug. "I'll talk to the Hermit, then see what I can do with the Awen."

When he pulled the Twrch Trwyth away, the king's face grew sour and dazed again. Erec succeeded in putting the Hermit's hand on the vial after a little tugging and a few choice words from the Hermit. But then a grin spread over his face and he began to laugh. "You're alive. And the king has his scepter back. This is wonderful!"

Erec pressed the vial between their palms. "Not so great yet, until I finish this quest without getting killed."

"So far, so good." The Hermit tittered.

"Any advice?" Erec asked. "I have no idea how to do this."

The Hermit shrugged. "No clue." He grinned joyfully, as if this was the best possible answer.

Why did he think the Hermit would help? "I guess I'll get started then." Erec pulled the vial away, and the Hermit's gaze grew cold and spacey.

Just to be safe, Erec held the vial tightly while he shoved the large rock off of the pit Melody had made. The open backpack lay underneath. Erec caught a glint of the sparkling colors in it, reminding him there were five Awen. Which should he attempt first? If the Trwyth Boar amplified the Awen's powers, things would get much worse here soon. He imagined the king and the Hermit in a rage like Jam had been in. Unfortunately, he had nothing to tie them down with. Maybe it wasn't a good idea to have them here now after all.

The king had made a bed on the field with his scepter and cuddled in it, sipping cocoa and scowling.

It made sense to connect the Awen of Beauty first. No matter how ugly it made him or his surroundings, at least that wouldn't make it harder to go on. He also decided to do the Awen of Knowledge last. That would be the hardest, and he probably would be unable to do anything after that.

He lifted the backpack from the pit with a stick and pulled out the glowing green dodecahedron. Even though he held the Trwyth Boar in his other hand, everything around him turned scary and awful. The cliff near his side was dark and menacing, ink or blood running down its side. The swirling mists didn't help, distorting everything further. He felt fine, but he gagged when he saw his own hands. They looked like bones and spiky worms with waving feelers jutting from green slime.

Erec lifted the chain off his neck. He held the Awen of Beauty next to the small, pig-shaped glass vial. How did these connect? He touched them together in several places, and nothing happened. Erec tried not to look at his hands, pretended they were someone else's. How much worse could he look when this thing hooked up?

As he slid the Awen around the glass boar vial, a spark jumped suddenly out of the vial. He held the vial still, and a beam of green light burst from one of the pig's feet straight through the Awen of Beauty. The Awen then exploded into the light, becoming part of the green beam that shone brightly far out over the sea.

It had worked. Erec glanced nervously at his hands. He was surprised that they looked fine. No, more than fine. His hands looked spectacular. They had never looked a fraction this nice before. Could the rest of him look that good as well?

All that he could see around him through the fog was radiant with beauty. The king and Hermit looked spectacular as well—a bald Adonis and an aging teen heartthrob. He could not wait to attach the Awen of Sight next, so he could really see what was around him. He grabbed the glowing blue twelve-sided ball next.

But the instant he touched it, he was blinded. Everything turned black. Erec could hear the king grumbling in the darkness. Still, he could feel the Twrch Trwyth in his other hand, and he brought the two together before him. He moved them around each other, but the effort felt futile. How would he be able to tell when they were connected?

After more fumbling, a spark went off in the blackness. Erec held the Awen still, and soon a blinding beam of blue light shot out of another boar foot deep into the evening sky. The Awen of Sight exploded into the light and was gone. The mist on the island cleared. Erec could see again.

More than that, he could see everything. Fish swimming in the bottom of the sea, all the way from here. Distant treetops. If he focused, he could see right through the king to his beating heart and the little white nerves leaving his spinal cord, branching like trees. He squinted into the air and spied the edge of the Earth's atmosphere, right where outer space began.

Everything he saw was spectacular. It was breathtaking. He couldn't stop looking—into the beating wings of a hawk, at the dance of the sand grains under the rhythm of the waves—until finally he remembered there was more to do. He was excited now. This was amazing. How could people have died doing this? Nothing seemed dangerous at all.

What next? One look at the king and Hermit grumbling told him to choose the Awen of Harmony. How could they feel bad in the midst of this beauty?

Before he fished the gleaming red dodecahedron out of the backpack, he braced himself. When he picked it up, with the Trwyth Boar in his other hand, it would make him explode in fury. Would he know enough to handle it?

Erec stopped. Know enough? Of course. He would have to do the Awen of Knowledge first. He started a chant in his head. *Touch these things together. Move them around each other. Touch these things together. Move them around each other.*

The moment he grasped the shiny yellow ball, he stared off in a daze. No thoughts or questions troubled his mind. Everything around him was so beautiful. He just wanted to look at it.

But he kept hearing a chant. *Touch these things together. Move them around each other. Touch these things together. Move them around each other.* What things? He had things in his hands he supposed. *Touch these things together. Move them around each other.*

He put his hands together and moved them around each other. Soon, this touched off a spark. A beam of yellow light burst from the glass boar's snout, and the Awen of Knowledge blew up, fusing with the beam and forming a huge bright yellow spotlight on the cliff side.

Everything was clear. Perfectly clear. Knowledge filled him— everything he'd ever wanted to know.

In that moment, Erec realized that if he had chosen the Awen of Harmony first, he would have died.

Erec marveled at the beauty of how everything had been put together. He understood now why he had been picked for this task, the choice he would have to make, and he wondered what he would end up deciding. Life itself seemed to spread out before him, unraveling all its mysteries. Any small problem he might have had, any concept he might not have understood, were child's play now.

He regarded the king and the Hermit, who were snarling at each other, with compassion, as if they were tiny children. The Hermit understood more, and even though both were sharper now that the Awen of Knowledge was connected, they were so unaware. He even felt pity for Baskania, his never ending search for complete power, and what it had done to him.

It was time to attach the Awen of Harmony, before King Piter and the Hermit started fighting.

He knew exactly what to do. This would be the hard one, of course. That was clear now. People in the past had either picked this one early, and killed themselves in anger, or picked it after the Awen of Knowledge and destroyed themselves and everyone around them when their perfect knowledge mixed with perfect hate.

This is why Erec had been chosen, he knew now. Only he could possibly protect himself from the red Awen. There was only one way to block its complete hate. And that was complete love. He had to bring his dragon eyes out.

It was easier than ever to turn his eyes around. Love surrounded him. The beauty of the earth. His father trying his best. Dragons, dragon eyes, Bethany. Love filled his every pore, pumped with every beat of his heart. He was ready.

Thick white nets of Substance hung around the Awen and the Twrch Trwyth. Of course this part of the island would have more

Substance than the rest of Upper Earth. The Awen was collecting it, but only the Twrch Trwyth could secure it.

He grasped the sparkling red Awen of Harmony. Its power surged from its closeness to the Trwyth Boar. Waves of fierce hatred raged through him. Life was a sham, a rotten tragedy with pathetic saps playing the clueless actors. Everyone should die a merciful death, get out of this pigsty.

But he was ready. Love fought back. The Substance itself filled him with a love so deep it melted his anger. He saw the wonder in the tiniest insects, the grand cliffs before him. He could feel his dragon eyes fighting the rage that seared through him. Hope made him bring the red Awen close to the Twrch Trwyth.

But hatred began to take over. He was tired of being a pawn in the sick game the Fates were playing, pushing him across a painful, rotten board until he turned into a king. What then? Ruin his life with the scepter? Rule over the pathetic peons who were all selfish, mean, and power mad themselves? Why bother? Where was the good in it?

One look at the king made him want to hurl the red Awen straight into his face. What a mess he had made of Erec's whole life. What was it with him and these "mistakes"? He just sauntered along, destroying everyone else, and Erec had to deal with it? Not this time. Erec would put the red Awen in the king's hands, make him hold it, show him what it was like to deal with mistakes.

The hate was winning. Only a long look at the Substance, absorbing its beauty, kept his dragon eyes from turning back into his head. Love poured out again.

He could feel the two forces inside of him: the love battling the hate. Sharp emotions flared in him one way, then the other. He tried to focus on love, but then hate would start to conquer him again.

Love. Sometimes the word resonated, echoed deep inside. Other times it felt like an empty promise. Erec did not know how long he sat there, fighting himself. Every time he began to bring the red Awen close to the Twrch Trwyth his anger would spiral.

Love. He focused on June, Bethany, the dragons. Finally, in a burst of hope, he turned his love inward. He loved his hatred. Loved himself for it. Loved his anger. Accepted it fully. Loved all the terrible things that his hate pointed out to him. Loved the pain, the stupidity, just because they were real and there, and it was all a part of him anyway. He could feel love surrounding the hate, covering it like a shield.

And when he tried to bring the Awen to the Twrch Trwyth, this time he could do it. He slid it around until a beam of red light shot from the boar's tail, far into the woods. The red Awen exploded into the light.

At last Erec understood the meaning of the word "peace."

CHAPTER TWENTY-SEVEN

A Letter to Erec

KING PITER GRINNED and the Hermit laughed. "You did it!" the Hermit said. They broke into applause, making Erec laugh so hard his stomach hurt.

"I'm not done yet," he said.

The king looked around in wonder. "It's beautiful here."

Erec agreed. The gray of the sky matched the eyes of his birth mother, Hesti. Skylarks swooped in perfect swan dives. No choreographer could plan a more perfect dance. The tips of the heather danced in perfect time to the beat of the wind, the harmony of the waves, the music of the Substance, and the rhythm of his own heart.

Every ounce of hatred had seeped out of him, leaving him tired but filled with complete love and understanding. He could feel a deep connection to his father, the Hermit, and the universe itself.

The last Awen would be easy, he knew. "Ready for a little rumble?" he said with a grin.

Erec fished the black Awen of Creation from the backpack. He would have little time, so he moved fast. As soon as he grasped the shiny black dodecahedron with etched symbols on its twelve faces the earth crumbled beneath him. Giant boulders bounced down the mountain, and the cliff side erupted into a shower of falling rock.

Erec's hands worked swiftly together until he saw a flash. A beam of white light broke from one of the boar's feet, and the Awen of Creation melted away into it. The rumbling stopped. No more chunks fell around him. Everything was still.

Deep in a pit, Erec slipped the Trwyth Boar chain back around his neck. Five beams of light shot from it: white, red, blue, yellow, and green, forming big glowing circles on the dirt around him. A few thin rays of light shone from above, through the rocks and dirt that had caved in over him.

Right where the beam of white light was shining, small green sprouts began to pop out from the dirt. The Awen of Creation, he thought. The most miraculous Awen of all. He could spend years just watching what it could do.

But, for now, best to climb out of the pit and let his father and the Hermit know he was okay. Getting out was much easier than it would have been in the past. The Awen of Knowledge in the Twrch Trwyth told him everything he needed to know. It was like having a permanent cloudy thought, but he didn't have to turn into a dragon to know what to do.

He pushed the right rocks at the right angles and climbed out of the pit without a problem.

The king and the Hermit were overjoyed to see him. Erec was astounded. Rocks, boulders, and raw dirt littered the ground, but the land looked even more beautiful than any he had ever seen. He could live like this.

King Piter clapped his back. "Well done." Then he peered at Erec's chest with curiosity. "Your Amulet hasn't changed yet."

"I know," Erec answered. "I haven't completed the quest yet."

The king was confused. "But . . . it seems like you did a pretty good job to me."

"He still has a decision to make," the Hermit said.

It was true. Erec was not sure what he would choose. The decision he had to make was crystal clear to him. He could either plant the Twrch Trwyth deep in the ground, where it would burrow its way down to the Earth's core and stabilize the Substance.

Or he could keep it.

Erec sat on the rocky shore, gazing far across the sea. With his boosted vision, he could see deep into the woods of Avalon, then spot a squid on the ocean floor. This was the hardest decision he had ever faced. It meant everything to him. It was his life.

He knew what both options would bring, of course. The Awen of Knowledge made that clear. His choice was simple yet so hard to make. If he buried the Twrch Trwyth, he would be his old self again. A little headstrong, sometimes bumbling, but meaning well. He would not remember all the answers that he knew now. It would be a much smaller life, less meaningful, less beautiful. He would not be able to watch each wave swell and see the perfection in it.

If he kept the vial, he would move to a cave. He would want to live in nature, to best study how things grow. Every moment of the rest of his life—and his life would be much longer if he wore the Twrch Trwyth—would be an exercise in amazement. The things he could discover and bring to light would change the world.

And the Substance? That didn't really matter either way. Whatever he decided, it should be fine. He knew how to fix it now. That would be easy to do if he kept the Twrch Trwyth, since he'd have all the knowledge. Sure, burying the Awen would stabilize the Substance, keep the problem from getting worse. But it would not fix it. There was only one thing that would do that.

But he knew either choice he made should be okay. If he buried the vial, and lost the knowledge of how to fix the Substance, the Fates should help him figure it out through his quests. So that wasn't an issue.

Life would not be easy if he gave up the vial. The trials he would have to face were more than any one person should have to bear. But now he could see the beauty in that, too. The perfection of not knowing, of going through life with each day a surprise, an unfolding mystery.

Was this all about him? Well, it really was. People would die either way, unfortunately. He did not like to think about that. More mistakes would be made by more people. But that was a part of mortal existence. He could never change that. He was happier thinking about how life, in general, would improve with either choice he made, once the Substance was taken care of.

He wasn't sure he could really give up the Twrch Trwyth. Give up knowing the workings of the universe, feeling its harmony, seeing its spectacular beauty. That would be next to impossible. If he did, then he would fall back under the spell of that silly scepter again, he knew. The magic of the scepter paled in comparison to what he had now. Who needed to "do" things, mess with yourself or others, when all this wonder was before them? Power? There was no limit

THE SEARCH FOR TRUTH

to the power of the universe that he was one with now. But it was a peaceful power, a complete thing, not the searing addictive power of the scepter.

He had no questions, no misgivings. It was just a choice. Just one that would change everything forever. There were no right or wrong answers.

But there was one thing he kept coming back to. With the Twrch Trwyth he would live in all-encompassing love, knowing, understanding, and accepting. It would be wonderful. Without it, he would be like a child, his love, disappointments, grief, and fears mingling with hope, pride, and amazement.

Monks and mystics everywhere spent their whole lives trying to attain what he had now. But which way did he choose to exist? To be a peaceful, happy observer of the world, or a cog in its mucky, magnificent wheel, a simple link in its spectacular chain? Peaceful observation or spectacular immersion?

So he made his choice. And he smiled because the Fates had known all along what he would choose.

He wished there was more wisdom that he could leave for himself, but he knew that only certain things would be okay to let himself know. So he asked King Piter for his notepad and a pen. "The notepad is in your jacket pocket, Father. And I'd like the pen in your shirt pocket, not your Aitherpoint quill."

The king turned pale, but took out the pad and pen.

Erec wrote a note to himself, chuckling.

Erec,

Congratulations on your decision. You have picked the harder path, and for that I am proud of you. But it is the better path in the end. I'd like to leave you with a few words of wisdom. Use them as you will.

Choose the blue Awen ball first. The yellow one would be a disaster.

Give your father a hug. Forgive him for his mistakes. We all make them.

Things may look bleak at times, but never forget the love you brought forth today. If you could win over the hate of the red Awen with that love, you can win over anything.

Nothing can stop Oscar. It's written in the fabric of time. So just help him.

Give Bethany a kiss. You'll know when the time is right.

Put the coat on the coat rack.

There is good to be found everywhere, even in evil. And you can learn in the dark.

Sit Jam down and tell him how great he is and how much you care for him. He will protest and squirm, but keep going on and on until he looks like he'll faint.

No matter what happens, remember that this was a grand adventure and a wonderful experiment.

And most important, but most difficult, trust yourself.

Love, Erec

Tears rolled down his face as he walked back to the pit. He was not ready to give up the Twrch Trwyth, but he never would be ready. Using it longer would only make it harder. He cried for the tadpoles he would never really see, for the raindrops he'd never explore, for the life he was giving up.

Erec held the small glass vial shaped like a boar over the pit. Five bright-colored spotlights shone from it. It was spectacular.

He let it go.

The earth parted as the Twrch Trwyth fell, swallowing it up. The ground closed over it. Erec hung his head, feeling the great loss. Then he collapsed.

***

The Hermit thought Erec's letter to himself was a comedy sketch. He laughed so hard he rolled on the ground, slapping his knees, eyes watering. The king found it interesting but was as mystified as Erec about most of what he had written. "The coat and the coat rack?"

Erec shrugged. Kiss Bethany? He didn't know about that, either. But he did give King Piter a big hug. "I'm glad to know who my dad is now. Aoquesth said some pretty great things about you."

The king hugged Erec back, a big grin on his face. "Hey, look." He pointed at his chest. "A fourth segment is lit up on your amulet."

Erec lifted the Amulet of Virtues off his chest. A fourth segment glowed a sunny yellow. He was curious what the symbol written on it meant, so he brought his dragon eyes forward. It was easier than ever to make his eyes turn around now. All it took was just a memory, really, of all that love.

"Knowledge?" He was confused. "I have the virtue of knowledge? I don't think so. I just threw all that knowledge into a pit."

The Hermit cocked his head. "You forget, Erec. You once knew everything. That sets you apart, you know. All your past and all your future is inside you, in that little black box. It holds all the answers now. That is something that will be a part of you forever."

Erec frowned. "You mean inside that black box I still understand everything in the universe?"

"We all do," the Hermit said. "But not like you. You have it all spelled out in there, crystal clear."

Hmm. Erec wondered what he would choose to show himself the next time he looked into his future with his dragon eyes. At least he could trust that he'd show himself the right things, since that black box now had all the answers.

***

The Hermit giggled and bent over the lump of ground that had been a huge rift moments earlier. It had healed over, and already a raft of tiny sprouts were growing there. "A little light is shining from here." He picked something up from a tall tuft of grass. "Someone left you a present, Erec."

Erec walked over. In the Hermit's hand lay the glass Trwyth Boar vial, only now it was empty. But attached to three of its feet were tiny blue, green, and black balls. A red one was attached to its tail and a yellow one to its snout. He thought he could see tiny symbols on little faces around the balls, like tiny dodecahedrons.

"But why was this left here? I dropped it into the pit. It was supposed to fall to the center of the earth."

"It looks like you knew about it before, though." The Hermit giggled, tapping Erec's letter to himself.

Choose the blue Awen ball first. The yellow one would be a disaster.

"I don't get it," Erec said. "What does it mean to choose the blue one first?" He felt stupid, not knowing something that he fully understood just moments earlier. "I don't know what these things do."

"Oh, yes you do, silly Erec Rex." The Hermit slapped him on the back. "You know better than anyone."

Erec played with the vial and saw that the balls were attached to the glass boar by tiny stems. "If I break one off, it will do something. . . ." If he only knew what.

"Exactly." The Hermit nodded. Erec put the chain around his neck alongside his amulet, where it had been before.

King Piter stepped through the rubble of the Castle Alypium, tears in his eyes. Erec felt terrible.

"I'm so sorry about all this," Erec said. "I should have listened to you. You told me again and again, but I thought I knew better."

As annoyed as he had been with King Piter, Erec realized how his father had been right all along. Erec was not ready to take over as king yet. He still had a lot to learn. And King Piter was not ready to lose his power. The people of Alypium still needed him watching over them, whether they knew it or not.

The king's eyes were wet. "My plants . . ."

It seemed odd that the king was more concerned about some plants that might have died than the devastation before them. Smashed shards of pottery urns mingled in the dust with crystal fragments and splintered wooden floorboards. Mangled tapestries wound around crushed gargoyles.

Erec felt terrible. "Are you sure you can't fix it again?"

"It's unfixable," the king said sadly. "I can clean it up, though. That will be one of the last things I'll do with the scepter."

The thought made Erec uncomfortable. Had he stripped his father of that much power? "Why is that?"

"The castle was a big part of me, stabilizing me. It let me do great things with the scepter and not be as influenced by it. I'm at much greater risk carrying it now and using it."

"Can't you make another castle with it?" Erec asked.

"No." The king smiled kindly. "That was only possible once. Too much of me went into it. There's just not enough left."

Erec had really blown it. "Maybe I should use it to make my castle now. Then I can use the scepter without as much danger."

The king waved away that idea. "You're not ready yet. It would destroy you. I need to keep it until you build yourself up more." He pulled it slightly away from Erec. "You'll be able to handle it after the Fates prepare you with your other quests. Just give it time."

It didn't sound like there was much time. Erec would have to finish the quests quickly so he could take over before something bad happened to his father, or someone stole the scepter. But what would happen if he did finish all twelve quests? He would inherit his father's scepter, build a castle, and rule over Alypium. It made a little more sense now that he knew he was an heir to the throne. But what about the other two thrones? What had happened to his brother and sister?

Erec studied the king. "You said you knew the other two who were supposed to rule with me. That would be my brother and sister, right?"

The king nodded. "But they can't help you now, I'm afraid."

Erec tried to remember what the king had said about them. "One of them is missing, and the other has some kind of problem, and can't do the quests. Which one is missing?"

The king sighed. "I've spent a lot of time protecting your sibling from finding out about all this. I'm not sure it's a good idea to tell you now. I'll need to think it over, make sure it's not dangerous."

"And what about my mom, Queen Hesti? Where is she? I want to find her—" Erec stopped when he saw his father's expression. His chin was trembling as he looked at the empty space where the castle had stood. Remembering his missing wife seemed to be more than he could handle.

Erec decided not to push him now, after everything they had both gone through. But his mother was out there somewhere, and he would find her. And his triplet siblings, too. It would be nice to get to know them. He wondered if it was his brother or sister who was missing. Prince Muck-Muck or Princess Pretty Pony. Well, he would just have to find the missing one. That was all. It would be great to do the rest of the quests as a team.

"What will you do now? Where will you live?" Erec kicked a broken piece of a column out of the way as they walked. A shiver ran through him as he thought about living in Alypium without King Piter to protect him, or protect anyone, as well as he once had.

The king said, "I'll be spending some time in Avalon, I think. The druids were quite helpful there. But I'll be here, too, keeping watch.

I'll build a house with the scepter, for myself, you, Jam, a few servants. A doghouse for Wolfboy. Bethany will have her own area, attached. It won't be as nice as she's used to, though." He shrugged.

"But a lot nicer than what she had with Earl Evirly," Erec said. "I think as long as she's with you she'll be happy. She likes to think you're her father. I think she was upset to find out you're really my father."

He felt a twinge in the back of his eyes, where his dragon eyes were. The thought of Bethany made him frown. Something wasn't right, it seemed, but he didn't know what. Was she in some kind of danger? There was no real reason to think so. Maybe he was just worried about her being upset.

While he was thinking about it, Erec stumbled over a cement block and fell down a hole onto some steps. "Where do these go?" He trotted down the stairs, then saw they led into the twisty tunnels under the castle. "The catacombs," he called up the stairs, then came up. "Nothing's guarding them now."

"Then this is where our house will be," the king said. He stood awhile, as if calculating the house's size. Wind whipped through his hair and cloak.

"What's that?" Erec pointed at a large object sticking out of the rubble. They walked closer and saw gold gleaming through the dust.

It was the king's huge throne. Beside it sat the Lia Fail, the stone that screamed. The throne and rock stood miraculously untouched, perched on a small circle of wood floor. Everything around it had collapsed.

"I think the house will contain this as well." The king smiled. "Glad one thing is still in its place."

"So we'll have a pretty big house, with a throne room and huge catacombs below, and servants? Not much else from the castle I'd miss, anyway." Then he remembered something. "What about the pool table? In the game room?"

The king knew what Erec was talking about. "Posey used that to visit sometimes. It was also an escape route. Should be around that way." He pointed east. After wandering a ways, they found a wet spot around a tunnel of water. The king looked down at it. "I'll put a pool here, in our gardens, huh?"

"How will you explain this to the people of Alypium? Will they still think you're their king?"

King Piter had already considered that problem. "I'll tell them I wanted to downsize. That this was the next step in your becoming king. If they think I'm truly out of the picture, someone will build a castle for the Stain boys tomorrow. And try to get the scepter from me. I'll have a harder time keeping it safe now."

Erec could see the worry in his face. "I'll help too, Dad. But if you want people to think you're king, better make this house a nice one. Like a castle, right?"

"You got it. Walk over here." They stepped away from the water tunnel, where their pool would soon be. The king made a sweep with the scepter, and the rubble and mess dissolved into the air. Piles of plaster and wood rippled, then vanished. The ground swept itself smooth until a field of dirt appeared where the castle had stood. The debris and wreckage vanished from the castle gardens and the maze.

The king took a deep breath. With an effort, he stamped his scepter on the ground. A beautiful house with a few turrets and the flag of Alypium on top rose before Erec, building itself in fast motion. It was springing straight from the king's imagination into real life. Outside, around them, immaculate gardens arose. The sight was spectacular.

The king dropped the scepter. He looked stunned, desperate. "Hold my hands," he whispered hoarsely.

Erec grasped his fingers and felt him shaking.

"It's . . ." The king looked pained. "I forgot what that scepter can do. How bad it is. Without . . . without my castle to help me. Just hold me here for a while, so I don't pick it up again until I'm ready."

Erec squeezed his father's hands, keeping him from grabbing the scepter like he knew he wanted to.

The house was wonderful inside. Erec was sure he would not miss the castle at all, except for what it had meant for King Piter. Soon he heard barking and stepped outside. Wolfboy bounded up, knocking him onto his back. "Hey, boy." He wrestled his wenwolf dog a bit, scratching his ears. "Glad you're okay, pup."

He looked up and saw a surly Bethany and a shy-looking Jam approaching. When Bethany saw him, she looked around for somewhere else to go but gave up when Jam forged ahead of her.

Jam nodded at Erec. "Young sir. Bethany told me you discovered you are the king's son. Congratulations, sir. I assume you will be living with him here then?"

"Don't congratulate me," Erec said. "I kind of made a mess of things." He gestured at the quiet gardens where the king's castle once stood.

Jam smiled. "I'll be taking care of Bethany, then. We'll find a place nearby—"

"No way," Erec said. "You two are living here with King Piter. He planned it all out. Bethany gets her own whole section of the house, with her own servants." He laughed. "Bigger than where I'll be staying, I'm sure."

Bethany's eyes lit up, but she remained quiet.

Jam cleared his throat. "I can still live with the king?" He broke into a big grin. "Well, then." He dusted his butler coat off. "I'll have a lot to do getting things in order. Let's see how many servants we'll have to run the ship now." He strode toward the house with big steps, murmuring about fine cutlery and soup pots.

Bethany bit a thumbnail nervously. "Was it your idea for me to stay here? Or King Piter's?"

Erec knew what she was asking. He smiled. "King Piter's. All the way. It wouldn't be home for him without you. You know that."

She shrugged. "Yeah. But now that he has a real son, I can't imagine he'd have much time for a fake daughter."

"Bethany, don't be stupid." Erec threw a twig at her. "You'll always be like a daughter to him. Your mom was his best AdviSeer. She was almost part of the family."

Bethany stared over Erec's head. "I guess this kind of makes us siblings, then?" She didn't look too happy about it.

"Yeah," Erec replied. But he wasn't sure what he thought about that either.

Erec figured he'd follow the directions in his letter from himself. He found Jam in the huge kitchen suite in the house, directing traffic and polishing cabinets. "Jam? Can I talk to you a moment?"

"Of course, young sir. Tell me how I can assist you." Jam followed him to a small window seat that overlooked the pool. In the tunnel below it was the waterway system that could take them all the way to Ashona.

"Jam, this is really important to me, okay?"

"Yes, young sir?" He looked nervous.

"I want you to know, I really appreciate you. The things you're always doing for everyone else are tremendous. You are the most giving person I've ever met."

"No, really, young sir. That's kind, but not deserved." Jam blushed.

"I'm not done, Jam. I think you're great. Bethany thinks you're great. King Piter couldn't do without you. I mean, none of us could. You really are a good person. I mean it. Inside and out."

Jam was beet-red now. "Please, kind sir. I only do my job. Nothing more. I'm nothing special."

What had the letter told him to do? Keep going on and on until he looks like he'll faint. "No, Jam, you are special. You jumped right in to help me in Otherness. You stayed to fight with the Hydra and Valkyries even knowing you could have died. You are a true hero, Jam. I look up to you. Maybe someday I'll be as great a man as you are."

Jam was squirming and actually looked sick. "Stop. Really, I don't deserve—"

"You do. You are the meaning of the words 'brave' and 'kind.' You . . ."

Jam was pale. His head began to wobble in a circle like he might faint. Erec smiled and left him alone to recover.

When he walked back into the kitchen, Bethany ran into him. "There you are! Cutie Pie had another secret for me. It's the same thing. Balor and his brothers are stealing pie again, at the Green House."

"Why would they steal it at the Green House?" Erec asked. "Wouldn't they take it from other people's houses?"

"Maybe they're taking it there to eat." Bethany was working it out in her head. "I just put my stuff away, and I know just where the gag Serving Tray is. Let's whip up some treats for them to find, and leave them near the Green House. We can hide and watch what happens to them."

Erec felt a twinge behind his eyes. It wasn't a cloudy thought or even a premonition. But he knew something was not right about the pies. He just couldn't put his finger on it. "Don't go without me, Bethany, okay?"

"Yeah, of course," she said.

Erec's mother visited him with her glasses while he was roaming through the king's new house. He was glad she hadn't seen what this had looked like when it was all in ruins. It took a while to explain to her what had happened.

June's voice choked. "That's why he didn't want me to tell you? He said he had good reasons, but I never knew."

"I saw you when I went back in time," he said. "Do you remember me talking about meeting Olwen Cullwich back then?"

"It was ten years ago, Erec. I don't remember that at all." She paused. "Danny found a strange note in his coat pocket the other day. Something about clowns." Then she sounded uncomfortable. "Are you coming home soon?"

Erec thought about it. He had worn himself out with this last quest. It would be great to go back for a while after he helped his father settle in, and after he went with Bethany to see what the Stain brothers were doing, stealing pies. He still had a strange feeling about that and didn't want her to go alone.

It confused him a moment, though. He was living with his father in Alypium. Should he still also live at home with his adoptive mother? Then he realized—that was why June sounded nervous. She was wondering the same thing. Well, she didn't have to worry.

"Yeah, sure, Mom," he said, smiling around the room since he didn't know where she was. "I can't wait to come home again."

Bethany carried a cake in a covered platter she had found in the kitchen. Erec lugged a pie on top of a wrapped container of pudding. He shuddered thinking what was inside of them. The fake Serving Tray had done a good job when Bethany asked it to make the food look good on the outside. The first pie she tried had turned out too disgusting to think about. As for the pudding, a nasty rodent had popped its head out, making her shriek and drop the serving platter straight into the big pudding bowl. She brought her fingers close to pluck it out, but thought better of it. They would have to get the tray back later.

The Green House, a stately mansion, took up a whole block in the center of town. The front door was set back from the street. They found plenty of shrubs to hide in, but nowhere to put the goodies.

"Well, I have this." Bethany pulled her remote control out of her pocket. Erec felt a twinge of jealousy when he saw it. She'd had over a month to learn to use it better while he had been at home. "Let's see...." She pointed the remote control at the sidewalk leading to the front door and pushed a button. "Phero," she whispered.

A small coffee table appeared on the sidewalk.

Erec was impressed. "If you gave me that remote, I'd be lucky if I could move that table an inch."

Bethany looked pleased. "You just need more practice, that's all. Actually, I do too."

"I don't know. That seemed pretty good to me."

Bethany shrugged. "Only problem is, I don't know where the table came from. Don't have a great grasp of that yet. Someone, somewhere, is putting their coffee mug down and it will crash to the ground."

Bethany left the lids on the cake and pudding but put the pie out on the table uncovered. Then they found a spot behind some bushes that covered them completely. Several people eyed the pie when they walked by, but luckily nobody stopped.

"We should have left some sheep food out too, for Dollick," Erec said with a laugh.

After waiting and chatting about King Piter's new house, they almost gave up. "Wait." Bethany pointed. The Stain triplets were heading into the Green House.

"Hold on." Erec pointed his spy watch, the one that used to be Balor's, at the Stain brothers. It amplified sound from a great distance. He pushed and turned a dial. Balor's voice rose quietly from the watch. "... don't know whose it is. Just leave it. It could be old."

But Damon was drooling. "Pie ... I like pie. What kind is it?"

Bethany whispered, "Humble pie. Eat it."

"How am I supposed to know, bonehead?" Balor knocked on the bone under Damon's hat. "I didn't make the pie. Come on, let's go in."

Damon stood looking at the pie, then lifted the covers off the cake and pudding. "Oooh. Cake."

Bethany crossed her fingers. "Let them eat cake."

Next thing they saw, Damon was scooping handfuls of cake to his mouth. To their surprise, he looked like he was enjoying it.

"Uh-oh," Bethany whispered. "I didn't make the cake with the good Serving Tray, did I? Could it have made a normal cake?"

After Damon took a few more mouthfuls, Balor began to retch, and Dollick started to *baa*. "Look what you're eating, bonehead." Balor pointed at the cake.

"Cake," Damon said lovingly.

Bethany started to giggle. "I wish I could see it," she whispered.

"Is it good?" Dollick bent his head over the cake and took a bite out of it like an animal, then spit it out. "Yueicch! This is . . . bleeegh! Augh!" He coughed and spit.

"Pie." Damon stuck his hand into the pie and popped a wet handful into his mouth.

"What are you eating?" Balor sounded furious. "Look at that!"

Erec laughed so hard he had to cover his mouth with his arm so no one would hear. Soon Bethany was doubled over, hand on her mouth, pounding the ground in merriment. "Serves 'em—" She hiccupped. "Serves 'em right for stealing pies."

"C'mon, you two freaks," Balor said. "Let's get inside. Dad said Bethany will show up before long. He wants to talk about plans."

"What?" Bethany whispered. "Could that be me they're talking about? What's going on?"

Damon ate another scoop of pie, then he got a funny look on his face.

"Oh, no," Balor said. "What's wrong now, Damon? If you're going to—"

Damon turned around and started throwing up onto the grass. Balor and Dollick looked the other way.

After Damon finally stopped, Balor said, "What do you expect if you eat disgusting, infested glop? You idiot. Let's go in, unless you're going to blow chunks again."

Damon held his stomach like he wasn't sure, then looked back at the pie. "Pie . . ." he said with admiration.

"The only *pie* you need to worry about is the pie locked away inside," Balor said. "The pie that will bring Bethany to us."

Bethany gave Erec an incredulous glance. "Huh?"

But Damon gulped another scoop of the disgusting pie on the table. Balor shook his head in his hand. "You idiot. Now you're going to barf again."

Dollick looked like he could not handle watching. He wandered onto the lawn, dropped down, and munched some grass.

"Bethany loves pie," Damon said, taking another bite. Then he gagged and threw up again.

"Yes, she does. Dad says pie will bring her to us. We gave her cat Cutie Pie the message, twice now. So as soon as she gets it, she'll come right away." Balor raised a finger at Damon. "Now don't be stupid and go calling him 'Dad' again. He doesn't like that, okay? Just say 'Shadow Prince,' like before."

"I just don't get it," Bethany whispered, stunned. "Are they all crazy?"

"Dumb name, anyway," Balor said. "Who would name a kid Pi?"

It was not until then that Erec realized they had been talking about Bethany's brother, Pi, all along.

Bethany was pale. Her mouth hung open in shock. She had just learned that she even had a brother a few months ago. He traveled with the Alypium springball team, but she had been able to meet him and spend some time with him. He was the only real family she had, and Erec knew how important he was to her.

Bethany started to charge out of the bushes, but Erec grabbed her arm and pulled her back. "You can't go out there," he whispered. "It's a trap."

"They have Pi in there." Bethany's eyes were stormy. "I'm getting him out."

"How are you going to do that? They've been waiting for you. I don't know why they want you—maybe to trap me. But you can't just run in there."

"Erec," she whispered fiercely, "he's my brother. I have to try. Maybe you can go find the scepter. Right now Balor is just sitting there alone in front of the Green House with those two. I have to find out what's going on." She broke loose from Erec's grip.

"Bethany! No!"

"I won't go inside, okay? I'm just going to talk to them out here." She ran ahead toward the Stain brothers.

Erec slammed his fist into the dirt. Why was she being so stupid? Anyone could see her out there. He knew she must be out of her mind with worry for her brother. It was clouding her judgment.

He sunk his face into his knees. This was just what Baskania wanted. He had sent messages to her through her cat, Cutie Pie, to get her to show up at the Green House and save her brother. And now she was doing exactly that. At least the message had gotten flubbed by the cat before, so Bethany had thought the Stains were stealing pie from people. He wondered if Cutie Pie made it sound like that on purpose to protect her.

Little good that did. She went right in on her own anyway.

In a minute, Bethany stopped before the Stains, seething. "What have you done with my brother? Where is he?"

"Well, lookie there." Balor gloated. "We were just talking about you. Looks like my dad was right."

"Bethany loves pie." Damon nodded thoughtfully and gazed back at the rancid, oozing pie on the table.

"Damon likes pie?" Bethany asked. "You like this nice pie I left for you boys?"

Balor's eyes narrowed. "You did this?" He looked back and forth between her and the sickening slop. "How did you make it so disgusting?"

"Magic," she shrugged.

"You don't know enough magic to make these." Erec saw Balor push a button on his wristband. He cringed. Balor was letting someone know Bethany was there. She had to get away.

"Bethany!" Erec shouted.

But at that moment, Baskania appeared in front of her. Erec did not see any extra eyes on his face today. Baskania opened his hand, and a coil of rope shot from his palm, twisting around Bethany until she was wound tight from the neck down. The end of the rope formed a stake, planting itself in the ground behind her to hold her up. Erec was only too familiar with those ropes. He had been tied with them before. The only things that could undo them, that he knew of, were a silver knife, a scepter, and dragon claws.

Dragon claws.

He looked up at the faded blue sky. He wasn't in Upper Earth now, so he could do a dragon call. Dragons could come into Alypium—he knew that, since Patchouli had brought him near the castle. It would be dangerous for them, since the Alypium army was on the alert to shoot dragons on sight. But this was an emergency.

Through his watch, Erec could hear Baskania talking to Bethany. He was laughing. "You made these tasty treats by magic? I wonder if you're telling the truth, girl. That would be no small feat. Hmm . . ."

He scratched his chin. "I might have to make you eat the rest of this cake, pie, and pudding. Unless, that is, you can *prove* to me you made these. I hate to be lied to."

Balor and Dollick were cackling with glee. Damon, on the other hand, looked upset. "Why does she get the rest?"

Bethany's face was pale, looking at the rancid, infested slop on the table through the tears in her eyes. Then she perked up, relieved. "I can prove it! It's in . . . the proof is in the pudding."

"It is?" Baskania said. "What's in the pudding?"

"The magic tray I made these with."

That seemed to interest Baskania. "Magic tray, huh? Reach in and get it, Balor."

Erec was relieved but surprised that Baskania wasn't instantly killing Bethany. He seemed to be toying with her. Why would he do that?

Then he realized. Baskania was using her as bait to draw Erec out. Erec closed his eyes with relief and concentrated on doing the dragon call.

Love. It took a moment to overcome the hate he felt for Baskania and the Stains. But his memory of his love conquering the hate of the red Awen flooded back. Then it was simple to bring his dragon eyes forward.

When his eyes turned, everything became green. Big knots of Substance hung in the air around him. He stared into the skies, beaming love into them and calling to the dragons. *Dragons! Help me. Baskania captured Bethany. He'll kill her.*

The Substance, the world, looked beautiful through his eyes. *Please, come quick! We're in danger.*

His concentration was broken by a scream. Balor had stuck his hand into the pudding and pulled out a plump rat by the tail, which was reaching up to bite him. He flung the rat into the grass and it scampered away. Bethany wrinkled her nose at him and stuck out her tongue.

"Must I do everything?" Baskania pointed a finger at the pudding bowl, and a gleaming silver tray rose from it, spotless. He snatched it and looked it over. "Nice. Give me an apple." A worm ridden pile of rotten apple mush appeared on the platter. Baskania tossed the magic silver tray behind him.

Damon started after it. "Apple . . ."

Balor knocked him on the head.

"Dad." Damon pointed at the apple. "Can't I eat the apple?"

Baskania sneered at him. "Do not ever call me that again, you idiot."

He looked at Bethany. "I'm so glad you showed up today. I've been meaning to have a chat with you, Miss Bethany Cleary. I think you have something interesting to tell me. A secret, maybe? Ever since I found out about it, I've been looking for you, but it seems you and Erec Rex have been traipsing all over the globe, from the hottest to the coldest spots." He sighed. "If only Rosco had told me that you had a little secret before I saw you last, it would have saved me a lot of time."

Erec felt his stomach drop. Baskania wasn't just using her to trap him. He had found out about the secret she'd almost told Oscar. The one he couldn't know about. Of course.

What had his cloudy thought told him would happen if Baskania learned the secret? Erec tried not to remember. But it was too hard to forget. Baskania would take Bethany with him back to his headquarters, she would die, and the world would soon end.

And now it was happening? Why wasn't he getting a cloudy thought? What was wrong with him?

He focused again on the skies. *Hurry, please! Baskania might find out a secret that will end the world!*

Baskania pointed two fingers at Bethany. "You will tell me the secret, now. The one you almost told Oscar before Erec Rex stopped you. I need to know what it is."

Bethany looked mesmerized. She opened her mouth to speak.

But then something appeared in the sky. Everyone looked up. Six dragons flew toward them. Erec nearly collapsed in relief. There were shouts of fear from the street, and people running.

With a wave of his hand, a shimmering bubble appeared around Baskania, the Stain boys, and Bethany.

Baskania laughed a crazy, high-pitched cackle of glee. "Erec Rex." He sang the words. "I know you're out there somewhere. And I'm going to find you now. You don't think your dragons scare me, do you? Remember this dragon shield spell? I already used it before with you, didn't I? Tsk, tsk. You don't seem to learn your lessons, boy."

Five of the dragons dove at the bubble, clawing at it to rescue Bethany. But the bubble resisted them easily. They breathed fire on it, bashed it with their mighty tails—but nothing happened to it. Bethany was untouchable.

Loud blasts from detonation bombs rang through the air. Gunshots soon followed as people joined with the Alypium army in its attack, firing at the dragons from a distance. Bethany looked at the bubble around her with horror.

Patchouli found Erec. "It looks like your friend is stuck. We can't stay long, under attack. Climb on and I'll fly you to safety."

"I can't leave her and her brother Pi," Erec said with a gasp. "He's somewhere in the Green House." Then Erec got an idea. "Maybe we can crash through and find him." He climbed on Patchouli's back and sailed above the Green House lawn. A black band of smoke whizzed past them with a loud whistle. The detonation bomb narrowly missed them, leaving a crater in the lawn where it exploded.

Patchouli signaled the other dragons to leave. She darted back and forth in the air with Erec, avoiding being a still target.

Baskania spotted him, though. "There you are, Erec Rex." His voice rang sharp through Erec's watch. "Why don't you come join our party? We have some tasty food down here waiting for you." He snickered. "Your girlfriend baked it. I'm sure you'll enjoy it."

"I'll be back, Bethany!" Erec shouted. "I'm going to find something for you."

Baskania's face broke into a sneer. He snapped his fingers and Pi Cleary appeared next to Bethany, in the bubble.

Pi was bound in rope like she was. They gazed at each other sadly. Erec was glad he could not hear what they were saying. It was too awful.

Now what would he do?

"You can't save Bethany and Pi with your dragon friend," Baskania called to him. "The only way is for you to come in here yourself. We can make a trade. You for them."

The last time Baskania made a deal with him, he had broken it immediately. Baskania said he would let Erec free if Erec gave him the Archives of Alithea. But when Erec handed the scroll to him, Baskania captured Erec. There was no way he would hold to his word in a "trade."

Baskania turned his attention to Bethany. He pointed his fingers back at her. "Tell me your secret."

"No!" Erec screamed. "Stop them!" He dove with Patchouli toward the bubble, sailing into it full force.

When Patchouli hit the dragon shield, she bounced off it so hard, Erec went flying into the grass.

Through his watch Erec heard Bethany say, "When you asked the Archives of Alithea to tell you the secret of the Final Magic, and where it was hidden"—she sounded like she was in a daze—"Erec asked it how old he was at the same time. And it told you both the answers to each other's questions. But Jam, the butler, heard both of the answers."

Erec pulled himself to standing, dizzy and helpless. What could he do? He didn't even have a remote control on him. Was there anything around?

And then the answer came to him.

Baskania spoke quietly, in shock. "Erec and his butler know where I can learn the Final Magic? Do you know too?" Recognition settled over his face. "You have the answer, don't you? You know what the scroll told the butler and Erec. What did it say?" His voice became harsh. "Where is the secret of the Final Magic?"

"No!" Erec shouted, running toward them.

Bethany sounded like a robot. "The secret of the Final Magic is hidden in the mind of the smallest child of the greatest seer of the first king of Alypium."

"The smallest child of the greatest seer . . ." Erec could see Baskania working out who that was. "The smallest child. Yes. I knew the key was in something small." He cackled with glee. "But *you're* the smallest child of Ruth Cleary, the greatest seer of King Piter. *You* hold the key I have been looking for all these years? You? What amazing luck. And you've delivered yourself to me."

Laughter like blades of icy steel erupted from his chest until he howled with mirth. "Somewhere in you, my dear, lies the Great Secret. You will show me how to use the Final Magic. Give me control over everything I desire, life and death. And"—he smiled, the corners of his mouth twitching—"if I can't find the answers from torturing you alive, I'm sure I can discover them when I remove your brain."

Erec fumbled with the tiny Awen balls on his chain. Which should he pick? They were his only hope, whatever they would do. Maybe the yellow one would confuse Baskania enough that he could rescue—

But then Erec remembered his own letter to himself.

Choose the blue Awen ball first. The yellow one would be a disaster.

He twisted the tiny blue dodecahedron, and its stem cracked off the empty glass boar vial. He ran closer and threw it at Baskania.

White smoke filled the air. At first Erec could not see a thing but white. But then his vision became perfectly clear. He could see the Stain boys looking around wildly, stumbling and falling. It was obvious they could see nothing.

Baskania looked around in a rage, blinded. He shouted, "You're still not safe from me, Erec Rex!" He pointed in the direction of Bethany and a puff of red smoke shot toward her. Erec saw it whiz past her, part of it touching her face. Her head fell limp on top of the coils of rope.

Erec ran toward her and Pi under the cover of the smoke. But Baskania opened his palm. Another of his rope coils unwound from it. Erec darted away as the rope shot toward him. It did not need to see to know where he was. He remembered how these ropes had chased after them in the water when he dove into the well of the Oracle. If the Fates had not intervened then, they would surely have been caught.

Erec stumbled back as the rope flew toward him.

It shot through the air, twisting, ready to capture him.

His heart sank. Baskania had won. When the fog cleared, he would be tied up on the grass with Bethany and Pi.

But, to Erec's surprise, the rope curved in the air and headed straight for his Amulet of Virtues. It dove into the amulet, plummeting inside and disappearing, the gold pounding on his chest as it went in. The disc slurped it from the air like a strand of spaghetti.

His amulet had never done this before. But, then again, he now had four segments lit up. The king had said it would get more powerful as he progressed.

The rope had vanished into his amulet, but Baskania was disappearing and reappearing in multiple spots, looking for him. Erec grabbed the rope-bound Bethany and Pi, one bundle under each arm, and ran.

The fog gradually receded as he tore away from the Green House, but it covered all of Alypium. It still gave him complete cover as he raced through the old castle grounds. Pi was heavy, but Erec felt surges of strength, and his adrenaline kept him going until he was inside King Piter's house.

CHAPTER TWENTY-EIGHT

Old Magic

J AM FOUND A silver knife and cut the ropes off a dazed Pi and sleeping Bethany. It was misty in the house, but the fog was not nearly as dense as it was outside. The windows looked like someone had painted them white. Erec knew he was the only one who could see the trees through it.

"Thanks." Pi looked him over in wonder. "I'm heavy, kid. Pretty cool you were able to carry both of us. How could you see to find us?"

"It was a magic thing that let me see you." Erec thought it was better not to mention his Awen. The fewer people that knew about them the better. He nudged Bethany. He wondered if having dragon powers gave him extra strength, too. "Wake up. You're safe now."

"I'll go get smelling salts," Jam said, "and some bandages for those scrapes, Pi."

But the salts did not even make Bethany's eyelids flicker. Nothing Jam could think of would rouse her.

Erec froze. He had forgotten until now that Baskania had knocked her out. The puff of red smoke . . .

He felt sick. What had that maniac done to her? Would she be okay? Erec huddled on the floor next to the couch where Bethany was lying, keeping watch. He was aware that time was passing, but he had no idea how much. Bethany would be okay. She had to be. Maybe when King Piter came back he'd know what to do. Or they'd take her to the best magic doctor.

Pi slept on a couch nearby. Finally, at some point, overcome with exhaustion, Erec fell asleep.

Hours later, King Piter appeared, waking Erec and Pi. He looked ragged. "Just got back from Avalon. I'm getting a Port-O-Door for the house soon. What's up with the fog?"

Erec noticed the king was not carrying his scepter, and he asked about it.

"I decided it was best that I don't hold it so much anymore," the king said wearily. "It's safely hidden for now."

Erec told him what had happened outside. "What do you think Baskania did to her?"

The king plopped into a thick chair. "Bethany told Baskania? Now he knows where to find the secret of the Final Magic? If he learns that magic, he will destroy the world. His power will be out of control." He was horrified. Then his mouth fell open. "Or maybe he doesn't know where it is. Either way, we need to protect Bethany from him now, and also . . ."

"Also?"

"Never mind. Baskania will come after her, though. That's probably why he put the spell on her."

"Can you tell what kind of spell it is?" Erec asked.

"I could with the scepter." A look of longing stole over the king's face. "But it's best I don't use it. I'd guess it's old magic, though. He'd want to keep her an easy target, unable to defend herself, or talk to anyone but him. He won't have hurt her memory—that's for sure. He'd want to keep that intact so he could drag the secret of the Final Magic out of her."

Erec shuddered. "How can we wake her up?"

The king looked worried. "It might not be possible. The reason those old spells are still used is they work so well. They're usually based on unsolvable riddles. Only a strong emotion could bring her out of the spell, but without hearing or understanding anything, she won't be able to have any strong emotions. She'll stay buried deep in her haze." He wrung his hands together then rubbed his face. "We'll take her to Ippocra Asclep. We'll take her everywhere. I just hope someone can find a way."

Erec saw tears in the king's eyes. It was really that bad?

The king sniffed. "I loved that girl like a daughter. Really, I can't see her go like this."

"Is there anyone who knows how to fix this?" Erec felt desperate.

"It's old magic," the king repeated. "She's pretty much Baskania's prisoner. She may start to wake up, which is even worse. Then she'll try to find him, like a zombie."

This was not possible. Erec was sick with the thought of her answering only to Baskania. If only he'd gotten there sooner. Why had he stumbled? Why couldn't he have seen it coming? It was all his fault.

"Young sir." Jam walked in to the room. "You can't sit next to that couch forever, sir. Would you like me to fix you a cocoa?"

It didn't seem fair for him to have cocoa if Bethany couldn't enjoy anything. She was barely alive. "No, thanks, Jam. I'm fine. Really."

"All right, young sir." Jam nodded.

Erec woke up on the floor, holding an uneaten piece of toast Jam had given him. He was angry at himself for falling asleep. The king had said Bethany needed to be guarded, right? He looked at her, so fragile and helpless, hating himself for letting this happen. He hugged his knees to his chest and watched her.

What had the king said about that old deep magic? It was based on riddles. Too bad Aoquesth wasn't here. He was good at riddles. Erec smiled to himself. Aoquesth wasn't here, but his eyes were. At least he would always be a part of Erec.

Only a strong emotion could bring her out of the spell, but without hearing or understanding words she won't be able to have any strong emotions. She'll be buried deep in her haze.

Erec dropped the toast.

The letter.

He got on his knees and leaned over Bethany, hoping. This was too strange to do. But he had to try.

Erec's lips touched Bethany's. Her eyelids fluttered. As he kissed her, she awoke, and kissed him back.

It wasn't a bad feeling, actually. For a moment he thought that he'd like to try it again, someday, in better circumstances.

"Erec?" She sat up, confused. "Where are we?"

"You're at home, Bethany. You're safe now."

She smiled at him, then lay down on the couch and fell asleep.

Light streamed in the windows in the morning. Erec woke up, his side sore from sleeping on the wood floor. He'd had a terrible dream, about searching for his lost mother in a fog. The dream ended with his old one—the awful memory of the father that was not his, the fake memory the Memory Mogul had given him.

Where was his birth mother, Queen Hesti, now? He knew from the inquizzle he asked that she was alive somewhere. What had happened to her? Was she with his lost, missing sibling? And what was wrong with his other sibling? He would have to find them all, and soon.

The king and Pi came into the room. Both of them looked devastated. Pi sat next to Bethany on the couch and put his hand on her shoulder. "Don't worry, sis," he said. "We'll find someone to help you."

Bethany sat up with a bright smile, and threw her arms around him. "Pi! You're all right! How did we get here?"

The king stepped back. "She's awake? But how . . ."

The Hermit appeared in the doorway wearing terry-cloth wraps around his waist and head. He did a small dance. "I know. Think of the letter Prince Poo-Poo Head wrote to himself."

The king's jaw dropped.

Erec felt a little awkward around Bethany the next day, but she seemed all smiles. They sat on the front porch. Bits of the agora peeked over their manicured lawns. "So," he asked, "you're not upset anymore about King Piter being my father?"

"Naw, I'm used to it," Bethany said. "It just felt like you took the only relative I had. I was jealous. My parents are gone. I'm not even related to Bea Cleary, that famous prophetess, which bummed me out. Pi travels all the time with his springball team, so I felt all alone. I had to see that the king still wanted me around, that's all. And I guess he does."

"I know he does." Erec smiled.

"And it doesn't make us brother and sister," she added.

"No." Erec thought about the kiss. "It does not."

She laughed. "You know, it's not every girl that gets rescued by a kiss from a prince."

Erec's face turned red. "Let's just . . . forget about that. Okay?"

"Okay, Prince Charming," Bethany teased.

"Great nickname." Erec grimaced.

"Better than Prince Poo-Poo Head." Pi popped his head out the door, then joined them.

"Oh, I almost forgot to tell you." Erec was glad to change the subject. "I found out about that memory I got from the Memory Mogul. The one I used to think was my father. It's *your* memory. I knew the man's voice was familiar. Turns out it was Earl's. I guess he was trying to ditch you when you were little, and Baskania, his boss, told him you might be useful."

Bethany stared in wonder. "So they cut a chunk of my memory out and you got it?"

Erec nodded. "It was just a small snip of your memory though. They must have taken the rest out before that."

The three of them stared at the city of Alypium in the distance. The flags on the Green House now stood higher than any other building.

"So," Bethany said. "You've been having my nightmares for me all of these years?"

"I don't know if it works like that." Erec smiled.

She leaned back on the steps. "Say hi to Danny and Sammy for me when you go back."

Erec was uneasy. Bethany was out of immediate danger, woken from her spell. But Baskania would be hunting for her now that he knew her secret—that she held the key to the Final Magic that he wanted so much. Erec wondered how Bethany could teach Baskania about the Final Magic since she didn't know anything about it herself. Maybe he shouldn't leave her here. . . .

Pi winked at him, seeing his discomfort. "Don't worry. King Piter and I will keep a good eye on this girl while you're gone, and Wolfboy, too. I hear you're heading back for a little break with your sibs?"

"Yeah." Erec nodded. "And my mom." Regardless of who his birth mother was, June would always be his mom.

One Thousand Years Earlier

T EN-YEAR-OLD THANATOS ARGUS Baskania saw the long line of people waiting outside his grandmother Cassandra's courtyard. Cringing, he ducked into her side yard. As soon as his grandmother saw him, she would chide him for being late and make him work the rest of the afternoon. And with so many people waiting, the healing would take forever. He probably would miss dinner, even. If he was lucky, he'd get a little bowl of olives and dates.

Best to put off work as long as he could. He knew a great spot in his grandmother's yard where she would not see him. He could spend time there with his new best friend.

Cassandra was an iatromantis, a healer-prophet, the only one in Constantinople. It wasn't a tradition here as it was in Thessaly, where he had been born. But even though there were other iatromantes in Thessaly and the other parts of the Empire that had once been Greek, Cassandra was the best.

Thanatos's grandmother loved that her bloodline was pure Greek. Straight through to Plato, she always said. She missed Thessaly, but they were lucky to have escaped when they did. Nine years ago she'd known to pick up and move, right before Emperor Samuil of Bulgaria attacked. There had been other battles before, with the Saracens. And of course, rogue crusaders galloping through. But this was the worst, and she had been wise to have gotten them out when she had.

Constantinople was okay. It was all that Thanatos remembered. His mother, Magda, hated it, but she hated most things. At least their emperor, Basil II, "the Bulgar Slayer," kept them safe.

Actually, if not for his grandmother's high expectations, life would have been great. He would have spent all his time uninterrupted with his new best friend. But his grandmother had decided that he should be an iatromantis, just like her. She said he had better natural abilities than anyone she'd ever seen. As if he wanted to spend the rest of his life fixing things for one person after the next.

Not that he wanted to play with other kids anymore. They just didn't get it. There were so many things more interesting than playing chase, tossing a ball, or throwing a discus around. His new best friend was showing him tricks he had never dreamed were possible. If it weren't for his grandmother's obsession with healing people, he would have disappeared with his new best friend and never come back.

ONE THOUSAND YEARS EARLIER

He knew he was through with other kids when Junius's father had taken a group of them to the hippodrome for the chariot races last Saturnalia, right before the Winter Solstice. He had been to the chariot races before, and he was excited about going. But this time a new spectacle awaited him. Slaves were brought into the arena for a show like the popular one in faraway Rome. They were made into gladiators and had to fight lions, other beasts, people with bows and arrows, and one another, with or without armor. The fights were gory and awful, and it made him sick watching the crowds enjoy them.

These were the people his grandmother expected him to help day in and day out?

Thanatos found a quiet spot behind some shrubs and relaxed. Time to call his new best friend. He had made up a name for her: Life-Song. That's because she was everywhere, happy, and he could hear her singing. If he sat very quietly, he could feel her presence.

In a few moments she appeared. He could not see her, but he could sense everything about her, and hear her too. She didn't actually talk, but he understood what she felt. And when he played with her in his mind, real things would happen around him. The other day he pushed a spot in Life-Song, and a tree in the distance fell over. He was delighted with this discovery. He knew just how he'd done it, just where he'd touched, so he tried it again and again. The tree leaped like a frog across the field, making him laugh. He didn't know how to put the tree back, but he would figure it out.

He would figure everything out. He wanted to learn what every bit meant, how to make Life-Song his own.

Today he found a rush of waves coursing through Life-Song that he had not noticed before. Interested, he moved them in his mind. It made her sing a shrill, sad note. Then somebody screamed in front of the house.

Sure he had caused whatever it was, he ran to see what had

happened. A woman in line had fainted and hit her head on the brick pathway. People rushed the woman to his grandmother. Cassandra closed her eyes and put her hands over both sides of the woman's face. "She'll be all right." Cassandra nodded. "Let her rest under the tree."

Then she spotted Thanatos and clucked her tongue. "Late again, Thaddy," she snipped. "Can't Magda get you out of bed in the morning? Why does she keep you in that place, anyway? You two should live here with me." She grabbed the back of his shirt and dragged him to his chair at the other end of the courtyard. "Look at all these people here waiting on you."

Yeah, right, Thanatos thought. Live here with you and slave away every minute of my day?

A man approached and bowed, saying his back was bothering him. Sighing, Thanatos closed his eyes and rested his hands on the man's back. He could feel the area that wasn't right, and he adjusted it in his mind. The man smiled, bowing over and over again. "Thank you, Thanatos."

He was about to drop dead when Cassandra finally took him into her house. Everyone had been cured. "You did a good job, Thaddy. I can see you're improving. But tell me," she said, gripping his shoulder, "what is it you do in my side yard every day?"

Thanatos blushed. "I'm just … experimenting." He didn't want to explain about Life-Song. She was special, for him alone.

Cassandra leaned down and squinted at him. "You're getting pretty good at working with the Substance. Making trees hop, for example. But be careful."

Thanatos was surprised she knew what he was doing. "What is the Substance?"

"It's all around us. Everywhere. That's what holds life, Thaddy."

She handed him a bowl of olives, which he wolfed down. "You can make it do things, I know. But you need to stop, okay? Leave it alone. What you need to get good at is fixing people. Concentrate on that. Playing with the Substance will just make you want more. And you can't do everything, you know."

"Why not?" Thanatos asked, confused. "I think I *can* do everything with Life-Song . . . I mean, the Substance. I'm still learning, though."

"Not everything," she repeated. "Some things are off-limits. And for good reason." Her eyes turned hard. "There is something called the Final Magic, Thaddy. Lets you do unnatural things. Create life, control people, steer the planet. If anyone says they can give it to you, run away." She waved a finger in his face. "It is not meant to be in our world. It's a remnant of a time long before ours. The Golden Ones had that power. Now only a few of them are left, and they are ghosts."

She leaned toward him and whispered, "I know what's happening, Thaddy. It has to stop. Now. I've been having dreams. Not good ones either. Every night I see them—the three of them—and I'm battling them."

"Three who?" He leaned forward, interested.

"The Fates," his grandmother said. "The dream's about a prophecy, and they won't tell me what it is. I fight them each night to find it out, even though when I'm awake it's the last thing I want to know. Of course, in reality I couldn't lift a finger against those three. But in my dreams, I wrestle them, force the information out of them. And last night I finally got it."

Thanatos waited for her to continue, until he was about to burst. "What did they say?"

"I won't tell you the prophecy," she said, her voice flat. "It was the secret of how to get the Final Magic. It's not right, Thaddy. I'm going to take it with me to my grave. And it involved you." She looked at him sternly. "You are the one who could learn it someday. But *don't*. Mark my words."

"But why would you have those dreams—why would the Fates tell you—if it's such a bad thing?" he asked.

His grandmother turned on him fiercely. "Because you've gotten too close with the Substance. It's never known a person before as a friend. I think it loves you. It wants you to have the Final Magic so you can know its deepest secrets." She clucked her tongue. "It doesn't see yet how that could never, ever work. The Substance has been giving me these dreams, Thaddy, because of you. Now, *call it off*."

Thanatos squirmed with delight. Life-Song wanted him to have the Final Magic, to know everything? She loved him. Who needed anyone else?

A breeze wafted in and blew a small piece of paper out of Cassandra's pocket. It spun in the air and dropped onto the floor. Thanatos picked it up and read, *It's hidden in the smallest—*

"What's hidden?" he asked, looking up sharply. "The Final Magic? Is it hidden in something small?"

Cassandra ripped the paper from his hand, her face white. "That is *not* the prophecy. It's just a note I jotted. Now go to bed."

She stormed away, leaving Thanatos with a dreamy smile.

AFTERWORD

COLONY COLLAPSE DISORDER (CCD), or the case of the missing honeybees, is not fictional, unfortunately. Millions of bees have vanished from all around the world in the past few years. Between 80 and 90 percent of the U.S. commercial beehives are empty, with similar findings throughout Europe, South America, and parts of the Far East.

Honeybees have met with tough times in the past, fighting diseases and losing their habitat. But now bees are simply flying away and vanishing without a trace. No bodies are lying on the ground, like with past bee problems. They are just up and leaving.

Nobody knows why this is happening, but if the situation does not change, it may cause serious ecological problems. A third of U.S. crops, such as apples, pears, cherries, melons, strawberries, and nearly a hundred fruits, vegetables, and nuts around the world are dependent on honeybee pollination. Bees are an important part of our food chain. What would life be like without them? Would other species die off as a result? What would a trip to the grocery store be like? Luckily, so far, we haven't had to find out.

Of course, there has been much research and guesswork as to

what is going on. Assuming that Substance leaking out of Upper Earth isn't the cause of Colony Collapse Disorder, scientists are pointing fingers in several directions. Mites carrying viruses may be a part of the problem. Others think the bees are affected by pesticides on the plants or by genetically modified crops. In fact, bees are often fed high-fructose corn syrup in the winter months. Beyond the implications of giving them a substance we know is unhealthy, and which may pass through into their honey, the high-fructose corn syrup itself is often made with genetically modified corn. Some beekeepers have even been found using sodium cyanide, illegally, in their apiaries, to get rid of pests.

Stress on the hives may be a part of the puzzle. Bees get trucked from city to city in the United States. Tons are shipped into California each November to pollinate the almond tree groves. Some hives get moved ten times a year, from apples to oranges to peaches, which is not easy on them. Droughts affect them as well.

Some people even wonder if the world's extensive cell phone network is causing the bees to get "lost," the radiation from the phone towers interfering with the bees' navigation systems. Reportedly, studies show that putting cell phones on hives keeps bees away. But how much this has to do with the problem is unknown.

It's possible that Colony Collapse Disorder is caused by a mix of all of the above problems together. Maybe our honeybees are giving up on us and moving to greener pastures that only they know about.

Of interest, the Mid-Atlantic Apiculture Research and Extension Consortium recommended that beekeepers feed their bees an antibiotic, Fumagillin, for fungal infections, in case it might have something to do with their disappearance.

Reportedly, organic bee farms, which do not put chemicals, cyanide, or pesticides in their hives, or give their bees antibiotics or high-fructose corn syrup, have not been touched by Colony Collapse

Disorder. They are also required to have plenty of forage area that has no pesticides or genetically modified crops. Just something to think about.

Maybe the Substance is stronger on organic farms. That's the answer I tend to go with.

—Kaza